Shades and Shapes in the Dark

Shades & Shapes in the Dark

First edition. May 17, 2025.

Publisher: Loridian's Laboratory LLC

Ebook edition ISBN: 979-8-9867942-5-9

Print Edition ISBN: 979-8-9867942-6-6

Written by Michael Kilman

Also by Michael Kilman

Watch for more at https://loridianslaboratory.com.

Table of Contents

For Joanna, who taught me how to confront my shadows

Rest in Peace my dear friend

May 28th 1967 – May 7th 2024

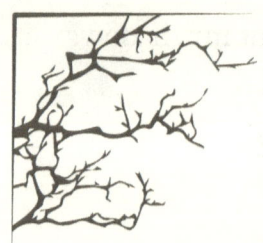

Chapter 1

The Crossroads of Life and Death

Those shades and shapes in the dark,
From which we draw our desires,
Shape our way of knowing,
Of where best to put our ire.

We cannot see the murky mists,
With eyes shut ever so tight
Where we leave behind only corpses,
And journey into endless night.

Oh how we take and take some more,
For thieving is our business,
We are a shadow of what we once were,
When we know only stiffness.

Wherever you go is where you are,
No matter how fast you're running,
No magic, nor wisdom, can set you free,
From your mind's endless cunning.

Come,
Let us wander through trains of thought,
And let the forms take their shape,

For having read this far already,
Know now, Reader,
There is no escape...

Tonight, she would stand before Demon for the last time. It was the last time because now, tonight, as the cold crept in under her skin on the darkest night of the year, and as the snow pelted her face with its cold harsh kisses, she would end it. She was tired of running, of hiding, of the manipulations and the games the living shadow had visited up on her these long years. Her torment would end before the sun rose over the snowy meadow.

Clarissa had not come here for suicide, far from it. She was no conciliatory party accepting defeat and suing for peace. There could be no peace between them. It was time to surrender to her fate, here, tonight, no matter what her fortune. She would finish the ritual, the true ritual. She didn't know if Demon could die, or if she could trap it forever like some bug in amber. Perhaps her plan would fail. Forty years of research, of questing for freedom from its gaze, left her with no definitive answers. But she had learned much and more. She stood there waiting for it, because, as they say, fortune favors the bold and her boldness was the sharpest of edges.

It had taken everything from her. Through the years it had stripped away all pretense of happiness, so that only unease remained. Only a species of longing stretched out through her loneliness as if a single gossamer thread, balancing all of her life, were holding her up. She was dangling. So what use was anything but surrender?

She stood in the eerie meadow, with trees bowing out away from the center, as if they were fleeing in fear. Any who came to this place, understood that need to run from the heart of the creature's den before it woke, even before they recognized the evil that lay within. The color was dimmer, desaturated, sometimes only shades of black and white. The sounds could hold no echo, and the snow and overcast sky enforced stillness.

This was where it all began forty years ago, when she was just a little girl. A cursed place. A place that marked its boundaries by the bones of dozens of creatures, some human. This was Demon's lair, but it was only the entrance. Years before, when she had needed to find power and answers, she had traveled to its depths, a space beyond reason or sense. She had fought her way out of that terrifying liminal space that lacked stability of form, full of terrors and wonders.

The wait was almost over. The invisible but familiar shroud descended around her. It darkened her vision and constricted her movement, a prophecy of Demon's arrival. Clarissa closed her eyes and took a deep breath, centering herself as she had learned to do from both Samira and Cathy. The constraints of the shroud slackened. She could not stop it from descending, but no longer would it hold her captive as it did in her youth.

Though Demon had only ever spoken to her a handful of times, Clarissa thought it would speak tonight. She had no reason to be certain of such a thing, but this was the end. It didn't matter that the fear nipped at any exposed skin the way the cold pulled at her edges. Nor, did it matter if she wasn't strong enough to defeat Demon. Her choice was born of revelation. For ultimately, all must stand at the crossroads of life and death. She would stand and be true.

It was only because of the snow catching the light of the full moon peeking through the clouds that she could see tendrils of form slipping through bare branches and trunks of trees leaking into the meadow like some sinister mist. There was no sound, save for the soft flutter of snowflakes as they gathered on the tall grass, sliding down to touch the earth and gather together. She wished she could gather like that with others. What a grand thing it would be to build something, some life with other people who loved her, with a purpose beyond survival, but Demon had made certain of her isolation.

It did not want her dead. At least she didn't think so. Its purpose was like a plague that left scarred survivors. Demon was a parasite. It was her fear, anger, and sorrow on which it fed. For it always appeared when she was possessed by potent emotions, or it cultivated those same feelings so that it could reap a bountiful harvest.

She called it Demon, though she didn't believe in deities. Some might argue that the existence of such an evil would demand a deity, but why should it? No, for Clarissa, gods and devils were just lazy stories that people told themselves to feel better about their lives. It would be so easy to hope that some god or goddess would come to aid her, to defend her, to send some sign to press forward. But in forty years of torment, she had seen nothing to suggest divine intervention. There would be no Deus Ex Machina. Here she was now, standing in the frozen meadow, forced into a confrontation with some supernatural being. She couldn't deny magic, she had command of some herself, but magic didn't mean there were gods or devils, heavens or hells.

At first, she had called it a shadow monster, but that wasn't right. Shadows couldn't kill. Light disrupts shadows. Demon disliked the light, but once, it had shown itself in the height of the noonday sun. It was a moment never long from her memory. She had lost two things that day, her greatest passion and a great love.

The wind picked up. It did not howl, but it shook the snow from the tops of the surrounding trees and cast flakes into the air like confetti shimmering in the moonlight. It would be beautiful if it didn't mark the coming of a monster. The wind was Demon's herald, its laughter.

The mist coalesced just inside the boundary of bones as a form took shape. She heard the crunching of feet in snow and frozen grass. She lifted her flashlight and shone it at the spot. Demon raised its arm to shield its eyes, taking a step back shifting its form, and then finding a temporary solidity. But there was no hiss or burning, or wince of pain, though she had bought the brightest flashlight available. After a moment, it let its long, jagged arms relax by its side. Spikes protruded every few inches, starting small at its wrists and then growing in size until they stood six inches tall on its shoulders. They reminded her of rotting teeth made of something like solidified tar. Its eyes were like giant black orbs, deep as the darkness and inhabited with a glowing red coal in the center of each. To stare into them was to feel a sucking sensation on your spirit. Clarissa knew from long experience that to stare into them was to risk everything. She stared at them now, fixing her will on Demon as it had so many times fixated its will on her.

It chuckled. She had never heard it chuckle before. It was more solid than she had ever seen it. Demon's black skin tightened around every sharp angle. She could see and count its sixteen ribs. Its torso was long, but its legs were longer. Its face was that of an upside-down triangle with rounded edges and long twisting horns at the top. It felt like a demon, and so she called it Demon. She wondered if its shape mirrored her thoughts of it.

As if it had plucked the thought from her mind it said, in a low rumbling voice, "Yes, something like that."

Its voice harmonized, as if several voices were speaking in union, deep and guttural but still clear and crisp.

"So you will speak, Demon?"

"Yes, you have come to the end now, and so we will speak of our contract." The growl was more like a purr, an animal vibrating its voice as it vocalized its intentions.

"You tricked me. I was a little girl. That contract was an accident."

It smiled, showing two sharp fangs among perfect white teeth. It was a vampire, but not a vampire.

"We all make contracts we don't intend. Sometimes we are born into them. Do you really think it was an accident?"

"You tricked me."

"Does that matter? You still gave me your blood."

"I didn't know what I was doing... I..."

Clarissa stopped and stood up a little straighter. She would not plead or grovel. She wasn't here to beg, she was here to destroy it once and for all, or die trying.

"I like when you call me Demon. You are right. It's not what I am, but it suits me well enough."

She wondered if she would get any answers, or perhaps she would only find the end of her life. But she must try, and the next question flowed naturally from her lips.

"What are you really?"

It said nothing. Nor did it move to step closer. Her flashlight still on it, she could see the writhing motion of its form. The red coals pulsed. For all its sharpness, there was no permanence in this form. It shifted depending on need, like all true power. Only its desire held it together, but soon it would drift apart like a dissipating mist.

"What are you?" Clarissa asked again.

"You should already know."

She didn't. She did have a suspicion, but far more doubt. Something itched in the back of her mind. Some revelation waiting to emerge. But will it as she might, it would not come.

"No, I don't."

It smiled. "Then you have already lost. You should not have come here if you didn't understand my nature."

"Haven't you had enough games?"

It chuckled with its low rumble, and she thought for a moment that it had tilted its head back with the laughter, but now it was impossible to tell. Gone was the form that reminded her so much of a demon. In its place, it warped and bent, as if taking parts of reality with itself. It squirmed as if there was nothing but a writhing black sackcloth full of pulsing insects beneath its dark outer layer.

"I never tire of the games. It is what I live for, live on. It is half of my being."

"Then what is the other half?"

Reforming its face, white teeth flashed below the red dots of its eyes. "So this is to be it, Clarissa? The night when the contract ends? Are you sure you're ready for the final confrontation? You can turn now and we can continue our game as it was, but two more will die."

"So there's a chance to save them?" A spark of hope betrayed the fear in her voice.

It said nothing, teeth and eyes gleaming.

Clarissa shivered. She wasn't sure if it was from the cold, or from the fear of what must come next.

Clarissa said, "No, this is it. This will end tonight."

The teeth flashed again in the middle of the billowing mist. "Quite a shame, rare is the victim that I can feed on for four decades. I cannot however, refuse a direct challenge. It is the core of the contract."

"Did you change my memory? Block me from seeing the terms of the contract somehow?"

"Of course, But humans always eventually push through to see the small print." It smiled.

She stood a little straighter. "Then I challenge you."

"Are you certain? For if you go through with this, after tonight, only one of us will remain standing. And if it is me—and it will be me—I will take your life and I will ring you dry of all your being, until there is nothing left but a husk, just like the others."

"Yes. I'm certain."

"And you would proceed knowing the stakes?"

"I'm not afraid to die."

This time, there was unmistakable laughter. It boomed on the wind, but there was no echo. "Now, now, why would I kill you?"

"But you said..." She couldn't finish. She thought she knew what Demon meant, but... the prospect of it was worse than anything she had imagined.

"If you lose, I will wear your skin for the rest of your life so that I can feed constantly. You will break loose the boundaries of my container and set me free for an age. You will be helpless to stop me. You will see the horror of what happens when you give into every craving. Just imagine the perversion, the vile acts, the unrelenting uses of your body and mind that I could enjoy for a century or maybe more. I can use my ancient knowledge to keep you going until your bones turn to dust."

"Why? Why would you do that to me? Why are you doing any of this?"

Demon only flashed its teeth.

She took a deep breath and felt the defiance rise within her. Yes, she was afraid, yes, she was tired, but her will was strong. Even if it would solidify her suffering, she had to try. Two lives depended on it. There were no others still standing. She swallowed hard, choking down her fear and anger, and said, "I know your secret. I know how to defeat you."

"Do you now?" The red embers pulsed. "You seem so certain. Tell me, how did you come by this knowledge? We both know all those years of traveling and study yielded no true answers."

She was afraid she was wrong. But a part of her was certain of the truth, the same part of her that had helped her press through the darkest days of the fugues Demon induced.

"Nothing lasts forever Demon."

"That's true, but our kind can span many human generations."

"And for how many generations have you been tormenting people?"

"Since humans first began dreaming."

Clarissa gathered her will and courage and said, "The answer was there all along, right from the moment I first encountered you."

The white teeth reflected the light of her flashlight as it said, "I have no such weakness."

She said it again, and felt strength in the words, "Nothing last forever Demon."

Demon chuckled, "Tell me, how did you discover this apparent weakness?"

She swallowed hard. "That's a long story."

"You traveled all this way in arrogance?"

"You don't believe me? That I have the tools to end you?"

"I don't. There is one way to nullify the contract, but no human has ever uncovered it and it will not mean my end. I am eternal."

"Nothing lasts forever Demon." She said, a third time, sharpening the words.

"Perhaps, but I will far outlive your kind. I have no weakness that you could exploit."

"Then let me tell you how I discovered it."

"Why waste time? It seems to me you only wish to delay the inevitable. Why fight at all? Simply lay down, surrender, let me inhabit you and be done with it."

A fire burned in Clarissa's breast and she felt her courage grow. She would finish the ritual and fulfill her promise to Monica and Annie.

"Because, Demon, I want you to see your end coming. I want you to learn how weak and pathetic you are."

It laughed for several moments. Something happened then. Something Demon didn't notice. For as it laughed, echoes returned to the meadow for the first time in human memory. But, Clarissa did notice and it brought her courage.

"Very well," said Demon. "Consider it a last request before I inhabit you and make a mockery of your species."

Clarissa could see it was excited to feed on the emotions that would rise from her story. It already knew the darkest parts. Reliving it all wouldn't be easy, but it had to be done. After all, this was her last stand, her one chance to end an ancient evil.

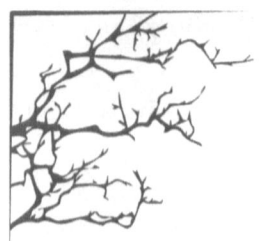

Chapter 2

The Meadow at the Edge of the World

Ever unbidden,
Never forgiven,
We are driven
on.

Always pretending
Never ascending
Past the unending
road

Open to seeing
Never agreeing,
From what you are fleeing
for

Mind your possessions
Never suppression
Be careful when you unlock that door.

There is nothing quite like the innocence of fast friendship in youth. For Clarissa, the girl next door, Monica, was a blueprint of the deep imprint young friendship leaves inside us. They met when each could barely form a sentence. They met first in a solitary sandbox behind Monica's house, where their parents had arranged a play date. It was in the rise and fall of sandcastles that they built their connection.

They were two girls, from two different worlds. Clarissa, born with red hair, green eyes, and a face full of freckles, she had only ever known the suburb she was born into. Monica, always the shorter, with dark hair and black eyes, had been born in her father's native land of Columbia and moved to the United States to be closer to her Mother's family when she was two years old. Monica came from a Catholic household, keeping the rituals of the church with her parents every Sunday. Clarissa's parents pledged to agnosticism and art. Both families were friendly enough and each girl played soccer until they were eight and grew tired of it.

Growing alongside each other, they lived more like sisters than friends. Each walked in and out of the other's household as if they belonged there. Neither set of parents minded much.

Clarissa's father died when she was six. The loss created a strange chasm between them, though Monica never knew it. The story of her father's passing was a tale that Clarissa could not share even as her friend comforted her in the aftermath. For what words would a six-year-old have for such a tale as that? Worse, Clarissa had seen something that night, some shape in the dark as her father took his last breaths just on the other side of the bathroom door. Because she could not yet comprehend what she had seen, and her father's death had loomed so large, the memory was forgotten until it was too late and Demon was already in pursuit.

Now, at nine years old, the only thing Clarissa understood was that her skateboard, the final gift from her father before he drew his last breath, was at the center of her universe. Her first talisman to ward off her depression, and her last tenuous thread to his existence. Before his passing, she would sit with her father on the porch as he smoked his pipe and read a book. Together, they watched the neighborhood kids, Margie and James, practice tricks on their skateboards up and down the street. Her father, noticing her interest, had gifted her the board, all bright yellow with purple flames licking the surface. It was Clarissa's greatest treasure.

By the time Clarissa was nine, the age in which Demon solidified the contract, she could no longer remember what her father looked like. Even when Clarissa stared at their family pictures, he seemed a stranger from another life.

At the height of the summer solstice of her ninth year, Clarissa met her fate.

2.   The woods of South Eastern Pennsylvania were thick, despite the city of Philadelphia carving out large swaths of forests for buildings and roads. But in the suburbs, plants and animals crept through neighborhoods, pushing back into their ancestral territory wherever possible. In the woods, ferns clambered up at the sky between trees, and most mornings were filled with mist and dew. For Clarissa and Monica, the forest was not a place of sorrow or darkness. It was a place of light and joy. They passed countless hours dashing in and out of the trees. The creeks and tributaries to the Delaware River were filled with living treasures and the girls uncovered turtles, caught crayfish, and sometimes tadpoles. Both girls fancied themselves tomboys and shied away from dresses. Neither of their parents minded, except Monica's on Sundays.

Near the park, and along the woods, were three waterfalls. Not huge falls, nothing that would inspire a painting or a poet, but for children, they were a playground. Two dozen large boulders jutted up out of the water at the base of the falls. In the summertime heat, when the scorching unrelenting sun of the Philadelphia suburb would catch fire, the girls sat on the boulders and let the spray of mist gather in beads on their skin and soak their clothes.

The day that Clarissa met Demon was one such summer day. It was the longest day of the year, a day when the evening twilight crept up, and the veils between worlds thinned. For at the height and depths of the light of the sun, things are thinner than they would be otherwise. In that thinness lay great power... or tragedy.

The two girls sat on the boulders, their legs crossed and facing one another, catching the mist on skin and clothes alike. Monica wore her backpack, which she had wrapped lovingly in a white plastic trash bag to keep the water away from her sketchbooks and library books. Clarissa's skateboard sat on one of the other nearby boulders a dozen feet below, away from the spray of the falls. She didn't want to risk a scolding from James or Margie if she rusted her bearings again.

"Do you want to make a game of it?" asked Monica. Her hair was matted with sweat, mist, and sunblock. Her soft round face, almost cherub-like, was red from the heat.

"Rock Hop? Again? We just played Rock Hop yesterday. Remember? After the skate park."

"I know, but what else are we going to do?"

Clarissa shrugged. "I don't know. Maybe we should go back and see if we could rent a movie and lay really still on the carpet at your house?"

Monica sighed, "Coolest place in the house."

Clarissa nodded. "In both of our houses. I wish we had an air conditioner."

"Denise Snyder got a pool this summer."

"She did? Seems like everyone is getting a pool but us."

"Yeah, and she told me neither of us are invited."

"She's such a bitch."

"Language," said Monica.

Monica was the peacekeeper of the two of them and she hated conflict, but she was the smartest person Clarissa knew.

"What? You know it's true, Mon. She probably doesn't even have a pool, she just wants to rub it in our face."

Monica shrugged. "You staying at my place tonight?"

"Can I?"

Clarissa tried to keep the eagerness out of her voice. Summers were hard at home. Her new stepfather, Ted, paced through the corridors, patrolling like some warden in a prison, exerting control over everything, tidying every crumb and speck. Clarissa wasn't even a messy person. She had cleaned that house top-to-bottom dozens of times with her mother before Ted arrived. Her room was tidy. But tidy wasn't enough for Ted. It was his domain; any hair out of place, and he would be on you. Not shouting, he rarely raised his voice. No, Ted asked in a deep nasally tone, "If you could please be sure to clean up after yourself," if even a single sock lay on the ground. He had no patience for messes. Even her mother wasn't exempt from his compulsion. When Clarissa's mother made her morning coffee, she couldn't leave it on the counter unattended for a single minute, or Ted would dump it out in the sink. That usually caused an argument. Coffee was the only thing keeping her mother going.

Monica said, "My Mom doesn't care. She's out all night, anyway. As long as we don't wake her up in the morning, she probably won't even know."

"It's kind of cool your mom is a night nurse," said Clarissa.

"Sometimes. But she sleeps a lot during the day and my Dad is a terrible cook."

"Yeah, well, at least your Dad isn't like Ted. He's so annoying."

"What about your Mom?"

"She just lets Ted do whatever he wants, it's like... like..."

"Like what?"

"I don't know. Sometimes, she looks at me and she just looks sad. I try to ask her what's wrong but... I don't know. It's like she hates me and doesn't want to deal with me anymore. I mean, she tells me she loves me and stuff, but she works so much and sometimes I feel like she almost prefers it that way, like she doesn't want to see too much of me."

"I thought she was working less since Ted came around?"

"No, he lost his job already and only works a few hours a week for a friend who owns a plumbing company. So my Mom's working two jobs again."

"When did that happen?"

"Two weeks ago."

"Why didn't you tell me?"

"I don't know. I guess I didn't want to talk about it."

There it was—the rift. It was hard for Clarissa to talk about her family or home life. She didn't want to think about it when she was out with Monica. She just wanted to focus on having fun.

Monica nodded and leaned forward, hugging Clarissa. The embrace lingered for a few seconds, and then, parting, Monica jumped up, the waterfalls behind her. Clarissa couldn't help but smile. Monica always seemed to know when a hug would help.

Monica asked, "What movie should we rent?"

"There's that one about the kids that play baseball and fight a monster. It looks kind of interesting."

Monica frowned, "Baseball? Do you even care about baseball?"

"They fight a monster. Monsters are cool."

"That's not what it looked like to me. It looked like it was about a bunch of stupid boys."

"Well, what do you want to watch?"

"That Sailor Moon movie is on VHS now."

"Monica, you literally dragged me to that movie three times when it was in theaters. I used up all my movie money from my Mom seeing that one with you."

Clarissa stood, herself, picked up a few pebbles off the top of the boulder, and threw them over Monica's head and into the waterfall. She loved to see if she could disrupt the flow, to somehow change the torrent, to reshape things around her. She enjoyed it, even when she knew it was fruitless.

"Dragged you? Admit it, you love Sailor Moon."

Clarissa put her hands on her hips. "No, you love Sailor Moon. I only went because you practically begged me."

Monica raised her arms in the air and said, "Moon prism power, make up!"

Clarissa rolled her eyes but couldn't suppress a smile. "How about we watch some skateboarding highlights?"

Monica's smile fell. Almost whining, she said, "Isn't that tape at your house?"

"No, I stashed it at yours. So I don't have to watch Sailor Moon."

Monica rolled her eyes. "I don't want to watch that tape again. I watch you skateboard every day."

"Well I need to study it if I'm going to compete one day."

"You really think you will?"

"Yeah, and I'm gonna win, too. Just like Margie."

Margie lived two blocks over and had befriended Clarissa when her father died. She taught Clarissa everything she could about skateboarding. When she was twelve, Margie had won a youth slalom competition.

Monica shouted, "Hey, you! What are you doing?"

Out of the corner of her eye, Clarissa saw a flash of color. She turned and saw someone crouching down on the boulder below, grabbing her skateboard.

Clarissa raised her hands to her mouth and shouted, "Hey! Put that down, it's mine!"

The boy, a few years older than both of them, with dark curly hair and wide suspicious eyes, froze. He looked around, not seeing the girls on the boulders just above him. Clarissa picked up a small pebble and threw it in his direction. It missed but clattered down on the rock just next to him. He looked up and caught Clarissa's eye.

At first, she thought he was going to put the skateboard down and apologize. He looked at it, looked up at the girls, and then, grinning widely, said, "Finders keepers, you little dweebs." He hopped from one boulder to the next, and after jumping across several large rocks, he dashed off into the thick of the woods with Clarissa's skateboard, the very one her father had given her, in his arms.

Clarissa's heart pounded. A rush of anger and panic sent spikes of adrenaline through her. She launched into action, leaping across the boulders as fast as she could and into the woods after him.

"Clarissa, wait!" Monica tried to follow but was slower than Clarissa. In a moment, she had left her friend behind. She couldn't wait; she couldn't lose that board.

She dashed through the woods after the boy. He was at least three or four years her senior. Despite his scrappy appearance, he was clumsy and slow. He didn't hide, he just kept running. Even in the moments when he disappeared behind the trees and bushes, she could hear the crash of his footsteps in the thick underbrush.

"Get back here! That's my board you... you thief!"

She could hear him laughing as he kept on. "Too slow dweeb! It's my board now."

Clarissa's legs burned, and she felt out of breath, but the desire to get her board back drove her through the pain. It was the one thing in her life that made her happy when so much else was wrong. And if she lost it, if she lost the one present her father had given her before he died, her heart would break open.

After long minutes of giving chase, she felt winded. She didn't know how much longer she could go on. But then, just as she thought she couldn't run anymore, the boy ahead stopped and caught his breath. Evidently, he didn't know she was still in pursuit. She ducked behind a large oak tree and waited as the boy surveyed the scene. She didn't dare stick her head out, not just yet, and besides, she could hear him if he started walking away. It was impossible to be silent, walking through so many layers of branches, leaves, and ferns. She closed her eyes, listening hard, and in several more moments, she could hear the slow movement of his feet.

This was her chance. The boy thought he had lost her in the woods. Now all she had to do was sneak up behind him. Then she could knock him down and take the board before he could get back up. It didn't matter that he was bigger than her. She could catch him off guard and run before he knew what had happened.

Carefully, slowly, she peered out from behind the tree. He was just on the edge of her vision but walking away from her. He stopped every few moments and looked around, turning in different directions. She smiled. He was lost. Then her smile faltered as she realized she was lost too. He had run a long way, and he had weaved around in several directions as he ran. It occurred to her that even if she were to get her board back now, she wouldn't know how to find her way back. These woods ran on for miles. Though, if she walked long enough, eventually she would find a river or a road. Hadn't her father always taught her that if you get lost in the woods, find a river or road and follow it? So that's what she would do.

After a few more moments, the boy picked a direction and walked on. Clarissa kept up, dodging in and out of trees and doing her best to keep as quiet as possible. She only moved when he did so he wouldn't be able to focus on her footsteps. He stopped a few times and looked around, her skateboard still under his arm. She hid behind trees as often as she could and after several minutes, she almost caught up. Then, she stepped on a tree branch, and the crack was so loud it made the boy turn around.

He was only a few dozen feet away. Clarissa charged at him. His eyes went wide, and he turned and ran through the woods, dodging left and right around trees. But she was close now, and even though he was older, he was in worse shape than she was. All those hours on her skateboard had given her a little extra endurance. She caught up, and with all of her strength, she shoved him hard. Her hand caught some pin or button on his jacket, and she felt the sharp pain in the center of her palm as something wet and warm flowed down her wrist.

Too late, she realized she had pushed him off a hill. She saw him go over the edge and disappear. He was just... gone. She heard something crashing through the brush below. Clarissa waited for several more breaths, afraid to see what she had done. Finally, she walked toward the edge and looked down. It was difficult to see between the trees and the undergrowth, but she could see someone lying at the bottom of the hill and just a hint of the colors of her skateboard nearby.

Clarissa felt first guilt, then anger, and then guilt again. She hadn't meant to hurt him. Why had he taken her skateboard? No, this was his fault. He was a thief. He deserved whatever he got.

She made her way down the slope. The decaying leaves from years of fall foliage were slick. Twice, she grabbed a branch to keep herself from pitching forward. Each time, she felt a sharp pain in her palm and left a smear of blood on the branches, but was too focused on her task to care.

The sun was close to setting now, and Clarissa knew the woods weren't safe after dark. Teenagers used the woods to party, and if they caught you out here, you'd end up with a beating or worse. The thief was probably out here meeting his friends and came a little early. Usually, the older kids didn't come down into the woods until after dark.

But how had time slipped forward so quickly? She hadn't been running that long, had she? It couldn't be more than four or five o'clock. She should have plenty of time before sunset. Her father had always told her that time was strange in some parts of the deep woods and that she should be careful. Normally she would have heeded his warning, but her board... she hadn't thought about what she was doing when she dashed into the woods after the thief. There was a sinking feeling growing in her stomach. Unease descended on her.

Then she realized she was alone. She looked around. The forest didn't look friendly. Monica was long gone, but it didn't matter. In moments, she would take her skateboard back from the thief and she would run back the way she came. Or at least, she would try to run back the way she came. She couldn't be that far from the edge of the woods, could she? Philadelphia wasn't a small city.

She stepped off the hill and right into a meadow. A deep chill gripped her, despite the sweat pouring down her face from the heat and her run. She couldn't put her finger on it, but this place was creepy. It felt wrong. That was when she noticed something odd at the edge of the meadow. Trees bent out and away from the center in every direction. It was almost as if someone had detonated an explosion here and it had blown the trees outward, forcing them to regrow in strange twisted angles. But there were no scorch marks or signs that anything was wrong. Even the leaves and branches pointed away from the center. Not one branch or leaf had the courage to grow toward the meadow. There were tufts of tall grass among the dirt, but even they seemed to bend outward. There were no birds here, nor any sign of any rabbits or squirrels. Not one flower flashed its color. The wind was still, but when she looked up, she could see a light breeze blowing at the treetops. It was as if someone had paused all motion inside the perimeter, a place with its own sense of time.

Clarissa took a step forward. Something crunched under her feet. Looking down she saw a white object poking out of a patch of grass. She knelt down to inspect further and saw... was that... bones? They were small, so they weren't human bones, but they were definitely bones. Now that she knew what she was looking at, she could see them everywhere. A few feet away, hidden half under moss, the skull of some creature stared up at her with empty eye sockets, as if to say, turn back. She looked to the left, and the right, and there were more bones ringing the edge of the meadow in a narrow band, as if marking a boundary. She swallowed, the lump growing in her throat, and crossed over the threshold and into the meadow where her skateboard lay.

3. She focused on her skateboard. It lay a few yards inside the meadow. It was odd because from above the hill, it looked like the boy and her skateboard were lying next to each other, just at the edge of the trees. Several yards further inside lay the boy who had taken her skateboard. She crept toward the unmoving form as if she was the thief and they had swapped roles.

A sense of urgency filled her like some unwanted insect crawling on the inside of her belly. The fear rooted her to the spot. Something was... opening, awakening, stirring as if it had slumbered for a thousand years. She trembled.

Clarissa took a breath and remembered what Margie, the older girl who taught her how to skateboard, always said. "You can't stop being afraid, but that doesn't mean you should give in to fear."

Clarissa repeated it to herself under her breath several times. It helped. She was being ridiculous. She needed her skateboard. It was hers, not the thief's, so why couldn't she shake the idea that she was the thief? Why, as she took step after step toward her prized possession, did the thought grow? Clarissa had done nothing wrong, or at least, the little shove she had given the boy hadn't seemed like a big deal.

A wave of dread hit her. It was unlike anything she had ever felt. Clarissa told herself she would just grab the board and go. The boy would be fine, wouldn't he? She could call 911 when she got out of the woods. The boy was too big for her to lift, anyway.

Determined to keep going, she clenched her fist and flinched with pain. Her right hand hurt. She looked down, and there, on her palm, was blood. A lot of blood. It had dribbled down her arm and was still bleeding. In the center of her hand was a large gash. What had been on the boy's jacket that could cut such a deep wound? She had felt pain when she shoved the thief, but she had no idea that she had torn a hole in the center of her hand. Some of her blood dripped onto the ground.

She followed the drops and saw that as soon as they hit the ground they vanished, as if the ground below was thirsty, eager for a drink. Compelled to do it without thinking, she held out her hand and let the blood drip on the ground on purpose. The hard dirt between the grass swallowed up the moisture almost instantly. She didn't like it. It made her feel ill and amplified that sense of wrongness. She needed her board back, then she could leave.

As she got closer to the boy, her plan hit a snag. Something was wrong. The thief still lay unmoving. That stillness disturbed her. Something in her memory stirred just below the surface. Her father's face flashed with a bubbling well of unease, but she pushed the memory down. If the boy wasn't moving, she couldn't just leave him there, could she? She would have to wake him up and help him find his way out. It was the right thing to do. It was something her father would want her to do.

She approached her board slowly, feeling fear grow with every step. The closer she got, the harder her heart pounded. There was the mingling of the deepest kind of curiosity and dread as she inched closer. She reached down and grabbed her board. For a moment, she thought it would be best to turn and run back up the hill, but something beckoned.

She took a few steps toward the center.

"Hello?"

There was no response. The meadow swallowed the echoes, like it had swallowed her blood.

Clarissa said to the unmoving form, "You know, you got what you deserved falling down that hill. You shouldn't have tried to steal my board."

Still no response.

"Hey! Did you hear me?" She practically shouted the words.

Nothing.

Clarissa took a few steps closer, raising her board up like a club. If he was faking or playing some kind of trick, she'd be ready. Then she was standing over him.

"Hey! I'm talking to you, thief!"

The boy didn't stir, and then she noticed something else. One of his limbs was bent in an unnatural direction. Truth hit her in the gut. All hope and light and laughter drained out of her. The reason his quiet disturbed her so much was because his chest wasn't rising and falling. Now her memory of that terrible night when she lost her father surfaced. The paramedics had broken down the door and for one moment she glimpsed between the two men and saw her father's body. Her father had lain still just like the boy in front of her. Clarissa's heart beat like drums in the darkness. Her limbs shook and for a moment she almost collapsed, but then caught herself.

Her voice quavering, uncertain, "Hey. This isn't funny anymore. You already stole my board. Knock it off, okay?"

She prodded his body with her foot. It twitched. She jumped back, an electric surge of terror. There was a smell, a terrible smell, like a mixture of shit and rotting garbage, but somehow sickeningly sweet, too. She gagged.

She covered her face with her hand, and said, "Come on. Seriously. Knock it off. I didn't mean to shove you down the hill, I swear. I didn't even know there was a hill... I... I..."

Before she could finish, the earth groaned, like thunder below her feet. The wind woke to a gale, and she struggled to stand. Then a loud crack, like the sound of a thousand trees snapping their trunks at once, echoed through her ears. Pain spiked and there was total silence, except for a terrible ringing. She felt something wet and sticky flow from her ears and reached up to see what it was. She looked down at her uninjured hand in amazement. More blood.

The world set about tearing itself apart. Wind uprooted trees and cast them into the sky, like twigs. The wind walled her in, blowing in circles around her and the thief. She was in the center of a storm, bones and branches and leaves and dirt encircled them, flying madly through the air. The ground shook and across the meadow, the earth cracked and danced up and down like someone was slamming their fist into a jig-saw puzzle.

Clarissa shouted for help, but the wind swallowed her breath and all the echoes. Feeling dizzy she fell to her knees. She just couldn't get enough air. Her body felt weak. It was growing harder to keep her eyes open.

Then, in a blink, everything stopped. The ground stilled. The wind quieted. The dead silence of the meadow returned as if someone had scooped all the noise of the world out and left nothing behind. Cracks in the earth sealed up, and the bones paused in midair and fell back in the exact spots where they had laid before.

Clarissa gasped and drank in the air. She took several more long, slow breaths and looked around. Where had all the color gone? All she could see were shades of gray and odd shapes in the dark. She looked down at her clothing. Clarissa had been wearing a red shirt and blue jeans, but now... the color was gone. Even the purple flames on her skateboard were gray.

There was a long silence. She tried to say something, but there were no words, no noises anymore, not even from her own mouth. She tried to scream, but though she could feel her throat tear from the effort, no noise emerged.

A thrumming sensation began. It started at her feet and spread through her body as it reached her mind. Then, the noise returned, though it was still without its echo. The thrumming continued, the meadow's heart beating.

"Hello?"

She didn't know who she was saying hello to. The boy couldn't hear. He was dead. But there was someone there. Every goose pimple on her exposed flesh raised in attention, and her heart pounded, synchronizing with the thrumming of the meadow.

It was coming. What that meant, she didn't know. But Clarissa knew it as sure as if someone had said the words out loud.

"Is someone there?" her voice trembled.

Out of the corner of her eye, she saw the boy move. She turned her head, and staring, she saw him move again. Was she wrong? Was he still alive? A glimmer of hope flashed in the colorless dread.

She leaned down next to the boy and the smell returned. She gagged again, almost dry heaving.

"Hey, are you okay? Say something if you're okay. Or just move your arm if you can't speak."

She reached down and touched the boy's back, placing her flat palm where his heart would be. He was cold. How could he be so cold? The oppressive heat of summer still lingered.

She withdrew her hand as if avoiding some trap, or the jaws of a predator.

"Please be okay," she said in a whisper. All pretense of anger, all sense of justice, had vacated her heart. She wanted only for the boy to stand up again, even if he was a jerk. Clarissa wanted them to walk out of this terrible place together. She didn't want to be alone. Something was coming, and they had to move fast.

She took a deep breath. She knew what she had to do, but she didn't like it. The thought of putting her hands on him again disturbed her. She felt dirty even placing a single open palm on his back.

Clarissa steadied herself, thinking of Margie's words. She didn't have to let the fear take control. Then she reached her hands down under him and felt the coldness press against her fingers. She turned him over with significant effort. He was bigger than she was by a head. After a moment of pushing, he rolled over onto his back and she watched with horror as the body flopped over exposing the truth to the sky.

She saw his face, saw the condition of his body, and stumbled backward. Then, Clarissa tried to scramble away like a crab, desperate to put some space between her and the rotting, stinking corpse.

She screamed. Still, there was no echo.

The remainder of the boy's face was frozen in a terrifying, haunted expression. His mouth was open wide, almost as if someone had used fishhooks in the corners, pulling it up into a maddening, terrified smile. The left side of his face that was pressed into the dirt, was partially decayed. Bits of muscle and bone peaked through patches where the skin no longer existed. There were claw marks down the center of his face, crossing the cavities that were once his eyes. Maggots crawled from each of the sockets, working their way around his face. There was no blood anywhere. And she knew that the earth had drunk up his blood, as it had hers.

Clarissa shuttered. Hugging her legs, she wept onto her knees. She closed her eyes. She knew that if she closed her eyes and took some deep breaths, the scary things would go away. Her father had taught her that. This couldn't be real. She needed to reset her brain because it was playing tricks on her.

Clarissa opened her eyes. The body was still there. She was still in this creepy meadow and her skateboard lay a few feet from the boy's body where she had dropped it. She had almost forgotten about it when she turned the boy over.

Nothing happened for several minutes. Panic faded and reason reasserted itself. She didn't understand. How could this be? The boy had only fallen moments ago, and though she was young and had never seen a decayed body before, besides the few scary movies she had watched at Monica's, she knew that there was no way the boy's body should look like this already. It had only been a few minutes, or had it? She thought of how the time had passed as she ran through the woods. Maybe time was different here?

"Okay. Okay... I gotta tell someone. I gotta get help."

Clarissa wasn't talking to anyone in particular. But the thought of telling someone, especially since she had pushed the boy, was almost as daunting as staying here with the corpse through the night. The darkness was spreading, and the last slivers of light were disappearing into the trees around the meadow. She didn't know where she was or how long it would take her to find her way back.

How did it come to this? Stuff like this always happened to her. Well, maybe not quite like this, but something always turned her world upside down. First, her father had died, then her grandmother. Then her stepdad moved in. All she had wanted to do was pass the time with her best friend and her skateboard.

But the darkness would brook no argument. It was coming, and she had to get out of there. She sensed, somewhere way down deep inside, that there were far more dangerous things in this meadow than teenagers playing their games of mischief.

Clarissa swallowed, stood up, grabbed her board from next to the boy, and slowly backed away. She didn't know who she was going to tell, but before she could tell anyone, she had to find her way back.

She took a few steps to go, and just as she did, the wind started up again. Across the meadow, she heard some rustling in the trees and underbrush. She turned toward it, but now it was too dark to see anything, and she didn't have a flashlight.

"Hello?"

She sounded like a parrot to herself. But there was no answer, no echo.

"Excuse me, I'm lost. Can you help me find my way back home?"

Branches cracked and popped on the other side of the meadow, just beyond her vision. She could only see the faint outlines of the trees on the other side, skeletons in the colorless dark. She thought of the bones on the ground. The cold crept into her and she hugged her skateboard, desperate for warmth and light.

"Please, I need help. This boy fell and..."

A long, loud groan, almost a growl, filled every corner of the meadow. It sounded almost human, almost animal, but it was neither. Terror filled every cell, and she realized that, just like in a dream, she could not move. Her legs felt heavy, her arms dead weight, her mind frozen, unable to do anything but listen to the reverberation of the noise. Something in her was screaming, begging her to run, to move, to do anything but stand here.

Long, loud labored breaths emerged from the other side of the meadow. There were more snaps of twigs and the wind gusted as a strange black mist rose and ate all the light that was left. She shouldn't have been able to hear the noises over the wind, but the wind seemed to carry it right to her ears.

A strange glow grew in the dark and permeated the meadow. Within the dim light a shadowy form, just barely visible, entered the other side of the clearing. Clarissa felt warmth and wetness between her legs as her bladder let go. Somehow the sensation of her urine running down her leg unfroze her, and with her skateboard in hand, she finally felt her legs unfreeze and she sprinted back up the hill from where she came.

She didn't dare look back.

It followed.

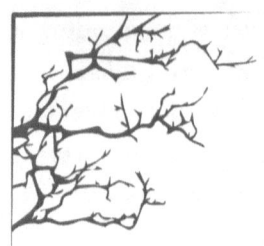

Chapter 3

A Long Way to the Dark

A long way to the dark,
But you'll have no trouble running,
Where the serpent's coils tremble,
With singular slithering motion.

There is no way to find here,
There's only a species of wandering,
Not even a flicker of hope or rest,
There is only ever wanting.

Alas, you beg and cry and crawl
Through bleakness, anguish, longing,
For a time when it hadn't gone all wrong,
When it wasn't your soul you were hunting.

C larissa ran, dodging trees in the dark. The furrows between the bark gave rise to creatures carved in the living wood of tree trunks. Eyes and knots staring, roots reaching like forked hands, to spear her, to grasp her, and hold her in place so the thing following could work its vile mischief.

The Light was the reason she knew it followed. In the meadow, she had seen it coming only because of its strange indescribable living glow. For that's what she thought of it as, a living glow, as if the consciousness of the shadow itself were its inner light peering outward, that both its intention and attention were what gave light to the forest beyond the deep darkness.

Clarissa risked a glance up. She could see a few stars winking in and out between gaps in the thick summer canopy, and there, above, were further hands reaching down. Flickering optical illusions created by the monster's glow. Leaves like padded tendrils tilting toward her. Another shudder of fear wracked her body and her movements slowed, as if she was running in a dream or a nightmare and could not escape because time itself proved traitorous.

She dared not risk turning back to understand its form. Even a momentary glance back might be long enough for it to close the distance. There was no curiosity in her, it had all been driven out with the decay of the boy's body.

Something brushed the back of her neck, just the barest caress, a terrifying tenderness. But with that touch, she felt a heaviness settle into her limbs. She pushed harder and her muscles burned far beyond exhaustion. Despite her efforts, despite the rapidity with which she moved her legs, she was slowing down. Gravity claimed her. The roots and branches slithered around her limbs.

"Noooo!" Clarissa screamed her terror. That single syllable was like a glass already full and spilling over.

Then something else in her, some deep stirring of anger born within an instinct to survive, roared to life. She shrieked, "Leave me alone!" The sounds reverberated through the trees shattering the silence.

The restraints of root and branch drew back, as if startled at the force of the words. For a moment, Clarissa thought she would break free of whatever power was slowing her down. She felt lighter, faster, stronger. She dashed through the woods and there, ahead, were street lights and the hope of pale concrete, orange and awash with light just a few dozen yards away. She was almost clear of the forest, almost to the road, where she could find help... perhaps salvation.

Her foot caught in a root. Time slowed as she flew forward, her skateboard cast aside into the underbrush. She tried to stop herself, reaching out to the air for a handhold, for anything, but could find no purchase. Her head smashed into the tree just in front of her. Stars filled her eyes even as blood trickled down her forehead. She felt dizzy and lightheaded. Knowing the thing was just behind her, she tried to pick herself up off the forest floor, crawling with every effort and feeling tree roots and underbrush beneath her palms. She thrust herself up, but just as she stood, she spun and fell.

Still, she did not give up. She crawled. Fallen branches and plants scratched her shins, and as her hands grabbed at the soil, trying to pull herself forward, she felt the pain of the wound in the center of her right hand where the jacket had slashed her open as she pushed the boy over the edge. For a moment she saw the image of her blood dripping into the soil of the meadow, saw the ground lapping it up.

"What did I do?" She whispered to herself as the strength to move forward faded. She heard something behind her, and not wanting to die face down, she rolled over onto her back and looked up through the branches of the trees, hoping to see the stars at least once more. She could not outrun it, not now. Inky blackness spread over her vision, like a thick cloud of smoke billowing around her. The stars and branches were blotted out until there was only dark. Then, somehow, the darkness got darker.

Clarissa knew, somehow, though she couldn't quite explain it, that she was inside the thing's intention, for that strange glow had vanished. Clarissa lay in the deadest of nights, where she couldn't even see her hands in front of her. All she could hear was the sound of her breath. All she could feel was the throbbing in every part of her body. She was a mixture of the ache of fresh bruises, and the burns and sharpness of scratches and punctures from her failed escape attempt.

Without warning, something wrapped around her, something that, when she saw it later in the light, she would think of as a black burial shroud. Her arms and legs were pinned, her body cocooned. It was not the cocoon of a caterpillar awaiting a magnificent rebirth, but rather the trap of a spider's web, a feast for later that left its victim struggling without hope until some beast consumed her.

Something grabbed her and dragged her for some unknown distance. Blinding pain surged through every inch of exposed skin. The forest tore at her flesh as the monster pulled her through the woods. Then it stopped and turned her, so she lay face-up, still. The shroud released and for a single moment she was able to move her arms and legs, until tree branches and roots shot out of the ground and restrained her, twisting down in the bare earth, rooting her to the spot. She struggled, flinging rage into her limbs for extra strength, but she could not fight it.

Clarissa could smell the earthen dampness, mixed with her own blood. She thought she could smell the decaying body of the boy again, perhaps nearby. Had it dragged her back to the meadow? She had no sense of time or distance. The darkness washed away all such considerations.

Something lit the darkness to a lesser shade. Through blurry vision she saw it there, standing over her. The monster's red eyes and shifting shapeless form danced against the black. The light both pulsed with radiance and absorbed everything around it, a creature of contradiction. There and not there. She shut her eyes waiting for the end.

It reached down and grabbed her face, squeezing her cheeks and opening her mouth. Something from its palm probed her lips, pushing past the boundaries of teeth and tissue. It slid down her throat. She tried to scream, but the creature swallowed the sound. Clarissa had the impression that it was drinking in her screams the way the earth had lapped up her blood. The object pushed past her vocal chords and down into her stomach.

It was hard to breathe with the obstruction. Fear woke her from her passivity. Her whole body shuddered, and she bucked and moved her core in every direction, pulling anywhere that there was the least bit of slack. It was sucking her under the earth, pulling her down into its depths. The mud and earth swallowed her legs. She closed her eyes and summoned the last wisps of her remaining strength. Then, with all her might, she pulled her right arm free.

Her eyes still shut tight, trying not to see the horrors in those glaring red coals in the center of its shifting face, Clarissa reached over and pulled her other arm free. Then she reached up and grabbed the thing down her throat with both hands and pulled on it. It was thick and sticky, pulsing with life. There was a strange bleating too, almost like a beeping noise from some malevolent machine.

It wouldn't come free at first, and she felt pain down in the depths of her esophagus. The pain grew as she yanked harder. Inch by inch, she pulled, never daring to open her eyes. Then it was out, and with it she vomited all over herself, coughed, sputtered, gasping in the dark air. Quickly, using her arms, she sat up and pulled at the roots tangling her legs, but her lower half was part of the earth now and she could not get them free.

Something struck her in the chest, hard at first, stealing her wind, but then slowly pushed her back down. The tree roots reached up to take hold of her arms again. Many tentacles in the dark, seeking to restrain her. She was so tired. She couldn't fight much longer. Something grabbed her whole body, and involuntarily, she opened her eyes and screamed.

2 Clarissa wasn't in a forest. She wasn't tied down by roots or branches. There was no shadow looming over her. She was in a bed. Several people stood around her. Blurry and through tear filled eyes she saw strangers, all in white and pale blue clothing. One wore dark blue. She didn't understand who they were. What had they done to her? What were they doing to her now?

One of them was trying to talk to her, but she could not hear through the pounding and pulsing of blood inside her skull. She screamed again, and as the person came closer, she lunged at them, striking something hard with her fist, fighting for her freedom. She thrashed and turned and moved as other arms rushed to grab her. And then they were pushing her down a third time and eight pairs of arms held her still. Restrained and helpless, her eyes caught the glint of a needle. She screamed and thrashed. What were they doing to her? Why? But there was no fighting. There were too many hands holding her. She watched as the needle poked past the edges of her skin and felt the sharp pinch as it worked its way through the muscle. First, there was burning, then a warmth spread outward from the pain and almost immediately she felt all the strength and fight run out of her.

Slowly, the hands let go, hesitant, wary, just like she felt. She sat up on her elbows, but it was so much effort. Five adults watched her, eyes staring, blinking, with mouths unmoving.

Clarissa wanted to plead with them to stop whatever they were doing, but she was so tired. Swinging her legs over the edge of the bed she planted her feet on the floor. She tried to stand, but her legs would not hold her up. Collapsing, she crawled on the cold tile. She worked for every inch she could muster. But her limbs stopped responding.

Clarissa lay her head down on the cold floor with eyes open, watching the gathering of shoes around her. She counted them. The floor smelled like lemon and cleaner, and sneakers. The scent of her whole world now. Beyond her world, she could hear conversation but could barely understand the words and could not comprehend their meaning.

"Jesus, that was a big enough dose for an adult."

"She's a willful one. It's probably why she survived out there in the woods alone."

Clarissa wanted to look up and see the faces of her captors, but she couldn't move anything other than her eyes. Then her eyelids grew heavy. She didn't think she could keep them open much longer.

"Come on, let's get her back in her bed."

"Doctor, should I remove the ventilator from the room?"

"I'd say so. And reach out to her parents."

Clarissa's eyelids closed, and she fell back into the shadows.

3   A dissonant arrangement stirred Clarissa from sleep. Each instrument entered her consciousness one at a time. First, the rising rhythmic beeping of medical monitors, relentless in their pacing. Followed closely by the sound of shuffling footsteps up and down the halls. Each step clacking with invading echoes. Then came a choir. A low din of a dozen conversations between doctors, nurses, patients, visitors, and so on. But this orchestra did not stand alone in noise. The other senses roused alongside the auditory dimension.

The potent, rousing fragrance of cleaning chemicals, of plastic, of sterility, triggered lengthy, looping memories of the moments she had shared with her father during his treatments only a few short years earlier before his inevitable death. Chilled hospital air pressed against any exposed skin. Had Clarissa opened her eyes, she would see all the familiar sights of a hospital room. She was unwilling to risk opening them just yet. Such an act would confirm with her own eyes where she was and the horrible thing that had happened.

She could not hide from the questions much as she wanted to. How had she ended up here? Was her nightmare of the roots and branches taking hold of her for some sinister purpose, real or imagined? Was it somehow both? Beyond the moments when the monster chased her, all was veiled in a thick, dark fog.

The most shocking memory to rise was that of the boy, broken and rotting on the forest floor. She shivered thinking of the maggots crawling over his half decayed skull and making meals of the remnants of his eyes. Had she killed him? It was only a push. How could someone die from a push? How had the body decayed so quickly? What happened to him after she fled the meadow? Had Monica chased after her? Who found her? She knew she was in a hospital, but what kind of hospital? Why had those people assaulted her and jammed that needle into her?

Clarissa slowly cracked open her eyes but didn't move her head. In that brief glance, she caught the image of every standard hospital room she had ever visited with her father. The white walls and machines by the bedside, framed with the pole that held a dripping IV bag, that this time, was hers. Hesitating, she stopped herself from moving too much. She recalled the five adults retraining her the last time she was awake. The pain of the injection site on her left bicep was still sore, and she held back from reaching over and touching it.

One of her most fearful memories of the days she spent in a hospital with her father was her discovery that some hospitals had places where people went for mental illnesses. She couldn't help but wonder, was she in one of those? Was this some kind of prison hospital for murderers? A lump swelled in her stomach as if she had swallowed squirming bees.

She remembered the time she got lost in the hospital during her father's treatments. Wandering into the psychiatric wing, though even now, she didn't fully understand what that place was, she found herself surrounded by patients and tasted some previously unknown and terrifying dimension of the human experience. That day, Clarissa had gone in search of the cafeteria. Her mother was working, and her father's treatments had run longer than expected. He sent Clarissa off to buy herself a snack, but Clarissa had stepped off the wrong floor on the elevator.

She wandered the halls until she reached an empty nursing station through a door that was propped open. At six, she was too young to read the signs warning her of what lay beyond. She quickly found herself in the middle of a group of patients. Later, as a teenager, she would learn about traumatic brain injuries and other mental illnesses, and she would understand that her experience wasn't really dangerous at all. But for a six-year-old, to find yourself surrounded by a woman muttering curses and threats to herself, a man who spontaneously took off his clothes and yowling in agony, and another with half of his face burned from some terrible war, was more than enough to leave a lasting impression. A nurse had found her only two minutes later and brought her back to her father, shaken and terrified, but few six-year-olds would have walked away from that ward unscathed by the memories of that experience. Her father had tried to explain the experience to her, but the monsters we make in our minds aren't easily dismissed by logic.

What made that moment worse was that it happened only a few months before her father's shocking and devastating death.

Clarissa never forgot that event, and now, laying there thinking of the nightmarish experience she had the last time she woke in this place, she wondered if she might be in the mind part of the hospital. Would they lock her away with the kind of people who scared her? She had killed someone. When she had tried to leave the bed before, they had come and injected her with something.

Afraid, Clarissa kept her eyes shut. Almost as if summoning someone with her thoughts, she heard two people coming down the hall. Clarissa thought of the needle, and the adults holding her down. Did they tie her back down? Carefully, with as much stealth as she could manage, she checked her limbs to see if she could move, and it seemed she could. That puzzled her, but she wouldn't take any chances.

Two sets of footsteps paired with two voices lurked just outside of the room.

First, a feminine voice said, "Is this the girl? How long was she missing again?"

A masculine voice said, "Three days in the woods and three more unconscious. But she woke up this morning. We gave her a sedative. It should wear off soon."

A sedative? She tried to remember if she had heard that term before. But she couldn't recall anything. What bothered her more was, if they were discussing her, how had she been missing for three days? Hadn't she just fled the meadow? Her stomach turned and for a moment she thought she might be sick, but she choked back the feeling, though she couldn't stop goose flesh from rippling up and down her body.

The woman said, "Yeah, I heard. Poor thing. Can you imagine what it would be like to be so young and wake up in some unknown place on a ventilator?"

"Nancy said she couldn't believe how strong she was. She landed a good hard punch to her right eye. She's gonna look like George Foreman after Tommy Morrison got hold of him." The man chuckled to himself.

The woman said, "What's wrong with her?"

"Well, there are a lot of minor wounds. Lots of bruises. The girl's pretty scratched up, got a large wound in the center of her right hand. She was a little dehydrated and twisted her ankle. She might have a concussion from a knock on the head. There's no sign of any kind of abuse, but maybe she hit her head harder than we thought, though when we did some imaging, there was no serious brain damage. I bet she's got a hell of a story. I hope she was just lost in the woods, but..."

"But what?" said the woman.

"You hear about that place where Henry and Jaleh found the other kid?"

"No."

Clarissa's skin tightened. Every hair stood on end. She wanted so badly to shift and move in her hospital bed, but she didn't dare. Were they talking about the meadow? About the boy she had pushed and killed? Had they seen the monster too?

"You should ask them when you have a chance."

"Why? Did something else happen?"

"They saw something real strange down there, along with several other people. There's been rumors about those woods for ages. When I was a kid, they used to tell spooky stories about that place."

"What kind of stories?"

"Well, there were lots. You know how some places just attract all kinds of tall tales."

The man paused for a second. Clarissa was certain they were hovering just over top of her and performing some kind of task, but was too afraid to open her eyes and see what it was. She heard a series of beeps and a popping noise.

Then he resumed, "Some kids used to say that American colonists massacred a bunch of Indians there at some point. I heard another story that there was some weird religious cult where people ate each other. But the one that always scared me was about a shadow monster from the beginning of time that ate people and then used their bones to mark its territory."

"Jesus," said the woman. "And so they found that boy's body at this spot? And where did they find her?"

"A few hundred yards from that meadow. She must have found the body, tried to run for help, tripped and smacked her head on a tree. Let me tell you something, I'd want to run from that place even if there wasn't a body. I went down there when I was a kid, and there were bones surrounding the whole place. After I went down there, I used to have nightmares about those woods. I think most kids around here did."

Clarissa thought she might be sick. A part of her stayed in the hospital, but the other part drifted back into the memory of the meadow. The boy was there in the room with her, rotting. She felt a pressure behind her eyes as if the maggots were in the back of her sockets, nibbling slowly through her vision to push out through the tissue, blinding her. She wanted so badly to rub her eyes, to open them to be sure that she could still see, but she was even more scared of the adults who had poked her with the needle earlier and kept herself quiet, though tears were building in the sides of her eyes, and she wasn't sure how much longer she could hold them back.

"So what did Henry and Jaleh see?"

"Just ask them. I'm telling you, you're gonna want to hear it firsthand from one of them. You won't believe it from me."

"She's shivering. Will you have the nurse grab a warm blanket?"

"I'll grab one. They're right down the hall."

Through the beeping of the monitor, Clarissa heard one set of steps walking away, crinkling plastic, and something that might have been the liquid in an IV bag. When she had come and visited her father in the hospital he had explained all of the unfamiliar elements of his experience. She was five when his treatments had begun, and six when they had failed. Every sound, every medicine, every liquid plugged into him, came with an explanation. He wanted her to understand, in part, because he thought he was going to live and wanted to explain why all the things happening to him were a good thing.

Despite that horrible night when her father had died on the other side of the bathroom door, she still remembered much of what her father had taught her. His time in the hospital and the things she experienced there were the sharpest parts of her young memory.

Then someone walked back into the room and two people were hovering next to her bed again.

"Than, Alex," said the woman.

"No problem," The man replied.

There was a moment of silence. Then warmth as one of the two laid the blanket down on her. Clarissa desperately wanted to open her eyes to see what the two people were doing. But even though it sounded like they were just doing routine tasks that she had seen in the hospital with her father a hundred times, she was too scared to open her eyes.

The woman broke the silence. "Can you imagine being in her parents' shoes?"

"I've got two girls, I don't want to imagine," said the man.

"What about the other child? Any updates?"

The sound of a pen scratching on paper came from Clarissa's upper left.

"Dead, long dead. Gary down at the Morgue said the body was in an advanced state of decay. Probably several weeks dead. But it's hard to tell, exactly."

"What killed him?"

A pause, a heavy silence that bore Clarissa's guilt on its back.

"The autopsy was... inconclusive."

Clarissa wondered what inconclusive meant. She had never heard the word before. She didn't like it. The man's tone made it feel like a dirty word.

The woman said, "Really?"

"Yeah, he's got a broken arm, but there's no sign of infection or anything. It's the strangest thing, Peggy."

"Exposure?" said the woman. "Maybe he had a heat stroke?"

"No sign of that, either. Gary's stumped."

"Weird.... Creepy," said Peggy.

Clarissa felt the blood pressure cuff tighten around her arm with a buzzing noise. She felt the pressure grow, and though it was deeply uncomfortable, she lay still listening, hoping for some answers, though in her heart she knew that neither of these two had much to offer.

Alex said, "The whole thing is like something out of the twilight zone."

"Come on Alex, tell me what Jaleh and Henry saw."

Alex sighed. "Oh, man. I'm telling you, it's better if you ask them. I don't even know if I believe it."

"Not even a hint?"

Silence for several moments and then Alex said, "Some kind of weird shadow, some strange weather... I don't know, just ask them."

They had seen something. Clarissa wondered if she could ask the two people they mentioned about it. The meadow was strange, but these two were wrong. She knew who killed the boy. It was her. Clarissa had shoved him down the hill and when she had looked over the edge after him, he stopped and he never moved again. She couldn't explain the decay, but even if she had pushed him into the lair of the monster and it had killed him, it was still her fault for pushing him. As soon as the police showed up, she was going to jail. Ted sometimes watched a show about police and trials, and Clarissa remembered that sometimes people went to jail because they helped with a murder. She knew her best defense was to keep her eyes shut.

Almost as if reading her mind, the woman asked, "You think the girl did it?"

The man scoffed. "What? No way. He was dead for weeks. The girl must have found the body and saw something in that meadow, stumbled out and got lost. That's what Ryla down in imaging thinks, anyway."

"Did the cops come by yet?"

"Yeah, twice, but since she's been out, there's nothing they could do. No doubt they'll question her the moment they can. The weird thing is, no one can figure out who this boy is. They're just calling him a John Doe for now."

"Did the girl's friend... what was her name?"

"Mary or Madeline... I can't remember. Something with an M, though?"

"Was it Monica?"

"Yeah," Alex said, "That was it. It's real weird. This girl's friend saw her take off after a boy who stole her skateboard, right?"

"Right," said Peggy.

Alex said, "So where's that boy? Who was he?"

"You think it's the same one?"

"How could it be? That John Doe is so decomposed that they haven't been able to ID him."

"What about his dental records?" asked Peggy.

"Most of the teeth were missing, so that won't help. The police are real eager to talk to this girl."

Clarissa's heart sank. So, the police would arrest her as soon as she woke up. She was glad she hadn't opened her eyes yet. She wasn't ready to face the police, to see the look on her mother's face when she found out that Clarissa was a murderer. No wonder they had restrained her in bed. She was a criminal. But what was that thing they put down her throat? Was it that ventilator they talked about? She had never heard that word either. She had never seen her father on one, no matter how sick he got.

"Where did you hear all this?"

"I got a friend down at the police station. Met up with him at that bar last night after I got off. He told me all about it. Creepy as hell, if you ask me. But hey, maybe it will end up on that show... you know the one... about unsolved cases?"

"Unsolved Mysteries?" asked Peggy with an answer quick as a flash.

"Yeah, that's the one. Maybe it will go down as one of those."

There was a pause, then Peggy said, "Hey, I gotta run and do my rounds. See you later?"

"Yeah," said Alex, "I'm pulling a double, so I'm not going anywhere."

"Will's out again?"

"Yeah... not sure what that's about. But it's alright, I got a week off after tonight. That's the only reason they're letting me pull this double."

"See ya."

The sound of footsteps on tile echoed as they faded in the distance. The only remaining sound was the song of the medical monitors.

Hesitating for a moment, but then realizing that she needed to get the lay of the land, Clarissa opened her eyes, stretched, sat up in her hospital bed, and looked around. She had to get out of there and fast before the police came. Or should she? Her father had always taught her to take responsibility for her actions, but she was so scared. She swung her legs over the edge of her bed. Clarissa thought maybe it was best to run away somewhere and think it through. She wasn't sure what the right answer was. Besides, that thing was out there, wasn't it? Would it come after her again?

Before she could move any further, someone cleared their throat. Clarissa looked around behind her and there, in the corner, sat a curvy woman wearing purple scrubs. She had a clipboard and was scribbling something down. She looked up at Clarissa.

The woman was tall, one of the tallest women Clarissa had ever seen. Her voice was soft but quavered a little, and Clarissa could see lines of wrinkles gathering in her forehead and strands of gray hiding in the woman's brown hair.

"Well, hello there. How are you feeling this afternoon?"

Surprised that she hadn't known anyone else was in the room, Clarissa blinked a few times and thought about it. She wanted to say something, but she couldn't find the words.

After a few moments' pause, the woman said, "It's alright, you don't have to talk just yet if you don't want to, but let me go tell the doctor, so they can come check you out."

Before Clarissa could say anything, the woman rose and was gone.

Then, all at once, she had to pee. She tried to put her feet down on the ground and realized that she had a long tube attached to her arm, and when she accidentally tugged at it, she felt a sharp pain in her left arm.

"Ouch!"

A soft feminine voice said, "You may want to take the IV with you if you're going somewhere."

A short blond woman with an amiable smile and curves similar to the woman who had just left, stood just inside the doorway.

"I am Dr. Moore, but you can call me Vanessa, if you like. May I ask where you are planning on going?"

There was a lightness in the doctor's tone that surprised Clarissa. If she was in trouble, wouldn't they be angry that she tried to get up? Then she thought better. If she was in trouble and they didn't want her to run, maybe they would be really nice to her just like on that show her step dad Ted always watched.

Clarissa pointed to the open door that led to the bathroom in the corner, hoping that would be a good enough excuse, and it wasn't like she was lying. She really needed to pee.

"Ah, I see." The doctor gave her a smile. "Well, that is also expected after waking up from a sedative."

Clarissa winced as she moved the crux of her arm and the IV needle sent small shock waves of pain up her arm. The woman wore a white lab coat over a light blue shirt. She had big rosy cheeks and her demeanor was as bright as a blue sky. There was something in the juxtaposition of the doctor's personality and the horror of the meadow that rubbed against something uncomfortable inside.

"Is that your first IV?" The doctor pointed to her arm.

Clarissa nodded. Her throat was dry, and she felt a little woozy. She sat back down on the hospital bed, feeling the urgency of her need to pee growing.

"How are you feeling?" The doctor paused and then said, "Oh, I'm sorry, you need to use the restroom, don't you?"

Clarissa nodded. A few strange noises came out of her mouth and just as quickly as she had opened it, she shut it again. No words would come. It wasn't so much that she could not speak, but somehow, she couldn't make her mouth move. It refused to obey her.

"Do you need help?"

Clarissa shook her head, but then paused, thought about it, and nodded. She couldn't easily get to the bathroom herself, not with this tube attached to her.

The doctor walked over, helped support her, got her to the bathroom, and then back to the bed.

Clarissa's stomach rumbled. It was so loud the doctor laughed.

"I bet you're hungry. We're going to do a quick exam and a few tests, and then I will get you something gentle on your stomach. You were just on a ventilator and feeding tube, so it's going to take your body a little time to get back to normal food. I heard you had a scary experience this morning with the ventilator."

Clarissa guessed the ventilator was the thing down her throat and she wanted to ask, but the words still wouldn't come. So she said nothing, she made no sign at all.

The doctor frowned. "Can you understand me?"

Clarissa nodded.

"Are you having a hard time speaking?"

She nodded.

"Are you experiencing any pain?"

Clarissa thought about it. Then she pointed to the IV.

"Anywhere else?"

Clarissa mentally scanned her body. Doing so seemed to activate some minor aches, but the only part that was still hurting was her right palm. It throbbed dully. And until she had thought about it, she hadn't really noticed it. She pointed to the center of her hand.

"Yes, that will probably hurt for a few more days. It's quite a deep wound. Anywhere else?"

Clarissa shook her head. She wondered how she could have such a deep wound on her hand when it was just a zipper from a jacket that cut her.

"Good. Listen, I'm so sorry about this morning. I know it was terrifying. You certainly aren't the first person to react to a ventilator that way, and you won't be the last. They can be scary machines, especially when something happens and you wake up on one."

Clarissa looked down at the white-tiled floor, and then up around the room at the yellow walls. She said nothing. Even if she could have said something, she didn't think it would matter. Terrifying wasn't strong enough of a word for the meadow. She didn't think the experience would ever drift far from her memory in the same way that the terrible night her father had died never left her. It was always there, lingering in the back of her mind, waiting to jump out at her like a monster in a closet.

"Your parents will be here soon. You've been here for several days and we told them they had to go home and get some rest. We told them we would call them back as soon as you were awake."

The doctor crouched down so she was at eye level with Clarissa. "We're going to get you all the help you need to feel better, okay? Then you're going to go home and rest."

Go home? So she wasn't in trouble? Was this some kind of trick? On Ted's tv show, sometimes the cops played tricks to get information out of guilty people. But mostly they did that in rooms with a table.

Clarissa trembled. She felt so awful, as if something had sucked all the joy out of her, a hollowing out of happiness. Inside, there was only a vacant space where the joy had been. There was something black descending over her vision. There had been something like that in the meadow. The entire world seemed a little dimmer, but it wasn't. Was she still dreaming? The doctor was still speaking, but she seemed distant.

"Clarissa? Are you alright?" asked the Doctor.

Clarissa's attention snapped back. As it did, a nurse entered the room. The first thing that Clarissa saw was her eye, swollen blue-black. She remembered flailing, and something colliding with her first. Here it was, her handy work. First she pushed the boy, then she punched the nurse. What was wrong with her? What would her father think of her if he saw what she had done? The world dimmed a little more, and the room felt smaller. It was as if that black shroud from the meadow had followed her to the hospital and was pressing in at the edges of her vision.

Then there was fear, rising through all the discomfort of the IV, the endless beeping of monitors, the sounds up and down the hall of clacking footsteps. Fear pierced through it all with one thought. She hadn't gotten away. Was she still there? Was this a dream? Did the creature in the woods have her trapped in some sort of nightmare?

The nurse eyed her. There was little warmth in that gaze, just half-hidden resentment. It wasn't something Clarissa had ever experienced, but she would become familiar with that gaze in the years ahead. The nurse sat down next to Clarissa with a blood pressure cuff as the doctor wrote on her clipboard. She had watched her father endure this ritual many times before, but had never been a part of it.

Before thinking about her father and the blood that seeped under the bathroom door on that terrible night, words came rushing out, free from whatever blockage had held them.

"Am I going to get sick?" asked Clarissa.

Both the doctor and nurse stopped and looked at her.

It was the doctor who said, "Sick? Well, at this time we don't think so. We've treated all your wounds that might get infected and you've been on medicine to help prevent it. Other than some bumps and bruises, you seem fine."

That awful night, the one when her father had died in the bathroom flashed before her. Clarissa sat in front of the door, listening to the strange strangled sounds of her father's last gasps. She sat weeping against the door, not knowing what to do to help her father. A single rivulet of blood had seeped out under the door and Clarissa had put her hand in it. It was that blood that never seemed to come off and sometimes she washed her hands extra times at night when she couldn't sleep.

But there was something else about that night that troubled her. Something that danced just on the edges of her memory. Some experience that, at the time, she could not articulate. She had seen something in the corner, hadn't she? Two pinpricks nested in shadows, red and glowing. Were they the same lights she had seen as the creature pursued her in the meadow?

The doctor interrupted the memory, "I think you're going to make a full recovery."

Clarissa looked at the doctor, and then the nurse with the black eye, and felt the shame rise in her all over again. She looked down.

"Is there something we should know, Clarissa? Do you feel sick?"

Clarissa shook her head.

"Well, if anything changes, you can tell us, okay? Our job is to help you get better."

Clarissa nodded.

The ritual resumed. As the nurse cycled through her tasks, Clarissa couldn't help but stare up at that big swollen eye. She had done it. She didn't want to look at it, but another wave of shame prompted her to say, "I'm sorry."

She was almost as shocked about the words as the two adults in the room were. The nurse looked up, startled. Then a series of different emotions cascaded across Clarissa's face. First, anger, then shame, sadness. Clarissa devolved into tears.

The nurse said, "It's alright. It's not your fault. If our roles were reversed I might have done the same thing." The nurse forced a smile, but it was clear to Clarissa that she didn't wear it well.

Clarissa nodded. "Wh... Wh... What'ssss a ventilator?"

The words were tough, hesitant, like chewing on a hard piece of meat that she wasn't ready to swallow. They were there. She could think clearly, but it was like her muscles didn't want to work.

The doctor, with a soft and warm tone said, "Are you having trouble speaking?"

She nodded.

The doctor answered, "A ventilator is a device that helps keep the air flowing to your lungs when you're sick or unconscious, and you were unconscious for three days. But it's also not the most pleasant experience, and to wake up on one when you don't know what's happening to you can be terrifying to anyone, even adults."

The nurse said, "So really, don't worry about it." The nurse had a thick South Philly accent.

It was the nurse's tone that made Clarissa feel a little better.

The doctor said, "Is there anything else you can tell me about how you're feeling?"

Clarissa tried to reply, but the words wouldn't come again. It was as if, by the very act of thinking about speaking, she couldn't do it. So she shrugged.

"You don't want to?"

Clarissa shook her head.

"Is it still hard to speak?"

She nodded vigorously.

"Well, there's a large bump on your head and you have a concussion. We already ran a CT scan on you and didn't see any serious signs of trauma but we could also run an MRI...." The doctor paused for a second, seeming to realize she was talking to a little girl, "Your brain is probably still catching up a bit. That you can speak at all tells me that maybe your brain is still just tired and needs to rest."

The nurse pressed her fingers into Clarissa's wrist and looked at her watch.

She knew she had hit her head in the dream, but that wasn't real, was it? Everything felt so strange. How could she have been asleep for three days?

The words returned. "Ho... oww did I hit mmmm mmm my head?"

The doctor said, "We were hoping you could tell us. You don't remember?"

"No, I rr.. ran out from the mmmm.. meadow b.. b..because that thing was chasing me, and then... I d...d... don't remember anything after that."

"What thing was chasing you?"

Both the doctor and the nurse were staring at her. Both had stopped what they were doing. Clarissa was old enough to know that it would sound insane to the adults. She was afraid to tell them. Worse, something inside of her was screaming at her not to tell them.

Clarissa lowered her head. "D...don't remember." She said instead. "It's all mixed up."

Speaking was growing easier now but it still took focus.

"But someone was chasing you?"

Clarissa nodded.

"Did they hurt you? Touch you in any way?"

She thought about the darkness, about the shadow reaching out to her and something going into her mouth, but that was the ventilator, wasn't it?

"D...d.. don't think it caught me. I... don't remm... remember. I jus.. just woke up here. But the boy..." She couldn't finish the sentence. It was like her mouth had forgotten how to form words. It seemed harder for her to speak of the moment than it did of anything else. Had something happened to her there that made her speech difficult? She strained to remember something, anything, but nothing surfaced.

No one spoke.

Finally, the Doctor said, "We can talk more when you feel up to it, okay?"

Clarissa nodded.

"Can I ask you a few more questions?" asked the doctor.

Clarissa nodded.

"Do you feel like you want to throw up?"

She shook her head.

"Dizziness? Disorientation? Tired?"

Clarissa felt both, so she nodded.

"Which? All of them?"

Noticing the ease of talking about anything but the meadow, Clarissa said, "Yes, all of them. My head hurts, and I feel dizzy and feel like I almost want to throw up."

"We can give you something for that sick stomach. But none of this is unexpected. Between your concussion and the sedative we used to help you relax and feel calm after you woke up earlier, both can cause these symptoms."

The doctor scribbled several things down on her notes.

"Any numbness? Tingling anywhere?"

"No. I don't think so."

The nurse concluded her ritual and said, "I'm gonna duck out to check my next patient."

The doctor nodded, turned back to Clarissa, and said, "Okay, I'm gonna check your eyes, ears, and mouth, alright?"

She did, and Clarissa waited patiently through each stage of the exam.

Finally, the doctor said, "Well, I think you're a very lucky girl. That concussion may cause you some problems over the next few weeks or months. But I think you're going to be fine. We're going to keep you here for at least another day for observation. I will let your parents know. But in the meantime, if you need anything or you want to talk to anyone about what happened, we're here to help. Okay?"

"Thank you."

Her voice felt so small. But so long as she wasn't talking about the meadow or what happened, the words were easier. She couldn't help but wonder why that was.

Clarissa watched the doctor leave the room and noticed that the room had grown a little dimmer, the darkness had thickened. The weight of everything she had done, killing the boy, and hitting the nurse, weighed heavily on her.

Clarissa sighed and turned her attention to the old television mounted up above her bed in the corner. She switched on the TV with the remote by the bed. All those days in the hospital with her father meant daytime television was familiar to her. The Price is Right was on. She watched Bob Barker and the contestants, half aware of what was happening.

She pressed into her memories, willing herself to remember those missing moments. But there was nothing there, only the darkness of ignorance. Did they say she had been missing for three days? What had happened during that time? What about the shadow creature in the meadow? Was the meadow just as strange and disturbing as she had remembered, or was that part of the dream, too? She thought of the ring of bones, the trees bending outward, how color and sound had behaved. Those had to be elements of a dream, didn't they?

But the two strangers who had checked in on her earlier had said someone else had seen something. So, she couldn't believe it was just a dream. Besides, someone was dead. His body had decayed faster than it should have. He was dead because of her. She slumped down in her bed. The guilt seeped into her heart as the inanity of the commercial breaks bleated like a wounded animal and filled the room with meaningless noise.

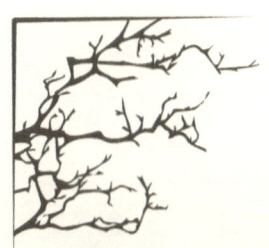

Chapter 4

Confession to a Murder

A little belief,
Can bring relief,
When traveling on a dark road.

But beware that need,
It's a kind of greed,
And can make your sanity erode.

Hold fast to the truth,
In great age or youth,
For only there is wisdom bestowed.

For time will tell,
In the ringing of the bells,
In the light,
All lies corrode.

"Ted, would you stop straightening the pictures and sit down?"

Ted stood opposite Clarissa's hospital bed from the door just in front of a window to the outside world. He paced relentlessly. His pacing wasn't unusual, but now Clarissa was sure he would wear out the tiles on the floor. Ted scratched the top of his balding head. His thick dark eyebrows and brown hair looked thinner than they had a few days before. He had small brown eyes and straight, even teeth. When he smiled, those teeth looked oddly perfect on an average man's face. He was slightly shorter than Clarissa's mother, which was saying something because her mother wasn't very tall.

"Sorry, Audrey, this whole place is just chaos. How do all these doctors and nurses even stand working here? Look at these cables." He pointed intently at the chords coming out from Clarissa's bed. "They're a mess. There's like six fire hazards in here and don't get me started on the plumbing."

Clarissa's mother rolled her eyes. She had the deep red hair of Clarissa, which was still thick and luscious, though the first signs of thinning had begun when Clarissa's father died. Her mother's slender fingers, sharp green eyes, beautiful face, and thick lips were the reason that after Clarissa's father had passed, most of the single men in the area had tried to court her. Her mother was never prom queen, but only because she had no interest. Audrey Lamont was an artist at heart.

Sitting next to Clarissa's hospital bed, her mother said, "He's been like this ever since you went missing."

It was a bit of a shock to Clarissa. She had never felt close to her stepfather. They were lukewarm at best, especially when he was acting like this.

Ted got down on his hands and knees and inspected something in the corner.

"Dammit Ted, sit down, and I mean in your chair."

He looked around, wearing a sheepish grin while on all fours. A wild look danced in his eyes. Clarissa had seen that look before whenever he was being... she searched for the word for a half a moment before remembering it. Ted was peculiar, her mother had said. Clarissa liked the word "weirdo" better.

But it was hard not to smile at his ridiculous behavior at that moment. Her mother caught that smile for just a moment, but then Clarissa tucked it away again, remembering where she was and why.

Ted said, "Okay, fine."

He stood up and sat on a chair in the corner of the room, thin lipped with arms crossed.

"He's cleaned the house a dozen times, Clarissa... a dozen. I'm going to kill him." She shot him a look.

Her mother and Ted had arrived about an hour after the doctor left. It turned out they had been in the hospital for three days and nights, all while she was unconscious. The doctor had to order them to go home and get some rest, food, and a shower because they didn't know when she would wake up. The doctor had promised if there were any changes, she would call right away. They had been gone all of an hour when Clarissa woke and both were sleeping, so they didn't hear the first phone call, nor the second. As they say, the third time was the charm.

There were bags under both of their eyes. Her mother's skin, sallow and waxy, looked tighter somehow. Each of their faces looked as if they carried a heavy load, but smiled through the work. Clarissa knew that smile, it was not that different from the smile her mother wore at her father's funeral, and that made Clarissa's stomach turn a bit.

"I'm so sorry we weren't here when you woke up."

"Mom, you don't have to apologize again."

Her mother's face showed depths of anguish. "You must have been so terrified. I'm so glad you're okay."

Clarissa shivered and closed her eyes for a moment and felt the tree branches coil around her legs, felt something slide down her throat. Felt the panics and screams stir in her all over again. She forced her eyes open and nodded gently, as if avoiding rousing the darkness with recognition.

Her mother looked away in shame.

Ted said, "So what happened to you during those three days?" His voice was colder, with no hint of frustration.

Her mother's head snapped around. "Ted. Seriously. Now?"

"What? I've been worried about her, too. Everyone wants to know."

Her mother sighed, turned back to Clarissa and said, "It's true. He might be a little insensitive right now," she said through gritted teeth and a brief, nasty glance to her left, "But he really has been worried about you, sweetie. He and two dozen other people walked through the woods for two days. Day and night."

"Two days? Did you find me, Ted?"

"No," he said. He opened his mouth to say more and then closed it. There was a long pause, and then he finally said, "But we found the other boy in the meadow."

A chasm of silence fell between them, a monstrous thing where something was nesting. Clarissa thought Ted might know what that thing was. She held her suspicion at bay, not because she was uncertain, but because she wasn't.

Finally, Ted said, "That place was... I don't know. I've never been anywhere like it, Clarissa. I thought that..."

She could hear the fragility in her stepfather's words, as if he needed to assemble the pieces from many sources to make sense of it. Clarissa understood. The meadow had no simple description, no coherence or cohesion. She could see that reflection in Ted's eyes, the one that she knew, without looking in the mirror, was in her own. That place had touched them both.

Clarissa was afraid to ask, but she had to know. "Did you see something there, Ted?"

Ted opened his mouth, looked at her Mother, and she gave him a sharp look back. He closed his mouth and said, "No, nothing. It was, uh... just really creepy, that's all."

Ted had seen something. She was sure of it. Some part of her wanted to probe and pry it out of him. But she knew from that cold sharp stare her mother had given him that was useless, at least for now.

Ted changed the subject. "A little girl found you."

"A little girl? Where was I?"

"You know where the baseball diamonds are, and those snack stands where we get water ice sometimes?"

Clarissa nodded. She shifted in the hospital bed so that she was sitting all the way up. She was tired of laying down, tired of sitting still.

"Then there's those basketball courts behind them, that back up against the woods?"

He paused for a moment and Clarissa nodded and sipped at the water the nurse had left her.

"Well, the girl was chasing a ball in the woods back there, and she stumbled on to you. Which was just the damnedest thing 'cause one of the search parties started through the woods right at that spot and never ran into you. Gives you the creeps, you know?"

"The creeps?" she asked between sips.

Before Ted could answer, her mother rushed to change the subject. "I'm just so glad you're okay. You can talk about what happened when you're ready."

It was useless though, she didn't remember. For the last hour, she tried to make the memories come back, to find some sense in that blank void of time where no memories would surface. She knew there was something in there, some black dread, the origin of the strange darkness that dimmed her vision even now. It was like a shroud, over a dead body. She had seen a picture of how ancient people had wrapped their dead in a blanket, once, in a museum, but the one descending around her was black. She didn't know why she thought of it as a shroud, but that's what it felt like. A burial. It was like watching her father's casket descend into the earth all over again.

Clarissa said, "I don't know."

"You don't know what, sweetie?"

"I don't know what happened to me. It's all just blank. I was running from the meadow, from that thing, and... then the trees were grabbing me, and I fought, and got free, and I woke up here."

Both her mother's face and Ted's turned ashen. They looked at each other for a long moment, as if communicating by telepathy. Their faces looked pinched and strained.

Ted said, "Thing? What thing? Do you mean a person? Was some person chasing you through the woods?"

Now she was certain he had seen something. The truth lay hidden in the layers of his voice. He might actually believe her. It was a hope of sorts, a light in all of this darkness. There was something in her that wanted them to believe her so badly, and another part that was terrified that they just might. A life of similar contradictions lay ahead of her.

"That boy in the meadow? I pushed him down that hill. It was an accident. I didn't even realize it was a hill until I looked over the edge and I saw him at the bottom...." She swallowed hard, not wanting to say the next words, but forcing them out anyway. "Mom, he wasn't moving."

Their silence urged her on.

"He was the one who stole my skateboard, so I chased him through the woods, and when I finally caught him, I shoved him to try to get my skateboard back. He was bigger and older than me, so I thought if I pushed him, I could grab it before he got up and ran away."

Still they waited, listening. She hesitated, looking at both of their faces for clues to her fate. But there were none. Only the beep of the hospital monitors filled the silence. A single person walked down the hall just outside the door. But now, with the day fading, there were fewer visitors.

"So, I followed him down into that meadow, because on the ground next to him was my skateboard. I thought maybe he was just knocked out."

Should she tell them about how the ground swallowed her blood? About the ring of bones? The strange trees? The color and sound both vanishing? Clarissa thought of her dream and waking up on the ventilator. How much of what she had seen had happened to her? Was the whole thing just a dream? How could anyone believe her if she didn't know the truth, herself? She was so stuffed full of questions that she thought she might be sick with it. All structures inside, all the things she thought she knew, were unstable.

But there was some ground to stand on. Ted had seen something. She wished she knew what it was, because then she would know how much to tell them. Even if Ted had seen something, it didn't mean he would believe her, and she didn't think her mother would at all. She, the skeptic. Even her paintings contained undercurrents of her rationalism.

Clarissa's mother seemed to sense her distress. She reached out and grasped Clarissa's hand gently. "Go on, we're listening."

Clarissa took a deep breath. "So, I got down to the bottom of the hill and that place was super creepy. There were lots of animal bones and stuff, and I realized the boy wasn't moving. So I turned him over, and..."

Rotting flesh and the smell of decay stirred in her memory. She feared that the scent had taken up permanent residence in her nostrils. She tried to push away the flash of memory, a face melting in the elements, patches of skin missing and muscle exposed, with maggots chewing out the last remnants of eyes, leaving no flesh or tissue behind. It was hollow; the flesh was hollow. And she thought... all flesh is hollow.

Clarissa looked at her mother. She looked at her step-father. She stared for a long time. Her mother squeezed her hand again.

"He was dead," said Ted. They were loud words.

Both she and her mom looked up at him. A ripple through the fabric of silence. His words broke her trance. Oh, how her memory could take her captive, hold her hostage to her fears in a spiral of agony.

Ted said, "It's a hard thing to say sometimes. I saw the body Clarissa, it scared me too... I..."

Ted's words, like her mother's hand, grounded her. Everything felt so unreal, so difficult to comprehend. Ever since the doctor left after examining her, she had wondered, had everything really happened? Already her memories made her feel like she was chasing a ghost. Ted's words changed that.

Clarissa wept. It was a sudden eruption, a ring of emotions orbited her, pressing their gravity until she could not hold back the tears.

Her mother wrapped her arms around her.

"I was so scared, Mom." Clarissa sniffed and rubbed her nose on her mother's shoulder, letting the tears soak into the cotton. But it was warm and familiar, and that made it a little easier. Though, she wished her father was here, too.

"Shh, I know sweetie, we were scared too." She could feel her mother's tears drip and then run down her bare arms, the same place where Clarissa's tears tread, so that their sorrow united.

To her surprise, Ted stood and wrapped his arms around both of them the best he could. It helped. It made her feel like, even though Ted wasn't her dad, his spirit was with her at that moment.

After several tearful moments, they broke their embrace. Ted sat back down in his chair. Her mother stayed by her bed, holding hands. Clarissa felt lighter, the room brightened, as if the shroud drew back and let the light of the sun pass onto her for the first time since she had stepped into that meadow.

Still, a question burned in Clarissa, or at least, one above the others.

Clarissa asked, "Did they find out who the boy was?"

Ted said, "Well..." Ted looked at her mother, then back at Clarissa. "No, they haven't figured that out yet. All they know is that he's been dead for a while."

She remembered what those two strangers that afternoon had said while they thought she was sleeping, but she had wanted to hear it again from someone she knew.

"Go on sweetie. What happened next?"

Clarissa looked around, having almost forgotten that she was even telling a story. But she pressed on. She was almost finished.

"I... after I turned the boy over something appeared at the far side of the meadow. That place felt so awful. I think it lives there. I think it was eating him, somehow."

There was something in Ted's expression. His fists clenched, his jaw set. She had never seen that look on his face before, nor the tension rising around him. He looked pale, almost angry. Though it wasn't quite that. For a moment, she thought he might speak, but Ted said nothing.

"What was it?" asked her mother.

"I don't know how to describe it, but it was like a shadow, and it was coming for me, chasing me. So I grabbed my skateboard and ran back up the hill. Then, like I said, I thought I tripped, and all around me tree branches and roots pinned me down and held me still. Then one went in my mouth and...and I woke up and attacked someone. Later, the doctor told me it was just that machine on my face." She paused, then said, "I may have accidentally punched a nurse."

Her mom, wide eyed, said, "Punched a nurse?"

Clarissa thought maybe the doctors would have already told them this, but they didn't.

"I didn't know what was happening. I woke up, and they had tied me down, and that thing was on me."

Ted started laughing. They both looked at him.

"What's so funny?" asked Audrey.

Still chuckling, he said, "I'm just imagining that poor nurse having to explain to all her friends and family how a nine-year-old socked her a good one."

It was a little funny. Clarisa smiled and her mom did too, though Clarissa thought it might have been with some trepidation. It made Clarissa feel a little better about her accidental assault.

"But Clarissa, sweetie, you don't remember anything after...the thing chased you?"

She nodded. "Nothing. But you believe me...don't you, Mom?"

There was a pained look on her face. "Well, I don't disbelieve you. Our minds have a way of filling in the gaps when we're scared."

Ted said nothing. He stood up, crossing his arms. All the humor had left him just as quickly as it had come.

"What does that mean, Mom?"

"Well, I'm sure someone chased you. I'm sure something terrifying happened to you..."

Her mother broke off. They were dancing around it. Her mother looked so tired, so frail, like she would just turn to dust, or like something was eating her, draining her. That scared Clarissa.

"I don't want to talk about this anymore, Mom."

Her mother's face shifted, lightened, the depth of despair that lived in the lines of her face seemed to shrink, but only a little.

"That sounds like a good idea. I think we all need rest, and now that we know you're safe and the doctor told us you're okay, I think we can finally get the rest we need."

Ted saw something in the corner and walked over. He pulled a handkerchief out of his pocket and picked up some crumbs off of the floor, examining them.

"Please, Ted, sit down."

Ted looked around, frowned, and sat on the padded bench under the window.

"The doctor said she wants to keep you at least another day or two for observation, just to run a few more tests and make sure you're okay. So I brought you some things to keep you occupied."

"Like what?"

Her mother smiled. "One moment, I left them in the hall."

Her mother disappeared behind the curtain and then came back with two things. The first was a duffel bag that Clarissa suspected was full of stuff to make her feel more comfortable, and the second thing was...

"Oh my god, my skateboard!"

She almost jumped out of bed to grab it, but thought twice when she felt her IV tug at her and a short sharp pain climbed up her left arm.

Her mother had a big smile on her face. "Yes, they found it next to you in the woods."

She felt the dark shroud dissipate. The room was full of light and happiness again. Her mother handed it to her. She hugged it and pressed her face against the top of the deck.

"Thank you, Mom." She could barely keep the tears at bay.

"Of course, honey. I know how much it means to you. And I just know that your father was watching over you when you were out there in the woods."

Ted had a sour expression on his face. He got up and started checking all the cables that ran from her bed to the monitors. He hated that skateboard. She did not know why. He seemed to hate both James and Margie, too, but for no apparent reason.

"Ted, will you please sit down." Her mother's tone courted anger.

He was worse than usual. Clarissa couldn't understand why. There were a lot of things she didn't really understand about Ted.

"I brought you your two favorite tapes. The nurse said they will bring in a VCR for you in a little while so you can watch them."

"X-games and The Hobbit?"

"Of course. I also brought you a few changes of clothes and a box of tasty cakes for a snack, once the doctor says you're okay eating regular food again, that is."

She leaned forward and hugged her mom. "Thanks. You're the best Mom, ever."

Clarissa opened the bag and started riffling through it. There was a book in the bag that she didn't recognize.

"What is...The Sword of Shannara?"

It was a thick book. Clarissa hadn't ever seen one so big before. Its size almost begged you not to open it.

Ted said, "One of my favorite fantasy books. It's kind of like The Hobbit, except instead of a ring, it's a magic sword. I thought you might like it. I know it's really long, so I thought we could read some together in the hospital to see if you like it."

Clarissa stared at the cover, where two adventures stared at a magic, glowing sword. She flipped open the cover and read the description. It actually sounded pretty interesting. She had just read The Hobbit a few months before, and she had loved the animated film ever since she could remember.

"Thanks, Ted."

He smiled and nodded, but said little else. It was strange that he seemed so muted. She wanted to know what he had seen, and if anyone else had seen it. He fidgeted and twitched in his chair. She still didn't quite know what to think of her stepfather. He could be such a pain in the ass, but sometimes he seemed nice.

Ted said, "So, has the detective been by, yet?"

"Ted," said her mother.

"What?"

"She just woke up."

Before her mother and Ted had arrived, Clarissa had thought long and hard about what she would tell the police. She was supposed to tell the truth to the police, wasn't she? And she wanted to, sort of. She was afraid to tell them about the boy, how she had shoved him. And, well, about all the other stuff that no one was going to believe. She wished Monica had been there; someone, anyone, who had survived to make her feel less crazy.

"Am I...am I going to jail?"

"What? Jail? Why would you think that?" asked her mother.

"I...I killed him."

Her mother said, "Sweetie, that's not possible. We already told you, no one knows who that boy is, but we know he had been down there a long time."

"I did Mom. I don't know how his body got all decayed so fast. It didn't make any sense. He fell, and I turned him over to check on him, and he looked like that."

"But you couldn't have." Her mother's words were a little more firm this time, a wall guarding reason.

Clarissa remembered the sting she felt when she shoved him. She looked down at her right hand and the wound that was already healing.

"I know I pushed him, Mom, because that's how I got this." She held up her hand for them both to see. "When I shoved him, my hand caught on something on his jacket and it cut open my hand."

She wasn't going to tell them about the earth drinking her blood, or any of the other weird details. She wouldn't describe the monster, either. She was sure of that now. She had given them an edited version, because in her mind, her mother would never believe her if she didn't.

Both Ted and her mother looked at each other but said nothing. She knew they didn't believe her. But she couldn't decide if that was a good thing or a bad thing. On one hand, if her parents and the doctors both seemed to agree that she couldn't have killed that boy, maybe that was part of the dream, too? What about the police, though?

"Jacket? Clarissa, it was 93 degrees that day. No one in their right mind would wear a jacket."

Why hadn't Clarissa thought of that? She pictured the boy as he was when she and Monica had first seen him. He had been wearing a jacket. It wasn't a heavy jacket or anything, more like a windbreaker, but her mother was right. Why in the world would he wear a jacket if it was so hot?

Her mother said, "I think maybe it's better if we stop talking about all this stuff right now and just get some rest."

Her mother stroked her hair. It felt nice. Clarissa couldn't remember the last time she had done that and somehow, in that moment, she felt a little better. But the shroud, the darkness, was still there, even if she couldn't see it. She gripped her skateboard, which she vowed never to let out of her sight ever again.

Softly, as if she whispered a bedtime story, her mother said, "Sometimes, when we experience something really terrible, our mind tries to make sense of it by filling in gaps. Our memories play tricks on us. It's why when you ask two people about the same event a few weeks later, their stories won't match."

As Clarissa relaxed into the safety of her mother's presence, she couldn't help but think that there was only one person who knew the truth of what had happened down there.

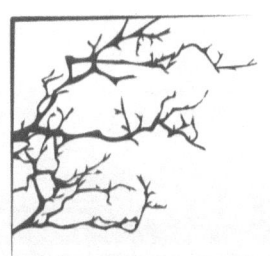

Chapter 5

To Tell the Truth for the First Time

We never really want truth,
When a story will suffice,
We seek to live/laugh/love,
Desiring comforting advice.

Truth brings tragedy,
Scattering who you think you are,
It forces us down dark corridors,
A dangerous path we must journey far.

No one wants the truth,
About the person they have been,
For if you look too deeply,
You might find a grievous sin.

C larissa's days after the hospital knew no rest, nor healing. Every moment was anxious with the expectation that something was around the next corner, that the sounds of machines and sliding curtains hid something sinister behind them. She feared she would cross through a doorway and find herself back in the meadow or the forest, bound by the creature that had followed her out. There was an overwhelming sense that she had woken something there. That crack, that trembling earth, that angry wind, were much on her mind.

Nothing seemed real. She expected to wake from a dream again, to find herself in some other place, some other reality. And there were those missing days that neither she nor anyone else could bring to accounting for any semblance of balance or release. The missing memories were a monster that stalked every conscious hour. Her curiosity clawed at those days, filling the cracks in time with her greatest fears and anxieties, a mortar of misery to some ramshackle existence.

Had the creature done something to her? Where had it gone? Was it still out there? Would it be back? Had she imagined the whole thing? What happened to the body of that other boy, the thief who had led her to that horrible place? Was she responsible for his death?

Clarissa remembered her father had once told her that a life full of questions and curiosity was a life of light, and hope, and growth. But this endless probing was devoid of wonder. A seed planted in a season of discord would bear the bitterest fruit. Clarissa knew, deep down, that there was some terrible truth to uncover. Something had happened to her, but there was no merchant to ask after the cost. Later, when she discovered the whole truth, when those missing days returned to her, she would descend into madness. For the cost was more than anyone should ever bear. But some carry burdens far heavier than others, and few are offered a choice they understand.

The social worker who had visited her daily in the hospital and spoken with her parents as Clarissa prepared to go home, had said that traumatic events sometimes steal memories, and that Clarissa's parents should consider having her see a therapist to work through the experience. Ted had said that therapy was for mentally ill people, that all Clarissa needed was to get home and get back to her life. After all, he said, people died all the time and finding a body in the woods was terrible for a small child, but life was unfair.

Since money was tight, her mother stood in silent disagreement.

Clarissa's nights home were haunted with shadows casting shapes on her walls. The wind and streetlights, and the light of stray cars at late hours, cast claws from the tree branches through windows. The first night home, Clarissa had screamed with the passing of the first car as it created shapes in the dark. Her mother, who had taken off of work for a week to be with her, spent the night in her bed, holding Clarissa, helping her feel safe. In her mother's embrace, she slept. The next morning, Ted brought home a blackout curtain to shield Clarissa from the shadows.

The second night home, Clarissa screamed in the pitch black, for now that shadows couldn't form from street lights and passing cars, her eyes made terrible pictures in the blackness so that she could not escape the images of the boy's rotting corpse decaying in front of her. She could feel the maggots crawling on her as they fled his body. The tangy smell of rotting flesh, like the sickeningly sweet smell of sewage, burned into her nostrils. It never strayed far from her mind. In the deep dark of her bedroom, even with the distant city noises, all her senses seemed focused on the worst of all things.

Clarissa's mother spent the second night with her to ease her terror.

On the third day home, Ted took down the blackout curtain. Instead, he put up a short strand of Christmas lights that pulsed with a soft glow. On the third night, there was no screaming. Instead, nightmares.

When Clarissa closed her eyes, she ran from the meadow all over again, the branches reaching out to hold her down so that the thing that lived in the meadow could take possession of her and use her for its sinister purpose.

Clarissa fought back, struggling and straining under wood and earth, fixing her to the forest floor. Breaking free, she ran and stood at the front door of her house. The door, normally white, was blood red. It seemed to drip and ooze, and as Clarissa grasped the doorknob and turned it, her hands grew slick and sticky with blood.

The house was empty, stark, clean, bleak. All colors were muted, all save the doors. All were red. She called out for help, for warmth, for comfort, for some acknowledgment that this was a place of safety and love. There, like a ghost, standing at the top of the stairs, looking down at her, was her father. His face was all soft angles, and suddenly, Clarissa found herself longing to be in his arms, to look up and see his gray eyes, to nuzzle into his chest the way she used to when they would watch movies together.

Hope filled her, for though she knew he had died on that terrible night three years gone, Clarissa's tenuous grasp on reality promised her that perhaps he was still alive somehow, that maybe everything would be alright.

Running toward him and climbing the stairs, her movement slowed. She looked up, desperate to reach him, but found that the stairs were covered in ferns, and branches, and roots, growing up from the floor and holding her in place. Clarissa reached down, desperate to pull herself free, but her hands, still slick with blood, made the roots slippery. She wiped her hands on her clothes, but they would not come clean.

Looking up at her father, she pleaded for help. But his eyes had turned from their cool gray-blue to a darker shade of red, like those same terrible orbs in the meadow.

Her father turned and walked to the bathroom and shut the door. Panic consumed her, and she pulled again at the roots, her fingers slipping. She couldn't let him go in that bathroom, not again. She wrapped the end of her shirt around the roots and yanked herself free. Running up the stairs, she dodged the snaring roots and vines waiting for her and charged the door, slamming her body against it. The wood groaned with her efforts. She was bigger now, older. Maybe she could save him this time.

Despite its complaints, the door did not budge. Clarissa pounded, shouting, calling to her father, knowing exactly what was happening on the other side. She remembered the single hand print, streaked in blood, smeared above the toilet, pointing to the crumpled body like some great red arrow. She looked down at the blood covering her hands, and there, out of the corner of her eye and to her left, were two crimson eyes, wrapped in the shadow of the corner adjacent to the door.

A claw slipped out of the shadow, taking form as it reached for her. Forgetting the door, she backed away. Tripping, she fell over the banister and tumbled not to the first floor of her house, but into endless darkness, tumbling as long as her life would carry her.

2. Clarissa opened her eyes early on the fourth morning home, waking from the press of darkness. The sun hovered just below the horizon. Most people were still sleeping before the long summer day began. For a long time she lay there, unmoving, staring at the ceiling, uncertain of what horrors might emerge.

After a while, it was the boredom and the hunger that convinced her she was awake. In the end, it is the mundane and the simple things that can bring us the certainty of our waking state, for dreams and nightmares alike, present grand arguments, and the simple, small things often go unnoticed.

Clarissa ventured downstairs where her mother sat at the dark wooden table, reading a book with a cup of coffee steaming in the new light of the day. A few shafts of light peaked in through the curtains, illuminating the leaves of some of her mother's potted plants on the tiled kitchen counter.

Her mother looked up as Clarissa walked into the kitchen. "Good morning, sweetie. Did you sleep okay?"

What could she say to that? Too tired of all that had happened, Clarissa said simply, "Fine, Mom."

Her mother looked her up and down, appraising, calculating, and then asked, "Would you like me to make you some French toast?"

Clarissa nodded. It was her favorite breakfast food. "Yes, please."

Her mother smiled and stood, making her way around the kitchen to grab ingredients and the large aluminum mixing bowls for the batter. The sound of pots and pans clinking against one another as her mother gathered her materials felt like a kind of musical comfort to Clarissa.

Her mother placed the cooking implements on the counter, next to the ancient black stove.

Her mother said, "Clarissa, there's a detective coming to speak with you this morning."

"A detective?"

Clarissa shuddered. She wanted to run back up to her room and lock the door. It was finally happening. Regardless of what her mother and Ted had said, she was going to jail. Even if the creature had killed the boy, she had pushed him down into its lair. She was responsible for his death.

"She just wants to talk to you," her mother said, in an even and calm tone. "Because of the other boy. Everyone is looking for answers."

Clarissa nodded. But inside, the dread wrapped its way around her heart, holding her still.

They were both silent for a while. It seemed the only sound was the wooden spoon on the side of the aluminum bowl as her mother mixed the ingredients. Then, her mother dipped the bread in the bowl and, one by one, laid down the soaked bread on the griddle. Normally, the sound of the sizzling, and the smell of vanilla and cinnamon, would wash away any anxiety, but not then.

Reading her daughter's concern in the silence, her mother said, "You don't have to worry, Clarissa. You have done nothing wrong."

But what did her mother know? What did anyone know?

"I pushed him, Mom."

Her mother turned, leaning against the counter, and frowned. "That's not possible, sweetie. He was dead for weeks before you got there."

Clarissa didn't argue. There was no point. But something occurred to her. What if... what if she had been there for weeks? The color, the sound, the feel, everything about that place was strange and disturbing. Maybe she had killed the boy, and because time was funny in the meadow, the body had decayed in front of her. She couldn't help but think of how fast the day had faded when she chased the boy through the woods.

"Sweetie, as long as you tell the truth, everything will be fine."

Her mother turned and flipped the French toast.

Clarissa didn't want to talk about it. There was no point. She didn't even really understand what had happened to her, and she doubted this detective would, either.

"Where's Ted?"

"Oh, off on one of his errands to find parts to fix the house."

"Fix the house? What's broken?"

A long sigh took precedence over sizzling slices of bread. "You know how he his...his condition. He...well...."

Her mother trailed off and slid the finished pieces of French toast onto a plate for Clarissa and put them in front of her.

Her mother didn't need to say anything. Earlier in the year, she had found out that Ted had been fired from just about every plumber job in the area. At first, her mother had thought that he had a drinking or drug problem, but that wasn't it. Instead, it was his obsessive need for balance, order, control. Her mother had called up Ted's former boss, Pat McKenry, because she couldn't get a straight answer out of Ted, and being newly married, she was worried that she had made a huge mistake.

McKenry had told her that Ted would spend all day at a house for a simple job. He would rearrange the pipes and do extra hours of work that was well beyond the scope of the project. He couldn't stand for things to be out of order. If he saw even the tiniest flaw anywhere, he would go out of his way to fix it. Several customers complained when he showed up the next day to fix something because he said that he couldn't sleep the previous night. He was up thinking about their sewer lines he told them, and had to go back to fix them or he wouldn't get any rest.

Some customers were more than happy for the free work and welcomed Ted back. That worked out for some, but others found that a week of constant work and water outages was more than they wanted or expected. For a while, McKenry had tried sending Ted out with a partner, and that had helped, but he couldn't be trusted on his own. Pat McKenry had said he liked Ted a lot, but he wasn't playing with a full deck of cards, and ultimately had to let him go.

That's when Ted came clean. Clarissa's mother had cornered him and demanded an explanation. Clarissa listened in at first, before both adults realized she was there. When they finally discovered Clarissa had been listening, her mother asked her to come in and sit down. "This concerns you too, I guess," she had said. After all, Ted had already taken apart sections of the house to fix it on two dozen occasions.

Neither her mother, nor Clarissa had noticed at first. The house was eighty years old and overdue for repairs. Ted had fixed everything. In the first months of their new marriage, Audrey Lamont was overjoyed at Ted's enthusiastic efforts to bring her house to full repair. But now, after a year of marriage, everything that needed fixing was fixed.

As Ted explained his condition, Clarissa struggled to understand the meaning of some words and sentences. He had gone to a doctor at some point. The doctor had said that he has a disease in his mind that makes him obsess over things. He cried as he confessed, and even Clarissa felt bad and hugged him. Because it turned out that it wasn't entirely his fault that he was such a pain in the ass.

"That's why I proposed so quickly, Audrey," he said. He explained he waited to move in until after the honeymoon. As long as he was happy, he could keep most of the compulsions at bay. The moment he felt stressed, he couldn't help himself. He knew that once he got fired, he wouldn't be able to hide the truth anymore. The longest he had ever held a job was two years. By the time he had entered Clarissa's and Audrey's life, eleven places had fired him and word had spread of his problem.

Her mother was furious, but she fumed with a blank expression as Ted explained his way around his particular quirks and habits. After that night, there were several more days of arguments, though Clarissa caught only snippets of shouting through the walls on a few occasions.

But in the end, her mother had admitted that she, too, was rushing into a relationship. Audrey had been desperately lonely and exhausted from working endless hours. She, too, was eager to rush in. She did love Ted. So they placed a bridge between them, because a rift had formed, and it would take time for the storms and winds of life to wear the mountains away and wipe the slate clean.

For now, her mother had realized she had another person to care for, to nurture. In some ways, that seemed to make her feel happy. Later, looking back, when Clarissa was an adult herself, and wanted so badly to be a mother, but couldn't because Demon was always on her heels, she would wonder if sometimes people pick partners to placate that instinct.

But it was hard going.

They were a fractured three. Each one tormented in their own way. Her mother had never really been the same since her father's illness and death. Ted had sometimes brought light into her eyes, but wounds that come from a depth of love like her parents had shared can take a lifetime to heal. Sometimes they never do.

Ted more than pulled his weight around the house, and that helped. He was a decent cook, too. Sometimes he burned things, but mostly her mother came home to leftovers in the fridge. Occasionally, he would leave her notes with the leftovers. Clarissa read one once, curious. It was a simple note, one expressing gratitude for her hard work. And that was when Clarissa had decided that maybe Ted was okay.

As Clarissa finished her French toast, there was a knock on the door. Clarissa's stomach dropped.

3   Clarissa waited in her seat, and her mother went out of the kitchen, and around the corner to the front door. Clarissa slipped out of her chair and followed silently, peering just around the corner so she would have a good view as the woman entered.

Her mother had already opened the door, and the detective stood just inside the threshold. She was a well-rounded woman of medium build and height. Her hair was shoulder length, and her eyes and nose sharp. A small hook-shaped scar circled her left eye. She wore a gray pant suit, with a pink shirt peeking out.

"Good morning," said her mother.

"Good morning," said the woman. "I'm detective Corrin. It's nice to meet you." The woman held out her hand and Clarissa's mother took it. "You must be Audrey Lamont?"

"Yes." Said her mother amiably enough, though Clarissa noticed a little edge under her voice. "Come in. Can I get you some coffee? French toast? I just finished cooking."

"It smells wonderful in here, but I had a big breakfast. Coffee will be just fine. Black, please."

Her mother welcomed the detective in and Clarissa dashed back to the kitchen table to pretend that she hadn't been watching. She shoveled a few pieces of French toast in her mouth. The syrup dribbled down her chin, and she wiped it away with her sleeve as the detective walked into the dining room.

"Well, hello, you must be Clarissa."

Clarissa said nothing. She didn't know what to say. Here was a woman that might be her jailer after today. Instead, she looked down at her food, trying not to think about everything that had happened to her.

"I'm detective Corrin, but you can call me Andrea."

Clarissa's mother poured coffee into a mug and handed it to the detective who, still standing, loomed large over Clarissa.

"Hi," said Clarissa. Her voice sounded small and mousy.

"How old are you, Clarissa?"

"Nine."

"My daughter is ten."

Clarissa's mother said, "Oh really? What school does she go to?"

"Ben Franklin. Where do you go, Clarissa?"

Clarissa didn't answer. Instead, she put more French toast in her mouth.

"Clarissa, it's important you answer the detective's questions."

"It's alright, I'm sure I'd be nervous if a detective came to talk to me, too. And Clarissa has been through a lot."

The detective smiled at Clarissa and then said, "Ms. Lamont, would it be okay if I talked to your daughter alone?"

Her mother said, "I don't think that's a good idea. She just woke up and-"

Clarissa surprised herself, resigning herself to her fate and cutting her mother off. "It's okay, Mom."

Her mother opened her mouth to argue, but nodded slowly, gave Clarissa a look as if to say, I'm not really going anywhere, walked out of the room, and went up the stairs to her bedroom, shutting the door behind her.

The detective sat at the table across from Clarissa. She pulled a notepad and pen out of her front breast pocket. Her smile was warm and gentle, her eyes kind. She reminded Clarissa of the way her mother used to look at her before her father had died, but with a different hair and eye color.

Clarissa's guts squirmed with eels trying to break free. She wasn't convinced that the police believed the same thing that her parents did. She had killed that boy when she shoved him down the hill. It didn't matter if there was some sort of strange supernatural force at work. He was dead, and she did the pushing. She was nine, and she was going to prison. She wondered what that would be like. Would she have to go to prison with grown-ups? Would they lock her up with other murderers? All the possibilities tumbled through her brain, tormenting her. The guilt and the consequence both collided in her mind, a steady beat of harmonic unrest.

"I'm just here to ask a few questions, Clarissa. Is that alright?" She clicked her pen.

Clarissa nodded. "Okay."

She needed to tell the truth. She knew that. Her life was over. But confessing would be hard.

"How much do you remember about what happened?"

"I remember a lot about some things, but I don't remember anything after I ran from the meadow...I...."

Clarissa fidgeted. She poked at her French toast and looked away. The fork trembled in her hand.

"It's okay. Just relax. You're not in any kind of trouble here, alright? I just want to know what happened so we can better understand the situation and find some answers for this boy's family. That's all."

Clarissa didn't quite believe she wasn't in trouble, but the detective's words helped a little, anyway.

"Let's start with what happened the afternoon you got lost in the woods."

Clarissa tried to hold back her guilt, but her confession burst out of her mouth. "I killed that boy. I'm so sorry. It was an accident."

Clarissa couldn't look at the detective. Her fork fell to the floor with a clang, the sound ringing out. She pulled her knees to her chest, wrapping her arms around them and burying her head. "I...I...just pushed him and then he fell." She sniffled, her words muffled as she spoke into her legs. "I was angry because he stole my skateboard. My father gave it to me. I...I didn't mean it, please...please, don't send me to jail. I know I deserve to go, but I...."

Tears leaked out. She couldn't help it.

There was a soft tap on her shoulder and as she looked up, the detective held out a box of tissues. Clarissa grabbed some and wiped her nose.

The detective kneeled down next to her and, with a soft voice just above a whisper, said, "It sounds like you had a terrible experience. I promise, you're not in any trouble, Clarissa. No one is investigating you for murder, or assault, or anything else."

"You're...not?" She sniffled and used a tissue again. "I don't understand."

"We don't believe that you killed him. But we want to find out what happened. I need your help for that."

Clarissa's words burst out again, "But, I pushed him down a hill."

Andrea looked like she was about to say more, but then said, "It's important that you tell me your side of the story before I give you any more information. Sometimes when we give someone information, it makes them accidentally change their story. So, I need you to tell me everything before I give you any answers. Can you do that for me?

Clarissa nodded, but still wondered if it was some kind of trick. Then she thought better of it. After all, there was no need to trick her. She had already confessed the worst thing she had done.

The detective settled back into her chair, then took a sip of coffee from the white mug Audrey had given her.

"It's really important that we don't skip anything. So I want you to start at the beginning, and we are going to go over every detail, alright?"

"Every detail?"

Clarissa couldn't help but wonder what this woman would say if she told her about the blood and the bones. What would she think when she told her that the whole earth shook, or how the wind had blown in a temporary tornado?

"Even the tiniest, strangest thing you experienced."

"Even if it sounds...."

"Crazy? Yes. Sometimes it's those crazy details that lead us to answers. Even the smallest details could help our investigation."

The detective took another sip of coffee, and Clarissa leaned over, picked up her fork, and poked at the last few pieces of French toast on her plate. They were getting soggy from the syrup. Clarissa hesitated, still uncertain if she should tell the edited version she had told her parents, or everything, as the detective requested.

"Tell you what. Instead of thinking of this like the police questioning you, let's think of it more like a trade of information. Tell me what you know, and I can tell you some things that we know. Now, I won't be able to tell you everything because we're still investigating, but what I can share might answer a few of your questions."

"I think I can do that but...."

She let her sentence hang in the air. A vulture's feather.

"But?"

"Well, it's just that some of it is really strange, and I don't know if you will believe me. The other parts are all blank, like, I don't know what happened to me between the time I left the meadow and the hospital. It doesn't make sense...none of it does."

"Just do the best you can."

Clarissa nodded and launched into her story. She told the detective about sitting on the boulders and her pursuit of the boy through the woods. Clarissa told her how she caught up with him, and when it was clear they were both lost, she ran out and tried to push him down and take the skateboard. Then, with tears in her eyes, she described how the boy fell and how, when she peered over the edge, he had stopped moving.

"And then what happened?"

"I...that place was really strange and scary."

"Strange how?"

"Something was...I don't know. There's something wrong with it."

Andrea nodded her head. "Yes, it feels strange there."

"You've been there?"

"Of course. We had an entire team out there investigating."

"The trees, and the animal bones...and then...that shadow."

"Shadow?"

"There was something there...maybe the thing that was eating all those animals."

"Tell me more. No matter how weird or scary it is, tell me everything. You never know what little detail might help us crack the case."

The words poured from her. With the telling, Clarissa felt a weight lift off of her, as if the burden of the experience had shifted from her to the detective. Clarissa told Andrea about the ring of bones, about her cut hand and the blood sucked up by the earth, and all of the other oddities that she experienced with her various senses. She finished with the rapid decay of the body, the strange shadow monster appearing at the edge of the meadow, and her flight.

"And after that, I don't remember anything. I remember leaving and running from whatever that thing was, and then I woke up in the hospital on the ventilator, and punched that nurse on accident."

"Yes, I heard about the nurse." The detective smiled. "Don't worry, she isn't taking it personally. In fact, she had a good laugh about it with me. She said you're the strongest little girl she ever encountered."

That made Clarissa smile a little, but it faded into the guilt of the boy's death.

"And there's nothing else you remember?"

"No...but, the boy...I killed him...I...."

In a soft voice, the detective said, "That's just not possible Clarissa."

"What do you mean?"

"Do you know how sometimes, when you turn off your light at night in your bedroom, your eyes and mind can play tricks on you?"

Clarissa nodded, thinking of the second night home when Ted had installed the blackout curtains.

"Well, I think maybe this is one of those times. I think your mind was playing a trick on you."

"I...I don't understand."

"Well, we examined the boy's body. And I want you to know that it's clear he had been dead for at least a few weeks, long before you even got there."

"But that's not possible." She paused a breath, recognizing the echo of the detective's words. "He stole my skateboard, and I ran after him to get it back."

"Yes, and your friend Monica confirms a boy stole your skateboard and ran off into the woods with it. So that part of the story troubled me."

Clarissa said, "Maybe that shadow did something to his body? Maybe it could make it decay faster? What about the bones and the trees?"

Detective Corrin put down her notepad and pen, and took another sip of coffee. Then she grabbed Clarissa's hand and gave her a soft and reassuring smile. "Yes, I saw the bones. Yes, I think the trees are strange, but his death wasn't your fault. Look, even if you're right, and you pushed him, and he fell down and died, you still wouldn't go to jail. It was an accident and you're only nine years old. A nine-year-old, I might add, who has been through quite an ordeal. No one is arresting you."

This all made even less sense than what Clarissa had seen in that meadow. How was it possible that his death wasn't her fault?

"But I pushed him. He never moved again after that."

"I don't think you pushed him."

"What? What do you mean?"

"Clarissa, I think what's happening is that you had a traumatic experience, and your mind is trying to make sense of it."

"What's a traumatic experience? I don't understand."

She had heard the word traumatic before, but couldn't remember where. She reached for the definition. Instead of an answer, the image of her standing in front of her bathroom door, with her dead father inside, floated in her mind's eye, but she couldn't make sense of it.

"A traumatic experience is when something awful happens to us. Sometimes, when something awful happens, our mind has to protect itself because it just gets too scared. And because of that, sometimes you forget on purpose, or your brain makes up a story to help protect us from that fear."

Clarissa said, "So I don't remember what happened to me after the meadow because...it was something terrible?"

The detective's expression changed to one of pained discomfort. She squirmed in her chair.

"Yes, well, you hit your head, so it's also possible that nothing happened in those few days. The doctors said you had a concussion, which can also mess with your memory a bit."

"So you think that me pushing that boy was my mind playing a trick on me?"

"Yes, something like that. Do you know what I think happened?"

Clarissa shook her head. She thought maybe it was best to play along. None of this made any sense, and she had the sneaking suspicion that something horrible was coming. Whatever was happening, it wasn't over. In fact, she felt an increasing sense of dread, almost like she was back in the meadow. Out of the corner of her eye, she saw something move. She looked to the corner of the room where several shadows gathered, and her heart pounded.

There was something there, something moving. It was only just a hint of a flicker, something that if she had blinked at the wrong time, she might have missed it.

The detective turned and looked, searching the same corner as Clarissa, and then turned back.

"Are you alright, Clarissa?"

Clarissa shifted her attention from the corner of the kitchen to the detective. That sense of dread was growing in her, almost drowning out her emotions. It felt like when she had run through that forest and had known that something was just behind her. It felt like when those roots and branches had taken possession of her. That sense of darkness, that shroud, descended on her.

"I...."

"It's alright. Again, you're not in trouble."

Clarissa said, "But how could I not be?"

"I understand why you might think that, but here's my theory. I think there were two boys."

"Two boys?"

"Yes, two boys. The first boy stole your skateboard and ran into the woods with it. You chased him like you and your friend both said, and after a while, you both got lost in the woods. You said, yourself, that you lost sight of him a few times while you were chasing after him, right?"

She thought about it for a moment, then said, "Yes, but he was easy to follow because he wasn't good at being quiet, and there wasn't anyone else around."

"But you lost track of him, didn't you?"

"Yes. I did, but I found him again."

"Is it possible that you didn't push him at all? That maybe the boy who stole your skateboard ran down into that meadow, saw the body, dropped your skateboard because he was so afraid, and then ran in a different direction?"

Clarissa shook her head, "No, I don't think so. I know I pushed him. It's the one thing I'm certain of."

"How can you be sure when so much of your memory is missing?"

"Because of my hand."

Clarissa held up her hand. The cut was still healing, but it would be gone in a few more days, and didn't hurt anymore. "Something on his jacket was sharp and cut me. That's how I know I pushed him. Then, like I said before, when I got down there, the ground drank my blood."

Detective Corrin's face changed several times. Then she looked thoughtful for a moment and said, "Okay, maybe you pushed him. But you said that hill was really steep, correct? You told me that after you pushed him, you waited a few moments to look over the edge. Then you looked over the edge and he was lying there motionless."

Clarissa nodded. "Well, it was hard to see through all the trees into the meadow from the top of the hill."

The detective nodded, as if satisfied. Somehow Clarissa thought she was trying to convince herself of something. She wondered if the detective, like Ted, had seen something strange or disturbing. She wondered again at what Ted had seen.

"So, two boys, okay?" said the detective.

"Two boys?"

"Yes. The one you chased and shoved, and the one who was already in the meadow."

"What do you mean, already in the meadow?"

"There was a boy that you chased through the woods. But there was another boy who was already dead in the meadow."

"But I know I pushed someone. So where did he go?"

"I think you pushed that boy. I think you cut your hand on something on his jacket. But you said, yourself, that you couldn't see the bottom, right?"

"Yes, that's true, but...."

"So, it was two separate people and your mind is just filling in the gaps."

The detective scratched out a series of notes on her notepad.

"But what about the other stuff, like the bones, and the wind, and the sound, and the ground drinking my blood?"

"You told me that the reason you punched the nurse was because, when you woke up, you were having a nightmare about trees trying to grab you, didn't you?"

Clarissa nodded softly. She put the fork back on her plate, no longer hungry.

"But that was after I ran from the meadow, when my memory was weird."

"But what if most of what you experienced was just a dream brought on by your head injury?"

"It wasn't."

The woman's smile was still warm, but somehow it felt...well, she didn't know the word for it, but it felt like the woman was looking down on her, almost mocking her or dismissing her because she was only nine, and Clarissa didn't like it.

"Clarissa, what if when you were going down that hill into the meadow, you hit your head then, and not later, when you were running away from it? I slipped and fell going down that hill, as did two others who investigated the site. So, what if you fell then and hit your head, and seeing the body triggered a nightmare just like the ventilator did?"

Clarissa frowned. She had remembered almost falling and catching herself, but this all seemed wrong. Why was this woman trying so hard to dismiss her? Clarissa was glad she hadn't told her mom and Ted about the weird parts, now. They would have dismissed them just as much as this detective had.

"I don't know."

"The mind is a powerful thing, Clarissa. And our memories deceive us all the time. It's why we can't just rely on a single witness in court. We have to provide other evidence, because sometimes people will convince themselves they are right about something, even if it's wrong."

Clarissa didn't know about any of that. But this woman was a police officer. Her father had always taught her that police officers were helpers, like a firefighter. Maybe she knew better? But the body, the ground drinking her blood, the wind, all of it just felt so real. It had to be real, even if the detective didn't believe her. There was no point in arguing.

The detective said, "Okay. Fair is fair. Now it's your turn to ask me some questions. I will answer whatever I can."

Clarissa thought about what she wanted to know most. She had a lot of questions, but most of them weren't anything the detective was going to know for sure, especially since she didn't believe Clarissa's tale. So, she went with the most obvious question.

"Who is the boy?"

The detective frowned. "Well, that's embarrassing. We don't know. Our best experts tried to identify him several ways, but so far, no luck. We had an artist do a composite sketch that we released to the media."

"A composite sketch? Do you mean you drew his face?"

Clarissa imagined a black and white sketch of a face with missing eyes and holes in flesh. Maggots squirmed all over the picture. She shivered, hugging her legs to her chest again.

"Well, we drew what his face probably looked like before...whatever happened to him."

"You don't know what happened to him, do you?"

The detective looked away for a moment, then looked back. Clarissa could see the answer in her eyes.

"You don't know who he is, or how he died." It wasn't a question.

The detective shook her head slowly. All warmth had leaked out of her, just as the color had leaked out of the meadow. Clarissa felt that sense of dread come back in.

"Will you tell me when you find out?"

"Yes, well, as long as it doesn't interfere with the investigation. But we will tell you, eventually. Do you have any more questions for me?"

Clarissa thought hard, but what else could she possibly ask this woman? The police were just as confused about what had happened as everyone else.

"I don't think so."

"Alright then, I'll let you get some rest. But please, if you need anything, feel free to call me."

The woman handed her a business card with the words "Detective Adriana Corrin" and "Delaware County Police Department". Below was the woman's phone number.

Andrea said, "I'll give one to your mother, as well, in case you lose it. Rest up, Clarissa. You've been through a lot in the last week, and in time, it will feel like nothing more than a bad dream."

The woman drained the last of the coffee cup, then gathered her pad of paper and pen, and put it back in her pocket. The detective went back to the front door and called out for Clarissa's mother, who appeared promptly. Her mother and the detective talked for several minutes, and though Clarissa could clearly hear what they were saying, she wasn't interested. She felt the shroud around her. Clarissa heard the door close and her mother walked back into the room. Clarissa hardly noticed. When her mother asked her questions, she answered in single flat words.

The detective had also seen something down in the meadow, something horrible. It had scared her, just like Ted. She was certain of that now. She had pushed that boy into a monster's lair. Adults always seemed to struggle with the idea of monsters. In all the movies, the parents never believed the kids. That was also true in books.

It wasn't over. No, whatever had happened to her down in the meadow was only the beginning.

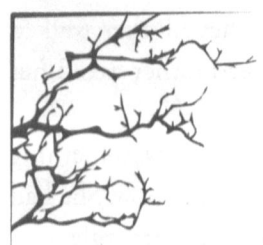

Chapter 6

The Red Eyes Adjacent to Tragedy

Red eyes linger,
On a fracturing moment,
With mind sent scattering,
While gathering fragments of memory.

A herald came seeing,
Hungry for what might be,
Adjacent to tragedy,
An arbitrator of Samsara.

A deal made,
A road taken,
Ignorance is unreliable,
When we are born to crimson lives.

Days collapsed into one, stitching uncertainty into each sunrise and sunset. Such is the way of trauma and tragedy, especially when the knowledge of what happened is kept in closed vestments. Clarissa lost track of everything that made sense. Nine suns rose and fell after the detective's visit. Each day's passing bore little consequence. In that time, she watched *The Hobbit* dozens of times and ate little. She stared at the flicker of the screen in her bedroom and let the credits roll to the end, so the VCR would automatically rewind the tape and she could start again.

There were nightmares, a swelling of terror when her eyes closed. Nor did it fully retract when she woke. The boy's body swam into the center of her consciousness often, an unwanted visitor knocking at her door with the bloody rise and fall of twilight. Even in moments when she sat and ate cereal in front of the TV, the smell of the body would waft into her nostrils, sticky and unyielding. Death was a relentless reminder, a constant companion, a shape in the dark.

Clarissa's guilt was a cloak that she wore in every waking moment, a certainty that sometime soon, the police would come to arrest her. It was the primary reason for her disinterest in her skateboard. The local police were notorious for their dislike of skaters. James and Margie had each been arrested a dozen times. The judges knew James on sight, and called him "hoodlum" and "thug" when pronouncing a sentence and pounding their gavel. It was a good thing James's father was a lawyer, though with each offense, he and his father hated one another a little more.

There were several mornings where Monica came knocking. At first she was turned away when Clarissa refused to come down. But when she persisted, either Ted or her mother had let Monica come up to the room. Though, even when Monica sat in her room for hours, Clarissa lay there staring up at the ceiling or watching *The Hobbit*, trying to understand what had happened to her, offering only short answers and clipped opinions. Monica sat sketching and outlining the world in pencil, and tried to cheer her friend up.

Worse, that strange shroud that she had experienced in the aftermath of her journey was a frequent visitor. The world seemed dimmer, darker, more dismal. It hung over her like a fog, encouraging indifference.

Then, on the tenth morning after the detective had come and gone, a rescue party came to liberate Clarissa of the black garment that filtered her perception. Three people staged an intervention.

2. Clarissa's bedroom door slammed open. James and Margie said in unison, "Time to get up, buttercup!" The voices were strong, cheery, and as full of vigor as the deep summer cicadas.

Clarissa, having heard steps creeping toward her door, drew a pillow over her head, pretending not to hear. She kept her breath slow and steady to feign sleep.

She felt someone get on her bed, the depression on the left side grew and she rolled toward it. Her whole world shook as someone pulled the pillow and blankets off of her. Monica jumped up and down on the bed.

"Come on, Clarissa! Moon prism power, make up! Let's go! It's summer and you're missing it!"

James, ever the adopted brother from another mother, said, "It's time, Clarissa."

His voice carried the resonance of a master instructing a pupil. There was no compromise in his tone.

Clarissa flinched, and thought she knew what James meant, but, keeping her eyes squinted shut, she didn't respond. It was too much to leave the house, to face the height of the sun when she had become accustomed to the nocturnal kiss of the shroud.

Margie laughed. "I saw you twitch when James said that. We know you're awake and you're coming with us."

In a sing-song voice, Monica said, "Snake Hill time! Snake Hill time!" It almost sounded like a gloat, even though Monica didn't have any interest in a skateboard, only her sketchpad and her books.

Margie said, "Yep. It's time for your test, young grasshopper!"

"Wax on, Wax off!" shouted Monica, who was still jumping up and down.

Clarissa still squeezed her eyes shut, balled up now with fists clenched. There was no way she was leaving this room. Even if she was, she certainly would not take on Snake Hill or risk the wrath of the police.

James made a trumpet with his mouth, and now Clarissa felt two people jumping on the bed next to her. Realizing they weren't going away, Clarissa opened her eyes and rolled onto her back. Monica was standing right above her with the biggest shit-eating grin Clarissa had ever seen.

"Yes!" said Monica. "Victory at last! I'll bring your skateboard!"

Monica jumped off of the bed, grabbed Clarissa's skateboard, and ran down the stairs with it. She knew that Clarissa would follow her skateboard wherever it went. It was her father's heart, the last present he ever gave her before his terrible end. Margie jumped off of the bed and followed.

James said, "Ten minutes, and then we'll be back up here if you don't come down."

Clarissa gave him a dirty look. But James just smiled.

"Monica will make you pop tarts."

"The police are already after me James...I...I can't."

"Bullshit, Clarissa. You know damn well my dad would get you off. How many times has he gotten my charges dropped? My ass would be in jail a dozen times over if it wasn't for him. You ain't got no excuse."

"But-"

He cut her off. "Butts stink, Clarissa. You're coming, like it or not."

Clarissa grumbled, but James went out the door and pulled it shut behind him. Clarissa swung her legs over the edge of the bed and stood up, stretching. The shroud was still around her, and she felt weak and tired. All she wanted to do was climb back in bed and lay there, but she knew that the trio downstairs would never allow that to happen.

She was afraid of the police, but James was right about one thing. His father had bailed him out many times. He wasn't a bad kid. Mostly he got charged with trespassing or vandalism for grinding on rails where he wasn't supposed to.

At that moment, she hated the three of them. She hated their stupid, smiling faces. She hated that they were forcing her out of the house. Later, when she traveled the landscape of the country alone, she would reflect on the value of those three friends. She would think about how they had pushed her to laugh and smile even with the surrounding shroud. But now? Now she wanted to scream at them.

She threw on some clothes, and as she did, she tried to think of a compromise. Sure, they wouldn't let her sit around anymore, but there was no way she was going to tackle Snake Hill. She wasn't ready. So far as she knew, no one her age had ever done it on a skateboard. Plenty of kids did it on bikes all the time, but on a skateboard? The thought of flying down that hill at some insane speed, dodging cars and mailboxes, and Mrs. Lampree's weird sidewalk sculptures, were almost as scary as the idea of going back to the meadow. No, she would find some other place to skateboard. She wouldn't budge on that.

But as she descended the stairs, she stopped short of turning the corner and listened, just out of sight.

"Snake Hill? Are you sure, James?"

"Yeah, Mrs. Lamont. She, like, really needs it, you know?"

Clarissa's mother really liked James. After Clarissa's father had died, James had come over several days a week to teach Clarissa everything he knew about skateboarding, and about life in general. He had given Clarissa knee and elbow pads, his old ones from when he was a kid, he had said. Though, James was only five years her senior.

James said, "She's ready. I can feel it. She was ready before...." He flushed with embarrassment, "You know...." He rewound and said, "She's totally ready and I think maybe it will help her cheer up."

Her mother said, "I suppose it's true that sometimes we just need a win to get back up and keep going. Alright, as long as she wears a helmet."

Clarissa made a face from her hiding place. She hated wearing a helmet. It always tugged at her long red hair, and she always had to brush it out afterward.

"Scout's honor, ma'am. I'll make her wear one."

"Me, too," said Margie. Though, they wouldn't make her do any such thing. "And don't worry, she's got the skills. She's a way better skater than I was at her age. Snake Hill is kind of a...skater initiation ritual. No one takes you seriously until you've done it."

What Margie said was true. Most of the other skaters would chase you out of the skate park unless you were with someone who had conquered

Snake Hill, or if you had done it yourself. Clarissa knew she needed to do it, but last time, she had stood at the top, ready to plunge down that mountainously steep road...and she froze. Her stomach squirmed with writhing eels, and vertigo took hold of her.

Margie had said that most people freeze the first time they stand up there, but when Clarissa had asked if she had frozen, she had said that she had done it on the first try. Everyone knew Margie was one of the best skaters around, but she finished by saying, "I was eleven, Clarissa. I didn't try it 'til later because I was too scared. Most people do it after ten."

Clarissa had said, "So, I can wait another year, then."

Margie had laughed at that and said, "James won't let you. You're too good, girl. He ain't gonna let you waste your talent."

Sure enough, here they were. Clarissa now had less than six months before her tenth birthday. She took a deep breath and went around the corner into the kitchen, dressed and ready.

"Good morning, sweetie," her mother said. "It's good to see you up and out of bed. Are you ready to head out with your friends?"

Clarissa shrugged. "I guess."

James said, "You guess? No, no, no, Clarissa, there ain't no guessing with Snake Hill. You gotta get pumped."

James, who always had his walkman in his pocket, refused to upgrade to a discman like everyone else, saying that CDs were lame, and skipped when he was on his skateboard grabbed it off of his belt and pushed it into Clarissa's hands. "Here," he said, "Listen to this."

Clarissa, knowing that if she didn't, he would just put the cassette in the stereo and crank it up, took it and put the headphones on her head. James reached over and pressed play.

It was so loud that Clarissa immediately jumped back and then turned it down. Van Halen's *Running with the Devil* was playing at full blast.

"Really?" said Clarissa, "Van Halen sucks, James. Don't you have anything better to pump me up?"

"Van Halen is classic, Clarissa!" he shouted, pumping his fist. "And when you ride Snake Hill this morning, you're gonna feel like you're riding on the devil's back. Best get your mind right, grasshopper!"

Margie, Monica, and even her mother, laughed, and then, for the first time in what felt like a lifetime, Clarissa laughed too.

The shroud pulled back a little.

3 Blinding sunlight bounced off the surface of cars. A shimmer of heat hovered over the pavement as Clarissa glanced down Snake hill. The mid-morning heat had already soaked up the dew that the deep green grass had gathered the night before. Already, Clarissa could feel waves of heat swelling in the summer sun, and she could tell that she wouldn't be able to be outside in the afternoon, at least, not without a pool or soaking their shirts first.

James skated up next to her in his JNCO jeans and said, "You got this, Clarissa. Just remember everything I taught you...stay loose, knees bent, head forward and-"

"Keep most of my weight over the front truck." Clarissa cut him off.

"Right." He slapped her shoulder and smiled. "Proud of you."

She smiled back, though she was having second thoughts as she peered down the hill. It seemed much steeper than she had remembered, and much longer, too. She wondered how fast she would go. If she wiped out, it might be stitches, or a broken bone, or worse. So far, she had avoided breaking bones, but as she looked down Snake Hill, she thought she might break something today, especially if she had a collision with one of those weird sculptures half-way down. She had to avoid the sidewalk at all costs.

Margie pulled up behind them, kicked the tail of her board and caught it by the top, her medium-length brown hair blowing in the gentle breeze. Clarissa thought she looked like a superhero, like Rogue from X-men, maybe. She wore a jean jacket and baggy black pants, despite the heat. Margie always wore that jean jacket, with buttons and slogans all over it.

"You ready, Clarissa?"

Clarissa nodded, though she didn't feel ready. Glancing down Snake Hill a second time, she felt butterflies in her stomach. She had gone down several hills before, but none were as steep, as long, or as winding.

Margie laughed. "Scares the shit out of you, doesn't it?"

"No. I'm just...thinking about my route. Like James taught me."

She tried to look determined and unafraid. Margie was really cool and even better than James, even though he was two years older than she was.

James said, "She's got this. You should've seen her over on Winona Street last month. She did that hill like a champ, and she caught air."

"Air, huh? You didn't tell me that. Nice," said Margie. "You're ready, Clarissa. Remember what my dad always used to say?"

Clarissa nodded, "You can't stop yourself from being afraid, but that doesn't mean you should give in to fear."

"Totally."

Clarissa trembled. Margie and James both looked at each other. Monica was already waiting at the bottom, though none of the three could see her. She was around the last bend, which seemed like a million miles away to Clarissa.

James bent down in front of Clarissa. He was a full head taller than she was. James said, "I know you got this. You wanna fly right?"

That made Clarissa smile. In a low voice just above a whisper, she said, "Yeah, for my dad."

James nodded.

Clarissa swelled with emotion as the image of her father came clear for the first time in a while. She had tried not to think of him much lately. The hole inside her heart was still wide open, exposed. Though three years had passed, it seemed like only yesterday that she and her father had sat on their front porch on a summer evening, and she had said those words. "Daddy, I want to fly like James and Margie".

The two had raced up and down the street all evening on their skateboards. But Clarissa's favorite part was when they went fast. That night had only been a few weeks before....

James grabbed her shoulder gently, brotherly, shaking her out of her reverie.

Knowingly, he said, "Your dad, he's looking down on you right now, you know that? He's gonna give you some extra courage, kid. You're gonna crush this hill. "

Clarissa felt a lump in her throat and she looked down. She didn't know if she believed that, but she felt a little braver thinking about her father. He would have wanted her to do this, she was sure of it. She looked down the hill again. It didn't look as bad. She gathered her courage, looked back up at James, clenched her fists and said, "Yeah. Let's do this."

They lined up their boards at the top of Snake Hill and stared down. It was a one-way street, and cars could only park on the right hand shoulder, meaning the whole left side was clear. On the left was a chain-link fence that led into a playground outside of Clarissa's elementary school.

James said, "Alright, on the count of three."

Clarissa felt her guts tighten, but she took a deep breath just like Margie had taught her at the top of the half-pipe, and thought about staying loose. She relaxed her arms and legs. She was going to do this. There was no turning back now. She looked up at the sky, wondering if maybe her father was up there. She decided she was going to pretend that he was, whether it was true or not.

James started the countdown. "1...2...3...Go!"

Margie and James pushed off hard, trying to catch speed early, racing to be the first to the bottom, both fearless as they sped down the hill. Clarissa gave only a little push, and let gravity take her, not wanting to start off too fast, so she could get the hang of the hill and feel it out like James had taught her.

Slowly at first, but then moving faster, she skated down. She banked left at the first bend, and then right. She wobbled a little, but then crouched down to get her balance. Then she was going faster than she ever had before, far faster than she wanted to.

Nerves and stomach clenched tight, and Clarissa wobbled. She felt her heart sink. She wasn't going to make it. Clarissa took another breath and leaned into her board. Then another turn came, and she veered far right, almost into the cars, narrowly missing a mirror. She over-corrected and wobbled, waving her arms in the air, knowing that this was it. She was heading right for Mrs. Lampree's sculptures up on the left sidewalk.

The curb came up on her, and with all her effort she jumped it, caught a crack on the sidewalk, and almost ended her run on Snake hill right there. Though she wobbled, somehow she managed to regain her balance.

But now, the large plaster object-part hippo, part lion, part monkey, and who knew what else, grew in size as she approached it. It was as tall as she was, and as she plunged toward it, her speed increased despite the cracked sidewalk stealing some of her speed. She trembled as it inched forward, already imagining the feeling of her bones breaking with the collision. Fear gripped her, an icy hand on her will and heart pulling her down just like gravity.

Something changed in her then, something she didn't expect. The fear fell away and anger replaced it.

"No!" She shouted. "No, no, no!"

With each utterance, her anger grew. She thought of everything that had happened to her so far. She thought of the loss of her father, of the boy stealing her skateboard, of everything she had experienced in the meadow, and she knew that she could not let it stop her anymore. She was here. Her father was watching her from somewhere beyond. She was on this hill, and she would not let it defeat her. Courage and anger mixed inside her, a blend that she would come to rely on, because sometimes, to override fear, another powerful emotion can smother it.

Time slowed down. In that moment she found a new kinship with her body and board, and made the slightest adjustments to her stance. The plaster statue was only a few feet away as she restored her balance. She dodged out of the way of the ugly plaster sculpture just in time, then jumped off the sidewalk and back onto the smooth, recently re-tarred road.

The road flattened for a moment before the next drop. With her restored balance, she crested the next lip of the hill, then began her descent down the final straightaway. Her speed increased until she was certain that she couldn't go any faster, though the fingers of fear tried to grasp her again. But now, she could see James, Margie, and Monica waiting at the bottom, skateboards and sketchpad in hand. One hundred yards to go.

Clarissa stood up straight with her knees only slightly bent. She raised her arms like wings. Something let go. The anger dissolved, her fear fell away, and she felt the rush of wind on her face and hair. The wind in her ears silenced all thoughts. She could smell the freshly cut grass, see the colors of flowers in front yards and joy filled every part of her.

Clarissa was flying. At that moment, she really thought she felt her father watching her, flying with her somehow. As she crossed the finish line, her three friends greeted her with cheers, hugs, and praise. Clarissa had done it, and all the other skateboarders in town would hear how she, only nine, had conquered Snake Hill. For the first time since the meadow, she felt happy. As long as she could fly, everything would be alright.

4. Margie's mother was never home. It was the greatest appeal of the place, especially for James, who hated his parents. Clarissa had never actually been inside the single-wide trailer before, nor in a trailer park. Margie's father had died when she was a toddler, and her mother, never having graduated high school, lived life much the way Clarissa's mother did, working virtually non-stop. They had found kinship in lost fathers.

The trailer had a bedroom on either end, with a combination living room/kitchen in the middle. A single small bathroom sat across from a large storage closet on the left side of the trailer. The living room was relatively clean with only a few dishes in the sink, but as they moved past the yellowing wallpaper and into Margie's bedroom, Clarissa couldn't help but think that Ted would have a heart attack. The small bed in the corner was framed in stacks of clothes, and the couch on the other side was covered in skateboard and guitar parts. Margie's one working guitar leaned against the back wall, and three others lay around the room in various stages of disrepair.

Clarissa thought it was the coolest place she had ever seen.

James said, "Can I use the phone?"

Margie said, "What for?"

" Duh, to celebrate Clarissa's baptism on Snake Hill."

Margie shrugged. "Sure."

James turned around and headed for the phone.

"Baptism?" asked Monica, her face confused. Monica moved a few tools aside on the couch and placed them on the floor so that she could sit down. "But my baptism happened when I was a baby, and Snake Hill isn't a church."

Margie laughed.

"It's like a metaphor," said James, from out in the living room. He had the phone off the cradle and was already dialing a number. "You know, like a baptism by fire? Haven't you ever heard that expression?"

"Oh," said Monica. "Well, how are we going to celebrate?"

"Pizza, kid!"

Clarissa said, "But I don't have any money."

"It's on me, kid. If Vinny is working today, he'll give me a free one, anyway."

Margie said, "Vinny's a guy James works with over at Empire Pizza."

Margie sat on the edge of her bed, and Clarissa sat on a pile of clothes on a chair. They could hear James talking to someone on the phone, placing an order. After a moment, he hung up, came back into the room, and sat down on the couch next to Monica. Clarissa surveyed the posters around the room. A poster of Alice in Chains, and a poster of Soundgarden, were up above the bed. Margie also had several pictures of female singers on stage that she didn't recognize.

James said, "Pizza's on the way." He reached into his pocket, pulled out a cigarette, and fired it. He offered one to Margie, who declined.

"Your dad's gonna send you off to military school if he catches you smoking again," said Margie.

James shrugged, "That's why I'm smoking here. Besides, your mom ain't gonna notice. She smokes two packs a day."

Margie shrugged back and said, "So, how does it feel, Clarissa?"

Clarissa couldn't help but smile. She had been nothing but smiles since she had crossed the finish line. "Like I'm on my way."

"Damn right, you are!" said James. He blew out smoke. "I bet in a few more years, you could kick some ass in a competition."

"You think so?" asked Clarissa.

Margie said, "Hell, yes. Your form in that last stretch was perfect, and so were your wings."

Monica said, "It was so cool, Clarissa. You really looked like you were flying!"

Monica opened her sketch pad and showed Clarissa a drawing she had made of her victory. It was just a quick outline, but Clarissa saw the sculpture she had narrowly avoided just behind her, framed by the cars on the other side of the street. There she was, with little zoom lines coming out of her. Instead of her arms out, they dangled at her side in what James said was perfect form. Monica had given her angel wings. A look of determination and joy lived in the pencil lines that made up her face.

"Is that what I looked like? Minus the wings, I mean?"

Margie said, "You looked like a rockstar. Coolest kid on the block today.

"It was truly impressive," said James. Especially, how you stopped yourself from wiping out. It's a hard thing to snap out of once stuff goes wrong. But you caught yourself, and you navigated that sidewalk and Lampree's little art gallery like a champ. You better be proud of yourself."

Monica put her sketchpad away, and they all sat in silence for a moment, all beaming in friendship and Clarissa's victory.

James said, "I bet you feel a lot better now, huh?"

The warmth of Clarissa's accomplishment guttered out like the wind blowing out a candle. It was like James had dumped ice water on her. The image of the boy's body flashed before her with that barest hint of a reminder, and the room dimmed just a little.

Clarissa said nothing, but her frown was a tell.

Margie punched James in the shoulder. "Shut up, man. Let her bask in victory and pizza."

Clarissa shook her head. "No, it's okay. It did help. Thank you for making me get out of bed."

Monica said, "You lost the bet, Margie! You owe me five bucks."

Clarissa asked, "What bet?"

Monica said, "The one where I bet her you would thank us for making you come." Monica stood up, put one hand on her hip, and the other palm up, for her payment.

James laughed and said, "Damn, she got you, Margie. Pay up."

Margie did, standing up and pulling cash from her wallet, forking it over. She sat back down.

"So, like, do you want to talk about it?" asked James.

"Talk about what?" asked Clarissa.

It took her a moment to register exactly what he was asking and then, all at once, she realized he was asking about the meadow.

"Oh. No. Not really. I mean, there isn't much to tell, anyway."

Monica said, "I told you guys, she doesn't remember anything."

"But what about the body? Was it all gross, like people are saying?" asked James.

Margie punched him again. "Shut up, James. You're not supposed to ask."

"Ouch." He rubbed his arm and took another drag of his cigarette before saying, "Sorry. I'm just curious."

Clarissa said, "It was just really scary. I don't want to talk about it."

Something in her almost refused to talk about it, anyway. She had the sense that talking about it would be obscene, like swearing in a church, or watching those bad adult channels her mother had caught Ted watching one time, that led to a terrible fight between them.

At that moment, she thought of her father and his death. Though, she couldn't really understand why. Later, she would know why. Because later, when she was alone that night, she would remember something about the story of her father's death that she had blocked out. Something so frightening that she had made herself forget, something not unlike what had happened in the meadow.

Suddenly, Clarissa was crying, and Monica was hugging her. James and Margie just looked at each other.

"What's wrong, Clarissa?" asked her best friend.

"Nothing, Mon. I just...I miss my dad, and he...well...I wish he could have seen me on Snake Hill today, flying. He...he gave me that skateboard the night he died."

Margie said, "Damn, really?"

"Yeah."

"You wanna talk about it?" James asked.

Margie slugged him again. "Shut up, James."

"Jeez, Margie," he rubbed his shoulder, "You're gonna leave a bruise. I'm just trying to let the girl talk. Isn't that important, or something? My court-mandated counselor said it's important to talk about our feelings."

To her surprise, Clarissa found that she wanted to talk about it. She had never told Monica the entire story, and Monica had never pushed her to talk about it. Clarissa was the only person who knew the whole truth. She hadn't even told her mother everything. She had been afraid her mother would blame her for letting her father die in the bathroom.

"Okay," Clarissa said.

"Okay, what?" asked Margie.

"I'll tell you about what happened to my dad."

"You will?" asked Monica who was still half-hugging her.

"Yeah. I've never told anyone before, so...maybe James is right. Maybe I should tell you guys."

Clarissa began her story. As she did, the shroud descended further, and when halfway through her telling the pizza arrived, she still continued to talk, even with her mouth full.

5.   The night Clarissa met death, her father sat in his favorite chair, watching his favorite show. He echoed the laugh track. Clarissa laughed too, though she could understand none of the jokes. Her mother was off working at a gas station. Her father's strange illness had taken precedence over everything. She could feel the tension between her parents, as if there were so many strings tugging at each of their hearts that they might snap.

Clarissa and her father shared a bowl of popcorn for their Wednesday night ritual. Her father's favorite show was something about a court at nighttime. She didn't know why that made it funny, but she thought the really tall person on the screen was interesting because he was as tall as her father. She wondered if she would be that tall one day.

"You want some chocolate milk, sunbeam?"

"Yes, Daddy."

Her father stood, tottering, a leaning tower, then he staggered carefully toward the kitchen, grabbing the walls for purchase. Clarissa had an idea that maybe she should get her own milk, but she wasn't tall enough to reach for the glasses. Her father always said that milk tastes the best when you drink it out of a glass. She watched him go, worrying that he might get sick, so she followed him to the kitchen.

Her father steadied himself, opened the fridge, took out the chocolate syrup and the milk, and mixed it in a glass.

"You like watching those neighbor kids on their skateboards, don't you?"

"Yeah! I love watching them fly."

He chuckled at that, and quickly it turned into a long, rasping cough. He almost dropped the milk, but steadied himself again.

"They fly, huh?" His voice was gravely from the phlegm and blood in his throat.

"Yeah, when they zoom down the street, or the grab the back bumper of a car and go so fast!"

He handed her the milk with a metal spoon sticking out of the top for mixing. She swirled it together before sipping.

"Well, I don't know if they should be grabbing onto any cars, but they definitely do look like they are having fun, don't they?"

She nodded.

In the other room, she could see the roll of the credits on the TV.

"Is it time for bed, Daddy?"

"Actually, sunshine, I want to make tonight special."

"Special? But isn't it a school night?"

"I'm sure Mrs. Morely won't mind if you're a little sleepy tomorrow."

She thought hard. Special times usually only came during birthdays and Christmas, but both her birthday and Christmas were at the end of the year, and it was almost summer. She was almost finished with first grade now, and wondered if that meant there would be more special days ahead.

"Yes. I've been noticing how much you like watching those skateboarders, and there is this movie with skateboarding in it."

"Like a cartoon? Is there a skateboard show now?"

She took another sip of her milk, leaving a chocolate mustache. Her father leaned over and wiped her upper lip with a napkin.

"Well, not quite like you're thinking. No, this movie is about a boy who travels back in time. But he loves to skateboard, too."

"Back in time? What does that mean?"

"Well, he has a machine, a sort of car with special powers. And he can go back into the past."

"Like yesterday?"

Her father smiled. Somehow, that smile erased his illness. It made him shine like the sun. Even now, when the bags under his eyes were as dark as soot, and he was so pale that he looked half in the grave, the smile still made it vanish for a moment. But then the smile faded.

"Well, yesterday, of course, but imagine if you could go back long before you were born."

Her bright green eyes widened. "Like when those big pyramids were built, or dinosaurs?"

"Yes, like that."

"Does he skateboard on the pyramids? Does he meet a stegosaurus?"

Her father laughed. "No no. Nothing like that. But he takes his skateboard with him back in time. Do you want to watch it?"

"But what about bedtime?"

"I won't tell your mother, if you don't." He winked.

She tried to wink back, but she could only close both eyes, or none. She couldn't understand how people could close just one eye. This made her father smile again.

"Oh, and there's something else."

"What?"

"Another surprise."

"What is it? A dinosaur?"

Her father laughed and said, "Well at the end of the movie, I'll show it to you."

"Can I have the surprise before the movie?"

He chuckled and leaned against the kitchen counter. "I think it's better if we wait. Would you like some more popcorn, sunbeam?"

"Okay. Then can I have the surprise?"

Smiling he said, "Movie first, okay?"

"Okay." She was disappointed, but she supposed if the movie had skateboards, she wouldn't mind waiting.

He went down the hall into the pantry, and she followed. She didn't want to leave him alone. Something about the idea of leaving him alone scared her.

She worried that if she did, she would never see him again. So she stayed close, not letting him out of her sight. He grabbed an aluminum foil ring of popcorn, then traveled back to the kitchen and put it on the burner. He walked back to the living room, pulled a VHS tape out of a grocery bag, and put the tape into the VCR.

"The machine is hungry, huh?"

"Hungry?"

"Yeah, Daddy, it eats the tapes."

"I suppose it does look like that, doesn't it?"

"We are eating popcorn, and the machine is eating the tape, and everyone is happy."

Her father paused. There was an unusual look on his face, something she had never seen before. It looked like sadness, but it wasn't that. "Yes," he said, "Everyone is happy, aren't we honey?"

And she was happy, or so she thought. For the time of tears was over, and when that ended, when she had cried all her tears out, the next thing had to be happiness. But then, her mother was still crying.

"Mommy doesn't seem happy lately."

He nodded. "Mommy is having a hard time with my sickness and with having to work so much. She hasn't had much time to paint, and painting is one of the things that makes her happy. But she's lucky she's got a wonderful little helper like you."

"But your sickness is getting better, right, Daddy? You don't have to go to the hospital anymore."

The popcorn started popping on the stove. They walked back to the kitchen. After a moment, her father reached over, switched off the burner, then poured the container into their big metal bowl. He cut off a chunk of butter and mixed it in, sprinkling a little salt on top. Clarissa thought the smell of popcorn was a happiness all its own.

"You are getting better now, right, Daddy?" she repeated.

There was something inside her that told her he wasn't, and it worried her. The tears were gone now, but there was something else there, something she didn't like, and it lived in her stomach.

"Well, we'll see. I'm doing the best I can to get better."

She walked over to him and hugged his waist. "You have to get better soon, Daddy, because I want to go camping in the Poconos again."

"I want that too, sunbeam. Come on, let's sit down and watch the movie."

She thought maybe he was crying. His eyes looked wet and red, but she couldn't tell for sure. He took her by the hand, led her back to the couch, and they sat down. She cuddled up against him, putting her arms around him. He felt boney and fragile. She wished he didn't, but she snuggled against him even tighter.

The movie started, and Clarissa loved the opening scene with the strange machine that made breakfast. She asked her father if they could make one just like it, and if they could get a dog, and if they could get a car that was a time machine.

As the credits rolled she asked, "Can I have a skateboard?"

A smile spread across his face. She thought it might have been the biggest smile ever.

"It's funny you should ask that."

She looked at her father, puzzled. "Why?"

"Well...I'll be right back. You wait here. I want you to close your eyes."

"Why?"

"It's a surprise."

She had almost forgotten about the other surprise. "Okay! I will close my eyes so tight that no light will come in."

He laughed and got up. She could hear his footsteps leave the room, then, suddenly, he was back in front of her.

"Okay, open your eyes."

She did. There, in his arms, was the most beautiful yellow skateboard she had ever seen. Purple flames licked up the length of the board. Purple was her favorite color, and she had never seen purple fire before. She reached out tentatively and spun one of its wheels, just like she had once spun the wheels on Margie's skateboard.

"Wow...it's so pretty, Daddy."

"Take it. It's yours."

"Really?"

"Yes, really."

He handed it to her. She held it reverently, as if it were the most sacred thing. She hugged it and felt the coarse surface with her hands. It was the best surprise she could imagine.

"You're the best daddy, ever."

He didn't say anything, but his eyes were watery again, and his whole face was a smile.

"Can I take it outside and try to ride it?"

"Well, it's a little late for that. You can tomorrow morning. After breakfast we will take it for a spin, okay? There's something else too.... " He handed her an envelope. "But, you can't read it 'til later. There are lots of big words in it, and it's really for when you get older."

"What does it say?"

"Well, mostly it says how much I love you."

That made her whole heart smile.

"I love you too, Daddy."

She looked up and saw that he was crying. So, his tears hadn't run out, either. Why had hers run out? Wasn't this a happy moment?

"Why are you crying?"

"Oh, I'm just so happy you're my daughter, sunbeam. I'm so very lucky, and I wish...that...well...."

"Wish what?"

"Wish that I got to see you grow up."

She didn't understand what that meant. Later she would. She would think of those words for the rest of her life.

"But, you are seeing me grow up."

He smiled, wiping away the tears, and said, "I know. I just...I know. Excuse me, sunbeam. I need to use the bathroom. He put the envelope on the counter and headed to the upstairs bathroom.

Clarissa touched the skateboard with something like awe. She couldn't wait to fly with the other kids as they rode down the street. She knew her father had just said that she couldn't grab onto the bumper of the car, but the boy in the movie did it and he was fine, wasn't he? Yes, she would try that as soon as she could. And maybe she could trick some big old bully into driving a poop truck, and then she would laugh, and laugh.

There was a strange sound upstairs.

"Daddy?"

Clarissa panicked. She shouldn't have left him alone. Her mother had said she was supposed to watch him carefully and call for help if they needed it. But the bathroom was a safe place, wasn't it? She put the skateboard on the couch and climbed the staircase as fast as she could.

"Daddy, did you hear that noise?"

The sound happened again. It sounded like something wet tearing, then there was coughing, and a gurgling noise. The smell of vomit and blood drifted under the door.

She put her ear up to the bathroom door.

"Daddy, did you hear that?"

"No...don't...I...."

The noise came again. A long horrible noise, a wretch, a cry, a groan, a dirge. Then silence.

She knocked on the door. But there was no answer. Then she tried to turn the doorknob. It was locked.

"Daddy? Are you okay?" Her voice trembled.

There was no answer. No further noises from beyond the door.

Fear crawled over her, like a swarm of insects. She rubbed her arms as if scattering them away. She didn't know how she knew, but she knew something was very wrong.

"Daddy? What was that noise?"

Still nothing.

She knocked on the door harder. It made her knuckles hurt.

"Daddy?"

Still nothing.

She shouted. "Daddy! Daddy! Daddy! Daddy! Please Daddy! Answer! I don't want you to be sick anymore. Daddy?!"

She fell silent.

Then something took hold of her, some raw emotion, and she slammed her little body against the door.

After several more minutes of pounding on the door and screaming, she collapsed on the ground, crying. She lay there for several minutes, not knowing what to do or how to help. Then, she remembered what her mom had told her to do if she needed help. She ran downstairs, picked up the phone, and dialed 911.

A woman answered.

"Hello, 911. What is your emergency?"

"My Daddy, he's sick. He stopped answering in the bathroom, and there were these scary sounds in there...."

The operator said, "Can you tell me your name, sweetie?"

"Clarissa Lamont."

"Okay, tell me what happened."

Through tears, Clarissa did.

Later, she would remember that she was crying, that her tears hadn't all dried up. And she would see again at her father's funeral that there were still many more tears inside her. They seemed endless, and somehow she knew that her life would be full of tears, that the sadness would always be with her.

The operator said, "Do you know your address?"

"I...I can't remember." She thought hard, and then the street name came to her. "It's Tasker Circle. But I don't know the address."

"That's okay. We can use the phone to find out where you are, okay?"

"Okay."

"We're going to send help right away. Where is your mother?"

"She's at work."

"Do you know the name of the place where she works?"

"It's a gas station down the street, but I don't know its name."

"Okay, hold on, help is on the way."

And help was on the way. In a few minutes, an ambulance arrived. The paramedics broke down the door, and she saw in the gap between their bodies that her father was covered in blood. There was no life in his eyes. It didn't even look like her father, but like some doll that was made up to be just like him, some husk where her father used to live. The smell was almost unbearable.

A police officer grabbed her by the hand and took her out on the front porch. She asked Clarissa questions, and Clarissa answered the best she could, but she kept looking back to see if her Daddy was okay.

"What's wrong with him?" The tears were still streaming, her vision blurry.

The police officer said, "He's very sick. We're, uh, taking him to the hospital to have him looked at. Your mom will be here soon."

Some neighbors were peering out of their windows, or standing on their porches watching. Clarissa saw them, and they saw her. But at that moment, they seemed so very far away.

The paramedics brought out a long stretcher with something black on top of it, some kind of bag. Clarissa stared at the strange black form for a moment, then she stood up and bolted over to the stretcher. Her father was inside that bag, she just knew it, somehow.

As she retold this story to her friends, she realized that the shroud was just like that black bag that had surrounded her father.

"No!" She screamed. "No, no, he can't breathe in there! Open it up! It's too dark in there, he will die if you don't let him out! He's really sick!"

She jumped up and she tried to get to the zipper in the center of the bag, but she couldn't reach it. Quickly, a set of arms scooped her up and held her back as the two paramedics put the stretcher in the back of the ambulance. Clarissa fought to get away. She kept screaming and flailing, fighting the policewoman who struggled to restrain her.

Then her mother arrived. She wrapped her first in her arms, then carried her inside and wrapped her in a blanket. Her mother's face was pale, and she looked as if she had aged a thousand years. Her mother sat her down on the couch, and told her to watch the TV while she went outside to talk to the police.

Clarissa watched her mother leave, watched the ambulance pull away down the road. She did not turn on the TV, only watched out the window. She tried to hear what her mother was saying, but after several minutes her mother collapsed to the ground, shrieking into the night. Several of the neighbors nearby came and gathered around her as the police officer drove off. They were talking to her, picking her up, sitting her on the porch, hugging her.

After a few minutes, several of the neighbors went back to their homes, but Monica had appeared, and Mary, Monica's mother, followed Clarissa's mother inside. As they walked through the door, they saw her standing by the window.

Her mother, her voice shaking, said, "Clarissa, I'm going to need you to go spend the night at Monica's so I can go to the hospital with your father, okay?" Her mother's eyes were dark red circles mixed with the black of her mascara. She squeezed a tissue wadded up in her hands.

"I want to go be with Daddy, too."

"No, honey. They...they don't allow children at the hospital at this time of night."

Clarissa frowned. "But.... "

"No "buts", honey. I have to go alone tonight, okay? We'll talk about it in the morning."

"Is Daddy going to be okay?"

"He...."

But she didn't finish the sentence. She couldn't cross the gap between her husband's life and her husband's death, not yet.

Monica grabbed her by the hand and said, "Come on, Clarissa. My mom said we can watch the My Little Pony Movie and have a sleepover on the couch."

"But isn't it a school night?"

Monica's mother, a short, curvaceous woman, with brown kinky hair and dark brown eyes, said, "Well, I think maybe we can have a special day tomorrow."

There were so many special days and surprises lately, and Clarissa didn't understand what that meant. But it felt like it meant something was wrong. She didn't like it. But she knew she couldn't go to the hospital, and she was happy to see her friend Monica, who looked half awake in her My Little Pony pjs. Monica's mother had curlers in her hair, and was wearing a nightshirt and sweatpants.

Clarissa followed everyone out the door, but just as she reached the top of the steps on the porch she realized that she had forgotten something. She turned and bolted back to the couch, grabbing the skateboard, hugging it tight, and then showing it to Monica as she stood in the front door, saying that she hoped her Dad could see her ride it soon.

Her mother, who was watching on the sidewalk, started sobbing, turned away, got into the car, and drove off.

Clarissa stood there in the doorway, trying to understand what had happened. Her father was sick, and they were taking him to the hospital. He had been to the hospital many times. But then she thought about how much blood there had been in the bathroom, and how the vomit had smelled different. She turned and looked toward the stairs, up at the bathroom door that stood yawning open.

She thought she saw something there, some shape or form she couldn't understand. It was moving. The door was moving on its own. Monica saw it, too. They watched as the door slammed shut with a violence and force that Clarissa had never seen before. She jumped and quivered. The girls looked at each other. That slamming door would haunt Clarissa's nightmares for a long time after, eventually fading away from time and memory, until her retelling.

Mary turned and glanced up at the girls from the sidewalk. With her voice artificially cheery, she said, "Well, come on, let's get you two settled."

The girls followed. Clarissa carried her skateboard. For the next several years, she would barely put it down. She would take it with her to school every day, and it would share her bed every night, and when she thought about her father, she would pull it close and imagine he was there, hugging her and calling her sunbeam, and she would think, the sun has already set.

They walked up the sidewalk and went inside Monica's house. After a few minutes, they were laying on the floor with sleeping bags and pillows, watching the Ponies go on their adventure. Before long, Clarissa was asleep.

6.   "Jesus," said James. "I had no idea that you were there when your dad died."

Clarissa sat there silently, clenching her fists and feeling the waves of emotions from that day cascade over her. Her heart ached, and she had wiped many tears out of her eyes as she told the end of her tale.

Monica jumped over and hugged her. Clarissa loved her for it. Monica had been there with her through it all. In the days that followed, she had slept over at Monica's many nights while her mother had taken care of the funeral arrangements, and visitors had come to pay their respects. But the next morning, after the ambulance had taken her father away, had been the hardest. Clarissa knew the truth without being told. Her father was dead. It wasn't a mystery. There was no place in her heart for denial. But when her mother told her what had happened, that her father's illness had claimed him, it had made it harder, somehow somehow.

Monica broke the hug and went for another slice of pizza. She chewed noisily. Clarissa had lost her appetite after the first piece. The telling had taken away her sense of victory and courage. And there was something else, some part of the story that was missing, though she couldn't put her finger on it. She tried to dig around and feel for that extra thread, but there was nothing to pull. Clarissa picked up her skateboard, hugged it, and spun one wheel while deep in thought.

Margie, who looked somber and quiet after the tale, said, "Give me a cigarette, James."

"Thought you were quitting."

"Shit, not now."

With a furrow in her brow, Monica said, "Potty mouth."

"You know it," replied Margie.

James handed her one and pulled the lighter from his pocket. Clarissa looked up at her and saw that her eyes were red and puffy, too. Had Margie been crying?

Margie said, "I don't really remember my Dad. Just the way he laughed. That's what I think about, you know? He kind of cackled when he thought something was funny. I always thought he sounded like that witch from the Wizard of Oz."

Margie blew a puff of smoke. She pulled her cigarette up next to her face. Her eyes reflected deep oceans of thought with little glowing embers from the cigarette reflected in them.

"But what happened to you, Clarissa? Can't say I'd prefer that." Margie took a long drag on the cigarette and then exhaled, blowing smoke.

"But you gotta remember the good stuff too, you know. Your dad gave you that skateboard. He loved the hell out of you. He couldn't help it. He had some bad luck. And you can't forget what you did today."

James said, "Yeah. You kicked ass, kid. Ain't no one can take that away from you."

Margie said, "I've watched my Ma struggle a lot. You know what she once told me?"

Clarissa shook her head.

"She said, 'Margie, life is gonna kick you down sometimes. When it does, you gotta kick back.' My Ma didn't graduate high school, but she's smart as hell. Her whole bedroom is filled with books. So I figure I should listen sometimes, I guess. But you know what I know?"

Clarissa looked over at Monica, who was chewing so noisily that even Margie stopped.

"Sorry," said Monica, though it came out through a mouth full of pizza.

Margie shrugged and looked back at Clarissa.

"You did that today. You kicked back. Don't forget how you took on Snake Hill and won."

In a small voice, Clarissa said, "I won't."

"You're god damn right you won't!"

"Potty mouth."

Margie just grinned. She seemed to like to get a rise out of Monica a little.

Margie said, "You know why you ain't gonna forget Snake Hill, Clarissa?"

"Why?" She was sincerely curious, expecting some other insight to come out of Margie's mouth.

"Cause we're gonna do it again, right now."

"What?" said Clarissa and Monica at the same time.

James laughed. "Told you before, kid, she's relentless."

"You gotta get those wings on straight, again," said Margie, who was already standing up and picking up her board. "One more run this afternoon to remind you that no matter what happens, you kick back."

The four of them went out the door, and again, Clarissa conquered the hill. This time, she did it without ending up on the sidewalk, and when the four of them stood at the bottom again, she had to admit that she felt a little better.

Afterward, she and Monica walked home toward the sunset.

For some of us, the sun sets on our childhood long before we indulge in the many firsts of adolescence. The bleeding reds and purples of that descending sun pierce through the veil of our innocence. They leave us gasping for breath in that collision of light and water on the shores of our existence. Some live in that perpetual twilight, and when death comes in with the tide, they fight it with the futility of emptying the ocean with a single plastic cup. Some surrender to the inevitable, laying down as the waves wash over them and the light fades below the horizon. But some peer over the edge, across the unknown, and then wade into the water, reaching to understand and hoping to find meaning in the churn, or at least a semblance of peace.

7.   Several hours later, Clarissa lay in bed, with winking string lights keeping the darkness at bay. The double victories on Snake Hill had helped. Still, she felt something deep down inside her. It was a strange pressure in her chest, a looming dread. Later on, she would come to think of it as heart sickness. There was something behind her grief, some terrible truth. It throbbed in her chest and then, like a cold lump of fear, it pushed its way into her mind.

For there was something else she had seen the night of her father's death. Something that she had pressed down deep inside her because she was too scared to understand it.

She shut her eyes tight, willing the memory away. But it was too late. It came to the surface in full force and the shivers of fear rattled her bones.

Instead of simply reliving the memory, she stood down the hall from the bathroom door. There she was, standing there, watching her six-year-old self pounding on the door.

Her younger self pleaded, "Daddy! Daddy! Daddy! Daddy! Please, Daddy! Answer! I don't want you to be sick anymore. Daddy?!"

Young Clarissa fell silent. Then she stood back up and slammed her body against the door for several minutes, until she finally slid down with her back against the door.

Then, the younger version of herself saw something terrible, something in the corner, nestled within shadow. The memories of what she had seen that night flooded back into her, so she had a kind of queer double vision. She saw both her younger point of view and her nine-year-old point of view simultaneously.

In the shadows, something swirled and stirred. A kind of vortex or whirlpool appeared and then, there, gleaming, were too bright red eyes. As the eyes glowed brighter, the semblance of a face took shape in the dark, and with it, a fanged smile of razor-sharp teeth. Nine-year-old Clarissa knew at once it was the creature from the meadow.

Arms formed in the whirlpool and reached out of shadow and onto the floor. At the end were two terrible sets of four-fingered claws. They were so sharp that they left small holes in the thin brown carpet as they dug for purchase, pulling a long snake-like form of a body from the portal. It clawed forward again, and again, coming closer and closer to six-year-old Clarissa.

The shroud closed in tightly around nine-year-old Clarissa, holding her still. Clarissa struggled to break free, to rush out and pull her younger self away from the creature that slithered ever closer. It was only a few feet away, using the carpet as hand holds, like a climber scaling a cliff. When its face was only two feet from her younger self, it stopped. It reached up with one of its long claws and touched Clarissa in three places-forehead, jaw, and cheek.

Not only could Clarissa remember the terrible blinding pain, like every nerve ending had been set on fire inside her body, she, the observer, could feel it now, too. As the shroud restrained her, both she and her younger self screamed in blinding agony. It felt as if something pushed out from the inside of her skull. The only thing she could think was that there were maggots in there. Maggots like what happened to the boy in the meadow, maggots that would burst out of her eyes and then feast on her face.

The pain peaked, a discordant crescendo like all the strings inside a piano snapping at once. Then, the agony evaporated almost instantly. Clarissa blinked her eyes and saw the creature retreating backward, using its claws to push itself back into the shadowy portal from whence it came. Except it didn't entirely disappear. Instead, it turned its gaze down the hall toward nine-year-old Clarissa. She felt the burn of its gaze and, for a moment, there was a brief resurgence of pain before the eyes dimmed and the shadowy thing vanished beyond the gradation of shades in the dark.

She looked back at the bathroom and saw something else, something that would puzzle her for a long time. The six-year-old version of her was staring at her. Now that she saw it, she remembered that night, that she had seen something strange, had seen what she thought could only be an older version of herself. There they were, two versions of herself, past and present, staring at each other across time.

Clarissa opened her mouth to say something, but the scene faded from her sight, then her eyes opened and she was in her bedroom She lay flat on her back, staring at the ceiling.

Had she just had a nightmare? The memory of the past still clung to her, but was that because she had just dreamed it, or was that because she had really just...time traveled, somehow? You weren't supposed to experience pain in dreams, were you? She couldn't remember.

It occurred to her that there was one way to verify if she was dreaming, or if that memory held any truth. Her mother had told her once that memory was a funny thing. It seemed to change on you all the time. So she needed to investigate. Quickly, she swung her legs out of bed and adjusted her pajamas, which were twisted and awkward as if she had been thrashing in bed, or fighting off the shroud.

Quietly, she opened the door. There, down the hall, looking out over the railing and into the house's entrance, was the bathroom door. It stood just at the top of the steps. At the other end of the hall was her mother's and Ted's room. She could hear Ted snoring lightly as she crept down the hall. Her heart pounded in her ears as she reached the spot where the creature had come out of the wall. She looked carefully at the shadows and the corner, and saw nothing. She poked and prodded the spot for several minutes, feeling her fear lessen as she could find no evidence of the creature's malevolent gaze.

She slumped against the wall, feeling relief for a moment. Then she traced the path of the creature with her eyes and thought she saw something. The fear regrouped and hit her like a hammer. She squinted and looked again at the floor leading to the bathroom. Gooseflesh tightened her skin, and the room felt suddenly cold.

Slowly, carefully, she got down on her hands and knees. It was dark, so it wasn't easy to see, but she put her nose almost to the floor to be sure of what she was seeing. Her mother had never replaced that carpet. It was the same one from that terrible night.

Her heart thumped even harder, and suddenly it was hard to breathe. She saw them. In the carpet were a series of tiny tears where the creature's claws had gripped the floor to pull itself from the portal. Once she saw one, she saw them all. They were like animal tracks, but so much worse.

Struggling to breathe, Clarissa leaned back until she was sitting on the floor. Her eyes were playing tricks on her, that's all. All of that was impossible, wasn't it? Swallowing and taking a deep breath, she looked again. Sure enough, the claw marks were there. It had been here; she hadn't just made it up. She was certain of one other thing then, too. That thing from the meadow, whatever it was, had something to do with her father's death.

And It had seen her.

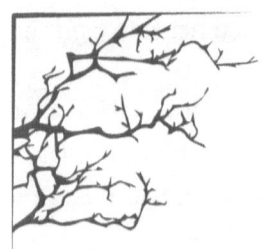

Chapter 7

If It Bleeds It Leads

News is a coffin,
With truth(s) unforgiving,
An offering to the dead,
And vicarious living.

Unless...
You are the story,
Unfolding before your eyes,
Stealing away your solid ground,
With a malevolent surprise.

Salt of the earth,
A pillar of the damned,
Corrupted by gossip,
Your heart and soul jammed.

The summer sweltered. With heat haze on the streets and sweat on every brow, Clarissa, Monica, James, and Margie became prisoners of summer, though Margie tried to bust out. The papers had called it the heat wave of the century, and for nine days that summer, beginning July 22nd to August 1st, the red of every thermometer in the greater Philadelphia area hovered around 102 degrees Fahrenheit. Margie had shown up on the morning of the 25th, bright and hopeful that Clarissa would skateboard with her. James had already declined, and Margie had said, "The skatepark is totally empty. It's like a freaking ghost town, Clarissa, come on."

It wasn't that Clarissa wasn't willing or deaf to Margie's pleas. She had tried the day before when the temperature was 101, but after an hour, she had felt like a hard-boiled egg. So, with the temperature on track to break 104, Clarissa declined and closed the door. She was thankful that Ted had gotten a big freelance gig not long after her stay in the hospital, and had sprung for a window unit air conditioner in the living room.

Clarissa, her mother, and Ted all sat in the living room, with the single AC unit on full blast. Even at 11 a.m., it was still warm enough in the living room for Clarissa to sit there in her green and blue one-piece bathing suit. Her mother had seen the sense in Clarissa's wardrobe and changed into a flamingo-pink version, complete with a wet towel wrapped around her head. Each of them took turns soaking in a cold shower to keep cool until Ted complained about the water bill. Ted only wore gym shorts, his increasingly large beer gut glistening with sweat.

There had been no formal breakfast that morning. No one had any interest in turning on the stove. Clarissa wondered if their air conditioner would survive the summer. It moaned in random cycles, a bellyaching mechanical tone that drew worried gazes with each complaint.

Clarissa watched *X-Men* on her favorite Saturday morning cartoon channel, and ate a bowl of cereal. Her skateboard sat next to her, propped up against the couch. Ted sat reading the newspaper, wiping his brow with a dish rag every few minutes. Twice, Clarissa had seen his frustration with himself for letting his sweat drip on the floor, so now, he focused on wiping up every drop he could off of his increasingly bald forehead. He was losing the war against his body's attempts to cool itself, heaving exasperated sighs.

Her mother, off of work because the restaurant she currently worked at, Charlie's Ribs and Steak, had a broken AC, had begun her day with painting. However, it was already hot enough that she said her paints weren't mixing the way she wanted them to. So, instead, she sat with a sketchpad in her lap. Every once in a while, she would swirl her glass of water and mix in the ice. She had told Clarissa once that she did that to keep it cooler longer, though Ted had mocked her logic before her mother had snapped at him. Clarissa didn't know what to believe.

Every half hour, or so, her mother would stand up, put her sketchpad down, far away from any drinks, and throw a few more ice cubes in her drink. Clarissa couldn't help but wonder if it was an excuse to open the freezer and stand in the cool air for a moment. When Clarissa had tried that earlier, Ted had scolded her and nagged about the power bill.

It was when *X-Men* wrapped up and the next program began that something in the paper caught Ted's interest. At first, he turned the pages softly, but then after a moment, he seemed to flip back and forth between two specific pages, making enough noise that both her mother and Clarissa took notice. Muttering to himself audibly, Ted looked up at both of them, paused, and then froze, realizing that their gaze was on him. He blinked for a few moments, opened his mouth to say something, and then closed it again. Ted seemed to think about something for several minutes, and just as Clarissa had turned her attention back to the TV, he finally spoke.

Though his words were calm, there was an edge in his voice. "Hey, Clarissa, do you remember the name of that detective who talked to you a few days after you got out of the hospital?"

Clarissa's heart froze. The crystals of ice in her veins traveled to her fingertips and toes as her heart pounded. The shroud dimmed the room a fraction. She hadn't thought about the detective in weeks, but now, with her name ringing in her ears, she felt sick to her stomach. How long had it been since she came to speak with her? Three weeks?

"Did you hear me?"

She turned and looked up at him. His face was pale, his tone agitated. Gone was the wooden politeness only a question earlier. Had she done something wrong?

"Well?"

"I...I don't know."

Her mother said, "Ted, what's your problem?" All her mother's patience had dried up with the heat.

He looked over at her mother as if he didn't remember she was in the room, then back to Clarissa and said, "Sorry, I...it's the heat, that's all. But, Clarissa, you don't remember her name?"

His tone was only slightly apologetic. What was bothering him? Clarissa couldn't understand his expression. Later when she was older, she would, but now; that thin mask of calm hiding a veil of terror just below it was unfamiliar.

"Ted, what's this all about? She's only nine. Why would she remember the detective's name? That was at least a month ago."

Ted shook his head. "No, Audrey, it was twenty-four days ago. I marked that date on my calendar, June 30th."

Her mother replied, "We aren't all obsessed with schedules and dates, Ted." She didn't even try to hide the irritation in her voice.

"Clarissa, it's really important. What was her name?" His voice trembled a bit.

The tremor in his voice was an earthquake, altering the destiny of everyone involved. A silence possessed the room. Everything felt heavier, more serious. All the agitation in the room evaporated. Her mother's irritation fermented into fear, a poison, an intoxicating beverage.

Her mother said, "Ted, you're scaring me. What's going on?"

Ted considered, then said, "Audrey, you have her card, don't you?"

"I...I think so. If I do, it's up in the bedroom junk drawer. Why? Ted, what's this all about? Did something happen to the detective?"

Ted's face bore the truth like a grinning skull, his features sunken and sallow, all pretense of joy bled away like a decaying corpse. Later, Clarissa would think that the news of that morning had brought him his first gray hairs, scattered around the bald patch growing on his forehead.

He didn't answer her Mother's question. Instead, he got up quickly, not with his usual meticulous attempts to prevent the chair legs from grinding against the wood floor, but with enough speed that the chair went crashing to the ground. In a very un-Ted-like fashion, he didn't even stop to pick it up as he dashed up the stairs. Her mother stood slowly, silently, as if afraid to wake an angry beast. She picked up the chair, her eyes locked on the stairs that lead up toward the bathroom.

Clarissa's heart pounded. She swallowed, following her mother's gaze. Her mother wasn't looking at the bedroom door where Ted had disappeared-she was looking at the bathroom door. Did her mother know something? Had she seen those red eyes adjacent to the door?

She turned toward Clarissa and said, "Do you know what this is about?"

Clarissa shook her head. But it was a lie. Something was wrong, and it had to do with the monster from the meadow.

A moment later, Ted came running down the stairs, waving the card in his hand.

"Got it!"

In his excitement, he almost tripped down the last stair, but caught himself. He hurried to the chair and put the detective's card next to the newspaper, looking between the two several times. Clarissa felt the weight of it on her and wanted desperately to know what Ted was doing, but she didn't dare move from the spot. Immobilized. But her fear could not dampen her curiosity. It was a sore in her mouth that she could not help poking with her tongue.

He read the card out loud. "Detective Andrea Corrin"

Then he read the paper out loud. "Detective Andrea Corrin."

He swore under his breath and rubbed the top of his head, something he often did when he was worried or fretting about something that needed done.

"What's going on, Ted?" her mother asked.

"She's...," he swallowed and paused, as if gathering his courage, "...dead. Audrey."

Ted looked up at Clarissa again, that same look of fear in his eyes, and said. "She's dead," a second time, as if he had to say it again to believe it.

He looked ten years older, and so did her mother. Clarissa trembled. The room darkened another degree. The Detective she talked to was dead? Had the monster killed her? Why? Then it struck her.

Clarissa said, "She went down to the meadow too...."

Ted was silent.

"Didn't she, Ted?" asked Clarissa.

Slowly, he nodded his head. Just above a whisper, he said, "Yeah, she did."

"Didn't you also go to that meadow, Ted?" asked Clarissa.

Ted looked at her for a long time. The only sound was the air conditioner doing its best to keep up with the hot day. Ted blinked several times. Clarissa thought he was trembling, but she couldn't be sure. His posture was rigid and still.

Her mother broke the silence. "How...how did she die?" She swallowed, an audible click in her throat.

Ted's eyes drifted from Clarissa and over to her mother. "What?"

"How did she...die...Ted?" The word 'die', separated from the others, quarantined in her speech.

Clarissa waited, holding her breath. She wanted to be wrong so badly. Maybe it was a car accident, or maybe she died in the line of duty. A hope for the damned, the cursed.

He looked down at the paper. "Audrey...she...I better just read it."

He lifted the paper up in front of his face, his Delaware County accent extra pronounced with the careful reading of each word.

"Detective Andrea Corrin, a veteran of the Philadelphia Police Department, died yesterday under what one inside source said was mysterious circumstances. The police have yet to release details, but Corrin's elderly neighbor had discovered her body when the detective failed to have their regular morning tea together. Her neighbor, who wished to keep her name anonymous, was quoted as saying, "The body was badly decayed, almost as if it had been there for weeks. But that was impossible, because we just had tea yesterday morning." The official cause of death is still pending. But with the strange condition of the, and another recent body found in the woods in a similar condition, the FBI has become involved in the investigation. When asked, the FBI would not comment on the possibility of chemical or biological terrorism."

"There's more," said Ted, "But that's the gist of it."

"What else does it say?" asked her mother.

He gave her a sharp look. "We'll talk about it later."

"Later? Ted, this is weird. That woman wasn't here that long ago and she's dead? It's so strange, it's just like...."

Her mother stopped what she was saying and looked over at Clarissa. Her face flushed and her mother said, "Ted, can you help me in the garage? I want to see if I can get those paints to mix again."

"Sure, Audrey." Ted looked long at Clarissa as he said those words, then both adults walked quietly out of the room and to the garage. There was nothing quiet about the set of their shoulders, or how each step they took weighed heavily on the floor. Clarissa knew that they were talking about her. She wasn't stupid. After all, she had left her childhood behind in the meadow. There was something else too...ever since the meadow, she understood things more clearly, though she couldn't be certain why.

Once they shut the door, she got up and walked over to the door, and put her ear against it. She couldn't hear what they were saying, for both were speaking in harsh whispers. At first, it sounded like the hissing of snakes. As the harsh tones escalated into mumbles, she could tell they were arguing, but not what they were arguing about.

Finally, she heard her mother shout, "That's ridiculous, Ted! There's no way that's true."

Clarissa heard the slap of footsteps on concrete coming toward her. Quickly, she ran back to the living room floor where she had been sitting. She had just sat down when her mother flung the door open, stomped over to the kitchen table, grabbed the keys from the key ring next to the sink, turned, and walked back out to the garage.

Ted said, "Where are you going?" He sounded confused and hurt. "Come on, Audrey, let's talk about this."

She pushed past him and got in the car, shouting. "There's nothing to talk about, Ted! You damn well know what you're implying. You will not discuss this with her! " She glanced at Clarissa, but only briefly.

Was her mother saying that Ted wasn't allowed to discuss the death of the detective with Clarissa? Who else could it be? What had they argued about, exactly? Certainly something about the detective and what had happened, but what was their fight about?

Her mother practically ran out of the garage door and got into the car. Clarissa got up and walked to the door where Ted stood, watching Ted's desperate attempts to bring her mother back. The outer garage door hummed to life and lifted to let a shimmer of heat inside. Just as it opened, her mother sped out, her car crunching over the curb as it hit the street with speed. A car coming her mother's direction swerved out of the way, honked its horn, and the driver shouted obscenities. Clarissa watched as her mother sped off before anyone could say anything.

Clarissa took a risk. "Ted, what did you and my Mom talk about?"

Ted, still framing the door, stared at her for several long moments and Clarissa could almost feel him balancing the scales in his mind, trying to decide what the right thing to do was.

All he said was, "Spider-man's on. Want to watch it together?"

Surprised, Clarissa asked, "You like Spider-man?"

"Of course, I grew up reading the comics. I always loved it when he fought Doc Ock. Those mechanical arms were so cool. Even as a kid, I always wished I had four extra arms so I could fix things."

The music of the show's theme song played, and Ted sat on the couch. Clarissa followed. She wasn't sure what to do or say. She knew that whatever they had talked about in the garage was important, but it didn't seem like Ted would speak of it. He never was the forthcoming type. He always struggled to speak directly.

As *Spider-Man* played, she couldn't help but think of the detective. Someone else was dead, and only a few days before, that thing from the meadow had seen in her that strange dream memory. After the show ended, they retreated to their own activities. Ted went to work on something in the house, and Clarissa went back to reading since skateboarding was out of the question.

She was reading *The Elf Stones of Shannara*. As she did, she had the strange feeling that the author was tapping into something real, or at least some version of the truth. In the book, a special magic tree held creatures from the Demon realm in a prison, a kind of world next to their own. The tree was dying and if the characters didn't restore it in time, then all the evil would be unleashed upon the world. It made her think of the meadow and of the creature, the boy, and...the detective.

That sick feeling of fear filled her belly and she couldn't help but wish that magic was real. But, she thought, if that creature was real, if it really could make a portal into her house, if it could change forms and shapes, then wasn't magic real, after all? Did that mean that there was good magic out there, like the Elfstone? If so, where and how could she find it? She thought she had better ask Monica and maybe, just maybe, it was time to tell Monica everything. If she couldn't tell her best friend what had happened, who could she tell?

Ted, covered in grease from working on god-knows-what in the house again, walked back into the living room where Clarissa was sitting and said, "Clarissa, I've been thinking."

Here it was. He was going to tell her what the fight was about. Clarissa sat up straight, eager and terrified in similar measure.

"About what?" She slid her favorite bookmark into the book and put it next to her on the arm of the gray couch.

"Have you told anyone else about what happened to you down in that meadow?"

Clarissa shook her head. Monica hadn't asked. Clarissa suspected it was because she was a scaredy cat. Any time James asked, Margie had smacked him, saying that Clarissa would tell them when she was ready. She was nervous about telling them. What if they thought she was crazy?

"Good." He seemed satisfied with this answer and Clarissa saw something in his face change, though she wasn't sure what it was. He seemed more relaxed, somehow.

He said, "I don't think we should really talk about any of the weird stuff that happened earlier in the summer to your friends or anyone else, okay?"

"What do you mean?"

Her mother and father had always told her it was important to talk about the things that bothered you, but Ted wasn't her father. He was Ted. Ted had kept that secret about his illness until after he had married his mother.

"Well, it's just, some people might think all that stuff is pretty weird. And it might be a good idea to keep it quiet and not talk about it. You don't want people to think you're weird or anything, right?"

He paused, but Clarissa didn't say anything. He ran his hand through his thinning hair.

"Look at me, Clarissa, I don't have many friends 'cause people think I'm weird. Trust me, you don't want to end up like me."

Clarissa thought about it, and Monica, James, and Margie. She didn't have many friends, either. Lots of people already thought Clarissa was a little weird, and she wasn't looking forward to going back to school after everything that had happened that summer. At nine, she already understood that word got around, and people were bound to ask her about what had happened to her in the woods. Was Ted right? Should she keep it all to herself?

Ted continued, "All I'm saying is, people can be pretty mean sometimes, and you never know who might take it the wrong way, you know? You don't want to lose, say, your best friend over it, right?"

Clarissa nodded slowly. He wasn't wrong. What if Monica thought she was weird or she scared her so badly that she didn't want to be friends anymore? She was suddenly glad that she hadn't told Monica anything else about the night her father had died. What would she have said if she had? Would they still be friends?

"Okay," said Clarissa.

"Okay?"

"Yeah. I don't want to talk about it much, anyway."

It wasn't entirely true. She could feel the story ache inside her, whispering that it wanted to be told. But she thought Ted knew better. After all, he had been a weirdo his whole life and needed to hide it to keep people from hating him. So he probably knew better than she did.

"Alright, but let's not talk about it to anyone, okay? I mean, let's not even bring it up again in the house."

"Not even with my mom?"

"No. Not her, either."

"But, why not?"

"Well...," he seemed to pause and think for a moment, rubbing his chin. "Did you see how upset your Mom got just now?"

Clarissa nodded.

"She's pretty sensitive about everything that happened, and I think it scares her. So I don't think she really wants to talk about it. So it's best if you don't bring it up."

Her mother had always told her that she could tell her anything, but Ted was right. Her mother did get really upset. She had never seen her drive away like that before. It worried her a little. Maybe she couldn't stand the idea of thinking about what happened in the meadow? Or was it something else? Clarissa had to ask.

"What did you talk about in the garage?"

Ted hesitated, then said, "We talked about how you disappeared, mostly, and how much that scared us."

"But why did she get mad?" She could tell he was leaving something important out. Sometimes he talked to her as if she was still in kindergarten, and couldn't understand some of the bigger and more important things.

"It's hard to explain.... It's...well...grownup stuff, you know? I don't want you to worry about it. Your mother will be back in a few hours, but trust me, Clarissa. Unless you want her to get upset like that at you, don't bring up the topic to her, or anyone else, okay?"

It was strange that Ted had said that just after Clarissa was thinking about talking to Monica about all of this, but what could she say? Maybe Ted was right. Did she want to weird Monica out with the story? Sure, Monica was her best friend, but Monica also hated it when someone said a bad word. Could she handle something like a monster or dead bodies? Of course, Monica already knew about the boy's body, but maybe it would freak her out if she heard about the detective, too.

"Okay, Ted. I won't."

And she meant it, at least then.

Some skeletons knock at the closet door, a relentless pounding like in *The Tell-Tale Heart,* ever thudding and shuddering until you open it just a crack to silence its madness. Then the truth comes tumbling out, tinging the room with its dark secrets. For once something is out, it will never truly rest.

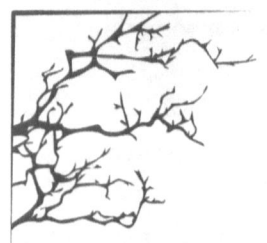

Chapter 8

The Burden of Secrets

Bearer, bearer of secrets and songs,
What do you carry when you aren't long,
For the world and its games, of tortuous ends,
When you can't share your secrets with your closest friends?

You poor scared thing,
So broken and bruised,
Perhaps you felt that you had nothing to lose.
The mistake you made, because you thought you could trust,
Left nothing behind but wind and dust.

The summer climbed to its greatest heat, and then ripened like a fruit into its autumnal form. With the arrival of September and the start of school only a week away, Clarissa finally found a sense of normalcy. It was true that the shroud still plagued her and that, on occasion, the world felt dreary, but with skateboarding and sleepovers she felt more like her old self. It was a lie, but a necessary one.

Clarissa decided that Ted was right. It was best not to talk about the thing from the meadow or any of those events. Monica didn't ask, and Margie and James were silent on the subject, so it made it easier for the days to evaporate without comment.

The creature that had haunted her gave no sign of its presence, and only the claw marks on the floor near the bathroom provided any evidence that it had existed at all. Sometimes, in the long hours of the night, when she stared up at the ceiling, eyes bleeding with exhaustion from some recent nightmare, she got up and went to the hall. She would crawl on hands and knees as silent as a mouse, and feel the scars left by the creature on the floor. She just had to be sure she wasn't crazy. Though she wished with all of her heart that it was the last she had seen of the creature, there was another truth lingering inside her. She had let it out. Clarissa didn't know what that meant, but she had snuck more than one of Ted's newspapers out of the trash, combing for any other strange deaths.

The news was silent on the matter of monsters.

A few days before school started, she and Monica went to the skate park. Clarissa was skating in the half-pipe when Michael, Andrew, and Tommy showed up, gliding in on their skateboards. Tommy was friends with James and Margie, but Margie didn't care for the other two. She called them the rat twins, not for any physical attribute, but because she said that they were "rat bastards". Though what that meant, Clarissa wasn't entirely sure.

Michael, the shorter bowl-cut, blond-haired kid three years older than Clarissa, spotted her. She noticed them talking and he said something to the other two. Tommy, with the flaming-red hair and freckles, and Andrew, with the shaggy brown hair and bushy eyebrows, stared at her, a strange smile on their lips and mischief in their eyes. Something about that look bothered Clarissa, and she pretended she hadn't seen them, hoping that they wouldn't approach.

Monica sat at the top of the half-pipe sketching like she usually did when Clarissa brought her to the skate park. Her pencil worked furiously across the page. She tried to sketch the whole park and Clarissa skating on the half-pipe. Monica had a long way to go in developing her skill and craft, but often, when Clarissa's mother wasn't working, Monica would ask a thousand questions about style and technique, and her mother was happy to oblige.

The three boys made their way over to her and Monica. Clarissa stopped at the top of the half-pipe, looking down on the three as they made their way up to her. She had a sinking feeling in her chest. They were up to something. Margie said that they were always up to something, and Clarissa wished that either she or James were with them. Clarissa looked around the park for any sign of her friends, but there was none. Normally, they were at the park at this time of day, but Clarissa hadn't seen them.

Tommy, who had a squeaky voice, asked a question first. "So like, what happened to you in those woods?"

Monica looked up from what she was doing. "Buzz off, Tommy."

"What? Everyone wants to know. The whole town is talking about it, especially after the detective."

Monica, who hadn't heard about the detective because Clarissa had followed Ted's advice and avoided the topic, asked, "What detective?"

"Where the hell have you been? In a hole? That shit happened weeks ago," said Andrew.

"Yeah," said Michael. "Where you been, in Stupidville, or something?"

Monica looked over to Clarissa, but Clarissa didn't say anything. How could she? It was her best friend and she hadn't told her about what had happened with her Mom and Ted. She couldn't tell if Monica was mad, but there was just a hint of disappointment in her eyes.

Monica turned back to the three boys, who stood at the bottom of the half-pipe. "I don't know what you're talking about."

Tommy said, "The freaking detective on the case about your little friend's disappearance, duh. How did you not know this already? She dropped dead, and her body was all weird and mangled like that boy they found in the woods."

Monica gave Clarissa a puzzled look. She was certain Monica would ask now. She wondered if James and Margie had heard about the detective. Clarissa had hoped that after several weeks people would have forgotten it.

Clarissa said, "I don't feel like talking about it."

"There," said Monica, always her staunch defender. "She doesn't want to talk about it, so buzz off, Tommy."

Michael, with mirth in his smile, always quick with a comeback said, "Buzz off? We just got here. Besides, no one wants you around, Clarissa. You're cursed."

It felt like a punch in the gut and nausea came with it.

"Cursed?" asked Clarissa.

"Yeah," said Michael, "My dad says you got bad juju or something."

Before Clarissa could ask what that meant, Andrew, who had the deepest voice of the three, said, "So, how'd you do it?"

Puzzled, Clarissa said, "Do what?"

"Let's go." Monica threw her things in her backpack, grabbed Clarissa by the hand, and pulled her down the half-pipe. Clarissa didn't mind being led away, she never much liked these three. But the boys skated down and surrounded her, even shoving Monica out of the way. They loomed over her, their shadows tall, their grins wolfish and greedy.

Clarissa shoved Tommy, but he was much bigger and wider than she was, and he didn't even flinch.

Clarissa who, despite her size, wasn't scared of them said, "Get out of my way, jerks."

They laughed and mocked her. "Get out of my way, jerks."

"Just leave me alone."

Michael said, "Not 'til you tell us how you did it."

"I don't know what you're talking about." Clarissa shoved Michael and he laughed at her pitiful effort.

Tommy said, "Bullshit, you don't. Look, we figured the first one was easy. You were in the woods alone with that other kid, and you probably just hit him over the head with a stick or maybe shoved him down a hill or something."

Clarissa's heart pounded in her chest. How did they know about her pushing the boy down the hill? Did that get out somehow? Only her parents and the police knew about that. Had she told Monica, Margie, or James? She couldn't remember. Would they have told anyone else?

Tommy didn't give her time to respond. "The second one, though, offing a cop? That's real impressive."

Andrew said, "It's witchcraft. That's how she did it. I told you guys. It's the only thing that makes sense. Bodies don't rot like that, at least that's what my mom said."

Monica charged into the teenagers, but they didn't budge. Even shorter than Clarissa, she crashed back into the ground. They didn't even turn to notice her, only swatted her away when she tried again.

Michael laughed and said, "Come on, tell us. Is it Satan? Did you make some kind of deal with the devil or something?"

"No. I don't know...I...."

Michael took her skateboard. Clarissa saw red.

"Give that back, jerk!" Clarissa tried to grab her skateboard, but he just held it up high where she couldn't reach it. She punched him hard in the balls and he doubled over, barely standing.

Michael, through gritted teeth, said, "Fuck you, you little bitch. You're gonna pay for that."

She tugged at the skateboard, but Tommy took it and threw it aside. "It's ours now, you evil little shit. What are you gonna do? Cast a spell on me?"

Andrew shoved her from behind. Michael, standing up again, caught her. Then he shoved her, and Tommy caught her. Andrew said, "Let's play pass the chicken until she talks."

They threw Clarissa around several more times. She felt like a pinball trapped in a machine, unable to do anything but slam into objects and ultimately fall. Andrew held her now, with her arms pinned behind her back. She struggled and squirmed to get away, and he twisted her arms hard. Clarissa cried out in pain.

Monica attacked Andrew over and over, trying to help Clarissa break free. But it was no use. The three were so much bigger and older than they were.

Tommy said, "You know, my dad said the Bible says we're supposed to kill witches. But maybe it would be enough if we just fucked you up."

A malevolent grin spread across Tommy's face. "I always heard that if you kicked a girl in the crotch it hurts just as bad as a boy. But I ain't never seen it. What ya think Michael, want to get a little payback?"

A large shadow loomed over all of them, and Andrew's jaw dropped open. Before anyone could say or do anything else, someone grabbed Tommy by the hair and pulled hard. Tommy cried out in pain.

Clarissa heard a loud thunk. Andrew cried out in pain and let go. Clarissa turned and saw Margie standing there with a big stick. Andrew lay on the ground holding his right shoulder.

"What the fuck is wrong with you?" said Margie, with fire in her eyes. "You're torturing a little girl...a goddamn fourth grader!"

James was standing there, arms folded, between Michael and the others. James was much taller than the three boys. The one holding Tommy by the hair was a giant of a man, someone who Clarissa thought wasn't just a teenager but a full-grown adult, and a big one at that. He was easily over six feet tall with muscles bulging.

James said, "Tommy, I thought you were cool. What the hell are you picking on Clarissa for?"

The big guy let go of Tommy and shoved him. Tommy fell to the ground, got up, and scrambled away, backing into his friends. "She's a witch, asshole. She's murdered two people already."

Margie said, "What the hell is this, the Salem witch trials? Some weird shit happens and you blame a little girl? God damn rat bastards."

Clarissa didn't know what the Salem Witch Trials were, but she would remember to find out later.

Andrew said, "We were just playing around. It wasn't serious."

The big man spoke. "Just playing around?" His voice boomed. All three boys were paying attention to him, and all looked scared. Clarissa couldn't blame them. His biceps were bigger than most people's legs. He took a step forward, and they slunk back. He walked up to them until they were back against a small concrete wall.

"You three have a very interesting definition of playing around. If I pounded a better attitude into you, would that just be playing around?"

"No...No, sir," said Tommy.

"We wasn't sticking around, anyway," said Andrew.

Margie stood next to Clarissa now, watching. Monica stood at her other side. James walked over and grabbed her skateboard.

Margie said, "Alright, Derick, don't murder them. Let the little piss ants go home."

Derick, the big man's name apparently, leaned in really close and said, "If I catch you messing with this girl again, boys, I'm gonna take it personally. You don't want me to take it personally, do you?"

Michael, the only one with any bravery left, said, "And who the fuck are you?" His voice trembled.

Derick got right up in his face, almost nose-to-nose. "Boy, I'm the one watching you now. Real close like." His words were so soft Clarissa could barely hear what he was saying. "I'm gonna be around here a lot from now on, and if you don't behave yourself, if you so much as laugh in this girl's direction, I'm gonna tear you limb from limb. Understand?"

Michael nodded quickly, the fear sparkling in his eyes. All his color and defiance drained away. "Come on guys, let's get out of here."

They grabbed their skateboards and ran. The five of them watched them go.

Margie was the first to speak. "You alright, Clarissa?"

She nodded. "Thanks."

Margie said, "Come on, let's go back to my place and get some ice cream."

Clarissa nodded. She and Monica grabbed their things and followed James, Margie, and Derick out of the park and back toward Margie's house.

"I don't think they'll bother you again," said James. "They're cowards."

Monica said, "What was that stuff about witches?"

Clarissa had the same question and was glad that Monica had asked.

Margie said, "Some of the conspiracy nuts in this town think that someone is using magic to kill first the boy and then the detective."

Clarissa said, "What's a conspiracy nut?"

James said, "Someone who believes in made up bullshit like it's real or something. Everyone knows there ain't no such thing as magic."

Clarissa wasn't so sure about that, but didn't argue. She thought of the creature in the meadow and the claw marks in the hallway. If that wasn't a kind of magic, what was it? Again, Clarissa wondered if there was some other kind of magic out there, one that could be used to help her if that creature came back. Maybe she could find something like an Elfstone or a Sword of Shannara? But how would she begin to find such things? She didn't exactly know any wizards.

Clarissa said, "They think I killed that detective?"

Monica said, "What detective? I don't understand. How come you didn't tell me about any of this, Clarissa?"

Clarissa, feeling her face redden with shame, said, "The detective who interviewed me...she's dead. And I didn't tell you because I didn't want to freak you out, or make you think I was weird or something."

Monica said, "Why would I think that? You're my best friend. You can tell me anything, Clarissa."

There was a deep note of disappointment in Monica's voice, and her eyes looked sad. Clarissa would never forget that look, even as she came to understand Demon's nature.

Those words would ring inside Clarissa's head over and over in the long nights ahead. Monica was her best friend and neither of them could remember a time when they weren't friends. Maybe Ted was wrong.

Margie said, "People are scared. When something weird happens and people die, they tell stories to try to make sense of it. At least that's what my English teacher Mrs. Becker said when we studied the Salem Witch Trials last year."

Clarissa said, "What were those?"

"Oh, back in the late 1600s, there were a bunch of people who were accused of being witches and having magic powers that hurt people. My teacher said some fungus made people hallucinate and think that supernatural things were happening to them. They blamed the women and executed them and, of course, it turned out none of it was real. People just blamed the weird things on these women."

Monica said, "Like Clarissa?"

"Yeah," said Margie, "Exactly, and those little rat bastards are just trying to look cool by confronting you. They're freshmen this year. Don't worry, Clarissa, James and I will make sure they get knocked down a peg or two, and Derick here will pound them if they bother you again."

Monica, always the curious one, turned to Derick who was walking just behind her and said, "Who are you?"

"Derick." He said with a grin. "I go to high school with Margie and James. I'm a senior."

"Super Senior," said James with mocking laughter in his voice.

"Yeah, yeah. Laugh it up, chuckles. Ain't my fault my Mom got sick. Besides, the football team needs me and the coach is happy to have me back."

"And so am I," said Margie, who grabbed his hand with a big smile. "How's your mom doing?"

"Better now. Doctors told her yesterday she's in remission."

"That's wonderful, Derick."

Clarissa noticed the smile in Margie's voice and felt something strange inside her. It was a weird, twisted sort of feeling that she didn't understand. She only knew that she didn't like seeing Derick close to Margie like that. She liked the big guy, especially after he had helped her, but she didn't want him near Margie. It made her...feel...something. There were no words for that sensation.

Clarissa kicked at a rock. She didn't want any of this. She just wanted things to go back to normal. She felt a pressure in her chest, a sense that it was harder to breathe. She couldn't stop thinking of what those three boys had said. Had she killed the detective, somehow? The thoughts swelled inside her as they walked several more blocks.

Finally, Clarissa said, "What if they aren't wrong?"

That stopped everyone in their tracks, and looking up, she saw that they were all staring at her, even Monica.

Margie said, "What?"

"What if they're not wrong? I mean, I'm not a witch. I didn't use magic. But what if there's something...supernatural happening?"

All four of them stood there looking at her without saying a word. Their eyes were full of longing and curiosity.

"I saw something down there in the meadow. Something I can't explain. There were bones and...and.... "

Tears came. Both Monica and Margie rushed to comfort her.

"Rat bastards," said James. "I'm gonna kick the shit out of them."

Derick, the giant, as Clarissa started to think of him, crouched down in front of Clarissa, a big friendly smile on his face. He was huge, but Clarissa could see the kindness in his eyes as he said, "Now, listen. Even if you did see some kind of monster or something down there, even if that's true, that would mean that none of this is your fault. Got it?"

"But what if I let it out?"

"Let it out?" asked Margie. Her eyes were sharp and focused on Clarissa.

"Yeah, what if because of something I did down there, I sort of let it out into the world and now it's killing people? Would it be my fault, then?"

Derick shook his head. "Why did you go into the woods in the first place?"

"Because someone stole my skateboard."

"Right," he said, "So, someone stole your board, and you chased after them. Let's say you ended up in some kind of monster's lair. Well, even if you did let it out, it's not like you did it on purpose, right?"

Clarissa wiped her tears from her cheeks. "I...I guess not."

"Well, Clarissa, there ain't no such things as monsters, but even if there was, none of this could be your fault, alright?"

Clarissa couldn't agree with him. She thought of the claw marks on the floor outside the bathroom. She thought of the thing she had seen coming after her in the meadow, of the bones, the wind, the strange sounds, the lack of colors. But most of all she thought of those eyes adjacent to the door, where her father lay dying. It was real. She couldn't deny it. But Ted was right. She might be able to talk to Monica about it, but not Derick, James, or Margie.

Derick stood up when Clarissa nodded her acceptance of his statement.

Margie grabbed Derick's hand, then leaned over and kissed him on the cheek. "You're so sweet."

Derick blushed and then, in a moment, they were all walking toward Margie's house, navigating the uneven sidewalks badly in need of repair. But her mind was still uneasy, still swirling around from one terror to the next. It was a nagging splinter in her mind. She just couldn't stop thinking about it as they walked several more blocks.

But before they got far, Clarissa said, "But what if monsters are real?"

James said, "They're not."

"But what if they are?"

They were all looking at her again, all waiting for her to say more. But she stood, silently.

Finally, Margie said, "Then we find a way to fight them."

Clarissa said, "How do we do that?"

"I don't know, maybe look it up in the library or something? Books have answers. I'm sure someone has thought of this before."

Clarissa nodded. Margie was right. If there was any place that might have information about a monster, it was probably the library.

As they arrived at Margie's, Clarissa couldn't bring herself to say anything more. What would she say? She didn't know this Derick guy, and both James and Margie didn't believe in the supernatural. That left Monica. Should she tell her? Was Ted wrong? Was it better to confide in her best friend? She didn't know. But she also knew that if everyone at school pestered her with questions like those three did today, she didn't know what she would do. She might just tell.

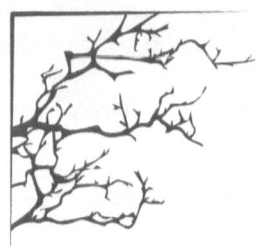

Chapter 9

The Festering Wound of Time

A clock strikes,
A crow caws,
Each second measured,
By the gripping of claws.

Its hunger grows,
The walls close in,
You thought it was over,
But it was about to begin.

When darkness comes,
As living night,
There will be no hope,
Only endless fright.

C larissa sat, white knuckled, gripping her desk. Looking down and staring at the grain in the wood, her red hair acted as a curtain, a shield from prying eyes. She couldn't look up. She felt the gaze of every single one of her classmates on her. Even her new teacher had stared when she thought she wasn't looking. They were furtive glances, but sharp as daggers.

The summer had ended. As she sat in her fourth-grade classroom on the third day, she felt the horrors of the summer fading behind her. There had been no sign of the monster since the newspaper, though the shroud was still a regular visitor. It was getting easier to sleep at night. Ted had found a part-time job for one of the plumbing companies as a consultant, and her mother was home more often. But here, in the classroom, she felt exposed to the glaring eyes of her classmates' morbid curiosity. Whispers and snickers punctuated every available silence.

Her friends stuck by her, but she could feel the stares everywhere she went. She had spent much of the last week either indoors or hiding. Ever since the incident with Michael, Andrew, and Tommy, she avoided the skate park, unless Margie or James were with her. Both were occupied with other things. Margie's boyfriend Derick took up much of her free time, and James...well, James had seemed to disappear lately and offered no explanations. When he was around, he had a funny smell about him, almost like a skunk. Only Monica was a regular ally as the fall drew closer.

The thing was, Clarissa couldn't go anywhere in town without stares. Even when they had gone to Penn's Landing and the Liberty Bell for a family day together two days before school started, someone had recognized her and followed them, snapping photos. Ted confronted the man and chased him off, but it ruined the rest of the day.

It wasn't long after that Ted discovered why people paid so much attention to Clarissa. One of his coworkers had brought in a copy of a local tabloid. The paper had run a photo of Clarissa without her mother's permission. The accompanying article weaved a tale of satanism and witchcraft with Clarissa at the center of the story. Apparently, she had wandered into the woods, discovered some sort of satanic ritual, and was now a part of something sinister, despite only being nine years old. The paper asked if Clarissa was responsible for the deaths, or just a victim awaiting her own.

Ted hadn't intentionally shown her the article, but Clarissa had seen him reading it one morning. When she asked about it, Ted had left the room and said not to worry about it, reminding her not to speak of anything that had happened to anyone. But Clarissa had clearly seen a picture of herself lying unconscious in a hospital bed. Someone had snuck into her room during the days she was unconscious.

The morning after she saw the tabloid in Ted's hands, she and Monica had gone into Davis' Trading Post a few blocks away from their houses. They found a copy, hidden behind one of the cramped aisles filled with leftover Fourth of July fireworks and magazines, and read it. Clarissa struggled with a few of the words, but Monica seemed to know them all. It was like watching an episode of Unsolved Mysteries. There were no answers, only lots of spooky questions.

Still, Monica didn't ask about what happened in the meadow, and Clarissa didn't have the courage to tell her. She couldn't stop thinking about what Ted had said, despite Monica's reassurances after the incident at the skatepark . She couldn't lose Monica, especially not now, when everyone else thought she was a freak.

Now that she was back in school, Clarissa felt like she wanted to vomit. She didn't know how she could stand all the staring and whispers. Mrs. Rollins, her fourth-grade teacher, took the roll, calling the names of each of the twenty-seven kids in her class. Clarissa put her face against the desk and smelled the wood. She did like that smell, and it made her think of Pretzel Day, which, coincidentally, was also today.

"Clarissa Lamont?"

Clarissa lifted her head and looked around. Everyone was staring at her.

"Yes, Mrs. Rollins?"

"I have assigned you to go fetch the pretzels at the end of the day."

The pretzels were part of an ongoing fundraiser for the school. Every week, one of the local bakeries would sell giant soft pretzels for half the price to the school, and the school would then turn around and sell them at full price and keep the extra money to help pay for school supplies. Being the kid to go get the pretzels for your class was the most coveted chore. Mostly because you got a free pretzel to do it, and there was also a kind of strange bragging right. So Clarissa sat up in her chair, a little brighter. Not only would she get to grab the pretzels, but she would also get away from the stares for a little while.

The day moved quickly. She and Monica ate lunch together, and everyone sat as far away from Clarissa as they could. Though they never stopped staring over their shoulders and whispering. Clarissa wished James, Margie, and Derick were younger, or that somehow she could eat lunch with them because, even with Monica there, she felt alone.

After she picked at her food for a while, she and Monica went out to play for recess. Clarissa brought her skateboard, and Monica her sketch pad. Clarissa wasn't allowed to use her skateboard on school grounds, but she had permission to bring it with her to school.

They both sat in the grass with their backs against the chain-link fence that rimmed the borders of the playground. It was a tall fence, eight feet high, and bordered Snake Hill. The grass poked through the links and a few birds chirped in one of the tall oak trees that sat just on the other side of the fence. The recess grounds were a large open field. In one corner was a baseball diamond with a large backstop behind it. But there was plenty of open space for running around.

Some kids played wall ball against one side of the building. Other children chased each other in a game of tag around some of the trees, and up and down the playground equipment. Clarissa was happy to be away from all of it. For the first time in hours, she felt like no one was looking at her. She breathed a sigh of relief.

"Hey," said Monica. "You should take Snake Hill home tonight."

Clarissa, who couldn't find a smile at the moment, only nodded.

"I want to see you fly again."

Clarissa looked up, "And what about you?"

"I'll race you to the bottom!"

"You can't win on foot. I'm too fast. That's what flying means, Monica, duh."

"Says you. I'm fast like Sonic the Hedgehog."

Monica put her sketchpad down, stood up, and shouted, "Gotta speed, keed!"

She ran around in a big circle and then came back, a smile on her face.

Clarissa couldn't help but smile, too. She was grateful for her friend. Monica sat down and went back to her sketches, pushing her glasses up on her face. She was trying to draw the school and the kids playing wall ball.

Clarissa waited for her to ask about the meadow, waiting for an excuse to tell her everything. But it hadn't come up, and Clarissa didn't quite have the courage to bring the topic up herself. Even reading the magazine, Monica had said nothing. In fact, Monica had changed the subject.

It was one reason Clarissa was afraid to talk to her about it. Monica seemed to want to avoid discussing what happened in the meadow. Clarissa couldn't blame her. It was scary to think of, and Monica didn't like spooky stories all that much, though she loved Halloween. Ted was probably right, it was best to keep it inside.

Clarissa thought of the detective and the boy daily, and her father's death was never far from her mind. It was as if all of the recent things that had happened had forced her to think about that terrible night outside the bathroom all over again. Snake Hill was the only thing that helped when it got bad. Monica seemed to sense that. She had gone up and down it several times in the last few days.

"Alright. Fine. I'll race you. But don't complain when you lose again."

"I won't," said Monica looking up from her sketch pad, "Because I'm not going to lose. You're gonna eat my dust, and after, you'll have to buy me a chili dog."

"Mon, you don't even like chili dogs."

"Yeah, but Sonic does and if I'm gonna be fast like him, I need the fuel."

Still sitting, Monica pumped her arms like she was running and made zooming noises. Clarissa burst out laughing, and they both laughed together for several moments. Finally, Monica pushed up her glasses and returned to her sketch. Clarissa ran her hands over her skateboard, thinking of Snake Hill and flying, a faint smile on her lips.

Then the shroud descended and darkness crept into the edges of Clarissa's vision.

Almost as if the shroud knew what was coming, two fifth graders peeled off from their group playing wall ball and walked in her direction. As they got closer, Clarissa's heart sank. They were definitely headed for her. It was like the incident at the skate park all over again. One of them had a small magazine rolled up in his hand. Even without looking, Clarissa knew what that magazine was...the tabloid.

It was Daryl and Rob, the enforcers of the school. The ones whom everyone tried to avoid. Daryl rocked a mullet with lightning bolts buzzed into each side. He was a short, skinny kid with a reputation for giving noogies and wet willies. Rob, whom everyone called Buffalo, after a fight where some scrawny kid with glasses had coined the phrase, had short curly hair that puffed up on top. He was a bruiser, a head taller than other kids his age, and not afraid to throw his considerable weight around.

Daryl approached and said, "Hey, heard you killed a cop this summer."

Clarissa sighed. "I didn't kill a cop."

Rob said, "You killed a cop. Everyone's talking about it. It's all I'm hearing." He waved the tabloid at her. "Says it right here."

Monica, who stopped sketching, looked up and said, "That's not what that article says."

"Sure it does," said Daryl. "You got some kind of power to curse people now or something?"

Clarissa said, "What do you want?"

"We want to know the details," said Rob.

"Yeah, like how the hell you did it?" said Daryl.

"And like, how you got the body to decay all quick. Did you use acid or something?" said Rob.

"Idiot. I told you, if you used acid, you would melt the body, not age it," said Daryl.

"Oh, yeah. Well, tell us how you did it."

"I didn't kill a cop."

"Look, we ain't gonna tell no one. We just want to know how you killed a cop. Like, did you take away their gun, or what? You been holding out some mad ninja skills, or something? We could use a ninja in our crew."

Monica said, "You guys are morons. She didn't kill a cop. You realize that the cop was killed, like, forty miles away from where we live, right? How would Clarissa have gotten to King of Prussia?"

Daryl crossed his arms. "Yeah, that's a good question. How did you get all those miles on your own? Did you take a bus?"

Clarissa grabbed her skateboard, stood up, and started walking away. Monica followed close behind, but so did the two boys.

"Come on," said Rob. "I bet Nick five bucks you'd tell us."

Clarissa felt the weight of it all on her. She started walking faster, back toward the school. Then she started running and Monica shouted, falling behind. Clarissa burst in through one of the doors, ran inside one of the lesser used bathrooms, went inside a stall, and sat down. She locked the door behind her. Tears flowed.

It would never end. Her reputation as a murderer would follow her around forever. No one even wanted to talk to her. She wished then that the monster had gotten her. That instead of running, it would have come and taken her and put her out of her misery.

She stayed there for a while. She didn't know how long. There were no clocks inside the bathroom, but she didn't want to leave. She just sat there with her elbows on her knees, on top of the toilet.

Finally, someone came in and knocked on the stall door. "Clarissa?"

It was Monica. But even knowing it was her best friend, she couldn't bring herself to say anything.

"Clarissa, are you in there? Everyone is looking for you."

"Why, so they can stare at the freak?" she sniffled and wiped her nose on a piece of toilet paper.

Monica said, "You're not a freak. You're my best friend."

Monica wouldn't leave, and Clarissa knew she couldn't stay there much longer. So she grabbed her skateboard, stood, and unlocked the door. Monica stood right there in front of her. Without warning, Monica flung herself forward and leaped in for a hug. Clarissa resisted at first, but Monica, so much smaller than she was for her age, was like a puppy who simply would not allow sadness to linger. Clarissa gave in.

"How long have I been gone?"

"Not too long, about a half an hour. But.... "

"But, what?"

"They already called your mom."

Clarissa's face fell. This was all so hard. She just wanted to be left alone, and now the entire school would talk about her for days.

"I guess we better go back to Mrs. Rollins's class. Do you think she will still let me get the pretzels?"

"Maybe. But if your mom comes, you might have to go home early."

Clarissa couldn't decide if that was better or worse. If she stayed at school, she would have to put up with all of those stares and whispers. If she went home, it might be even worse tomorrow. She hated school. Couldn't they just give her books to read at home, instead?

They walked back into the classroom, and there was Mrs. Rollins, on the emergency phone by her desk. She looked up.

"Actually, she just walked into the room. It seems Monica found her." She paused for a moment, listening. "Yes, well, let me talk to her and see what she thinks, and I'll call you back." Another pause. "Alright, I will call you back in a few minutes. Bye."

She put down the phone. "Monica, will you go join the other kids in the gym? I need to talk to Clarissa alone for a moment."

Monica said, "Okay." She hesitated, but only for a moment, and then Clarissa watched her go.

"Why don't you come sit up here with me?" Her teacher pulled out a chair from the corner so she could sit face-to-face with Clarissa. Clarissa sat down, but she couldn't look her teacher in the eyes. She was a mountain of guilt and shame.

Mrs. Rollins had a square face curtained by dark hair. She wore red cat-eye glasses, glasses that Monica loved and had asked her mother for repeatedly. Mrs. Rollins was a large woman, not just in width, but also in height. She was firm, but kind.

"You're not in trouble, Clarissa."

Clarissa looked up. "I'm not?"

"No. You just scared us a little, that's all. We were worried about you."

Clarissa nodded. She didn't know what to say.

"Monica told me what those boys said to you. They are with the principal now, having a conversation. It won't happen again."

Clarissa nodded. She didn't believe, though. In fact, she knew that with Daryl and Rob, a trip to the principal's office was so routine that they would simply shrug it off. She half expected them to find her again tomorrow and ask their questions.

"Oh, you poor sweet child. You've had a rough few years, haven't you? Your mother told me all about it. I want you to know that I will do my best to make our class a happy place for you, but I'm going to need your help, alright?"

Clarissa nodded. She had no idea how she could help.

"If you're having a hard time, it's okay if you come to talk to me. You can tell me anything."

Clarissa shook her head. "No, I can't."

Her teacher's expression changed, sharper somehow. As if something had really caught her attention. "Clarissa, is everything alright at home?"

"At home?"

"Yes. Is everything okay with your parents?"

"Yes. Why?"

Why was her teacher asking her this? What did her mom and Ted have to do with any of the miserable things happening?

"I'm just trying to understand. Why can't you tell me things?"

"Because you won't believe me and you'll think I'm a freak."

"Of course, I'll believe you. Whatever happened to you is not your fault."

"That's what the detective said. But she lied."

"Detective? Lied?"

Clarissa knew Mrs. Rollins had known about the detective. It was written in every stray stare the woman gave her. If Daryl and Rob were able to just come right up and ask about it, then it was common knowledge.

"I only told one other person about what happened to me, well, all that I could remember. And she didn't believe me, and now she's dead."

Her teacher was speechless for several moments. She leaned back in her chair, thinking. Was her teacher trying to get Clarissa to tell her the story? She wasn't sure if she should tell Monica or not, but she was certain she shouldn't tell her teacher or any other adults.

"Alright, Clarissa. Well, I just want you to know that if you need someone to talk to, I'm here. I will do my best to keep an open mind. I know that a lot of your classmates are staring, and I bet that's uncomfortable. But I think by next week, everyone will forget about it. A lot of the kids are just coming back from summer vacation and are just now hearing about the...the unfortunate events of this summer. Daryl and Rob were both out of town with their families most of the summer, and so I am sure their curiosity got the better of them."

Clarissa said nothing. She hoped Mrs. Rollins was right. Hoped that things would go back to normal. She didn't think it would, though. It was hard to ignore the shroud as it pressed up against her, dimming her world and squeezing her. Hard to ignore the stranger in Penn's Landing who had followed Clarissa and her family around.

Mrs. Rollins took Clarissa's silence as an agreement and said, "Now, your mother wants to know if you need to take the rest of the day off, or if you want to finish the day here."

"I don't know."

"Well, where do you think you would feel more comfortable?"

She shrugged. "I don't know."

"Well, it's one o'clock now, so you only have an hour and a half left in the day. Do you think you can stick it out?"

"Yeah, I guess I can."

"Alright. Why don't you head to gym class? I hear they have the parachute out today, so it might be a fun class. I'll call your mother and let her know she can expect you home at the usual time."

"Thanks, Mrs. Rollins."

"You're welcome, Clarissa."

2. There was only one word for the first week back to school-disaster. The shroud was thick and ever-present, a second skin. By the end of the week, Clarissa viewed the world like a woman wearing a veil at a funeral. The darkness never left her, and after Wednesday's events, her nightmares of the meadow returned.

Each day held an awkward encounter, laughter and mocking at her expense, or the endless, nearly unblinking stares of her classmates. She lived on an island, some far-flung area impossibly distant from the rest of humanity.

Through it all, Monica was there. Monica did everything she could to raise Clarissa's spirits. Monica let Clarissa watch her X-games tapes over and over again after school.

She drew caricatures of Daryl and Rob with giant buck teeth, enormous heads, and tiny bodies. It made Clarissa smile, but she had little laughter in her.

The truth of what had happened in the meadow, what had happened to her father, and perhaps what had happened to the detective, were a chasm growing between their friendship. Clarissa wanted to tell her friend, but knew that if Monica abandoned her, she would have nothing left. It was her greatest fear. So, all through the first week, she stayed silent.

Then, another week passed, and another, until they were on the edge of October. The mutters and stares died down, but the social isolation persisted. Clarissa hated school. Every night she dreamed of the meadow, and every morning she woke with the shroud tinging her vision with darkness. As the days shortened and the first week of October arrived, Clarissa had settled into her miserable routine, for there was no escape. She could see no way to make things better. James and Margie almost never came around anymore, and she still wasn't welcome at the skate park, so mostly she skated the streets when Monica couldn't hang out.

Then, after the first week of October, the creature from the meadow returned.

3. The 8th of October began like any other day for Clarissa, save one thing. She was sick. Or at least, she thought she was sick. She woke with aching limbs and a strange sensation of pressure in her chest that coupled with the feeling that she couldn't quite get enough air in her lungs. After some convincing, her mother let her stay home, but Clarissa soon regretted it. Daytime television was awful, and as she lay on the couch, she grew bored. Boredom brought with it an endless cycle of miserable thoughts.

By the time the end of the school day came around Clarissa felt physically better, except for the sensation in her chest. Instead of shrinking with the passing day, it seemed to grow. She had the nagging sensation that something terrible was about to happen. Dread filled every cell in her body. No matter what she did, or how she distracted herself, she couldn't shake the feeling. To her, it felt like the empty eye sockets of the boy crawling with maggots and staring up at her. It felt like death.

At dinner, she told her mother and Ted that she was feeling better, and asked if she could have Monica over for the night. She was afraid to sleep alone, though she didn't tell either of them. Ted scoffed and told her, "You stayed home sick from school today. You don't get to have a friend over." Her mother agreed. After dinner, Clarissa watched the Friday night programming for kids, *TGIF*, alone. The shows, like *Family Matters* and *Boy Meets World*, normally made her laugh, but with that terrible internal omen pulsing in her guts, the jokes felt as hollow as she did.

After 10 p.m., Clarissa went up to her room to settle in for the night. The chilly autumn wind battered against her window, and the limbs of trees shook and shuddered as they shed their colored leaves. Normally, she cracked the window and let the scent climb into her room, but the trees reminded her too much of the meadow. For just as the trees leaned outward away from the meadow's center as if running from the creature that dwelled within, the ones around her house leaned inward, an arrow pointing to her location, mapping her for a monster.

She sat up in bed with the string lights winking in the darkness. Clarissa shivered, despite having several blankets wrapped around her. Her skateboard lay in bed with her, as it did every night. She reached over and touched the rough surface of the deck, thinking of her father. In those moments, when her skateboard was close, she didn't think of his death, but of his smile and his laughter. She thought of how he smoked that pipe on the front porch as he read his books. Clarissa wished he was here now. She wished she could smell the pipe. He might know what to do.

She tried to read the skateboarding magazine that her mother had given her that morning, but something was wrong with it. All the color had bled from the pages. What was brilliant and beautiful in the light of day, instead, appeared tinted like an old photograph. Even the words seem to dance around the pages, swirling with incomprehension. Frustrated, she threw the magazine aside.

She tried not to think of the meadow, of the claw marks only a few dozen feet away, etched into the floor. Clarissa resisted thinking about whether she was responsible for the death of the detective, and wallowed in the guilt of the death of the boy who had stolen her skateboard. It was no use. She was alone, and there was no one there to keep her company except for her thoughts. Ted and her Mother had already gone into their bedroom to do whatever adults did when the kids were occupied. Ted had little patience for any fears Clarissa might mention these days. There had been too many nights since the summer where she had come knocking at their bedroom door, and she thought that even her mother was losing patience. She was a burden to them, and she knew it.

She slid down in her bed, unable to bar the flood of thoughts any longer. She wished Monica was there, wished she could tell her the whole truth. In those quiet moments of solitude and despair, she thought Ted was wrong, that Monica would be okay with the truth. It was so hard to be the only one to know those horrible secrets.

The only other person in the world who had known everything she'd seen in the meadow was dead, and Clarissa wondered if that wasn't an accident. Had the creature targeted the detective because of what she had told her? Or, and Clarissa thought this was more likely, some people who go down to the meadow catch the creature's interest and, ultimately, their death. But why had it killed the detective, and not her? Ted had gone to the meadow, and so had others. Why were they still alive? She had thought about that over and over again. If the creature was free, why wasn't it coming for her?

Unable to stand the silence, she walked over to her desk in the corner and turned on the radio. Her mother and Ted allowed her to listen to the classical station at night when she was struggling to sleep. It had been a recent compromise, and it helped Clarissa to relax. She climbed back into bed and tried to focus on the music. Instead, her thoughts swarmed her again, and a chill ran through her. Quickly, feeling as if she needed to protect herself, Clarissa made her blankets into a cocoon so that only her face stuck out. Then, she burrowed her head under the pillow. It was the best thing to do when she was scared. Every time she had one of the thoughts, she pushed it away and focused on the music. It was hard, though, for her mind kept trying to bring her back to her own fear.

Not long after, she fell asleep.

4.   Several hours later, Clarissa woke with dread as her companion. In the dark, still inside her cocoon, she heard the sound of her radio sour. The once peaceful classical compositions had transformed into a dissonant mockery. Violins screamed like nails on a chalkboard. The woodwinds mimicked a dying woman's moans, and the brass section, an elephant grieving one of its dead, blowing ominous sounds through its trunk. Worst of all were the drums, a diseased heartbeat with an irregular rhythm. Pounding, thumping, moaning, the room filled with the discord of the catastrophic orchestra, a dark omen of sound, and a promise that the creature from the meadow had finally arrived to claim her.

A small part of her was relieved that the wait was over and that she might finally know the end of her burden. In truth, that dark part of her was eager for the peace of surrender. The larger part, the one that knew she had only lived nine short years so far, and was suddenly aware of her own mortality, panicked. Her heart pounded in her ears, drowning out the sickening sound of the music. Pulling the covers tighter around herself, she dared not remove the pillow from her eyes. But it was growing harder to breathe, and she didn't know how much longer her shelter would keep her.

The wind howled outside, battering against the windows. There was a smell, a growing putrescence rising from somewhere in the room. It was the same sickeningly sweet stench that still lingered in Clarissa's nostrils when she thought about the maggot covered boy in the meadow.

"Please, no, " she whispered, the sound muffled through the pillow. "Please, leave me alone." There was only begging. For what else could she hope to do against such a creature?

Clarissa trembled in her cocoon, a caterpillar squirming in a chrysalis, but not eager to hatch at the wild terrors beyond her boundary. As the pressure in her chest increased, so did her sense of suffocation. The air grew stale inside her blankets. That, mixed with the terrible curiosity of whose corpse now lay in her room, and the terrifying possibility that it might be Ted or her mother, eroded the last bit of her will to hide. She had to breathe, had to see what fate beheld her.

Slowly, she untucked the blankets around her, lifted her pillow from her face, and peered out into the room. It was dark, at least, the string lights which she had left on, had lost their twinkle. Later she would see that the bulbs had all burned out. The only light was what entered through the window and the strange glow that emanated from one corner of her room, just next to the closet.

There was no corpse, no explanation for the origin of the smell. But though she had closed her window, it was open a crack. The curtains thrashed as the wind pelted them, bringing what felt like an arctic chill into her room.

Quickly, she stood and ran across the room, first unplugging the horrible radio. The sound died, leaving only the howling wind and thrashing curtains. Clarissa ran to secure the window and reached up to shut it, but it would not budge. She tried again, and with all her strength and effort, she slid it closed until it slammed shut, rattling the glass but not breaking it.

Before she could turn, she felt something warm tickle the back of her neck. A breath, or perhaps a light caress. She jumped and opened her mouth to scream, but found all the sounds had vanished. It was as if all of her fear had coalesced, dancing like rotting skeletons up and down her spine. She was afraid to turn around, afraid she might see the shadowy thing from the meadow there waiting for her. She didn't turn. She couldn't. Not yet.

Clarissa thought that maybe, just maybe, she was dreaming. She knew that sometimes in dreams, thoughts made things real. So, if she just kept facing the window, ignored the glow and didn't turn, she could wish the thing away.

The coldness in her spine did not diminish. Something pulled on her shoulder, almost like a skeletal outstretched hand. It was gentle, beckoning her to turn and look, to open herself up to its horrible touch. She fought the curiosity, because she knew from that day in the meadow that lingering too long could have terrible results.

Clarissa trembled. She couldn't tell if it was the cold, or fear, or both. The urge to see, to know, was growing to a fever pitch. It was an itch that, if ignored too long, would invite muscle spasms.

She felt the tugging again and almost collapsed into her fear, but did not turn.

"No," she said. "This is a dream. I'm okay. It's just a bad dream."

She didn't believe it. Not really. She knew that when she turned, because she would turn, that either the shadow would be there to greet her, or the boy's decaying corpse would be in her bed. There would be maggots oozing from his sockets, spreading on the sheets before they crawled around the room, infesting every nook, spreading their filth and rot until they crawled over her.

As if summoning the idea, she felt something crawling up the back of her leg, under her pajamas. Finally, the compulsion won. She brushed whatever it was off of her leg, trying again to scream but making no noise, and then stood stark still.

Slowly, she turned, noticing that the strange glow was growing brighter. Her heart pounded as she glimpsed her bed, where she expected the rotting corpse of the boy. Yet, there was nothing but rumpled sheets and blankets, and a pillow that half hung off the bed, ready to fall with the slightest disturbance.

To her relief, nothing disturbing greeted her. No shadowy creature, no rotting boy, nothing.

But there was something, wasn't there? Where was the glow coming from? It was faint now, and eerie green, as if the darkness itself had its own form of light. But as she looked around the room, forcing herself to look under the bed and in her closet, she saw nothing. Nothing was lurking in the dark, but neither was there anything emitting the glow. Then, it faded as if it had never been there at all.

Her terror abated. Gradually, her mind relaxed. She was safe in her room, her sanctuary. Clarissa looked at all of her posters of Tony Hawk and Nirvana, and she climbed back into bed. She sighed and closed her eyes, pulling the covers up over her, feeling the warmth and safety of her cloth cave. She tucked the corners up under her and did her best to make herself into a cocoon. Once done, she felt her eyes grow heavy again.

Before she was fast asleep, the fear returned, not in a gradual rising, but in a full-fledged terror, all at once and in a single moment. Her eyes shot open, alert and knowing that this time she would see something.

As she gently unraveled the top of her cocoon of sheets and blankets, and peered around the room, she saw a shape in the dark. Her eyes locked onto it. She found that she couldn't move. Her limbs were deadwood lying on a forest floor.

In the corner of her bedroom, where the shadows gathered in thick clusters, the glow pulsed. Something shimmered there, something was watching. Two red eyes, pinpricks of red in a wall of shadow, peered out from that corner. A set of gleaming white fangs appeared, but only for a second before vanishing back into darkness.

She wanted to call for help, but no sound came. Depth and form took shape around the eyes, not a true form, but something that kept shifting and changing, as if liquid poured out of the shadow. It grew in stature, spreading out from its corner and taking shape on the carpet. But the eyes stayed in that corner, and Clarissa could not break her gaze. She was transfixed.

She tried again to scream, tried to push against the soundless dark but nothing happened. Then she drew in a deep breath, and with all her effort and will, the scream rose from her throat, shattering the silence. The monsters shrunk back down into the corner and vanished.

Only a minute later, Ted and her mother, both looking disheveled and sweaty, barged in the door. Ted wore only shorts, and her mother a nightdress.

"What is it? What's going on?" asked her mother.

She pointed, her hand shaking furiously. "Corner." Was all she could say. It was like something was holding her words, keeping them away from her. She had to chase them down and pin them before they would rise to her throat. She wanted to tell her mother what she had seen and experienced, but for the moment, nothing else came.

Her stepfather turned on the light. There was nothing there.

"What are you talking about?" said Ted, clearly irritated. It was a rare night when her mother was home these days, instead of working at the 24-hour diner.

Her mother walked over to her bed, sat beside her, put a loving hand on her forehead, and caressed her face. Then she pulled Clarissa close into a hug and held her there.

"What was there in the corner, sweetie?"

Clarissa swallowed and focused on the words. To her surprise, they came flooding out. But it was a strange sensation, almost like someone else was speaking.

"The thing from the woods. It was there, in the corner. And I could smell...I could smell the boy who stole my board...I...." Her words were awash with tears and half-racked sobs.

Her mother rubbed her back and rocked her.

"Shhhh. It's okay, sweetie. You just had another bad dream. It's just your mind working through what happened to you, that's all."

"No, it wasn't a dream. It was real. The monster was here. It was coming to kill me like it did the detective."

Her mother frowned. There was a flash of guilt on her face.

Ted said, "What did I tell you, Audrey?"

Her mother turned and gave him a sharp look, and then said, "Would you like to lie on the couch and watch a movie to let your mind settle down?"

Wiping away tears, Clarissa said. "Yes. Please. Can I?"

"Of course. Everything is okay now. You're safe here."

Her mother grabbed a pillow and helped Clarissa carry a blanket down the stairs to the couch. She laid her down there and helped make her comfortable. All the while Ted watched from above, a disapproving frown on his face.

"What would you like to watch?"

"Can I watch *The Hobbit* ?" she sniffled.

"Of course. You know, I really enjoyed that film. I loved the book when I was a little girl. I like the way they animated it."

Her mother popped in a VHS, which was already rewound because Ted was a fanatic about making sure every tape in their library followed the dictum of 'Be Kind, Rewind', and hit play. After the FBI warning and opening credits, Gandalf magically teleported onto the screen and the film began.

Her Mother and stepfather went back upstairs, but not before her mother left a light on in the corner of the room and another on in the kitchen. The room was cozy, but not too bright, and it made her feel much safer. God, she loved her mother. She wasn't always there because she worked so many hours, but she was the best mother on the planet.

She fell into the spell of the movie, and as Bilbo cleverly tricked the trolls and the sunlight turned them all to stone, her eyes closed.

A few minutes later something else woke her. This time it wasn't a shadow, it was a noise. It took her a moment to realize that it was her mother and her stepfather arguing. She rose from the couch and snuck up the stairs. Gently, she put her ear to their door.

"No, that's not what I'm saying, Audrey. You can't coddle her. It's been months. She just had a bad dream, that's all. If you let her watch a movie down there whenever she feels scared, she'll just take advantage and tell you she's scared whenever she wants the TV."

"She's nine, Ted. She's had a traumatic experience. Two in three years, I might add. We don't even know what happened to her. For all we know, some pervert got his hands on her and she'll be scarred for life. Don't you remember what the social worker at the hospital said?"

"They're full of shit. Those shrinks don't know anything. Trust me, I know from experience."

"She wasn't a shrink, and she's worked with traumatized kids before. We have to keep reinforcing her sense of safety. They told us there would be nightmares, and flashbacks, and probably all kinds of strange behavior. We knew this was coming, Ted."

"So we just let her do what she wants?"

"Do what she wants? This is the first time in weeks, and it's a Friday night. She doesn't have to be up for school tomorrow. Who cares if she's up late?"

"Well, I'm not being quiet when I get up to go fishing with Al tomorrow. In fact, I'm gonna make it a point to be as loud as possible."

"Why are you being such a jerk?"

"She needs to toughen up."

"She's nine, Ted. This will pass. Kids are resilient, that's what the social worker said. We just have to be patient with her."

"You're coddling her. You always coddle her."

"Jesus Christ, Ted. My daughter has been through more than most adults have. She lost her father, and now she's gone through some terrible experience and found the body of a boy her own age. Then she was lost in the woods for three days. Three days, Ted. She's nine and my little girl was all alone. How dare you tell me how to raise my daughter!"

Ted muttered something Clarissa couldn't hear.

"What was that?"

Silence.

"If you just said what I think you said, I should throw your ass out on the street."

There was the sound of movement, of feet on creaking floorboards.

"Where are you going?" asked Ted.

"To sleep on the couch with my daughter."

Clarissa's eyes went wide. Quickly, while also trying to make as little noise as possible, she ran down the stairs and back to the couch. She jumped on it, pulled the covers over her, and closed her eyes. Just as she did, her mother came down the stairs. Quietly, her mother leaned over in the dimness of the room and kissed Clarissa on the forehead. Clarissa opened her eyes, as if she had just woken up.

"I'm sorry sweetie, I didn't mean to wake you."

"Mom? What's going on?"

"Shhh. Don't get up, sweetie. Can I watch *The Hobbit* with you tonight?"

On the screen, Bilbo was sneaking around a spider's lair, finding the Dwarves trapped in webs.

She feigned sleepiness, but after running toward the couch, her heart was pounding and she was wide awake.

"Where's Ted?"

"Oh, he's sleeping, sweetie. I just thought it would be nice to cuddle with you. We don't get to do that very often, do we?"

Clarissa said, "No. I can't remember the last time we did."

"It's been a while, hasn't it?" Her mother's voice was soothing and warm.

Clarissa shifted around and lifted the blanket, inviting her mother in. Her mother curled up behind her, and Clarissa felt the warmth of her mother's figure. Her mother's arms wrapped around her and pulled her close, and for the first time in a very long time, Clarissa felt the depth of her mother's love.

But out of the corner of her eye, she thought she saw something stir, some shape in the dark. And she squirmed her way deeper into her mother's embrace and drew the covers a little tighter around her neck. It was then that she knew the monster would be back, and that it wasn't going away.

5. It was a morning of blurry eyes and drooping spirits. Clarissa sat in her PJs watching Saturday morning cartoons, mostly bored and grateful for it. She felt safe in the daytime, and had all of the curtains drawn back, letting in as much light as possible. There was the lingering sense in the back of her mind that it would be back that very night, but she pushed it away and let the light wash over her for now.

Her mother left early, called into the gas station she sometimes worked at during the day. Ted stormed around the house, adjusting everything. Al had canceled the fishing trip for some last-minute emergency. Every end table or dresser needed to be realigned in each room. When asked, he would mutter about perfect balance and angles.

It was his most frustrating quality. Without warning, he would enter Clarissa's bedroom and straighten all the furniture. Sometimes, when he was pissed, he would get down on his hands and knees with a protractor and a ruler. Then, he would stand up, bitch about how dirty it was under your bed and that you had better clean it, and then storm out again.

He always behaved like that when he was angry, and while Clarissa knew they had fought about her, she wondered what Ted had said when her mother threatened to throw him out. Did Ted hate her? Did he think she was a murderer? He had said that her mother coddled her. What exactly did that mean? She guessed maybe it meant that she was spoiled or something.

Ted and her mother had been arguing a lot. It had begun after the story in the newspaper about the detective. That had to be what it was about. They had fought in the garage, too, that day, when her mother had driven off. She hadn't seen them fight like this since he had told the truth about his illness. Now there was another rift forming between her mother and Ted, and the bridge of the first one was swaying under the stress of those grinding tectonic plates.

She thought maybe Ted would leave soon or that her mother would kick him out. They were married, but Elise Fraken's parents had just gotten a divorce, so why couldn't Ted and her mother? She didn't know what to think of that. Ted had been around for a little while now, and she didn't hate him, exactly, and at least he always bought the books she liked.

Dinner that night was tense. Both adults knew Clarissa feared sleeping in her room. They knew it was Saturday night, which was still the weekend, so her mother would likely say it was okay. Ted seemed destined to fight, to argue again.

But he didn't.

When she asked her mother if she could sleep on the couch, it was Ted who immediately said, "Why don't you see if Monica wants to come stay the night and...," he paused, sighed, and said, "You can have a pillow fort in the living room and use the sofa cushions."

Audrey's face shifted from shock to smile. The kitchen transformed from potential turmoil into a place of laughter. The shroud over Clarissa lifted a little and the thought of Monica coming over made her feel so much better about the creature. It had run away when Ted and her mother had come into the room. It didn't seem to like other people much. If Monica was around, she should be safe.

Monica came over an hour later, already in her pjs. It was often like that. They lived next door to each other, so they always just went back and forth between houses, if needed. Each had a key to the other's house, anyway.

Monica brought a movie.

Clarissa smiled. "Always that one. Never the second one."

"What? It's the best one. They turn a train into a time machine. That's the coolest," said Monica.

Clariss shook her head in disagreement. "It's way cooler when Marty goes to the future, then goes back to an alternate 1985."

"Okay, but we haven't seen this one in a while."

"I guess that's true."

They went up to Clarissa's room and Clarissa changed into her pajamas.

"Hey, Mon. Do me a favor?"

"What?"

"When we go downstairs, don't say a word. Just follow my lead."

"Your lead? Why?"

Clarissa giggled. "You'll see."

They went downstairs. The floors creaked beneath their feet. Ted was on the couch, flipping channels. The girls looked at him. He looked at them. Both forces stood their ground, neither wanting to admit that the other was ready to take over the living room. Clarissa had figured out that in some ways, if Ted could mentally prepare himself a little, he struggled less. So, she gave him that and she could see the gears turning. Monica opened her mouth to say something, but Clarissa coughed once.

Ted sighed. "Fine. Just...let me get a beer from the fridge and my book. Please, just wait 'til I'm upstairs, and then first thing tomorrow, put the cushions back?"

Clarissa said, "Thanks, Ted." She meant it. She knew he hated pillow forts, it clashed against his meticulous nature, chaos in a space of order.

They built their fort and made popcorn. They watched the movie, and laughed and argued about which was best. As the credits rolled, and the house settled, Clarissa felt a tremor of fear as Monica turned the TV off, and the darkness climbed into their fort to sit with them.

It was a windy night, one of those gusty autumn evenings after the colors had turned, and the wind was catching the lingering leaves and scattering the remains of summer. So, with the house creaking, and the wind whistling through the ancient cracks in an ancient building, there was a chill in the air. Clarissa thought she could feel the cold, even through the blankets and the cushions surrounding their heads.

They had set up the two couches side by side so that they could lie next to each other like they were in bed. Then they made a roof of the cushions, leaving a little door to crawl in and out of for each girl. They finished with a sheet over the top. Clarissa lay facing Monica, watching her door, watching for the tiniest quiver in the breeze. But the air was still.

Clarissa didn't dare look out. Not after the monster had come the night before. It had crawled out of a corner, and there was no corner inside here, and besides, Monica was here. The two times she had seen it, she had seen it alone. She reasoned that Monica could help keep it away. Monica stared back at her in the darkness.

Monica whispered, "People at school are real jerks."

"Yeah."

"I mean, they don't have a clue. It doesn't even make sense. How could they think you got to King of Prussia on your own, without anyone noticing? It's not like you're an adult and have a car."

"Yeah. It's dumb." Her voice trembled a little more than she expected.

She wanted Monica to know everything. She needed her best friend to know the truth. But she was so scared to tell her she had pushed that boy down the hill, and then about the monster that was coming for her. Either she would think that she was crazy and none of it was true, or she would learn her friend was a murderer.

She wished that Monica would ask, because then-then-she would have permission to tell her everything.

"Clarissa, do you want to...," Monica hesitated.

Clarissa almost blurted out her entire story just with those first few words. It was so hard to be alone, to not have anyone believe you.

Monica started again. "Do you want to talk about what happened?"

Clarissa opened her mouth to speak, then hesitated. That sense of dread rose in her, that sense that she was in the meadow again, that the monster was coming. It felt like it was watching, waiting for her to tell Monica.

Suddenly, the words were tumbling out of her. She told Monica about chasing the boy through the woods, about how they had both gotten lost. She was working up the courage to tell Monica about how she had pushed him down into the lair of something horrible when there was a sound of heavy footsteps coming down the stairs.

Both girls were silent, listening. The only other adult home at the moment was Ted. Her mother was due back in the early morning.

"Clarissa?" said Ted.

She and Monica looked at each other. Then Clarissa said, "Yes?"

"Can I talk to you for a minute?"

Had she done something wrong? Was she in trouble? It was late. She wasn't sure what time, but they hadn't started the movie until almost nine o'clock.

"Okay?"

"Up in my room, please."

That feeling in the pit of her stomach, that she had done something wrong, took root.

"Be back in a few minutes."

Monica nodded and Clarissa crawled her way out of the fort through her little door. She looked up in the dark, and there, in the dim light coming in through the windows from the street lamps outside, she saw Ted standing on the stairs. He turned and walked up toward his room. Clarissa followed. When she reached his room, he welcomed her in and, looking down the hall first to see if Monica was nearby, shut the door.

She sat there, waiting for him to tell her what she had done. She couldn't think of anything.

"Clarissa, I think it's best if you don't tell Monica what happened in those woods."

"I...," she realized he had probably been listening. It was strange. Usually, Ted didn't do things like that. In fact, this was the first time she thought that he had listened in.

"Why not?"

"Do you remember everything that happened to you down there?"

She shook her head. "Not everything. I still can't remember those three days in the woods."

"Do you remember how scared you were?"

Slowly, she nodded.

"Think of how scary it might be for Monica if you told her."

Two thoughts competed in her mind. The first was that Ted should mind his own business, and with it, a surge of anger at his interruption. The second thought was that he was right. She hated that thought. Was it really fair for her to scare Monica, who didn't have any idea that some monster was hunting her?

Ted filled the silence. "I know this is hard to understand now, but sometimes it's better to keep your struggles to yourself, especially when they are scary. You don't want to scare Monica away, do you?"

"But...."

She didn't know how to object. She had come to believe that Monica wouldn't think she was weird, but she hadn't thought about the fact it might scare her. Maybe Monica wouldn't want to be her friend anymore because she thought Clarissa was cursed, just like the other kids at school and the skate park thought.

Hesitantly, she said, "Okay."

"Good girl. Now don't stay up too late, alright?" He walked over to the door and opened it. He said nothing else, but there was a strange expression on his face, one that Clarissa didn't understand.

She walked down the stairs and made her way back inside the fort. Monica lay there waiting. She was wide awake, eager to hear the rest of the story.

"So...what happened after you got lost with that boy?"

She thought about blaming Ted, saying that it was he who had told her not to share the story, but that felt wrong somehow.

"I'm...I'm really tired and it's late, and...it's really scary. Maybe we should talk about it when it's daytime."

Monica seemed to accept this, but was clearly disappointed. "Okay, we can talk about it tomorrow, or something. Maybe at the skate park?"

"Yeah, or something."

The girls had little more to say to each other, and it was late. Without the story to spur on their spirits, they faded into the night.

6   True to her word, the very next day at the skate park, Clarissa told the tale without even really realizing what she was doing. Monica sat in silence as she poured out everything from the moment she chased after the boy in the woods to the shadow's last appearance.

Other kids skated up and down the half-pipe while she and Monica sat on a bench. The kids gave Clarissa a wary look, but she had spoken softly enough that she didn't think anyone could hear her.

"So it's still after you?" said Monica, a little above a whisper.

"I think so."

"So you saw it twice now?"

"Yeah."

"And your parents scared it away?"

"Yeah, It doesn't seem to like other people when it comes around. But...I also feel like it's waiting for something."

"Like what?"

"I don't know."

Clarissa spun the wheels on her skateboard watching them turn round. They were getting worn and she would need to replace them soon.

Monica said nothing. It made Clarissa nervous.

Clarissa said, "I set it free, didn't I?"

"I don't know. You haven't heard anything else in the papers or news, have you?"

"If something else had happened, don't you think every kid at school would be talking about that, too?"

The sun beat down on them; it was unusually hot for October, but there was also a chill in the air, just below the heat of the sun.

"That's a good point. Are you sure when it came that last time that you weren't dreaming?"

"I'm sure."

Monica sat with that for a few moments. "Do you have any idea what it is?"

"No."

"Maybe we should try and look it up at the library like Margie suggested?"

Clarissa nodded. "Maybe."

They didn't investigate, not until the creature came again.

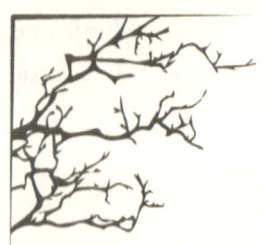

Chapter 10

The Shadow of Samhain

Come all ye, gathering shades,
The time of Samhain is at hand,
We will rise to rot and scatter,
Our blight across the land.

For the first of us comes at witching hour,
To seek his contractual prize,
Lust for power brings him strength,
With every victim's demise

But a bargain struck will not go unpaid,
A boon of power is owed,
It matters not who is struck down,
Nor the depth and breadth of your woe

For Samhain comes to deliver the third,
Into our Master's gaping maw,
Tremble not, for your strength comes soon,
Following the white raven's caw.

It was the last house of the night. That wasn't an accident or a coincidence. Clarissa had intentionally skipped the blue house with the fresh white trim on their first pass of the evening. When she was younger, the color of the house had reminded her of the sky. Even with the close of October, the lawn was the last to lay fallow for the year. The Halloween decorations were tidy. A happy witch here, a skeleton with a top hat standing with his bride there, and a few tombstones with clever sayings scattered across the lawn. All the decorations were friendly and neat. There were no cobwebs, no severed limbs, or giant spiders, no zombies or devils to be found. Sanitized spooky season. On the door hung a mosaic of a smiling jack-o-lantern that looked more cute than frightening.

It was safe to say Mrs. Everson's house was the best kept in the neighborhood, despite the single occupant's age. It was a prim and proper house, with every flaw painted over or carefully camouflaged. No other house on the block was so neat. Both Clarissa's and Monica's houses, which were a few doors up and across the street, looked to be in a state of disrepair in comparison. Mrs. Everson's faux perfection attempted to carry the weight of cracked and run-down houses that sat on either side of it, as if standing in judgment of them, though there was nothing wrong with them but time and age.

Mrs. Everson stood, stooped, on the edge of her porch just above her top step. Her eyes, framed by the deepest of crow's feet, were wide and watching as a ghost, a vampire, and what Clarissa thought might be a mummy wrapped in white strips, held out their bags and buckets in expectation.

"Trick-or-Treat!" said the three in unison.

"Well," said the woman, "Aren't you three just a delight. I have just the thing." Her voice quavered slightly, a reed of great age blowing in the wind.

Mrs. Everson reached down into her own bucket, as her left hand trembled just a little, without the help of her right to hold up her heavy bucket of candy.

"Since you have such wonderfully classic costumes, you each get a full-sized candy bar."

She looked up at Clarissa and Monica, who were standing there at the edge of the walkway. Was that a dirty look cast in their direction?

Out of the bucket, she pulled a full-sized Snickers and dropped it in the ghost's bucket, who said, "Thank you!" She then repeated this with the other two, each expressing their gratitude before turning and walking back toward Clarissa.

As the other children left, Mrs. Everson glanced up at Clarissa and Monica again. Clarissa's stomach twisted. As the town gossip, the old woman had fixated on one person in particular, as of late.

"We should skip her house," whispered Clarissa.

Monica, with a half-whine in her voice, said, "We already skipped it the first time. And it's the last one. She's giving out full candy bars. We can't pass that up."

Shaking her half filled pillowcase of candy, Clarissa said, "We have plenty of candy. Besides, she won't give a full candy bar to me. She never does. Every year it's the same thing. You get a full candy bar, and she gives me something small." Clarissa kicked the ground and clutched her skateboard in her left hand. The pillowcase full of candy swung in her right. "Last year, it was one of those crappy lollipops you get at the bank, and it wasn't even a good flavor."

"I'll share with you," said Monica, a big smile on her face. She pushed up her glasses. Her bright yellow wig was pushing them down, and she kept having to adjust it.

"That's not the point, Mon. She hates me. She's always hated me. Besides, Ted said to stay away from her. He said that she's the one spreading rumors about me."

"She won't know it's you."

"Because I put my hair up under my helmet instead of letting it stick out?"

In truth, anyone who saw Clarissa regularly wouldn't think much of her costume. It wasn't all that different from what she normally wore. She didn't wear a helmet, knee pads, and elbow pads when she skateboarded on the streets, but she sometimes did when on the half-pipe. It was her mother's rule, and Margie said that even the pros wore them on the half-pipe.

Monica said, "It will be quick. We'll say trick-or-treat, get the candy, and head back to my place for a scary movie. She's old. She probably can't even tell who we are. Look how thick her glasses are."

Under the thick glasses, the old woman wore a red cape and short, cropped white hair. Little painted red lines dribbled out at the corners of her mouth. She had tried to paint her face white, but it was uneven between the deep wrinkles on her face. Plastic vampire teeth hung around her neck. She called to Clarissa and Monica as the three other children walked past them toward the street.

"Come on, don't be afraid." She paused, and then said, "I won't bite." She laughed loudly at her own joke. Seeing their hesitation, Mrs. Everson made the trek down her stairs, taking them one by one. She seemed eager to approach.

Both Monica and Clarissa looked at each other. Clarissa turned to go, but Monica stopped her with a hand.

Clarissa whispered, "Forget it. It's not worth it."

Instead of responding, Monica walked toward the woman holding the big bowl of candy, saying, "Trick-or-Treat." She opened her pillowcase, but the woman looked past Monica, focusing on Clarissa.

Clarissa took a deep breath and strode forward, stopping several paces from where the woman was standing. She didn't want to get too close.

For a moment, Mrs. Everson appraised her. Clarissa felt the heat of her gaze. She hoped that Monica was right, and that the woman didn't recognize her.

Mrs. Everson said, "And what are you supposed to be, Clarissa?" not even trying to hide the sneer in her voice.

Clarissa stood a little taller and said, "Tony Hawk."

The old woman's brow furrowed. "Who is Tony Hawk? Is he some kind of undead creature? You look pale enough, and are those bags under your eyes real or painted on?" The woman flashed a sharp smile, and even without the fake fangs in her mouth, she bore a wolfish grin.

Clarissa spoke with pride for the man she idolized. "Only the greatest skateboarder of all time."

She presented her skateboard to Mrs. Everson, who, clearly not having noticed it before, scowled. It was a common reaction with older adults, but Clarissa knew Mrs. Everson hated them more than most. James and Margie had nicknamed her "the old bat", a nickname that had stuck amongst all the skaters in the area.

"It's not much of a costume, is it?"

Monica, trying to break the tension, said, "Trick or Treat," again. But Mrs. Everson didn't seem to notice. Her gaze was only for Clarissa, a gleeful malice dancing in her eyes.

Since Clarissa had told Monica everything about the meadow and the monster, things had been a little easier. Monica hadn't gotten scared or thought she was a freak; instead, she seemed relieved to finally understand what was happening to her friend.

For most of October, things had been better at school. The questions had faded, and most people simply ignored Clarissa once they realized she wouldn't talk about what had happened. At least, that was until the haunted forest had opened up in the third week of October. Their suburb of Philadelphia had an annual tradition. Behind the basketball courts at the edge of the woods, where they had found Clarissa after her disappearance, volunteers set up the haunted forest. It was the town's version of a haunted house. Every year, people would come from all over the community to walk a short, guided path through the woods, and wait for local volunteers to jump out and try to scare them. As soon as the annual haunted forest had opened, the town's curiosity returned, and speculation began anew.

Ignoring Monica, Mrs. Everson said, "You know, you, of all people, shouldn't idolize hoodlums. One of those terrible teenagers on a skateboard knocked over my mailbox with a baseball bat. I thought it was you, Clarissa, but they were much too tall. Skateboards are the work of the devil and those who use them are his minions."

Clarissa hugged her skateboard a little tighter with her left hand. She had told Monica they should skip this house, and now here they were, standing in front of the old bat. She couldn't help but feel a little angry with Monica.

"All I know is, my Dad gave me this skateboard. You know, the man who used to shovel your walk when it snowed? Or how about the time he repaired your porch, or changed your flat tire?"

Most people had loved Clarissa's father. He had helped a dozen neighbors repair their houses over the years. Clarissa was sure that would shut her up.

Mrs. Everson eyed her, smiled again, and said, "And look at what happened to him. A shame, really. He was a good man, once."

Clarissa felt something move inside of her, something warm. It bloomed into her face, a red rose, the thorns ready to draw blood.

"What's that supposed to mean?"

Mrs. Everson said nothing, a cruel smile painting her face.

Clarissa muttered under her breath, "At least my husband didn't leave me for a younger woman, you old bat."

"What did you just say?"

Clarissa hadn't said it loud enough for her to hear, nor did she dare repeat it. She knew she would get into trouble.

"I said, what did you mean about my father?"

Clarissa knew exactly what Mrs. Everson had meant, and the more she thought about it, the angrier she got. Her father had been a good person, which was more than she could say for this woman. Everyone on the block hated her. Even the police had stopped taking her calls because of her endless accusations leveled against her neighbors. Still, some listened to her rumors. Gossip was ever the currency, the tool to make people get in line and behave.

Mrs. Everson's eyes narrowed, a thin smile rested on her lips, but she said nothing more about Clarissa's father.

Monica, studying the exchange, tried again to change the subject and said, "And who are you supposed to be, Mrs. Everson?"

The woman looked toward Monica, as if noticing her for the first time.

"I'm a vampire, dear. A proper Halloween costume."

Clarissa hated the proud look on the women's face. She wanted to throw something at her. She clutched her skateboard a little tighter. The pillowcase, full of candy and in her right hand, was heavy. Clarissa twisted it thinking about how she had seen a bully hit another kid with a similar sack of candy only a half hour earlier.

Clarissa, with an edge in her voice said, "You're only wearing part of your costume. Aren't you supposed to wear your teeth inside of your mouth instead of around your neck? You look stupid."

The old woman let slip a momentary look of shock, but then huffed and said, "I'll have you know, young lady, that I have dentures, and I cannot wear fake teeth over top of them."

Mrs. Everson turned to Monica, looking her up and down with what Clarissa thought was a look of disgust, then asked, "Oh my, are you some kind of...," She seemed to search for a word for a moment, because what Monica was wearing wasn't obvious to everyone. "...Princess?"

Monica, smiling, and unable to hide the joy in her voice, said, "Sailor Moon!"

"Sailor...wh...what?"

"Sailor Moon. She's a kind of warrior. She protects the earth from evil with her friends."

Clarissa heard footsteps behind her and glanced back to find a werewolf, a Chucky doll, and a Ghostbuster heading in their direction.

The old woman looked over both of their heads and said, "Ah, now here are proper Halloween costumes."

Mrs. Everson, surprisingly quick and strong when she wanted to be, walked around Monica and Clarissa, and down the sidewalk, almost to the street. Before the other kids could say trick-or-treat, Mrs. Everson took an extra-large handful of candy and put it in the other kids' plastic buckets and jack-o-lanterns. Looking back at both Clarissa and Monica, she said, "Neither of those are even monsters. I only give out candy to children dressed in proper costumes. You two can move along."

Monica said, "But a Ghostbuster isn't a monster."

Mrs. Everson replied, "It's close enough. Your costumes are ridiculous. Your parents should be ashamed of both of you. Why, if I was them, I wouldn't have let you out of the house."

With fire rising inside her, Clarissa said, "I thought you said skateboarders were hoodlums? Doesn't that qualify as scary?"

"Hoodlums aren't monsters, they're just criminals, dear. Now, shoo, before I call the police!" She said it loud enough to be heard up and down the block.

Monica, whose face was a mask of shock and disappointment, said, "What for?"

The three trick-or-treaters did not say thank you or walk away. They watched the exchange with rapt attention. Other kids directly across the street or within listening distance were turning and watching, as well. Even a few adults who stood in their doorways handing out candy had stopped to watch when the word 'Police' was mentioned.

Mrs. Everson stared at Monica for a moment, then said, "Trespassing."

Clarissa said, "Trespassing? It's Halloween. We didn't do anything."

Mrs. Everson turned on them and, almost shouting, said, "Little girls who murder their own father, and make a pact with the devil in the forest, are not welcome here." She looked at Monica. "And neither are their accomplices." Her voice was high and shrill, lilting with glee and malice as if she had been waiting a long time to say this.

Rage swelled inside Clarissa. She put down her board, hopped on, and charged at the woman as fast as she could. Clarissa knocked Mrs. Everson's bucket of candy out of her hands. It exploded and scattered candy into the air, and with it came gales of laughter from some of the onlookers.

Clarissa turned around, did an ollie, and then, for the first time in her life, she did something she had seen Margie do a hundred times, but had never dared do, herself, before. She raised her middle finger at the woman, whose face was now a crimson mask of fury.

"Scary enough for you, you old bat?!" shouted Clarissa at the top of her lungs.

"Clarissa!" shouted Monica, running past Mrs. Everson and up next to Clarissa.

The werewolf, who until now, was watching silently beneath his mask said, "Dammmn! You go, Clarissa." His voice was familiar.

"Didn't think you had it in you," said the Chucky doll.

Mrs. Everson shrieked, "The police are going to hear all about this! I'll have them lock you away!"

But before the woman could do anything, the other kids dove onto the ground scooping up candy and shouting. "Free for all!"

Already, several other kids were charging in, eager to take this small vengeance on the town's aging bully.

With the woman's attention diverted by eight children around her feet, grabbing greedily, Monica tugged at Clarissa's arm.

"Come on. Let's get out of here."

Clarissa barely heard her. The fury churned, a terrible rapture born in a chrysalis of pressure. Clarissa considered taking another pass on her skateboard, this time swinging with her pillowcase for the woman's head. Her father had been a good man, and she fixated on the accusation. She hadn't killed him, she was sure of that; somehow, that monster from the meadow had, and before she had even gone inside its lair.

Mrs. Everson screamed at the children. She kicked one of them in the ribs and shouted, "Stop that! That candy is for all the neighborhood children, you ungrateful little bastards!"

More gales of laughter surrounded the woman, and Clarissa realized that the werewolf and the Chucky doll were none other than Daryl and Rob. For the first time in her life, she was glad to see them directing their energy toward someone who actually deserved it. Rob, the werewolf, punted the old woman's empty bucket far away, full of mirth and mischief, and Daryl bent over with gales of laughter, even as he shoved Snickers into his plastic bucket.

Monica grabbed Clarissa's hand and pulled. Clarissa hesitated for a moment, but when one of the other kids pushed Mrs. Everson down, and some adults rushed in to put a stop to the frenzy, she gave in and ran down the block with Monica and around the corner. They would need to circle around to the back alley later, when things settled down. Mrs. Everson would come knocking on their parents' doors, and though her mother and Ted were both out for the evening, Monica's dad would be home.

They ran for several blocks until they could hide among some trees in the nearby park. As they hid, they saw the flashing lights of a police car go by, followed immediately by an ambulance. Clarissa wasn't sure if that was for Mrs. Everson or not. They didn't exactly live in the friendliest area, and Halloween night provided all manner of excuses for masked mischief.

Panting as they stopped, Monica said, "That was kind of mean, Clarissa."

Clarissa turned on her friend, a bellows stoking her fury. "She deserved it. You heard what she said about me and my dad."

"But she's old. What if you gave her a heart attack, or something? My mom said that she's mean because everyone hates her, even her own kids."

Clarissa's anger, far from spent, needed a target. She said, "How can you take her side? I told you we shouldn't have gone to that stupid house, anyway. This is your fault."

Monica said nothing. She looked at the ground, letting her pillowcase full of candy slide into the dirt and yellowing grass. A few leaves fell around them and danced in a sudden gust.

"You knew she hated me. Even Ted said to stay away. But Monica needed her full candy bar. I thought you were a better friend than that."

Monica said nothing. The silence was oxygen, feeding flames.

"This whole town hates me, Mon. Everyone in school thinks I'm a freak. I wish I would have died in that meadow."

Monica looked up, her bottom lip trembled. Already, tears leaked from the corners of her eyes. Her voice fragile and small, she said, "I'm sorry."

She sniffled and wiped her nose.

The tears did not cool Clarissa's rage.

"I'm outta here."

Clarissa slung her candy filled pillowcase over her shoulder and dropped her skateboard to the ground.

"Wait. Where are you going?"

Clarissa put her foot on her board, ready to skate off.

"Away."

Monica dropped her pillow case, ran over, and threw her arms around Clarissa.

"No, Clarissa. Don't. Please. I'm scared. What if...what if it's out there?"

As if to punctuate the point, a gust blew through the trees above, cascading the last yellow, red, and orange leaves into a spinning, churning cloud around them.

Clarissa froze. It took her a moment to realize first what Monica was saying, and then, where they were both standing. Clarissa looked over to the edge of the park, and saw the gaping mouth of the trailhead, one of many that lead deep into the forest and toward where the meadow lay hidden. Her anger evaporated and a heavy chill crept up over her. She could feel something watching.

Monica, her arms locked around Clarissa, continued, "Be mad at me. You're right. I should have listened. I was a terrible friend. But Clarissa, I'm scared."

Monica's body trembled, and she held on tight. She continued, "It's Halloween. Aren't things supposed to be special on Halloween? It's the night that all the ghosts and monsters come out for real, isn't it?"

Feeling the gooseflesh rise on her arms and legs, Clarissa, trying to channel her mother said, "That's just in the movies, Mon. Monster's aren't...."

Clarissa didn't finish her statement, because now she knew for a fact that monsters were real. Her eyes drifted back to the trailhead. The sensation of something watching, something beckoning her back to the meadow crept deeper inside of her like the maggots had crept inside the boy's skull, eating their way out. She could smell the sickly sweet perfume of his corpse.

Still holding tight, Monica let loose another wave of tears, taking deep rasping breaths or sniffling between each phrase and sentence. "When you ran into the woods and then you went missing...I was so scared. I should have followed you...but...but I couldn't keep up. You were too fast, and I tripped and fell...," she sniffled. "And I broke my glasses. I couldn't see...." Monica bellowed, "I should have been there with you when that monster came. Maybe I could have helped somehow, but I'm a klutz." Her breath hitched, and she struggled to regain control. "I'm a good-for-nothing klutz. I'm so, so sorry, Clarissa. Please, forgive me. Please?"

Monica's tears leaked into Clarissa's shirt, and slowly she dropped her pillowcase and put her arms around her friend. She hadn't thought about how Monica felt about her disappearance, or even about why she hadn't followed her into the woods. Was she, Clarissa, the bad friend? Monica was so much smaller than she was, and she wasn't very fast, so Clarissa hadn't given it a second thought. She had been so focused on getting her skateboard back, her greatest treasure, that she had completely forgotten her friend.

"I...I didn't know about your glasses. I...it's...." Clarissa struggled to find the words. "It's fine. I was the one who left you behind at the falls. I'm sorry."

Monica sniffled. "It's okay." She let go and took a step back. "But Clarissa, can we please get out of here? I don't want to be anywhere near those woods. I feel like something is watching us."

Clarissa felt a cold plunge. Until Monica had said that, she could dismiss the feeling, but not now, not with those words, "I feel like something is watching us." She couldn't deny the fear that had taken possession of her. It was a sick thing, and with the dread came the shroud. The tendrils of darkness closed in on her. Her whole body burned with the desire to run.

At that moment, a loud and throaty cry came from just above their heads. Both girls jumped and looked up. There, above their heads, was a strange, winged creature. Clarissa had seen its like before, but instead of feathers as black as night, this bird had bright white feathers. It seemed to glow against the dark branches of the tree it occupied.

Monica said, "Is that a raven?"

"I...I don't know."

The creature cawed again.

"I mean the kind of bird that's in the Edgar Allen Poe story."

"I know what a Raven is, Mon. But they're black and that one is white...it...it almost looks like...."

"A ghost," finished Monica. "It's creepy."

The creature cawed again several times, cocking its head at odd angles, then flapped its wings in their direction, as if fanning some invisible flame. It spun around on its perch and repeated the motion.

"What's it doing?" asked Monica.

"It almost looks like it's waving."

Monica picked up her pillow case, and Clarissa picked up her. The creature did another circle of ritual motion.

"Let's go, Mon. I don't like it."

Monica nodded. "Yeah. Let's get out of here."

The girls started walking. The bird watched, and as soon as they were out of the park, across the street, and a few houses away, it flew forward and landed on a tree branch just above their heads. It did not repeat the ritual, but it watched them, cocking its head this way and that.

Monica, her voice trembling, said, "I think it's following us."

Clarissa looked up at it as it cawed again, as if asking a question. The deep sound resonated in the night, and gooseflesh prickled on the edges of Clarissa's skin.

"Yeah...," she swallowed, thinking of the shadowy creature that had come into her room, and wondering if this bird had something to do with it. "I think it is."

Monica said, "Do you think it's dangerous like in the Poe story, or that old movie, *The Birds*?"

"I don't know. Maybe. But we should head back to your house as fast as we can, so we don't have to find out."

"Where? We can't go back, yet. Mrs. Everson will knock on our parents' door any minute now."

Unsure of where to go, they kept walking at a brisk pace. The bird cawed several more times above their heads, performing its strange ritual, spinning and flapping its wings. Its black eyes stood out against the bright white feathers, feathers that almost looked like bones in the gloom. A strange mist gathered around them, swallowing their feet. With each step they took, the bird followed only a few trees or telephone poles behind.

"Let's go toward the skate park. We could hide in the playground equipment next to it for a little while," suggested Clarissa.

The skate park was on the opposite side of town from the forest, and Clarissa would feel stronger there, safer.

Monica nodded. "Good idea."

But as they turned left down a street, toward the skate park, the creatures flew in front of them and landed on the railing of a porch, baring their way and cawing loudly at them. It spun around several times and flourished its feathers.

"Let's just hurry past it," said Clarissa.

"I don't know," said Monica, her face fearful and dim. "What if it attacks us, or something?"

"This isn't that old movie, *The Birds*. It's not going to hurt us. Let's try."

Inwardly, Clarissa wasn't so sure, but what else could they do? Taking a few hesitant steps, Clarissa inched forward. The skate park was just a few blocks away. The creature didn't move as she walked past it. It watched her closely, cocking its head as she took several more steps forward. She stopped and turned, and saw that Monica hadn't moved at all.

"It's safe. Come on. I told you it wouldn't attack us."

The bird flew up and perched on a skeletal tree branch, cawed loudly several times, then leaped and caught the currents of wind with its wings. Monica watched it, unmoving.

"Come on. It's fine."

The raven leaped and swooped down at Clarissa and, talons out, it aimed for her head. Clarissa ducked out of the way just in time, feeling the creature scrape its talons across her helmet. Clarissa screamed and quickly got back up to her feet.

"Run!" said Clarissa.

It broke Monica's paralysis and both girls ran, fleeing in the opposite direction, the raven following not far behind.

"What about Davis's Trading Post?" asked Monica, already out of breath as they ran through the night, their footsteps heavy and hollow on the pavement. "We could...hide out there for a little while...I have two dollars from my allowance...so they...won't...kick us out."

Clarissa nodded, and they tried to turn up the street that led to the convenience store, only to find the White Raven waiting there in front of them, once again barring their passage and squawking loudly. It did another turn of a circle and flapped its wings.

"Shit," Clarissa swore.

Monica didn't correct her language, but grabbed Clarissa's hand and pulled her back in the other direction. Both shaking and terrified, they ran back toward the alley that led to their houses. The Raven pursued them. Every time Clarissa looked back, she found it just behind them. After several blocks, they ran up through the cramped alley lined with cars and trash cans. They barely dodged a car driving through the alley, with the driver yelling at them to pay attention. Finally, they ran up to the gate in the center of the tall, chain-link fence that led into the rear entrance of Monica's house, and quickly, Monica put the code into the lock that kept it shut from strangers.

Monica tore open the gate with the metal scraping on the sidewalk, and charging through, Clarissa slammed it behind her, as if baring the winged creature from entry. They ran through Monica's backyard, dodging an overturned bicycle, a few toys, and a sandbox that had become a small pond. They climbed up the cement steps that led to the back door.

Panting, they both looked around as they stood at the entryway.

"Is it gone?" asked Monica.

Clarissa said, "I think so."

They both looked up at the tall trees leering over the yard, crowding in toward the center like pointing fingers. Nothing. Their eyes ran down the length of the telephone pole wires that went through the center of one of the trees and into the house. Nothing. They looked at the woodpile stacked in the corner, used for when winter pressed in with its bitter chill to the old house. Nothing. Both girls let out a breath.

"Why did it attack you like that? Do you think it has something to do with the meadow?"

Clarissa, still sick with fear and adrenaline, said, "I don't know. But let's go inside."

Monica nodded. "Yeah. I don't care if we get in trouble. Not now."

They opened the door and went in.

2.   Monica was the oldest of three sisters. The youngest played just beyond the entrance on the thin green carpet with a toy matchbox car, a Barbie, and some duct tape. To the left, a passageway split off to some stairs that lead to a basement laundry room and the area where all three siblings kept most of their toys. The passage straight ahead led up a few small stairs to the kitchen, dining room, and beyond.

Monica, pretending nothing was wrong, leaned in and kissed her sister on the head. "Whatcha doing, Silvia?"

The six-year-old looked up with her brown eyes and braided dark hair.

"Making Barbie go on a magic carpet ride."

The first grader, dressed in a Princess Jasmine costume, hummed a song from Aladdin. Candy wrappers lay scattered around her, and she didn't seem to notice the chocolate smeared on the left side of her face.

"Go where?" asked Monica.

"Down the stairs, Sissy, duh. Want to help?"

Monica asked, "Why does she need to go down the stairs?"

The little girl rolled her eyes. "To fly, of course." She looked up at Clarissa and said, "You want to help, too, Clary? You like to fly!"

She had never said Clarissa's name right, so she always just called her Clary. Clarissa didn't normally mind, but she wanted to get inside, away from the door. She felt that sensation of being watched again and peered through the small window in the back door, checking for signs of the strange white raven that had chased them from the park. She saw nothing, but kept looking.

"Whatcha looking at, Clary?" said Silvia.

Clarissa, who was still searching, glanced back at Silvia and said, "Nothing...." paused, and then said, "Well, just a bird."

"What kind of bird?"

"A white one," answered Monica.

"I saw a white one. It was outside when I was trick-or-treating."

The girl imitated the cawing noise of the Raven, sending chills up and down Clarissa's spine. She and Monica looked at each other, and Clarissa felt the pressure of the shroud tighten around her.

"You saw it? Near here?" asked Monica.

"No, at Mrs. Everson's House. It was bright and beautiful, and I hoped it would drop a feather, but it didn't." She paused for a moment and then said, "Mrs. Everson's so nice. She gave me a whole snickers bar!"

Clarissa felt a stir of annoyance, thinking of the woman, but her thoughts passed back to the Raven. Had the bird been watching Clarissa at that house? She searched her memory but couldn't recall seeing it. But then, Mrs. Everson had consumed her focus, a vampire after all. Why the hell had that bird followed them? What was going on? What did it have to do with the meadow?

"Help, please!" said Silvia, whose hands were now tangled in small strips of duct tape.

Monica reached down and struggled with the duct tape for a moment, too. Like her little sister, she kept tearing off thin strips while the whole wider strip proved elusive. She handed it over to Clarissa, who looked back over her shoulder and through the window.

"I don't think it's there anymore, Clary," said Silvia.

Clarissa turned back to Silvia and helped with the tape. After a moment, she pulled several strips for the little girl. Sometimes Clarissa wished she had a little sister, but then Monica, six months younger than her, often felt like a little sister.

Eager to finish her masterpiece, Silvia lovingly took the duct tape and carefully wrapped it around the car and the Barbie doll. The car was far too small for the doll and duct tape stunted three of the wheels.

"I don't think that's gonna work, Sil," said Monica.

Silvia stood up and put the car on the trim, running parallel to the stairs. It slid, but after several feet, it slipped onto some stairs, stopped, and rested halfway down, a single wheel still spinning.

Silvia laughed and jumped down the stairs one at a time, and grabbed the car. Climbing back up to the top, she tried again. This time it slid a little further, but crashed with the same result.

"Wow! Look how far it went that time." Silvia jumped up and down, and then, again, taking one step at a time, retrieved her treasure. "A whole new world," she sang.

Clarissa looked back out the window again. Still nothing. Why had it stopped following them? She thought about how it had swooped down at her when they tried to go to the skate park. Why had it done that?

Monica said something to her, but Clarissa, staring out the window, didn't hear. Finally, Monica shook her gently.

"You okay?

"Huh? Oh...yeah."

"Are we going upstairs, or what?"

Clarissa nodded.

Clutching her skateboard and adjusting her pillowcase full of candy, Clarissa followed Monica up the stairs, leaving behind Silvia, who was still squealing with joy as she dropped the toy down the stairs another time. The familiar scent caught Clarissa's attention. It was a happy smell that reminded her of her grandmother's house before they had moved her into a nursing home.

Ted had set foot in Monica's house only once, and it almost broke his brain. Both Clarissa and her mother had laughed about that, teasing Ted for hours. Each corner of the house contained unique stacks of boxes, books, magazines, records, and so on. The place looked almost like the inside of a bookstore, except some of those piles were clothes and canned goods. When she asked Monica about it, she had said, "The house doesn't really have closets to store things."

The girls passed through the kitchen. Leftover enchiladas sat inside a pan on the stove. Clarissa always enjoyed the smell of Monica's kitchen. Both of her parents were excellent cooks. The girls walked through the dining room. The table, covered in a variety of envelopes and pieces of mail, featured postcards from all around the world. When Clarissa had turned over a few one afternoon with Monica, she saw that they were written in Spanish. At the bottom of each postcard, someone named Julio had signed their name. Monica had said that he was her uncle, who worked for the government, though Monica didn't know exactly what he did. Pictures hung on every wall in the dining room, some featured the elusive Julio, who, in several pictures, was standing with strangers from other countries and cultures.

They headed up the stairs, around the corner, and toward Monica's room. But there, standing in their way, was Monica's father. He was a short man, his hair thinning on top, and his black mustache twitched on his upper lip. Always stern and serious, he stood with his arms crossed...he always made Clarissa a little uncomfortable. Monica's mother, who was at work, was a short, full-figured woman, and always joyful. Clarissa preferred to be around her.

In his Columbian accent, Monica's father, Dominic Aguilar said, "You want to tell me what happened out there tonight?"

Monica, the ever-obedient daughter, opened her mouth to say something. Before she could, Clarissa grabbed her arm, halting her confession.

Clarissa said, "We went trick-or-treating. Look, we got our pillowcases half-full." Clarissa raised hers up to show him. Her arm trembled a little with the weight.

"So you had nothing to do with Mrs. Everson's accident?"

Monica said, "Accident?"

Monica's father eyed both of the girls, seeking truth. "You don't know?"

Both girls shook their heads. He looked at them again, searching for answers. But after a moment, he seemed to accept that they were telling the truth, at least about that.

"Strange, because I heard a rumor that this one...," he nodded in Clarissa's direction, "...harassed Mrs. Everson with her skateboard."

Clarissa, feeling a strange sense of glee inside at the thought of the woman having had an accident, said, "What happened?"

Dominic Aguilar stared at Clarissa for several moments, muttered something in Spanish under his breath, and then said, "They think she had a heart attack after those two...cabrones attacked her."

Monica's eyes widened, "Language!"

Her father looked at her, but said nothing else.

"A heart attack?" asked Clarissa.

She felt two things simultaneously. The first was that the old woman deserved it, but the second was a crushing sense of guilt that she might have killed someone else. It made her think of the boy who stole her skateboard, and how, when she found him lying outstretched on the ground inside the meadow, she had thought that he, too, had deserved it.

"Is...is she going to be okay?" asked Clarissa.

Dominic said, "I'm not sure. The ambulance took her away." He paused and then said, "You didn't harass her?"

Clarissa shook her head.

He turned toward his daughter and said, "Dime la verdad, hija."

To her credit, she looked right at her father and replied, "Es verdadero, Papa."

Clarissa didn't know exactly what they said, but she watched Monica's face flush red, and knew that her friend had lied about something.

Dominic stared at both of them longer, then said, "Don't stay up too late. There's leftovers on the counter if you want them." He turned and went back into his room. Standing at the threshold he said, "The truth always gets sorted out, eventually." Then he closed the door behind him.

Both girls walked around the hall and up to a second set of stairs. Wood paneling lined the third floor but didn't keep out the chill or heat. Monica liked it. None of her siblings wanted to sleep up there, and her sister, Dominica, who was only a year younger than Monica, swore it was haunted.

Monica's circular balcony bedroom overlooked the neighborhood, and it always made Clarissa feel like she was at the top of a castle.

Posters of Sailor Moon, Janet Jackson, Boyz II Men, and others lined the few walls between the wide windows overlooking their street. Her bed was an avatar of pink. A computer sat in the corner and sometimes they played video games on it like *Day of the Tentacle*. Monica was lucky. No one else Clarissa knew had a computer in their house. Monica's father worked as an engineer at some company, and occasionally they would upgrade their computers and give employees the chance to take an old one home.

"Do you think your dad knows what I did?" asked Clarissa.

"I'm not sure," said Monica. "But I told him you were telling the truth."

Clarissa nodded.

Monica said, "I hope she's okay."

Clarissa nodded, feeling that conflict inside of her again. If Mrs. Everson was alright, they would probably get into trouble. Neither she nor Monica had pushed the woman, so how much trouble could they get into? Though Clarissa had to admit to herself that she had wanted to hurt the woman, had wanted to make her feel pain, the way the old bat had cut her deeply with her words.

"I don't want to talk about it anymore," said Clarissa.

Monica nodded and said nothing, sitting on her bed in her Sailor Moon costume with her pillowcase of candy in her lap.

Clarissa put her skateboard in the corner, then dumped the bag of candy out onto the bed. Monica did the same. For several minutes they sorted their candy into piles of things they loved, things they hated, and things they were willing to trade.

"Snickers for a Reece's?" asked Clarissa.

Monica scoffed. "Are you kidding me? Reece's are way better than Snickers. How about for a Kit-Kat?"

"Uh, I don't know."

"Come on, you got like...eleven Kit-Kats and I only got three. It's a fair trade."

"Alright fine," said Clarissa.

They traded for a while, breaking only to cram candy in their mouths when the temptation became too much. Then Clarissa ran back over to her house and grabbed her PJ's. Ted greeted her when she came in, back early from a party down the street. He said nothing about Mrs. Everson, so she assumed that he hadn't heard anything yet. Instead, Ted reminded Clarissa not to say anything to Monica about the meadow. He didn't know it was already too late. She felt bad about that, but it also felt good that she no longer held the secret alone.

When she returned she found Monica was already waiting with both popcorn and a movie. Both girls sat leaning against Monica's bed, each mixing candy with popcorn as they watched *Ferngully, the Last Rainforest*. Neither was sure what to think. The tree containing the evil smoke creature in the center of the forest reminded them both of what had happened to Clarissa.

"I didn't like it," said Clarissa.

"Do you think that somehow the creators knew about the meadow, or something?" asked Monica.

"I don't know." Clarissa hugged her knees, rocking back and forth, trying to fight the chill.

"Do you think there might be a way to trap the creature again, like in the movie? Some kind of magic?

They had talked about that a lot over the last three weeks.

"Do you know where to find magic?" asked Clarissa.

Monica said, "Well...."

"It's not a good idea to go back there."

"Even during the day?"

"Don't you remember? It was afternoon when that kid took my skateboard. It's not safe. Besides, do you really want to go there, knowing what happened?"

Monica shook her head.

Clarissa, wanting to avoid talking about the meadow, asked, "Can we watch something else?"

"Sailor Moon?" Monica smiled hopefully. She still wore her costume.

"Please, no."

"Why not?"

"Because we watch it all the time."

Monica rolled her eyes, "Fine. What about *Honey, I Shrunk the Kids*?"

Clarissa shrugged. "I guess."

Monica changed into her PJ's, then both girls crawled into her bed.

As the movie started, Monica asked, "What do you think was up with that raven?"

Clarissa shook her head, pulling the covers up to her neck. "I don't know."

Monica snuggled into the blankets saying, "I think maybe we should head to the library tomorrow. We can add the Raven to the list of things to look up."

Since Clarissa had told Monica her secrets, Monica had suggested they go to the library pretty much every weekend. Clarissa liked to read fantasy books, but she didn't much care for the library. Most of those books were boring and Clarissa was a slow reader. Monica was the opposite. Her father had already started her on science fiction novels like *Jurassic Park*.

"I'm scared, Monica. I think it's going to come back any day now."

Monica frowned and was silent for several moments. Finally, she said, "Is there some kind of sign when it's about to come after you?"

Clarissa thought hard about the two encounters with the creature. Then she thought of something. "Well, just before it comes, the wind starts blowing hard."

Almost as if commanding it, there was a gust of wind that shook the house. The trees scratched madly at the exterior of the building.

Both girls screamed and pulled the covers over their heads, trembling.

Under the covers, Monica said, "Do you hear that?"

Clarissa, frozen, listened. At first she could only hear the movie. Then she heard something else.

It was coming. They could hear it approaching on the old, wooden, creaky steps that lead up to Monica's bedroom. It was quick, not slowly creeping forward like in the meadow. No shadow coalescing from mist this time. It was coming right for them both without hesitation. The shroud tightened around Clarissa and it felt hard to draw breath.

Monica said, "Oh god, it's right outside the door."

A thunderous knocking made both girls scream again.

Dominic said, "I hope you too are not watching anything too scary up here."

The shroud virtually dissolved and all of Clarissa's fear bled away.

Monica, who was also visibly relieved, shouted through the covers, "Sorry, Papa, the wind scared us. We're watching *Honey, I Shrunk the Kids*."

She jumped out of bed and opened the door for her father, who, seeing the TV, seemed satisfied.

"It's almost midnight, girls. You can leave the TV on but I want you to try and get some sleep."

"Yes, Papa," said Monica.

The wind howled again, the sound of an old woman moaning in terrible pain.

"Ah, I see," said Dominic. "The wind is full of mischief tonight."

He turned and walked back down the steps, shutting the door behind him.

Monica waited a moment, then climbed up to the window and looked down.

"Oh man, it's really windy out. Look, Clarissa, there's still a party going on across the street."

Clarissa climbed out of Monica's bed and walked over to the window. Below, an adult party was in full swing across the street, and some people stood on the porch with costumes on and beverages in hand. A witch's hat took flight, and the woman scrambled to grab it back. A man helped her, but even as he did, his red cape flapped hard and he drew it closer. The others, sitting on the porch, made their way inside.

Standing next to Clarissa in front of the window, Monica said, "When it came last time, did it give any other signs besides the wind?"

"Well, there was also this terrible feeling, like something was rotting inside of me. Like a big ball of fear that's stuck in your guts. It's horrible."

Monica's voice shook as she said, "Are...are you feeling that now?"

Clarissa thought about it for a second, then said, "No."

Monica, her face relaxing, said, "Oh, good."

Clarissa thought of something and then said, "I don't know if it will come with someone else around. So maybe if we are here together, it will be okay."

Both girls climbed back in bed.

"You really think so?"

"Well, when it...you know...hurt the boy, I was alone. I think he was dead before I crossed into the meadow. Then, when it came a few weeks ago, the second my mom and Ted came into the room, it vanished. When my mom slept with me on the couch it didn't come back. So maybe it's scared of other people, or maybe it can only appear to me, or something?"

"Do you think the detective was alone when it went after her?"

"I don't know."

"Why do you think it went after her?"

Clarissa hadn't figured that out yet. After she had told Monica the story about the detective, Monica suggested they try to find out who else had been in the meadow. Clarissa had asked Ted, since he was a part of the search party. He had given her a scolding look, but ultimately relented. He said he and five other people had been there. Ted wouldn't say who the other people were, but he had told her that no one else was hurt and to just let it go. To Clarissa, it meant that visiting the meadow wasn't enough to catch the monster's attention.

"I don't know. I can't figure that out," said Clarissa.

"Well, we'll have a sleepover every night then." Monica smiled.

"Our parents would never let us."

"They would if we told them the truth."

"Monica, they're never going to believe us. The only other person I told was the detective, and she didn't believe me."

"Well, I believe you."

"I know. Thanks, Mon. The few things I told my mother and Ted, they both ignored. They said it was my imagination filling in the blanks and they won't even let me talk about it anyway, remember?"

Monica frowned. "Okay, well, we just have to think of a good reason for endless sleepovers, that's all." Then she smiled.

Clarissa knew that was a long shot, but agreed. "Fine by me. Maybe we can switch off between houses, or something?"

Monica said, "Hey, maybe our parents can each adopt us and we can all live together. Can you be a part of two families at the same time?"

Clarissa giggled, "I don't see why not. But I think Ted's head would explode if we all lived together."

"Oh, man," said Monica. "Just imagine him running around trying to clean up all the piles around my house."

"Yeah, what if they fell on him and he was buried in your parents' stuff."

Imitating Ted, Clarissa said, "No, the angles in the room are all wrong...Ahhhhh help, I'm drowning in books!"

Both girls laughed for several moments before settling back down.

With the movie still playing in the background, Monica yawned and said, "I'm getting sleepy."

Clarissa yawned, too. She nodded. "Me, too."

Suddenly, a loud gale of wind buffeted against the house, making the walls rattle. It scared both of the girls, and they both pulled the blankets up over their heads.

Monica said, "Let's leave the nightlight on tonight."

"Good idea," said Clarissa.

They lay there, not looking at the TV, but hiding under the covers, staring at each other.

Soon the wind settled and not long after, both girls were fast asleep.

3 Above, a lightbulb flared to life for a single instant and then burst into brief brilliance before flickering out forever. Then the nightlight followed suit. Only the fuzz of the TV static shone in the darkness. The flickering static created a kind of pulsing wave of shadows, shifting in the strange shimmer. Slowly, something solidified in the static, that terrible static.

The loud pop of the light tugged at Clarissa's consciousness, an unrelenting pull toward alertness, and gradually she opened her eyes and saw the TV. All was fuzzy, then an image clarified. For one moment she saw the meadow. It was gone so fast that, later, Clarissa would doubt she had seen it, but its colors, awash in night, burned images in her retinas that lingered as the creature took precedence on the screen.

Slowly, it lifted one of its claws and pushed up against the boundaries of the glass that separated reality from fiction. The glass yielded like a living membrane, a viscous red liquid poured from the puncture as its first and then second claw penetrated the boundary. The TV bled with the terror born from its womb.

Clarissa wanted to scream. No sound would come. The shroud wrapped around her body. She couldn't even move, couldn't make any motion beyond the blinking of her eyes. A tear ran down her cheek, and that motion, that crawling motion down the terrain of her pores, was the only sensation she could fixate on to suppress her terror.

The creature's head pushed through, spilling its way out of the screen. Its slender body grew as it used its claws to pull its form through the portal. It was not entirely solid. Part of the creature smoked and shifted forms as it slithered forward until it plopped to the ground below the TV. Runnels of red poured from the portal and gathered in a puddle as it shifted again like a wet, half-solidified mass of black goo. It made a trail of red as it moved toward the bed.

She wanted to wake Monica, wanted to reach out to her friend, to warn her away, to tell her to run.

Monica didn't stir.

The shadow shifted, melting into the darkness. All Clarissa could see was that wide gaping mouth, full of sharp needle-like teeth that opened with glee. The shroud tightened around her, the blackness more acute. She could barely breathe as it approached. The world lost its form. She felt a depression in the bed as it crawled up toward her, a half-formed torso now, propped up on the edge. It paused its movement, then its limbs elongated, reaching up toward her, caressing her almost lovingly, as a claw stretched toward her face.

It was over. Clarissa couldn't move. She could not call for help.

Then, Monica was awake. She screamed. Clarissa saw the creature turn its gaze toward her friend, all of its teeth showing in a wide, malevolent grin. Footsteps pounded on the creaking wooden stairs outside the room. As quick as a single breath the creature retreated into the TV static.

The door opened, and Monica's father flicked the light switch several times to no avail. He reached back and turned on the hall light. When he saw Monica, a blubbering mess, he ran forward and scooped up his daughter, asking her to tell him what happened, what was wrong. She pushed words out in clumps, but none held meaning together.

Clarissa couldn't move. The shroud still held her captive. For several moments Dominic comforted his daughter, while Clarissa lay, her head propped up just high enough to see. Gradually, the shroud relaxed, and she shifted a little in bed.

Dominic said, "Clarissa, what happened? Did someone come into the room? I can't get a straight answer out of Monica. She said there was something at the end of the bed? Do you know what that means?"

Clarissa said nothing. She stared into the man's eyes. They were brown with a tinge of gray in the center, and she could see all the way down deep inside him somehow. She wanted to tell him the truth. With that urge came a kind of release of her verbal paralysis, and the words poured out of her before she could rein them in.

"It was the creature...."

"What creature?"

The words swam in her. She couldn't pin them down, but she needed to make him understand.

"The blood from the TV...it came out of the TV...."

Dominic, with a puzzled expression on his face, stood and looked around the room. "Blood? What blood?"

Clarissa sat up a little straighter. There was no trace of the creature or the blood that poured from the mouth of the TV, but still, the static flickered.

Dominic said, "What creature are you talking about? There's nothing here.

"I...."

She gathered her courage and opened her mouth. The words spilled out, just as the blood had from the TV, in a single gush.

"It's hunting me. I thought I was safe with someone else around, that it would only come if I was alone. It came a few weeks ago for me when I was alone, but now it came tonight, and it wants to kill me."

His expression shifted. He looked down at Monica.

"Did you see something?"

Monica, trembling, nodded her head.

"So, you both saw something at the edge of the bed?"

Both girls nodded. Dominic stood up, went out into the hallway closet, and came back with a flashlight and a spare lightbulb. He stood on Monica's bed, reached up, and switched out the lightbulb. He got back down off the bed and switched it on.

With the light, Clarissa felt better, and so, it seemed, did Monica.

"I don't see anything, do you?"

Then he saw something else. He walked over to the trashcan and looked inside. Clarissa knew it was full of candy wrappers.

He turned back to the girls. "I think I know what's going on here."

Clarissa said, "What?"

"Looks to me like you girls had too much candy. You know it's true what they say, having a bunch of sugar before bed messes with your head. It can give you nightmares."

Clarissa felt dizzy. It was so late and she was so tired. She could still feel the shroud pulled tightly against her. Though it had released to a great degree, the room was still darker than it should be.

"It wasn't a nightmare," said Clarissa, a tinge of frustration in her voice.

"What was it, then?"

"I told you, the thing from the meadow. The shadow creature who chased me through the woods."

Dominic frowned. He scratched his chin.

"You two just got yourselves all worked up. Let me ask you this, who woke up first?"

"What?" said Clarissa.

"You or Monica?"

"Me."

"Did you wake up feeling scared?"

Clarissa looked down. She knew now he wouldn't believe her.

With a sigh, she said, "Yes."

"Then you woke up Monica and told her there was something on the bed?"

Monica said, "No, Papa, it wasn't like that."

"Then what was it like?"

"I woke up, and Clarissa was lying in bed looking at something. But she was frozen and staring, and she looked sick. Then she started making this awful sound, like a gurgling noise, and then I saw something at the end of the bed, and it stretched out its arm for her."

Dominic said, "It was just a dream. That sounds like a really scary one, but it was just a dream, Monica. It's Halloween. Dios De Las Muertos, The Day of The Dead. You've seen scary costumes and decorations all night, and then ate a ton of candy."

"Papa, it wasn't movies or candy. Something terrible was here. I...I've never been so scared in my life."

Her father moved over and sat on her bed.

"Listen, hija. When I was your age, I was afraid of every shadow, too. Around this time of the year, when the days are getting shorter, and we talk of the spirits of our ancestors and other scary creatures, and then you fill your stomach with candy, it makes you feel more afraid. It's natural to be afraid."

Clarissa shook her head slowly, but he didn't seem to notice. It was over. No adults were going to help them. Why was it that adults always explained everything away?

"What about the light bulb?" asked Clarissa.

He looked over at her, his face calm, reasonable. "Perhaps that woke you in the first place, and when the whole room was dark, you saw shadows. The TV static can make strange shapes on the walls. It is just like when the wind scared you both earlier."

Clarissa shook her head, trying to refute the argument with that single gesture. She knew it was no use to go on, but something in her felt like she had to make him understand.

Clarissa said, "Don't you believe in God, Mr. Aguilar?"

He looked over at Clarissa, narrowed his eyes and said, "Why, yes, of course. I believe in Jesus Christ, our Lord and Savior."

"Do you believe in the Devil, too?"

Dominic frowned, looking at the floor, but said nothing.

"Do you?"

The man opened his mouth to speak but didn't seem to want to say anything.

"Mr. Aguilar? Do you believe in the Devil?"

He looked over at Monica for a moment, hesitating. "Of course." It was almost a whisper, but in the silence of the bedroom, it was as clear as if he had shouted.

"Do you think what happened to me in those woods was something evil?"

Again, he said nothing. But he shifted his body several times. He looked away at the floor, avoiding eye contact.

Clarissa said, "What if...."

He cut her off immediately. "No. Don't you dare say it. You're too young to know anything about this stuff."

"Was that little girl in the Exorcist movie too young to be possessed by something?"

He stood up, backed away from the bed, and looked at them both. His stare was icy, and fury brimmed just at the corners of his eyes.

"That was just a movie, and you are far too young to have watched it."

Clarissa, defiant, almost yelled at him, saying, "I didn't need to watch the movie to know it's about a girl possessed by the devil. There's evil in this world. That's what I'm trying to say. The thing that came after us tonight is evil."

His eyes widened, then narrowed. His gaze fixed on Clarissa. She could see something wild behind his eyes and felt afraid. Suddenly, she realized it was a mistake to have confronted this man. For the first time, she noticed the heavy crucifix around his neck. She thought of all of the pictures of Jesus and Mary in the house. Monica had once told her that her father was a very devout catholic, but the man before them was a stranger, someone steeped in his religiosity. Clarissa didn't fully understand her mistake until years later. Because what came next was her fault, and if she hadn't confronted Monica's father, everything might have turned out differently.

He said, "So, niña, you're attracting the Devil, are you? Is that what you're telling me?" His accent deepened.

Clarissa sat up against the headboard, trying to find some distance between her and Monica's father. His deep voice resonated through her. Monica sat in wide-eyed silence watching the exchange.

"No, that's not what I meant. I only meant to...."

Venom dripped from his words. "Because, Clarissa, it's either a nightmare, or it's some devilish creature following you around. And I don't know if I want someone around my hija, who's got the eyes of the devil on her."

Clarissa pressed on. She had no other choice but to try to make him see.

"Mr. Aguilar, please listen. I'm saying that if you believe in the Devil, couldn't there be other things out there that are evil, too?"

He continued on as if Clarissa had said nothing. "Which is it, Clarissa? Your imagination or the devil?" He trembled, barely holding back his fury. "Because like I said, I don't want someone hanging around my daughter with the Devil in tow."

Monica said, "Papa, stop. She's telling the truth. Something terrible was here."

He turned on her, his face red, "Silencio, hija."

He wasn't going to listen. Why did this bother him so much? Their plans of endless sleepovers, an unlikely proposition at best, was now completely off the table. What was she going to do? If Monica hadn't been there, it would have gotten her. If she had any hope of stopping it, she needed Monica's help. No one else was going to believe her.

Defeated and looking at the floor, Clarissa said, "You're probably right. It was just a bad dream from too much candy."

Monica said, "Clarissa? You know that's not true."

Ignoring his daughter he said, "I'm glad you're seeing sense. Now, why don't you go downstairs and pick out a movie that's happy and lighthearted? You girls can fall asleep watching something like that."

"But, Papa, it wasn't a dream."

He roared, "Enough, Monica! Even your friend has admitted it."

"But...."

"But, get a tape, and get yourselves both settled in. I'm done talking about this."

Monica nodded. Dominic turned, and with heavy legs, he went down the creaking stairs. He didn't slam his door, but he wasn't quiet about it, either. The girls got up, grabbed a copy of *Aladdin* from downstairs, hit play, and crawled back into bed.

With the movie in the background, Monica whispered, "Why did you agree with my dad like that?"

"Come on, Monica, nothing I was going to say was going to convince him. You saw how angry he was getting. What if...what if they don't let us have any more sleepovers?"

Monica nodded softly, then said, "Was it going to...?"

She didn't finish. She couldn't. The fear tugged at the corners of Monica's eyes.

Clarissa shivered, "Probably. Monica, if you hadn't screamed...."

Neither girl needed to finish the sentence.

Monica said, "I think it's time to find some answers. Tomorrow we'll go to the library."

"I think that's a good idea. Your parents don't have anything planned, do they?"

"Nope."

Good, we will have the whole day, and I think Ted's going hunting, or something, with a friend up in the mountains. So, if we need to check out books, we can bring them back to my place. Because we don't want your dad seeing us reading books after tonight."

"Why not?"

"Monica, didn't you see how scared he was when I mentioned the devil? That really freaked him out. Everyone in town is curious about what happened to me during those three days. Two people are dead and both their bodies decayed really fast. People stare at me for a reason. They're scared. So I think we better not tell them what we're going to the library to do. Or else it might scare even more people."

Monica nodded. "Yeah, you're right. Tomorrow we'll try to find some answers."

The girls lay in bed and watched the movie. Neither slept. When it ended, Monica got up rewound it, and started it again. Before the movie finished a second time, the sun peeked over the horizon, and both girls were deep asleep.

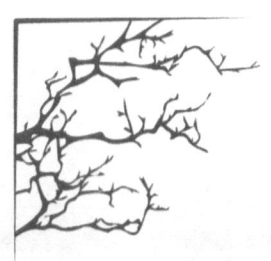

Chapter 11

An Investigation into the Nature of Evil

Three days you have,
no less, no more,
Once it bears witness
Though it's dark door

Three days to pray,
For the end to come swift,
Before your life,
Slips through your fingertips.

It comes in sevens,
Not in threes,
But if you look closer,
You'll see the woods from trees.

For once marked,
The clock ticks on
And in twenty-four nights,
You'll
Be
Forever
Gone.

"It's magic, Clarissa. There has to be some way to fight back. All we have to do is find out what it is. Every monster has a weakness," said Monica.

They stood in front of the library. It was a small, unremarkable building, but it was one of four in the South Philadelphia suburbs. Several trees with branches mostly bare and clinging to the last leaves of the season flanked the building on three sides. The single-story building glinted as the sun struck its many windows. Despite the calendar dipping into early November, the air was unusually warm, so neither girl wore anything more than a sweater and jeans. The smell of fall was fading. Out front, one of the librarians was already replacing Halloween decorations with turkeys, and Pilgrims, and Indians.

Clarissa, clutching her skateboard, said, "Yes, but not all monsters have a weakness. What about Michael Myers, or Freddy Kruger, or Jason?"

Monica said, "If they had a weakness, then there wouldn't be any sequels. They don't count. I mean actual monsters, not Hollywood. My dad says they would never kill off those monsters 'cause they are worth too much money."

"What do you mean by an actual monster?"

Monica shrugged, "A werewolf, or a vampire, or a ghost."

Clarissa rolled her eyes. "Mon, we don't know if any of those things are real. We only know that the thing from the meadow is real."

"Well, those are all monsters that people have told stories about forever. Some of them have to be real, right?"

Clarissa looked long at the library, of the people walking in and out. Would there be answers inside?

Clarissa said, "Maybe, but, we've never heard of a monster like this before."

"True." Monica puckered her lips, thinking. "But I bet once we find out what kind of monster it is, someone will have a way to fight it."

It was something. Clarissa wasn't as sure, though she was eager to try. What else could they do? They couldn't go to any adults for help, and James and Margie had vanished into their high school lives. All they had was each other. If Clarissa was by herself, she would struggle with the idea of library research, but Monica was a different story. Monica loved going to the library, and read all the time. Books spoke to Monica in the same way that Clarissa's skateboard spoke to her.

"You gonna be okay?" asked Monica. She smirked.

Clarissa barely heard her, she couldn't stop thinking about how the creature had looked at Monica. "Okay? What?"

"Well, it's just, you hate the library."

Clarissa turned and rolled her eyes. "I don't hate the library, Mon. I've gone in countless times."

"And rolled your eyes just like that every single time I made you come in with me." Monica tugged at one of her twin braids and pushed up her glasses, a big smile on her face.

Clarissa said, "Well, if I die, I won't have to worry about monsters anymore, do I?"

"Guess not!"

They both laughed.

"Besides," said Clarissa. "What choice do we have?" She frowned. "How do we search for something that we didn't even know existed?"

Monica shrugged. "I don't know. But I'm sure they've got plenty of adult books on monsters. It's too bad we can't go to the big one downtown. I'd bet they have lots more stuff there."

They walked in the door. The brown shag carpet crept up to the edges of the white bookshelves which wound around the rim of a central area. To the right was the reception desk and checkout. In the center, there were several tables where a few other people were reading. A man in a cowboy hat sat at one table reading a newspaper. There was a woman in a blue dress with thick eyeglasses, her face an inch from her book, reading with great concentration. A man with a cane sat with a book, turning pages faster than Clarissa thought anyone could read, but his eyes were focused and a strange sense of wonder played on his features.

"Where's the adult section?" asked Clarissa looking around.

"I...I've never been in the adult section," said Monica blushing.

"Isn't that where the books you like are?"

"No, that's in the section over there between adults and kids." She pointed to the back left corner. "That's where they keep all the art and music stuff. But the adult section is there." She pointed to the right. "And I've never been over there."

"Why not?"

"Well if I want an adult book, usually I ask my dad or mom to get it for me. They don't want me reading...certain things."

"What do you mean, 'certain things'?"

"I don't know...adult things, I guess."

"What, like a book on war, or something?"

"I don't know. My dad just said that little girls shouldn't read certain kinds of things, so he told me to stay out of the adult section without him."

"Well, your dad isn't here. And I don't think that we'll find what we're looking for in the kid's section."

Clarissa looked at the large number of shelves on the right side of the library. It was baffling how many books were in the world. She had never really thought about it before, because either Ted or her father had brought her books to read, or she mostly stuck to the school library.

Clarissa said, "How do we figure out which section has books on monsters?"

Monica said, "I guess we could try using the card catalog, but...," she hesitated, keeping her voice low. "I mean, the easiest way would be to ask the librarian, but do you think she will give us a book about monsters?"

Clarissa blinked. "That's what you're worried about? What the librarian would think?"

Clarissa glanced over at the woman. She had bright, red-rimmed, cat-eye glasses and a buttoned-up light blue blouse with ruffles. She dressed like she was sixty, but couldn't have been older than twenty-five. The woman caught Clarissa's eye and Clarissa looked away.

"Well, what if she tells my mom or dad about us looking up books on monsters?"

A voice from behind them said, "Can I help you girls find something?"

Monica almost jumped. Clarissa gave her a look, shook her head, turned, and said, "We need to find a book on monsters."

The librarian, whose face was stern, softened. She tapped her lip with her finger as she stared off into the distance thinking. "Monsters? Ah, well, you can find the Goosebumps series over in the kids section. There are a number of monsters in those stories. This way, I'll take you over there."

The woman turned to lead the way but Clarissa stopped her.

"No. Not fiction. We want to read about real monsters."

The woman turned and stared at both girls, a quizzical look on her face. Clarissa wondered if Monica was right, that they weren't allowed to go to the adult's section.

Then the woman smiled and said, "Oh, real monsters. Well, in that case, you'll be looking for the folklore section. That will be over in this direction. Follow me."

The librarian turned and walked over into the adult section and down several rows of books. Monica hesitated. Clarissa had to admit, she loved the smell of the library. All those books felt cozy, and it was true that stories had helped her get through some of the tough times in the last few months. She hoped that there was real magic. Maybe there were magic swords or elfstones out there like in the fantasy world of Shannara. If so, she hoped she could find one soon. She had a feeling it wouldn't be long until the creature returned for her. It might even come that very night.

"Come on, Mon." Clarissa grabbed her hand. The librarian stopped in front of a large bookcase. There were several dozen books on monsters in front of them.

"Now, let's see. What kinds of monsters are you looking for?"

Monica said, "Umm...what do you think, Clarissa?"

Clarissa said, "Well, we don't know." Thinking quickly, she finished, "We have to find a monster for a school research project, and we aren't sure which one to pick."

"A school research project? But it's November 1st. Your teacher assigned monsters after Halloween?"

Monica, catching on, said, "Well, we did a project on werewolves for Halloween. But we did such a good job with the last one, that our teacher asked if we could look into lesser-known monsters and do another class presentation...," She hesitated and then said, "...for extra credit."

The librarian clearly wasn't buying it.

"You girls know you can check out any book here you'd like, right? There are no age limits on books."

"There...aren't?" asked Monica.

"Of course not. It may be difficult for you to understand some of these books, however. And some stories are likely to be scary. But, well, when I was your age, I went through a monsters phase too. Do you know what kind of thing you're looking for?"

"Shadow monsters." Monica blurted out.

"Shadow monsters?" The woman looked thoughtful for a second. Then something flashed in her eyes. Clarissa knew what it was. Her heart sank. Had the woman seen the tabloid? Not to mention, Monica had just used her name.

For a long moment, the woman appraised her. It made Clarissa feel a little uncomfortable, but then the woman said, "Well, I'm not sure where to find shadow monsters. But you might start in some of these books up here." She pointed to a shelf with titles like, *An Encyclopedia of Monsters*, one that read *Ghosts and Demons*, and another title called, *Monsters of the Middle Ages*. But the one that caught Clarissa's eye was the one titled, *Lesser Known Monsters: A Complete Guide.*

"Would you like some help or would you rather browse, yourselves?"

Clarissa said, "We can look. So, we can take out any of these books?"

"Five books at a time, each. But you can look through as many as you want here. I will be over at my desk if you need anything." The librarian walked back to her desk. Clarissa watched her glance back several times as she did.

Turning back to the books, Monica grabbed several off of the highest shelf with the help of a nearby stool, and Clarissa grabbed several more.

"I guess it's good we got the whole day, if we want," said Monica.

Clarissa said, "I didn't think there would be so many books on monsters. It's gonna take us years to read through all these."

Monica laughed. "Well, we don't have to read all of them. Remember when Mrs. Rollins taught us how to look through the index and glossary in the back of the book? That's how you know if a book has something in it you want. Don't you remember that from class, Clarissa?"

Clarissa said, "Mon, you're the book nerd, not me."

Monica nodded, smiling. "True. But let's get started, I bet there are still at least twenty books that might be useful."

Each girl had several books stacked in her arms, and they made their way over to one of the tables and set to work.

2.   The day faded. A dozen books lay open, face-up, on the table in front of them. In one corner of the table lay a stack of books that both girls had decided weren't useful for their inquiry. They used the index and glossary in the back of a book to skim for information as their teacher had taught them. Clarissa buried her nose in one of the more promising books.

Monica, looking up at the clock, closed her book, and said, "That's it. I don't see anything even remotely like that creature we saw."

"Well, I think I found one," said Clarissa.

Monica perked up, "Why didn't you say something?"

"Well, I just started reading it a minute ago. So far, it's only sort of like the creature we encountered."

Here, in the light of day, it was easy to discuss the creature. So far, it had only appeared at night, and never around more than just the two of them. Even still, as Clarissa had read up on monsters and creatures all day, she felt fear sit next to her, a constant cold companion, invisible but ever-present. She couldn't help but wonder how many of the monsters she was reading about were real somewhere in the world. If one monster was real, it certainly seemed possible that others were as well. Would she be unfortunate enough to encounter others one day? That was, if she survived this one?

"What is it?"

Monica reached out to grab the book Clarissa held, but Clarissa drew it back, not wanting to lose her spot.

Clarissa said, "Well, we know it's not a physical creature like a vampire, or werewolf, or skinwalker, because it can dissolve into mist and make gateways."

Monica nodded. "Yeah, I think we can rule out cryptids too."

"Cryptids?"

"Oh, I just read that they're creatures like Bigfoot, or dragons, or the Loch Ness monster."

Clarissa nodded. "But we also know it's not a ghost, because ghosts are supposed to be stuck in one spot."

Monica shook her head. "No, I read in one of the books that some ghosts can haunt a person or an object. Like *Ghostbusters 2*, remember?"

"Oh yeah." Clarissa thought for a second, wondering if it could be a ghost. "But ghosts don't kill, right?"

"Well, Viggo did, so maybe?"

"Yeah, but he was like a sorcerer, and he was already powerful before he died. He wasn't a normal ghost."

Monica said, "Well, what if this thing that's following you isn't a normal ghost, either."

"Ghosts don't usually make people decay really fast, though, do they?"

Monica nodded, "That's true." She shifted in her chair and looked up at the clock again. "We better hurry, our time is almost up. My dad has a little Dios De Los Muertos ceremony to honor my grandparents after dinner, and I'm not allowed to miss it. Besides, I don't want my dad to find out what I've been doing all day."

It was on Clarissa's mind, too. She didn't want to anger Mr. Aguilar any further. In her mind, she could see the fear leaking from his eyes, could see how he trembled at the idea of a demon near his daughter. Clarissa knew that if she wasn't careful, he might try to keep Monica away from her permanently.

Clarissa said, "There's this creature called a Jinn. Some people claim they can sometimes appear as shadows on walls. They can also turn invisible or take different shapes. But that's all I've read so far.

"Can I read?"

Monica was a much faster reader. Part of the reason it was taking Clarissa so much longer to go through each book was that she kept needing to look things up in the dictionary. Monica used it too, but nowhere near as much.

Carefully, Clarissa handed the book over, making sure the marked page was still open at the right spot. It was a dusty tome, and some pages were torn and tattered. She couldn't help but wonder who had last read it.

Monica's eyes flicked over the pages for several minutes.

"Yeah, I don't know. It says that often there's some kind of bargain. Something sealed in blood? But you didn't make any kind of bargain, did you?"

"Blood?" A chill gripped Clarissa's heart.

"Yeah, it says here that you ritually cut your hand and squeeze the blood out as an offering to the Jinn. The Jinn will then appear to you and offer you a wish. It sounds like a Genie almost. But it's not like you offered it blood or anything."

Clarissa was silent. She hadn't quite gotten to that part yet. She had only just read about it appearing as a shadow on the wall when Monica had interrupted her.

Her palm ached with the memory of her time in the meadow. She saw herself squeezing the blood from her palm, then the ground drinking it up, and shuddered. The cut from the boy's jacket had long since healed, and there was the barest hint of a scar there in the center of her palm. The scar was almost crescent-shaped. Clarissa ran her thumb over it, thinking. She thought about how her mother-or was it Ted-had asked her why the boy would be wearing the jacket in the summer. The more she thought about it, the more strange it became.

Clarissa said, "Do you think...do you think I could have accidentally offered it blood?"

Monica looked over at her friend. "What do you mean?"

"I...," she paused, certain now that there was some connection between the blood she squeezed out of her hand and the creature. She looked up at Monica. "Don't you remember what I told you about my hand?"

Monica waited. She always did this when she knew Clarissa was going to keep talking.

"When I pushed that boy down the hill, something on his clothes snagged and cut my hand. Then...."

"Oh! I remember now. The ground drank the blood, right?" Monica shouted in excitement.

"Shhhh." Clarissa looked around the room to see if anyone was watching, but no one was. "Keep your voice down."

Monica looked around, and in a lower tone she said, "Sorry."

Clarissa continued, "But, I didn't make a deal or anything."

"Are you sure?" asked Monica.

"Well, yeah, I think I would remember...."

What did she remember? She remembered running from the creature, and then the nightmare when she woke up in the hospital. She had been in a coma for several days after they had found her, though the doctors still had no explanation as to why. So what had happened to her? Had she made a wish or a deal? There was one thing her heart desired above all else.

She thought of her father, thought of his smile, how he used to read and smoke his pipe on the porch, how she wished he could see her skate down Snake Hill and fly.

"You could have made a deal with it, Clarissa. Maybe you aren't allowed to remember that you made the deal or something. Maybe that's how it works?"

"Maybe. But Mon, if I did make a deal, why would it kill the detective? None of this makes any sense."

Monica nodded. "That's the thing that confuses me most. I don't understand what the boy and the detective have in common."

"Maybe he accidentally dripped blood in the meadow when he fell?" asked Clarissa.

Monica said, "But then what deal did he make?"

"I don't know. That's why I'm not sure this is a Jinn. What else does it say? Anything about making people age faster? What about the shroud?"

Monica skimmed for several moments, then said, "No, nothing like that."

Clarissa shook her head. "See, it doesn't fit."

"Wait. Here's another passage," said Monica, who traced her finger along the lines. "It says, Jinn can be good or bad. They can be followers of God or followers of Satan. The evil versions of Jinn are sometimes thought of as Demons. While they aren't necessarily the same things, Demons exist in several cultures and can appear in many forms. Demons are most known for possession or taking control of a host. Jinn are not known to behave the same way."

Monica looked up from the book. "It took control of you, right? You couldn't move? That's what the shroud does. You were totally frozen when it was reaching out for you."

Clarissa nodded. She hated thinking of it. Hated the dread she felt, the suffocating feeling of the shroud tightening around her and dimming her vision even as it fixed her gaze.

"It's not a perfect fit either, though. But it's the closest we've got," said Clarissa.

"For now." Monica stretched and stood up. "We can keep coming back and looking it up. But I also think maybe we should look up how to defend against an evil spirit."

"Why an evil spirit?" asked Clarissa.

"That's what both a Jinn and a Demon are. Didn't you see what the chapter name was when you were reading it?" asked Monica.

"No, I just followed the index to the page because it mentioned the word shadow monster."

"The name of the chapter is "Evil Spirits.""

Clarissa said, "So you think if we find something to defend against an evil spirit, then it might work for whatever this thing is, too?"

"Yeah, maybe. It's worth a shot, isn't it?"

Clarissa nodded as she stood up and began gathering books. "Yeah...," she sighed. "Yeah, we better find some way to defend ourselves, quick."

Grabbing several books up into her arms, Monica said, "You think it will come back right away?"

"I don't know. Maybe. But it was a few weeks between visits last time. But I don't know. I feel like it's not gonna wait."

"You think it will be back tonight?" Monica's voice trembled a little.

"I...I don't know."

With the fear standing between them, they stacked as many books in their arms as each could carry and began walking back toward the shelves. The librarian intercepted them.

"You girls should leave those books in the cart near the door. That way, I can put them back in the proper place. It's important that they are in the right order."

"Okay," said Monica, but it was clear that she felt uneasy. Clarissa felt the same. The librarian was helpful, and she had said that she had gone through a monsters phase, but that didn't mean either of them wanted her to know what they were reading. Especially with the way the librarian had been sneaking glances at them all afternoon. Clarissa was certain she knew who she was. She was surprised that the woman didn't come and ask about it like so many other people did.

They took several trips from their table back to the cart and then gathered their things. Monica her backpack with her sketchpad and notebooks, and Clarissa her skateboard.

Just as they walked by the librarian, Clarissa said, "Hold on, Mon, I got an idea."

Clarissa walked up to the librarian and said, "Excuse me, can you help me find a book on skateboards?"

"Of course," said the librarian.

3 The days were shorter now, and the darkness had claimed the sun minutes before. They walked into the cool November evening, the temperature already plummeting. Each girl shivered and crossed her arms as they walked, trying to stay warm under their sweaters, though for Clarissa it didn't help much with the skateboard in hand.

"Let's call it Demon," said Clarissa.

"What?"

"The creature. Let's call it Demon from now on."

"But I thought you said it didn't seem like that was the right answer? Wasn't the Jinn close too?"

"For now, let's call it Demon. If we figure out it's something else, we can change what we call it."

"Okay," said Monica, "Demon it is."

The air felt suddenly colder, and Clarissa couldn't ignore the wave of chills traveling up and down her spine. Somehow naming it seemed...dangerous, though she couldn't understand why. And what else were they supposed to do, call it 'the thing from the meadow'?

They walked several more blocks until they were almost home. Ted was sitting on the porch reading a book and smoking a cigarette. Clarissa always felt uncomfortable seeing Ted sit there, where her father used to sit. She didn't like it at all. Ted glanced at the girls as they approached. There was something on his face, some expression that worried Clarissa, but she couldn't quite figure out what it was. It made her feel nervous, as if she was walking into some kind of punishment or lecture.

"I'm gonna head in," said Monica.

"Goodnight. And thanks for helping me find that book on the Slalom." She said it loud enough for Ted to hear. She had held the book on Slalom firmly against the skateboard, but now made sure she held it in her hand so that Ted and her Mother could see it.

Clarissa watched Monica go and marched up toward the porch, past her mother's car. Ted said nothing. He just sat there in the dark, a circle of fire glowing in front of his face, smoke billowing down the porch like some dense fog. It didn't drift to the sky. It was heavier, like the feeling of dread building in her stomach. She was in trouble with her mom. She didn't know how she knew that, but she did. Ted didn't look thrilled either, but he said nothing. If he had been the one who was upset, he would have already started in on her.

As she walked through the door, she saw her mother sitting on the couch. The TV wasn't on. Her face was pale. Dark circles ringed her eyes. Her makeup was half done, she had on mascara but nothing else. It made her look more gaunt, almost ancient, as if she had aged a decade in a day.

She looked up and saw Clarissa, and said, "Where were you all day?"

"At the library, with Monica."

She narrowed her eyes. "Do I need to call down to the library and ask if you were actually there?"

Clarissa felt slapped. "What? Why would I lie about being at the library?"

Her mother stood and the anger on her face surged outward. Clarissa could feel the heat coming off of her as she approached.

"Because, young lady, when have you ever voluntarily spent time at the library? If you told me you were at the skate park, I would have believed you."

Remembering the book in her hand she said, "But look, Mom, I even checked out a book. We were at the library, I swear."

Her mother, standing tall now, fierce in her gaze, said, "Even so, that doesn't matter, does it? Because you know the rules."

Clarissa sighed. "I'm not allowed out after dark. I know, but Mom, it's only six-thirty. It's not like it's after my bedtime." She tried to keep the whine out of her voice, but what was the point?

"I don't care. Have you forgotten that it was only a few months ago that you went missing? Didn't you think of how it might make me feel if you were out after dark without my permission? And then I get this call from Monica's mother...."

"What...what did she say?"

"She said that you scared the hell out of Monica last night. That you claimed to see some kind of monster in her room."

Clarissa said nothing. What could she say?

"You know you're not supposed to talk about what happened in the meadow."

"I wasn't!"

The lie flopped on the floor between them, a big, ugly thing that neither could acknowledge or deny.

Her mother eyed her but didn't say a word.

"Okay. Fine. I told Monica some of what happened, but not everything. She's my best friend, Mom, and I'm...I'm scared. It won't leave me alone." Her voice trembled. "I really did see something at Monica's."

Overcome by it all, Clarissa threw herself at her mother, and her mother opened her arms and welcomed her. It felt warm and soft in her mother's embrace, and she buried her head in her mother's chest.

"I'm sorry, Mom." Clarissa sniffled.

"Clarissa, sweetie. I know all this is hard but, don't you see what happened? You told Monica and now Mr. Aguilar is furious at you. He thinks you're a bad influence on Monica. It's only because Mrs. Aguilar talked to him that you're even allowed to spend time with her still. You have to promise not to talk about this stuff anymore."

Clarissa felt the tears rising, a heat behind them. "But it's hard, Mom. I'm scared and I don't know what to do."

Her mother's tone softened. "I know, sweetie. Just, come talk to me when you're scared."

Ted was there, standing just inside the doorway. He wasn't saying anything, just watching. Why did Clarissa feel like he was waiting for something? What did he want? This was between her and her mother, and he had nothing to do with it.

"You don't let me talk about it!"

There was a hurt on her mother's face, and involuntarily she stepped back away from Clarissa.

Her mother's reply was softer, timid, "We're trying to protect you. Don't you understand?"

"Who cares if people think I'm weird, Mom? They already do."

Ted said, "It's not just about that."

Both she and her mother looked at him as he stepped in through the door, their attention and passions diverted from each other and toward him.

Clarissa, her voice trembling from the flood of emotions, said, "Then what's it about, Ted?"

Ted looked at her mother, and something passed between them. Her mother scoffed. "I don't agree with any of this, Ted. You know how I feel about it."

Clarissa couldn't understand what was happening between them. She'd heard them argue several times now. She knew that it had something to do with her, but what were they dancing around? What was at the center of the conflict? What did it have to do with her telling people about what happened? It wasn't like she wanted to tell strangers, she just wanted to confide in her friend and her family. But there was some semblance of guilt there, for she had told Monica everything, which it was against both her mother's and Ted's wishes, but what else was she supposed to do?

It was Ted who changed the subject back to Mr. Aguilar. "You told him you were possessed by the Devil?"

Clarissa shook her head. "No. It wasn't like that...I...I...."

The words were jumbled, spooled in incomprehensible loops. There were so many things she had to say, so many thoughts she wanted to express. Even as each thought formed, those behind them knocked each one into obscurity.

Her mother turned to her and said, "What was it like, then?"

"I...I...."

She felt the shroud shrink down around her, the dread climb up inside of her and nest. The world grew dimmer until the entire house felt as if it were in the shadow of twilight. Her emotions took hold of her, and before she knew what she was doing, she ran up the steps to her room and slammed the door behind her.

Once inside her room, she threw down her skateboard and crawled under her covers. She wanted to cry, but there were no tears. How could she make them understand? She had tried to make Mr. Aguilar understand, but that had only made things worse. Only Monica believed her, and now Monica's father was threatening to keep them apart.

There was a gentle knock at the door.

She reached out of her blankets, grabbed a pillow, and put it over her head.

The door creaked open, and Clarissa kept her eyes shut tight and pulled the pillow harder down on her head, wiggling into the depths of the covers. She wanted to bury herself forever.

"Go away."

She heard nothing. Only the sound of her own breathing under her pillow. The silence stretched out. After several minutes of listening, she slowly lifted the pillow off of her head, nosing her way out of the covers, peering out with a single eye.

Her mother sat in the corner of her room, her head in her hands. She was motionless. But as Clarissa watched her closely, she could see her breathing, her chest heaving as she tried to hide her weeping.

It was Clarissa's fault. Everywhere she went, people were sad, or scared, or angry, or...dead. Maybe a monster was hunting her, but she was a monster too.

Clarissa crept out from her hiding place, walked over to her mother, and knelt in front of her. She put her head in her lap like she used to when she was a little girl. Clarissa looked up at her mother to see her staring down. All of the worry and fear shone out from her eyes. Clarissa looked away. She wished she could tell her mother everything, wished she would believe her, but intuitively she knew she wouldn't. Her mother had always been a skeptic, in everything from religion to the supernatural. Her father had been the imaginative one, sharing strange tales he had heard, and weaving many more.

Her mother gathered her in her arms, not the way she did normally these days, with Clarissa gaining on her in height. This was how her mother had held her when she was much younger, cradling her in her arms.

"Sweetie. What happened at Monica's?"

Clarissa said nothing. What was the point?

"Please, Clarissa. I'm your mother. I want to know what's going on with you."

"You didn't believe me when I told you before."

She looked up at her mother's face to find a frown. It deepened far beyond her face, and sunk down deep inside of her. For a moment, Clarissa could see a hollowness there, one not too distant from the look her father's eyes had in the months leading up to his death. Later, when she was older, she would know that expression well. She would see it in the faces of others who struggled to survive alongside her. Simple futility.

"I will believe you this time. I promise."

Those words shifted something in her. Her reluctance faded and Clarissa decided to tell her mother about Halloween night. She opened her mouth to speak, but nothing came out. Fear swelled in her stomach. It was the words themselves that she feared, as if their terrible configuration would unleash the creature she now called Demon. But she tried to push on those words, to force them into being. She could not. They were stuck inside of her.

"Sweetie?"

She tried again. No words came.

"Are you okay?"

She tried some other words, any words. Something had stolen her voice. Had the creature stolen it? Or was this some evil of her own?

"Oh, my baby. I'm so sorry."

Clarissa lay there, feeling the warmth, but not even tears came.

Finally, her mother let go of her and sat next to her on the bed.

"I need you to talk to me. I need you to tell me what happened."

Clarissa looked up at her mother's face. Mascara ran down the sides of her cheeks. She smelled faintly of fried foods from her morning shift.

Then something shifted again. The shame had subsided. A receding tide. But what would be left behind? Fear filled that void. Her mother faded away, and she saw a tide of corpses, filling her mind's eye. There were no seashells on this beach; instead, the waters had left behind a graveyard of gnawed bones. Something had been eating the bones. Soft teeth, soft bones, so that each chipped away at the other. She traced the shape of the bones and saw the ring. The ring wrapped the meadow. When she looked down she was in the center of it, and off in the distance, past the retreating waters, a blackness began taking shape in the clouds.

Her mother was shaking her, yelling, and the vision broke apart.

"Clarissa! What's wrong with you?! Oh god, what's wrong with my baby girl?!"

Clarissa blinked and said, "Mom?"

Her mother said, "Oh, thank god," and hugged her tight, then pulled back so Clarissa could see her face. "That's it. We're taking you to see someone. God dammit, I should never have listened to your stepfather."

Her mother held her for a long time. After a little while she got up, picked up a book, and read to Clarissa. She lay there listening passively, thinking of Demon and how it had looked at Monica, how it had noticed her. She didn't like that. It felt...ominous.

She thought of all of the books they had combed through. She didn't know if that was what it was, a demon. But she had to call it something. Though intuitively she knew that naming it would give it another dimension, expand it somehow. For in naming something, giving it a symbol gives it depth and meaning, and helps to create a sense of reality that might not have been there before. And once named, something grows into its parameters, reaching the edges of the concept until it's bursting. Though something like this, the thing she now called Demon, could not really be contained, giving it such a name was to name her opponent, to give it a charge. After all, it tormented her, and what is a Demon but an arbiter of torment.

4. Clarissa woke and looked around. Her mother lay on her back next to her, still partially propped up with a book on her chest. The soft light of the early morning illuminated each of her mothers features, and Clarissa

stared a while. It had been a very long time since she had seen her mother like that and she couldn't help but think of her father.

There was something about seeing her mother lay there that reminded her of the times when she was little. She ached for that lost age. In that other lifetime, she would sneak into her parents' rooms on the weekends, jump on their bed, and wake them. Sometimes they would have pancakes, and all go to the park together.

Now she lived life partly in the shroud, in a house haunted by loss and pain. She tried to think of the good memories here, but with each day, with each visit of Demon, those good things seemed to evaporate. Worse, she was certain that anytime now, Demon would come for her and that would be that. It was hard to wake up to that reality. Clarissa wondered how many people her age woke with something sinister pressed into their thoughts. How many people wondered if this day was their last? Was she unique? She wondered if she would live long enough to find the answer.

She didn't want to die. A chill swept through her, her skin tightened with gooseflesh. But she told herself that she had just survived another night. Maybe all she needed to do was sleep next to her mother? But then she had thought about Monica and she knew her mother often worked through the night, and she didn't like the idea of sharing a bed with Ted. No, she and Monica would have to find some means of protecting themselves. It was the only way.

She focused on her mother again. Hesitantly, she tested her voice. "Mom?"

Clarissa shook her mother gently.

Her mother roused, blinking. She sat up against Clarissa's bedpost and looked around, confused. Then recognition crossed her face. She could see the fear set in behind her mother's eyes. At least they shared that.

"Clarissa? How...how are you feeling this morning?"

Her mother rubbed her eyes.

"I'm...okay, Mom. I think I'll be okay. Don't you have to go to work?"

"Shit. What time is it?"

Her mother jumped up out of the bed, opened the door, and ran down the hall.

For a long time, Clarissa sat up in her bed thinking. It was Sunday, so she didn't have to be at school, and she had agreed to meet Monica again at the library. Would Monica's parents let her go to the library again? They needed to find a defense, something to deter the evil magic.

In truth, Clarissa's sense of hope was tinged with dread. If a grown woman, a police detective no less, could find no method to stop the monster, then what chance did they have? But then, what if the creature had just shown up one night and attacked? Maybe that's what happened? If that was true, did it mean that she had an actual chance to fight it off?

Clarissa put on some clothes and went downstairs. Her mother scrambled around the kitchen, brewing herself some coffee, and searching for something while muttering to herself. Her mother had a way of forgetting things.

She saw Clarissa and said, "Sweetie, have you seen my keys anywhere?"

"No, did you check the fridge?"

Her mother cracked a smile at that. She had once accidentally left the keys in the fridge and Clarissa found them there by accident.

"Guess I'd better." Her mother opened the fridge door and sure enough, they were there, next to the milk on the top shelf.

Clarissa laughed.

Her mother laughed. Then she came over to the kitchen table and gave Clarissa a hug.

She pulled back and said, "I don't want you down near those woods, okay? Not even to the skate park."

"What? Why not the skate park?"

"Just, stay close today, okay? Just for the next week or two. Please? For me?"

Her mother rarely offered reasons for her demands. All Clarissa could do was shrug and accept it...and well, there was no point in arguing. Her mother would never know what she was up to, anyway. She would be busy at work for the next twelve hours.

Her mother grabbed a box of cereal, a bowl, and some milk. She sat down at the table and began eating. Clarissa joined her.

"Where's Ted?"

"Oh, he went out of town with a friend this morning. They're headed to Atlantic City. He is throwing a friend a bachelor party because he's getting married."

"What's a bachelor party?"

Her mother sighed. "You're almost getting to that age, aren't you?

"What age?"

"Never mind. We'll talk about it when you're a little older. A bachelor party is a kind of saying goodbye to being single before you get married."

"Why?"

"I guess it's symbolic, a ritual of sorts. I never really understood it."

"Did Dad have one?"

"No, your father and I eloped."

Puzzled, Clarissa asked, "What does that mean?"

"It means that we went to Paris together, and spent a summer there when we were in college. At the end of the summer we got married, and we didn't tell anyone what we were doing. We just sort of did it."

"You didn't tell anyone? Not even Grandma? Weren't they upset they couldn't be at your wedding?"

"It's complicated. Your grandparents didn't like your father very much. It's hard to explain. And anyway, I have to get going or I'll be late."

"Okay. Thanks for staying with me last night, Mom. You're the best Mom, ever."

Her mother smiled. "Thank you, sweetie. We'll talk about all this later, okay?"

"Alright, Mom."

Her heart ached to see her mother go. She wished things could be normal, that she and her mother could go to the park together or bake cookies like they used to do. She even missed running errands with her mother.

"Be good, sweetie. There are leftovers in the fridge for dinner, and lunch meat and cheese for lunch. Please don't go far."

"Okay, I won't."

It was a lie. She didn't ask about the library because it was across town and probably outside the bounds of where her mother had meant. If her mother asked her later why she had gone to the library, she would just plead innocence.

Clarissa spent the morning watching cartoons. There wasn't much on Sunday mornings, all of her favorites were on Saturdays. Lots of churches took over the channels on Sundays, and it was so boring. She watched anyway. After she ate a sandwich for lunch, she called Monica. She would be back from church by now. Monica answered and agreed to meet her at the library in an hour.

It was four hours later that they had a breakthrough.

5. "I think I found something," said Monica.

Monica held a large, green, leather-bound book in her hand. The leather was cracked and weathered, and there were water stains on some of the pages. It was titled, *Myth, Monsters, and Magic: A Guide.*

Excited, Clarissa stood and walked over to her friend. "What is it?"

Monica, all grins, said, "I think it's a way of defending ourselves. We can't attack it or anything, but look here."

Monica pointed her finger at the sentences in the middle of the page. The letters were tiny despite the book's large size, but Clarissa's eyes traced the words.

"There are many kinds of evil spirits in the world, and certainly more varieties than are listed in this chapter, but there is a common defense that is said to work against all such malevolent beings. According to some hermetic records, a circle of protection could act as a deterrent. The circle could be made of a variety of ritualistic symbols, but for the most part, a simple circle of salt with three key symbols inside of it would suffice. The reason often cited is that Salt, in the hermetic and later alchemical traditions of Europe and the Middle East, was considered a grounding agent. It was said to be symbolic of the physical world of man. Thus, it was thought that evil spirits could not cross a line that represented the very thing of which they could never truly be a part."

Clarissa said, "Do you think this is real? Like it will really work?"

Monica, a smile still on her face, said, "Yes, I think it will. He says how he himself tested it against an evil spirit and it couldn't cross the line. But he said it has to be a circle around whatever person or place you want to protect, and if the circle is broken for any reason it won't work. He said that some people tried to protect whole houses, but the problem was, even a little wind could ruin the circle, so he recommends creating one in an indoor space where rain or wind wouldn't mess it up."

Clarissa felt hope surge through her. "Do you think that we could put a circle around our beds? Would that work?"

Monica nodded. "Yeah, I read the rest of the chapter, and he just gives examples of the ways it worked. He said when he encountered a boy who had visits from an actual demon, the circle of salt around the boy's bed kept it from getting to him. It could still come in the middle of the night, but it couldn't get past the circle."

Excited, Clarissa said, "Does it have to be a special kind of salt or something?"

She kept thinking that this was too good to be true. She knew there was a whole large bag of salt in the cupboard for cooking. But it couldn't be that easy could it?

"At the end of the chapter, he said that we could do it with regular old table salt."

"That's it?" asked Clarissa. "All we need to do is use the salt we have in our kitchens to protect ourselves?"

Monica nodded, "As long as the circle isn't broken somehow, it's supposed to protect you."

Clarissa said, "Maybe it does make sense."

"What do you mean?"

"Well, remember what was around the whole edge of that meadow?"

"A circle of bones!" Monica shouted and quickly covered her mouth.

Clarissa looked around and saw several sets of eyes staring at them. The librarian among them.

"Sorry! We're reading books on monsters." Monica said, audible enough for the watchers to hear. Several of them turned back to their own books or newspapers quickly.

"Yeah, it lives in a magic circle, so maybe...."

Monica finished for her, her voice lowered to a rough whisper, "Maybe a circle can keep it out."

"Should we keep looking for another answer?" asked Clarissa.

Monica shook her head, "This is the only chapter on defending yourself against evil spirits I could find, and if this works, then we won't have to worry."

"Well, it could still come and scare us right?"

"Right, but it couldn't hurt us. Clarissa nodded, and inside she felt lighter than she had since Demon had made an appearance almost a month ago. Something told her that was going to work. It had to.

The girls packed up their things shortly after and left the library with hope in their hearts.

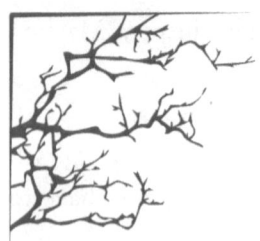

Chapter 12

A Herald in the Wind Calling Forth the Shadow

Inside the circle of salt and will,
Past the light at the shadow's edge,
You won't find peace and rest until,
You give your total and solemn pledge.

The age of magic is back at hand,
As Archons watch from up on high,
They want to see what power you'll command,
They want to know if you'll see past the lie

A weapon forged is what you need,
A ritual to make things grow,
The contract's terms made you bleed,
But with it comes a power bestowed

The first science is back, reborn
You must learn to know it well,
The road is long and full of scorn,
Until you weave that final spell.

I mpressed by her own stealth with sneaking in and out of the pantry, Clarissa closed her bedroom door behind her and opened the bag of table salt. With her right hand, she reached in and scooped out salt with a measuring cup. She descended to the floor and made a circle around her bed as the library book instructed. Then she drew the three ancient symbols, placing each inside the ring. The book had said that it did not matter where the symbols were, so long as they were inside the circle and faced toward the heavens. She cast the symbols, made from torn notebook paper and etched in crayon, under her bed. Each contained a wish, but each wish was the same as the others. Refuge. For what greater wish is there on heaven and earth when we are besieged by something we cannot control or avoid?

Clarissa did not yet understand the word talisman, but in the coming days, when many fell at the hands of her monster, she would revive that ancient craft. Or rather, she would understand later, that when she had freed Demon from his prison of bones, she had awoken other forces as well. The seeds within her blood awakened things in distant lands that had long slumbered, waiting out the age of reason. For Clarissa, there were magics to be found, and a blade to forge, but all of that was ahead of her, a yet undiscovered country. Now, in her early years, she double-checked her circle of salt and made extra sure all the symbols were facing up.

Clarissa climbed back into bed, pulling the covers up to her chin, watching, waiting. There was hope in her heart. Inside the circle and under her covers, the shroud felt lesser in some indefinable way. It was still there, but it felt distant, more subtle. Despite that, it was difficult to keep the skepticism gifted to her from her mother at bay. It was a nagging, tugging idea that the magic protection circle wouldn't work, that it was too simple for something so diligent as the creature that had crept into her life. Beyond her mother's embedded worldview, she simply wasn't that lucky. She often felt that the forces of heaven and hell had conspired against her to ensure her misery. And likely, it would again tonight.

Still, she had to try. For what else could she do? She shifted in her bed, uncomfortable, some of the salt had clung to her clothes and she could feel the grit grinding against her as she lay in her pajamas, waiting for Demon to arrive. Inside her was the barest hint of a wish that it would take her this night. There was a temptation to rise from her bed, break the circle, and be done with it. At least then there would be peace. But then, it was hard for Clarissa to be certain of an afterlife. Her mother had refused to say that her father was in a better place, had insisted that his essence had scattered to the wind, like so much sand on a beach or the salt fragments digging into her skin.

Monica had said otherwise. She claimed that since Clarissa's father was a good man, he was in heaven, waiting for their reunion and reliving the best moments of his life. Clarissa hadn't questioned her friend, but privately had wondered why such a benevolent deity would take her father from her. Worse, now she wondered why such a god would allow a creature like Demon to exist. Even if her father was in heaven, Monica's description worried her. For how many moments in Clarissa's brief span had possessed joy? Before her father's passing, her memories were foggy and limited. After his passing, there had been so much discomfort and pain. There were so few moments of joy for her to relive. She hoped that would change and realized then that she really did want to survive the night. How else could she know what happiness was possible?

Clarissa would fight back as best as she could. It was what her father would have wanted. He wanted her to fly. Thinking of him, she pulled her skateboard close, hugging it as some children might hug a stuffed animal.

The wind fell silent. The room, awash in stillness, hummed in her ears. She swung her feet over the edge of the bed, careful to stay inside the circle of salt, and crept around, checking every inch a second time. As she and Monica had walked home, they had recounted the exact wording. Monica had wisely scribbled it down in her notebook so they could review the instructions several times. Nothing must break the circle. The book had recommended making a line of salt as wide as a human hand, and to do it somewhere indoors. It warned that some spirits could conjure weather out in the wilds, but so long as windows and doors were shut tight, they were safe. The book had even recommended placing a towel under a door and hanging extra curtains or blankets on the windows to keep any possible airflow from desecrating the circle.

With Clarissa's check complete, she crawled back to bed. Though she was still skeptical, Clarissa reminded herself that it was a circle she had stepped into and offered her blood in the meadow. She could almost see the bones if she closed her eyes, see the strangeness of that place, where color, and sound, and light, and time were but shades of themselves. If a circle of salt kept it out, then what did a circle of bones do? She would have to ask Monica what she thought...if she survived the night.

She longed for the closeness of her friend, or perhaps even her mother. But it was of no use. Tonight, her mother worked the graveyard shift, and tomorrow she and Monica had school. There was no refuge beyond the hope of salt. If it came tonight and the circle did not work, she would not need to worry about Mrs. Emerson, or Daryl, or Rob, or any of the others who would be full of questions come sunrise.

She pulled her blankets up to her chin, casting a glance into each corner. Clarissa would not cover her eyes. Like a sore in your mouth that you cannot stop poking with your tongue, she had to look, had to know if it had come for her.

Her mother had said nothing about Mrs. Emerson. Ted had surprised Clarissa when a neighbor had come to the door that afternoon to tell of her and Monica's involvement. It was Anna Smith, the next-door neighbor of Mrs. Everson, who shared a version of what had happened. When she finished making her accusations, Ted had asked his own questions. Listening from down the hall and out of sight, Clarissa discovered that the woman hadn't had her heart attack until well after Clarissa and Monica had fled the scene. It had been the two large boys who had pushed the older woman and tormented her that caused the heart attack. When Ted pointed this out to Anna Smith, she had argued that Clarissa had started it. Pushing back, Ted had told the woman that the two girls were simply trick-or-treating and that, "The old bat probably got what was coming to her, anyway."

Clarissa, who had been peeking from around the corner, saw the look of shock and surprise flash on the woman's face. As their conversation grew more heated, Ted exchanged a few rude words with her before slamming the door. He silenced Anna's argument, but not her gossip.

Clarissa loved Ted for it. Clarissa didn't know quite what to think of her stepdad, but in that moment, when Ted had defended her, she had felt the first swell of pride for him. Later, she would discover that Ted had a reason to hate Mrs. Everson, for her rumor-mongering had cost him one of his best jobs.

The floor in her room creaked and Clarissa sat bolt upright, letting all other thoughts drop away. She sat in the dim illumination of the string lights, totally still, waiting, watching for any sign of Demon. The floor creaked again, but it was a familiar noise, the sounds of the house settling. With that, Clarissa settled herself, though her mind continued to dance a frenzy.

She wondered after her friend. Had Monica snuck in salt as she had? Would she make sure the ring remained unbroken? Then she thought better of it. If there was anyone as meticulous in her preparations and planning, it was Monica. Monica had already won the science fair, and once a spelling bee. She was ever the overachiever, ever the one to whom Clarissa always trailed behind in skills of the mind. Still, she could not help thinking about how the creature had looked at Monica on Halloween night. The thought unsettled her, and her stomach churned with rotten butterflies.

Clarissa lay, in an ocean of emotion and thought, letting the waves lift her up and down. The red glowing light of the digital alarm clock on her desk blinked in minutes. She traversed a sea of anxiety and then hope, back and forth. She kept her eyes open as long as she could, but then the minutes on the clock jumped by tens every time she blinked. Her last thought before sleep claimed her was that she should check the salt circle one last time.

2   Clarissa woke to the howling of the wind, whistling through the cracks in her old window. Nearby, shutters, and branches, and trash cans thrashed about in the high wind outside. The moment she opened her eyes to the dimly illuminated ceiling, she knew Demon was there. She could feel its presence, a kind of malevolent pressure against her mind. Swallowing the lump in her throat, she lay still on her back, afraid to move, afraid to look. She felt the greed of its gaze. Her flesh crawled. Her eyes watered.

She tested her body to see if the shroud had restricted her like before. She was free to move. She gathered her courage and her will, closed her eyes, and lifted her body, hoping against hope that she was wrong, that her monster had passed her over that night, and would forevermore.

If it was there and the circle did not work, it would claim her. Some part of her knew that it would not take her in her sleep, that it needed her and the others it had claimed, to be awake. It wanted its victims to know what was coming. Clarissa tried to open her eyelids but could not. She trembled, knowing that if she saw it, she would scream...if it let her. The cold of the room wrapped her up, even as she drew the blankets around her. She wanted to draw the covers over her head and hide.

She took a deep breath, and then, gathering her courage, opened her eyes.

There it was. Looming just outside the circle. Its red eyes and shifting form, bobbing back and forth, left and right. It circled around and even pushed up against the wall at the head of Clarissa's bed, probing for weakness. But Clarissa had moved the bed a few inches from the wall. She had waited for Ted's nightly dishwashing routine so he wouldn't notice. She knew he would notice in the coming days, but for now, the circle remained unbroken.

It popped in and out of form, bursting like smoke and then reassembling itself in rapid succession in a different spot around the bed. Each time it pressed up against the circle, it stopped short, as if pushing against invisible glass. She could feel its anger, a heat that pushed through the salt barrier. For though it could not move past her protection, there was no place its hate could not reach.

A smile escaped her lips. She didn't want to tempt fate by taunting it, but she could not contain the hope welling up inside her. It worked. They had a way to protect themselves from Demon. Triumph filled her heart as she watched it continue to struggle to break through the protection circle.

Clarissa thought that if there was a way to protect themselves, then maybe there was a way to stop it, or even kill it. There was some reason for the circle of bones, and tomorrow, when she shared her victory with her best friend, they would begin their investigation afresh, with the knowledge that there was some magic in the world for them to harness. For what was this circle of protection but a kind of magic?

Doubt cast its shadow, its own shape in the dark. What if it was faking? What if it was toying with her? Clarissa had to be sure. As terrified as she was to tempt the creature to action, she had to know the strength of the circle. She stood on her bed, defiant, staring down Demon. The creature stopped assaulting the circle, shifted to its familiar demonic face hovering at eye level and stared at her. Its red eyes glowed in the writhing face of shadow and smoke.

"You can't hurt me now, can you? The salt works, doesn't it?"

It said nothing, did nothing. She wondered if it could speak, if it was intelligent, or if it was like some rampaging beast going only where its appetite directed. It would only take a few years for Clarissa to realize the bright intelligence behind those red coals and the depths of Demon's manipulation.

"Well? What are you waiting for? Come get me!" Her voice trembled a little. She tried to sound confident and unafraid, but staring at the creature she felt terror shaking her core. All she could do was keep pushing it away.

It only stared at her.

"What's wrong? Not strong enough to get through a little salt?" she paused, trying to think of something to say to provoke it, much as she didn't want to. "You coward. You can't even get to a little girl, can you?"

Nothing. It didn't move, it just sat still, watching her, a predator waiting for its prey to expose its throat so it could clamp down and end the chase.

"I dare you."

Still nothing.

"I double-dog dare you." She felt a little foolish saying that to Demon, but she wasn't sure what else to do to test the strength of the circle.

Then all at once, she knew what she had to do to provoke it, knew what it wouldn't be able to resist. She swallowed hard, standing there on top of her bed, not breaking eye contact with the thing from the meadow. She took another deep breath, gathered her will and courage, and took a step off of the bed.

Immediately, it moved to the spot opposite her, just outside the circle. Its form shifted and flowed in and out of nothing, as if it had tendrils lingering somewhere beyond the visible world.

Clarissa couldn't help but wonder what would happen if she put her arm outside the circle while her feet remained inside it. She thought it might break the spell of protection, so she had to be careful. She put one foot in front of the other, an inch at a time. As she crept closer the creature spread its form wider, its shadowy tendrils prepared to grab her and scoop her up in a deadly hug. Then, at last, her toes touched the very outer edge of the salt. She was careful not to damage the circle, and then she looked up at the creature.

Its eyes stopped bobbing. Its form stopped shifting. All that stood before her was something sharp and black and covered in spikes and claws. Its form grew in size, but its face stayed level with her own. She thought that she saw it sprout what looked like wings, but she dared not look away from the eyes. Clarissa trembled and feared losing her balance, but stood fast.

Drawing on her last bit of courage, she tempted the creature again.

She whispered, "Come and get me, you coward."

All at once it moved, the black tendrils forming into arms and claws, the legs drawing up into a more recognizable form, but the head stayed at the same level. It struck.

The breath scared out of her, Clarssa fell backward. Even as she fell, all of her fear welled up in her as she felt the barest hint of the salt scrape against her toe. The shroud descended around her and she wanted to scream, but she found that fright had stolen all of her volume. She struggled and found that though the shroud had darkened the room, it did not restrict her.

She looked up and there the creature stood, exactly where it had been. Swallowing the lump in her throat another time, she looked down and saw that a thin thread of the line of salt remained. Her foot had scraped it, but there was still about a half of an inch of salt at the border. The circle was not broken.

Quickly, she slid back into bed and under the covers. Still, it did not move, but it took a familiar shape. Demon was now as it had been on that first night, when the dark mist coalesced and she had seen it for the first time, standing in the center of the meadow and moving toward her.

But it didn't pass the circle's edge. She was safe. It had tried to trick her into breaking the circle and failed.

Still, this was no peace, only a temporary ceasefire between hostilities. She knew that if she stepped outside the circle, or if the circle was broken, it would claim her in an instant. Clarissa lay back down and shivered. She didn't know what to do. She thought that she was safe, but how could she sleep while knowing that it was there? Was it waiting for her to fall asleep so that it could somehow sneak past the salt? Could it break the circle itself, somehow? But if it could, why hadn't it done it already? With each passing moment her sense of safety grew.

For the next several hours, she fought to stay awake, afraid of what might happen if sleep claimed her. It never moved, never wavered, it only stared with its red eyes, watching her all the way from the edge of the misshapen circle of salt. And Clarissa stared back as the night stretched long. Eventually unable to help it, she closed her eyes.

She woke with the first rays of sunshine peeking into her room. Demon was gone. She laid back down, feeling safe for the first time since she had entered those woods in pursuit of the thief, all those months ago. She didn't rouse until her mother, fresh off the graveyard shift, came to wake her up for school.

3   Monica didn't come to school the next morning. In the dark corners of Clarissa's imagination, a singular moment played on repeat. That moment on Halloween night, when she, Clarissa, had been pinned down by the shroud, and Demon's claws crept up her bed to take her life. Monica had screamed. She relived that scream over and over because she had to. Had it seen Monica? Would it go after her? Or was it just looking over in surprise as any human, animal, or monster would? She couldn't remember.

Monica's desk, the one on her left, sat empty. It felt like someone had punched Clarissa in the chest; her heart ached. Several times, Clarissa reached up and touched her heart almost unknowingly as she stared at her best friend's desk. Where was she? Hadn't she tried the salt? It had worked for her, but had Demon, angry from his failure to get to Clarissa, turned its attention to Monica? Was her friend nothing but a decayed corpse? Would she return home to find her friend carted out in a body bag, just like her father? She could almost see it, a pair of men pulling a cart out with a black bag on top. The bag much smaller than her father's, because it was Monica-sized and Monica was so small, even for her own age.

When people asked Monica why she was so small, she would say, "It's 'cause I was born early. I just couldn't wait to get out into the world." Clarissa had heard Monica's mother repeat that catechism many times. Along with, "God always has a plan, Clarissa," and, "Faith is the most important weapon against the bad things in life." But what faith, Clarissa wondered, would empty a body bag?

Should Clarissa have faith now? Faith that her friend was alright? She didn't think that was what Monica's mother had meant, but...she thought back to that night again, trying hard to recall Demon's reaction to Monica's scream. Was it after Monica now?

Clarissa couldn't help but wonder after her encounter the night before. The creature had stopped just beyond the salt. It stared at her like a dog waiting behind a fence, ready to pounce if you crossed into its territory. Was it an intelligent creature, or was it more like a hungry animal? Because, if it was more like the second, then maybe Monica wasn't in danger at all. Did she have to have faith in that?

"Psst."

Clarissa looked up. Veronica Marsh, the snooty, rich, blond girl who always wore a dress, was tugging on the sleeve of Clarissa's sweater.

Clarissa pulled away, pretending to focus on the spelling assignment that they were supposed to be working on. She glanced up and saw that Mrs. Rollins still sat at her desk grading papers. Her teacher turned a page, eyes focused on reading someone's answers. Clarissa looked down at her own paper again, and realized that she hadn't filled in a single one.

"Psst." Veronica tugged again.

Clarissa looked up and, recognizing that ignoring her would not work this time, she whispered back.

"What?"

"Where's your bestie? Is she in the hospital like Mrs. Everson?"

Clarissa stared daggers, but it only summoned a wicked grin on Veronica's face. Clarissa wanted to pull out all of her perfect blond hair. She and her followers were always prancing around the school, acting like they were better than everyone else because Veronica lived in the biggest house in the neighborhood.

Veronica glanced up at Mrs. Rollins and made sure that she was clear to lean in close. "What really happened on Halloween? Did you curse her? Did the monster from the woods come after Mrs. Everson, too?"

Emily Young, Veronica's best friend who always did her best to match Veronica's style, leaned in and whispered, "I bet Monica found out about the curse, and so you cursed her, too."

Both girls giggled. Clarissa almost wished she could find a way to send Demon after them, if only to scare them, so they would leave her alone.

Clarissa couldn't believe the words that came out of her mouth next. When she thought back, she would wonder if she was just scared for Monica or if she had just had enough of the constant taunts about the second-worst thing that had happened to her in her life.

In a horse whisper, Clarissa said, "Listen, you little bitch, listen real good. If you aren't careful, that monster will come after you. He doesn't like people who mess with me, not ever. You notice the people who have ended up dead? The boy who stole my skateboard, and the cop who was questioning me?"

Both girls' expressions changed. "What about Mrs. Everson? We heard she was being a bitch to you."

Clarissa realized that she had fallen into their trap, and more anger welled up in her chest. This was what they wanted. They had tricked her and now, no matter what she said, everyone was going to think that she was a murderer, that it wasn't a monster who had done the killing. Worse, she wondered if she might get arrested for what had happened to Mrs. Everson. Wondered if, after everything that had happened, they would throw her in jail and then there would be no circle to protect her.

She tried to think quickly to figure out some way to answer so she wouldn't get the blame for that, too. But fate intervened, though whether for the better or the worse, she would learn soon enough.

"Come on," said Veronica, still whispering. "Tell us what really happened."

The teacher was standing over top of them and her voice boomed, "Girls, are you focusing on your assignment?"

Veronica said, "I'm trying, Mrs. Rollins, but Clarissa is threatening me. She said she's going to send a monster after me like she did with all the others. She told me that after Mrs. Everson, she cursed Monica."

A sea of mutters filled the room, waves lapping up every word with a deepening fascination.

"Liar!" shouted Clarissa with a force that surprised even her. "You lying bitch."

Gasps rose from all corners of the room at the word Clarissa used in front of a teacher. In the recess yard, all of them had experimented with bad words, but always when an adult was out of sight.

The teacher cleared her throat, raised her hand, and then said, "1,2,3, eyes on me."

The students, from months of practice, all turned their attention to the teacher and said, "One, two, eyes on you." But there was a note of disappointment in it, a whining moan in the synchronized sound.

Mrs. Rollins said, "First of all, Monica is just fine. The reason she's late today is because she had a dentist appointment. She will join us later in the day, children."

She looked around the room to make sure all eyes were still focused on her. Despite their initial disappointment, she had their attention now. Every person in that room wanted to hear what she had to say because here was someone who possessed authority, and to all the children, this was next door to truth.

So Mrs. Rollins need not bother to check for their attention again, and the moment she realized that, she went on.

"There are many rumors flying around about the events surrounding what happened to Clarissa last summer. Now, children, when we have a question, what do we do to find an answer?"

A girl named Julie with a bowl-cut hair style raised her hand and was called on. She said, "Investigate."

Mrs. Rollins nodded. "That's right, and how do we investigate?"

Veronica, now obviously trying to score some points with the teacher so that she wouldn't get into trouble, said, "We go to the library to find facts."

Mrs. Rollins stepped back from her position standing over Clarissa and Veronica and made her way back to the front and center of the room as she spoke. "Yes, excellent Veronica. And it's quite ironic that you, of all people, should have that answer."

Veronica, looking confused, hesitated a moment, looking around at her supporters for answers, but found none. She said, "Why...why is that, Mrs. Rollins?

"Because, when we are looking for facts, what is it important that we do not do?"

Andy McGuire, the tall kid with a mop of dusty brown hair, raised his hand and was called on. He said, "We don't make assumptions about the facts. But we keep an open mind."

Veronica still looked confused. Mrs. Rollins didn't skip a beat. "It is a rather large assumption that a nine-year-old girl has some kind of power to control a monster. This is not a storybook. We investigate the world through science and reason. And then, only when we have closed off all the avenues of truth, will we allow for supernatural deductions."

She paused again for effect. "Further, it's a very large assumption that Clarissa, who has barely spoken a word all year, and who has never been willing to bring up the events that surrounded her disappearance, would have threatened to sick some monster on you."

She took a breath, and then said, "Now, please return to your assignments. The next person who interrupts our work time will have detention."

The entire class sat stunned. Clarissa couldn't believe that she would not get in trouble. Nor could she believe that Mrs. Rollins had stood up for her. Most of the year, so far, her teacher had become annoyed with the constant interruptions that other students asking her questions had caused. Clarissa realized, for the first time, that maybe an adult was on her side. Maybe Mrs. Rollins could help her somehow? Maybe she could tell her the truth? Mrs. Rollins was all about science, but then, Clarisssa had tested a hypothesis with salt last night, hadn't she? Yes, maybe she had an ally.

Unfortunately, Clarissa would never truly get the chance to find out.

4.

Clarissa picked at her fluffernutter sandwich, alone at the cafeteria table. Normally, the combination of peanut butter and marshmallow fluff was her favorite thing the school lunch offered, but today she wasn't sure if she could eat. Veronica may not have understood what had happened, but she knew that the teacher had made her look like a fool, and she'd be ready to take it out on Clarissa. At least she knew that Monica was safe now. Clarissa wondered how long it would be until she returned from the dentist. She couldn't wait to tell her about the circle and how Demon reacted.

Several of her classmates had already come up to her asking her questions about Halloween night, but left disappointed. Angry, Veronica had threatened her and had followed her to her seat, demanding information, but after a few minutes of Clarissa completely ignoring her, she gave up. The other teachers on lunch duty were watching and there was little Veronica could do. Besides, a dozen students had tried for two months now to get something out of Clarissa, and she had told them nothing.

Finally, when lunch was halfway through recess, Monica sat down next to Clarissa at the cafeteria table.

"Hi!"

Clarissa immediately hugged her friend. "Jesus, Monica, do you know how badly you scared me?"

"Language!"

Clarissa smiled, "That's not a bad word."

"It's taking the Lord's name in vain, and my Dad said it's as bad as saying a curse word."

"Whatever, I'm just glad you're here and you're okay."

Monica pulled out her Sailor Moon lunchbox and opened it. "Sorry, I didn't know about the dentist this morning."

"It doesn't matter. I have something to tell you."

Clarissa could see Veronica and her friends all staring at her.

Monica, her face stern, said with a hint of trepidation, "Good news or bad?"

"Good," Clarissa whispered. "Really good." She leaned in closer, "It worked."

Veronica stood up and walked over with two of her friends, Emily and Amber. Amber was a redhead like Clarissa, but with a face so crowded with freckles that her skin looked spotted.

"So what are you two talking about?" asked Veronica, with her hands on her hips, looming over the both of them.

"Nothing," said Clarissa.

"None of your business," said Monica.

Veronica said, "I think it is. I think it's everyone's business. I think-"

But she never finished. Just then, Daryl and Rob entered the cafeteria and everyone fell silent. Both of them had big grins on their faces and knew that all eyes were on them.

Veronica got up quickly and walked over to the pair. Clarissa knew that they would almost certainly spin a tale where they were the heroes. A crowd gathered around them, and based on their wild gestures, they had already begun their tale.

"Now's our chance," said Clarissa. "Come on."

"Where are we going?" asked Monica, quickly shoving food back into her lunchbox.

"To talk in the recess yard while everyone's distracted."

Monica smiled, "Great idea."

Clarissa grabbed her tray, and as quickly and quietly as she could, dumped her food in the trash. She couldn't eat it, anyway. Her stomach was all tied up in knots of excitement.

The girls found the furthest corner they could on the playground, one where they could see anyone coming from a long way away. But no one was outside yet, and even when they did venture out, most would be a part of the Daryl and Rob fan club, hanging onto their every word as they told the story again and again of how they had almost killed an old lady. Clarissa was grateful for the distraction. Those two would talk about their adventure for days and keep all of the attention away from her. Once it dried up, they would be back with their relentless pursuit, but for now, she had some peace.

They sat down against the chain-link fence, Clarissa holding her skateboard close, a smile on her face. Monica opened up her lunchbox, pulled out a baloney sandwich, a strawberry kiwi juice box, and began munching.

"It worked, Monica."

"The salt circle?"

"Yes. It tried to get past it, but it couldn't. It sat there for hours, just staring at me."

Clarissa told her about how she had gotten off of the bed and almost broke the circle trying to make sure it worked.

"That's creepy," said Monica with a mouthful of white bread and baloney.

"Yeah, really creepy, but it couldn't get through. It worked. What about you? Did you try the circle?"

Monica swallowed her food. "Yes, but it never showed up. I think it's just after you. I know you said it saw me or something, but maybe it was just surprised I was there."

Clarissa nodded, "Yeah, I think maybe you're right."

Through another bite of food, Monica said, "Did it do or say anything else?"

"No, I mean it moved all around the circle trying to find a way through, but mostly it just stared at me. After a while, I fell asleep."

"Do you know what this means, Clarissa?"

Clarissa nodded, all smiles. "Yes, it means that magic is real."

Excitement lay inside those words, and with them, great hope. Now that they knew how to protect themselves, they had a greater resource—time.

"Yeah, and it also means there's probably a way to stop it, or trap it, or...."

"Or kill it." Clarissa finished.

Monica paled at that, but nodded slowly.

"It must have to do with the circle of bones. Maybe they sort of trap it or something?"

Monica nodded, "Yeah, I think it must. But we'll have to go back to the library again and read more. We could look up magic spells surrounding bones and blood. If we can figure out what the bones mean, maybe we can stop Demon.

"Do you want to go after school?"

"I can't. My mom has to take me shopping for winter clothes."

"Oh." Clarissa didn't try to hide her disappointment.

Monica took the last bite of her sandwich and smiled. "Don't worry." She chewed. "Now that we have a way to defend ourselves, we have all the time in the world to figure it out."

Monica was wrong.

5.

The wind was up. But it had been for several hours. Since she and Monica had parted company, the wind had battered against the old house, making the walls creak and gasp at the onslaught. Clarissa didn't know if the wind was Demon's construction, or simply a windy Autumn night that heralded not a monster, but the coming deep cold of an East Coast winter.

There was no moon in the sky. As she peered out the window from her bed, she saw only the soft yellow glow of the street lamps between moving branches. The closest one would occasionally turn off. Then, with no warning or pattern, it surged back to life again. Each burst of light rippled down her nerves, sending shockwaves like thunder. Her heart would not stop pounding, raging in her ears and her chest.

It was coming again tonight. Clarissa was sure of it. Yes, she had the circle of salt, but she didn't like the idea of it standing there and staring at her again. She sensed Demon's hunger, its craving. She was sick with it, a sludge that lived in her guts, festering with maggots. Clarissa wondered if the others had felt this before Demon had killed them. She wondered if the detective had experienced the shroud and felt that terrible dread. Some intuition told her that no, the shroud was just for her, the one that had let it out of its prison. After talking with Monica she was more certain that the bones were a cage and her blood was the key. Tomorrow, when they returned to the library, they would try to find out.

As the house settled and all felt quiet, Clarissa tiptoed down to the kitchen. She reached up into the cabinet to the left of the sink, where her mother kept all of the baking materials, and found the salt. As quietly as she could, she climbed back up the stairs, avoiding the spots that would betray her with creaks of age. She had swept up the salt early that morning. Her mother had seen it and said nothing. Perhaps her mother was just too tired to comment, but Ted wouldn't let it go. So, now she would forever have a nightly ritual of a salt circle, at least until they ran out. Then she would have to find some way to get more. But for now, she had plenty to last for a few weeks.

She crept back into her room and made a circle around her bed, placing the symbols underneath again, as she had the night before.

For a long time, Clarissa lay there, unable to sleep. Even with a sense of safety, there was still something dark dancing in the back of her mind, some nagging feeling that tonight it would break through, no matter what she did. So Clarissa lay there, awaiting her fate, reviewing everything that had happened over the past several months considering the creature's behavior. She couldn't think of anything that she had missed, any hole in either her or Monica's plans. She knew that the salt would work, so why did she feel like something terrible was about to happen?

Eventually, she fell asleep. When she opened her eyes again, something had changed. A strange glow emanated from the corner of her bedroom, from the spot where the creature had entered the first time.

She whimpered. Even with the salt, she knew something was different. She felt a kind of surge in the power of her fear, and some deep part of her knew that the surge of fear matched the surge of the power Demon commanded.

That strange mixture of darkness and light grew, an alchemy, a fusion, born in sacrifice. Clarissa pulled the blankets up to her chin and tucked them between her neck and chest, keeping her hands free. The glow almost seemed liquid. Her eyes played tricks on her. Something would move in one of the corners of her room, and each time she shifted her gaze, she found it was only an illusion.

She was so tired, yet could not return to sleep. The deepest dread rose up inside of her, filling her to the brim, and several times she felt that the only way to ease that sensation was to scream. Finally, the feeling overwhelmed her, and tears leaked out from the corner of her eyes, even as she checked the circle of salt again and climbed back into bed.

Through tears, trembling breath, and pounding heart, she said. "Please. Don't kill me. I don't want to die."

As if answering, the wind roared to life. The trees bent and swayed, casting shadows from the streetlamps onto her wall. She risked a glance and the branches seemed like elongated fingers, claws ready to rake her body, digging deep and tearing flesh. It would break the circle, she was sure of it now.

The wind howled like trumpets twisted out of shape, some awful death knell, bringing with it the dread.

It was coming. Not in silence like the night before. Now Clarissa understood that last night it had just been teasing, and tonight, with the wind as its herald, it had come to reap her at last.

All the weight of loneliness captured her and thrust her into despair. For this time, no one would come to save her, and the salt wouldn't work. Monica wasn't there to scream and break the trance. Nor would it be like it was in the forest when...but there was blackness there, no curtain of night raised in revelation. Even now, in this moment of terror, she could not help but wonder what had happened during those three missing days. For she knew that her escape had not been accidental. Something or someone had helped her to break free.

She reached for the memory, pushing past all of her fear and trying so hard to unlock that door, to understand what came and went in that missing time. The answer to the riddle of Demon was in those moments. Every part of her knew it. There was something about...the blood and...an agreement. What had she agreed to? She saw herself in some strange, otherworldly place, where the trees looked like something out of Doctor Suess, but with darkness clinging to each branch.

She pushed harder for answers, deeper, but there was only blackness. Minutes passed. Sometimes she would look at the clock and see that not even a single minute had claimed her life. Then sometimes she would blink, and the clock would slip ahead several minutes, as if time had lost all sense and reason, and dwelled only in chaos. It was all relativity, the gravity of Demon at work.

The shroud pulled tightly around her, constricting her breath despite the salt circle. She couldn't move anymore. Her limbs wouldn't respond. But her head could move, so she stared into that corner, not daring even to look at the clock.

The shadows danced in the corner, swirling into their strange liquid pattern. This was it. It would pull itself from the shadow like it had done from the TV and take her life. She took a breath. Then she took another. Counting each one, she waited for her last.

The shadows swirled, unchanging. One minute passed, and then several more. They smeared together as the swirl of dark hypnotized her, transfixed her. She felt her will weakening, felt the crash of exhaustion colliding with her spirit. When it came through that dark doorway, that portal from wherever it dwelled when it was not in this plane of existence, she would be too weak to fight. Her hope was the salt, but she had lost all faith in it. How could she think Demon would be stopped by something like that?

But it had, hadn't it? Torn between fear and reason, it was difficult to breathe. The shroud pulled so tightly that she was lightheaded and dizzy. She gulped the air, never feeling relief from breath. Panic took her, and yet she couldn't move her limbs. She wanted to thrash, to fight, but she was under Demon's power, waiting, a bug trapped in a cocoon that the spider had woven around it for later feeding.

Breathing grew more difficult. The world grew dimmer. Clarissa struggled to stay conscious, knowing that it was waiting there, waiting in the doorway until all her fight was gone and she could only just see its claws stretch out across the salt to claim her. Then there was blackness. All forms washed out of living memory. A great wave had hit her, and she was underwater, floating in a void somewhere between dream and waking. She wanted to surface, to break free again, but she did not know which direction to swim.

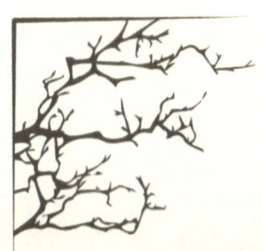

Chapter 13

When No Light Remains

When no light remains in uncertain terms,
And the death knell chimes,
Forever rattling your skull,
And the guilt,
A tide of tears and blood
Rippling,
Rippling like a stone in the pond.
Afraid of collision,
Concession,
Acquiescence.

Then comes the watcher with wings of white.
A reflection of the moon,
A tale of its own,
For on branded wings, it takes flight,
Stamped it is,
In the rhythms of solitude,
In servitude,
But never civility
For what purpose is peace,
In the lion's den?
But then...
There was Daniel.

Follow the white raven.
For white rabbits can never fly from the darkness,
Only descend to the depths.

Clarissa's eyes sprung open from all of the fear bottled at the bottom of her being. It was a force, electric and startling. She gasped for air, for the breath that the shroud had stolen. Her first instinct was to scream but there was no breath for it, and as she drew in long gulps of air, shafts of sunlight caught her eyes with a glimmer.

She was alive. The restraints of the shroud were gone and she moved experimentally, searching for the limits to her movement. Clarissa found no such limitations. She sat up, looking around, wondering if she was alive or dead, wondering if Demon had come. Grasping at her memories, she recalled the salt circle, and peering over the edge of her bed, saw that it was still there, undisturbed.

She slid to the edge of her bed and let her feet fall over it. She felt the grit of the salt as she planted her feet firmly. It had worked again. Two nights in a row it had tried to break through, and both times it had failed. She sighed in relief. Rather, she tried to sigh in relief. Something still felt wrong, something gnawed in the pit of her stomach, though she couldn't quite identify it.

That's when she heard it. A flutter of wings, and then a caw. She turned and saw it sitting on the outer ledge of her window. It tapped the glass as she turned and saw the white raven, its beady eyes staring, its head cocking back and forth.

The cold started at her feet and climbed to her scalp, pulling her skin taught.

"Go away," she said, hardly finding her voice at first. She tried again. "Go away!" she shouted this time.

For a wonder, it did. It pecked the glass one more time and then flew off.

It left behind that nagging dread. Something had happened, something terrible. But what? The salt worked. Then she thought of Monica. Surely, her friend had used the salt circle. Monica had used it the night before, so why wouldn't she do it again? But what if she hadn't? Or what if it had not worked?

She threw on her clothes and ran down the stairs.

Her mother stopped her and greeted her with a soft smile. "You're up a little early."

Her mother's smile faltered when she saw Clarissa's face.

"What's wrong?"

Clarissa opened her mouth to say something, and the words tumbled free in rapid order.

"It came again last night, but it didn't come for me. It came for Monica. We have to go check on her. It was the wind. And the shroud. It was here, and it went after Monica instead, and we have to go check on her, Mom. I have to go over there, now!"

She ran to the front door and put her shoes on.

Then her mother was there. Her voice soothing. "Sweetie, you just had a nightmare, that's all. You got scared again recently. So when you fell asleep it was already on your mind and you had a nightmare."

Clarissa couldn't keep the panic and fear from her voice. "No, Mom, that's not all. I was up all night. I didn't sleep hardly at all."

"And that's why you had a terrible dream. You have night terrors. I got them when I was your age, too. Some people get them bad. But they go away eventually."

Clarissa, in her panic, almost shouted. "No, Mom. We have to go check on her, now!"

Putting her shoes on, Clarissa walked to the front door. Her mother barred the way. Her arm a lever that Clarissa could not lift.

All the warmth drained from her mother's tone. There was still kindness there, but Clarissa knew that she would not let her out of the house. "Sweetie. I need you to come sit down on the couch and talk to me. It's six thirty in the morning. Monica won't be up for at least another half an hour for school. Remember how angry her father was last time?"

How could Clarissa forget? But it didn't matter, she had to know if Monica was okay. The white raven had come again, and now she was sure that had something to do with Demon. An omen? Was that what it was? An omen?

"Listen, I made you an appointment with a therapist next week. It's important you talk to someone about all of this. So just come sit down and I'll make you some tea, and we can talk about this."

Clarissa didn't have time for this. Her heart was pounding. Every ounce of her wanted to shove her mother out of the way and run out the door. For the first time in her life, she wanted to attack her mother. She didn't care if

Mr. Aguilar was angry again. She didn't care what time it was. She had to know if Monica was okay.

"Get out of my way, Mom." Clarissa's voice was cold and seething with fury.

It was a slap in the face. Her mother's mouth gaped. Shock followed anger. "Clarissa, what's gotten into you?"

"I'm going over to Monica's, and I'm going to make sure my best friend is still alive."

"Still alive? Clarissa, I know you're scared but...."

Her mother never finished. The shimmer of red and blue lights flashed against the curtains surrounding the door. Then, a single sharp bark of a siren, a single call, a death knell, one Clarissa would remember every time she saw an emergency vehicle for the rest of her life. Both she and her mom walked to the window, and each pulled one curtain aside. A police car and an ambulance had pulled up to Monica's house. Their lights were flashing, and two paramedics rushed to the door. As they did, a second police car pulled up.

The world dropped away. Time vanished. It seemed that single second passed as the paramedics went in and out of the house. Then she saw a police officer talking to Monica's father on the front lawn about something. With agony on his face, the lines of age crescendoed to new heights. Hollow eyes, spilling tears, begging, pleading, but Clarissa only heard mumbles from this distance.

"My baby girl!" Mr. Aguilar shouted, his accent thicker than usual.

Clarissa fixed her attention on the house, watching the front door, just as she had watched the dancing shadows the night before. The paramedics rolled a stretcher inside. Clarissa's stomach fell out. She had the sense that she was reliving the past, that she had rewound her life, back to when she was six again.

Then the paramedics came out with a stretcher, a black bag on top. A shroud for Monica, but one that would never retract again.

All at once, Clarissa understood the shroud, and why it had constricted her the night before. The shroud was that body bag around her father, and now Monica. Demon had told her what it was doing, for she had no doubt that the moment she had lost consciousness as the shroud squeezed out her air was the moment that it had taken Monica's life.

A strange, high-pitched whine filled the room, some distance away. Clarissa half-wondered at the noise. But inside, something tore. Her mother shook her, gentle at first, shouting her name, then harder, rattling her bones, as Clarissa's childhood tore away.

She couldn't hear her mother, but her throat hurt, a deep burn, and she realized that she was making the noise. She was keening, a term she was too young to know yet, but not too young to feel the wound to her soul.

Clarissa didn't remember throwing herself past her mother and out the door. Or how her mother had scrambled to catch her. Nor did she remember running full speed toward the paramedics, only to be blocked by Dominic Aguilar from reaching Monica's rapidly decayed body.

She only vaguely remembered that Mr Aguilar, mad with grief, had charged her, screaming that she had the Demon in her, that the devil had taken her soul. Later, Clarissa remembered the dull ache as her skull collided with the ground. He might have killed her, but Ted, appearing as if from nowhere, had come running and punched Dominic as the police rushed in to restrain him.

"Take me instead, please." She moaned to Demon as she lay face-up on the sidewalk. "Take it back. Please. I'll never do the salt circle again if you bring her back."

There was no answer. Just stares from the adults lifting her, checking her for injury.

Clarissa's words, "Take me instead, please," and a picture of Monica's room with a salt circle broken, would end up on the front page of every tabloid in town. Even legitimate newspapers covered the mystery at length. Written below in the body of the text in every article across the greater Philadelphia area were words like death cult, satanic ritual, three rapidly decaying corpses, and possession, a Satanic Panic redux. After all, if it bleeds, it leads.

But before Clarissa lost consciousness from her second concussion, she would remember the look on Dominic Aguilar's face. He screamed at the heavens as tears raced down his cheeks. In handcuffs, he threw himself again at Clarissa, held back by Ted and two police officers. He raged at everything.

But the image that most mirrored in her mind was the body bag loaded into the ambulance to take Monica away forever. As she closed her eyes, she heard the ambulance doors shut. Her last thought was that she would never befriend anyone again, lest Demon come for them.

2.   For three days, she lived in the hazy outlines of the surreal. She was conscious, but it was hard to think and when she did, there was nothing else but Demon's victims dancing like skeletons in her mind. Three were dead now because of her. For now, she understood that the unknown boy lay at her feet somehow, too. Demon orbited her, a permanent satellite. Clarissa had spilled that blood in the meadow and summoned Demon. There was no denying her role in the death of all three. She was at the center of it, even if the police wouldn't put her in jail.

No child of nine could carry such baggage. Few adults could weather that storm and survive. So, Clarissa collapsed. For two days, she thought of ways she could lure Demon back to her. In one half-hearted mad moment, her mother had stopped her as she ran out the door and toward the woods, toward the meadow where it had all begun. But watching her closely, Ted and her mother went after her, caught her, fighting her the whole way home. Her mother wept with her that night, and they both lost themselves in the tangle of tears, like in the time after her father had passed.

Demon did not come back.

Another day passed. The police came with their questions, but there was nothing to be said or done. They asked after the salt circle, and told her that Dominic Aguilar had fought with his daughter over it the night before, that he had swept away whole portions of it when he saw it in the middle of the night. He had accused his daughter of witchcraft and swore that Monica would never see Clarissa again.

With that news, Clarissa understood what had happened. She was shielded, but Monica was not. Demon was hungry, so it went for the unprotected child, as all predators would. She should have let it take her instead, then Monica would still be alive.

There were no charges brought against Clarissa. How could there be? The police asked Clarissa and her mother if they wanted to press charges against Dominic Aguilar for assaulting Clarissa, but they declined. Both parent and child knew the pain of that kind of loss, that it takes your mind from you, that you drown in sorrow and lash out at the world in previously unimagined ways. Clarissa knew she was guilty. She deserved far worse than what Dominic had done.

The murmurs began again. The papers ran headlines that inflamed the friction in town day after day. After the satanic cult story, some of the more reputable papers tried a new tactic, accidental exposure to chemicals or biological weapons. Perhaps, they said, Clarissa, who still seemed to be at the center of it all, had some sort of immunity or protection. But in the tabloids, the articles on demonic forces and possessions were plentiful. Clarissa's picture was everywhere, sometimes as the lone survivor of something terrible, sometimes as the cause of something sinister.

The day of the funeral came. There was much debate on whether or not Clarissa should attend. Her mother argued that Monica was her best friend, and she needed to say goodbye and have some closure. Ted argued that they weren't welcome, and that Dominic Aguilar might hurt Clarissa again. In the end, her mother won, though the family decided to attend only the internment, not the wake or viewing.

Clarissa was too numb to care. She was hollowed out as if all emotion had been drained from her. Maybe that was the way Demon liked it. Maybe the reason it killed Monica was so that could have a longer-lasting and more sustaining meal for Clarissa. She wondered if it fed off of others indirectly. Perhaps a funeral was a buffet.

At the funeral, rain splattered on her umbrella, steady and unrelenting. It had already been raining for three days. The bone-cold November rain threatened to turn to sleet or snow as the mourners navigated around puddles and the massive mound of mud near the large empty hole. It wouldn't be empty much longer.

Clarissa watched the casket with Monica's body as it was lowered down into the earth. The casket was black, black like a body bag, black like the shroud that wrapped her even now. The shroud was tight; she drew breath through clenched teeth. Her mother guarded her every moment, never leaving more than a few feet between them.

Clarissa didn't see Mr. Aguilar anywhere. He was missing from the crowd. All faces took turns staring at Clarissa, then the casket, and back again. The accusations were in their eyes. It would always be in their eyes. Clarissa traded glances with Mary Aguilar. She held Clarissa's gaze for several moments. Her eyes were different. There wasn't an accusation there, but a question. But there was and never would be a path to asking.

Even in the bleak gray of the steady, drizzling storm and the bone-soaking cold, a shadow appeared on the ground in front of her. Clarissa turned, and there, looming over her, was a man with broad shoulders and a mustache that had turned gray in a single week. Most of the thinning hair left on his scalp had turned gray now, too.

In a low rumbling voice, he said, "You took my little girl from me. You're not welcome here."

Mary walked around toward them to intervene. Both Ted and Clarissa's mother stood ready on either side of her as the man confronted Clarissa.

Clarissa kept her eyes focused on the puddle she was standing in, on the black rubber boots keeping her feet dry. She said, "I'm sorry." She couldn't meet his eyes.

Mary stood on his left now and said, "Dom, let her be. She's just a little girl. She couldn't have caused this."

"God dammit, Mary. Look at her. She's got the devil in her. She took our little girl from us and you want me to just accept it?"

Mary said nothing. Perhaps that was the most courageous thing. For what words could be a balm to such tragedy?

The entire crowd had circled them, watching the tall man with the wide shoulders wearing a large crucifix on his chest and the little girl in galoshes. The only sound was the patter of the rain on the umbrellas. Mist rose from the breaths of those that surrounded them. All were eager to see what came next. They hung on to Clarissa's misery with a desire not dissimilar from Demon. Voyeurs, all.

Ted broke the silence with a softness in his voice. "Dominic, I know you're angry. I would be angry, too, if it was my daughter. But how could this be her fault? You heard what the police said and-"

"-Fuck you, Ted. Your step-daughter is in league with the devil. It's the only explanation." He muttered curses in his native tongue. "Three people are dead. All three are connected to her. No one knows what she did in those woods, not a single goddamn person. For all we know, she's playing some kind of sick game with demons and Satan himself."

There were murmurs from the crowd. Some sounded sympathetic, others troubled, curious, hissing. They were greedy for answers, but if there were no answers, they would settle for sensation.

"Now listen, Dominic-"

Dominic Aguilar lunged forward to punch Ted. Ted, flinching backward, slipped and fell in the mud. Dominic jumped on him. In seconds, both men were rolling around in the mud, splashing in puddles, and trading in blows. Mary screamed. Clarissa's mother pulled her away from the fight. Several people jumped in to pull the two apart. Finally, several pairs of hands restrained both men. Both stood across from each other, faces full of mud and bruises, twisted with anger.

Each lunged again, but the priest, who had stood by before this moment, stood between them.

"That's enough, Dominic."

"Father, she's got the devil in her."

The priest shook his head. He walked over to Clarissa, kneeled before her in the mud, and tilted her chin up to look into her eyes.

"Oh my dear, there's no devil in you. This is not your fault. Do not carry the burdens of evil on your shoulders. There are forces far beyond us, both good and evil. But good will triumph, don't you doubt it. The Lord works in mysterious ways."

"She's evil, Father. She took my little girl. Somehow, she killed that detective and she murdered that other boy. Everyone in town knows it."

The priest shook his head slowly, looking up at Monica's father, but still kneeling in the mud. Rain cascaded down the man's solemn face. "No, Dominic. Look at her. Really look at her."

Clarissa could feel the weight of everyone's gaze.

"Evil. I see evil," said Dominic. His certainty was unrelenting.

"No. You see someone to blame. Someone, whom you confessed to me, tried to get you to see the nature of the evil that was plaguing your daughter. You came to me in grief and told me what this girl had said to you. Told me how terrified she and your daughter were before she was killed. This girl warned you, and you blame her. Clarissa is innocent. She's afraid. She's lost her father, she's been through something terrible that none of us understand, and now she's lost her best friend, yet you would attack her and her family."

The crowd hung on every word.

The priest stood and walked over to Dominic, who was still being held by two men.

"The loss of a child is one of the greatest crosses any parent can bear. It is not right that you should try to force this girl to carry your burden. She has so much to carry, herself. Remember, Dominic, God has a plan."

Mr. Aguilar's right eye was already swelling underneath some of the mud caked on his face. But his glare was like fire. He threw off the arms of the men holding him and turned to leave. As he did he stopped, looked over his shoulder, and said, "She's evil. You mark my words, more will die because of her. She's in league with the Devil."

Mary Aguilar followed him.

The men holding Ted let him go. Ted walked over and kneeled in the mud in front of Clarissa as the priest had.

"Listen, Clarissa. I know you might think I don't understand what you're feeling, but...I lost my best friend when I was eleven. A drunk driver hit him. It's when I started... cleaning. I...this isn't your fault, Clarissa. None of it is."

Clarissa didn't want to talk, but something in her spoke the words for her. "Getting hit by a car is not the same as being killed by a shadow that's hunting me."

The crowd hissed and murmured. They traded glances with one another, wondering at Clarissa's words. Everyone listened with rapt attention. By the next day, the story of the shadow hunting a little girl would be in the papers. It would become a legend long before Clarissa was fully grown.

Ted said nothing. Clarissa's mother grabbed her hand.

"Come on, sweetie. Let's go home."

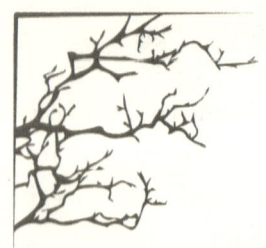

Chapter 14

New Shapes In the Dark

Tell her,
Tell her that...

New shapes come to sever you from stillness,
From stiffness
From what was,
Because
You are trapped,
Kidnapped
By emotional possession
Breathing in your obsession
Stuck in a cycle of regression
And this rumination on transgressions
It's stunting your progression.

Don't believe everything you think,
Or you'll sink
Into the circle of bones
Where Demon roams
There is no home
No rest,
No ease,
No peace,
No silence,
Only self-inflicted violence

Tell her,
Tell her to...
Turn and see the sun,
It's always there.

T hings did not improve after the funeral. Her mother was fired from one of her jobs, though the others kept her on. There was no explanation for her termination beyond meaningless babble. But later, when the angry letters arrived at the house, when strangers came knocking on the door asking if they could perform an exorcism or investigate paranormal activity, it was clear why her mother had been fired. No one would hire Ted either, not even for a single day. He was twice cursed, first from his mental illness, and second from association.

All good will amongst neighbors vanished. Mrs. Everson, now recovered, pacemaker in her chest, shared sinister, gleeful grins whenever Clarissa came close. The rest of the neighbors kept Clarissa in quarantine, vanishing at her or her parent's approach, leaving only shadows in the corners of her eyes.

James and Margie came for visits on occasion, but as Clarissa repeatedly refused them, they came less and less. Clarissa did not want Demon to notice them like it had noticed Monica.

The house felt dimmer. In the days ahead, the shroud barely lifted. It kept Clarissa fixed in place, almost unmoving. Her stomach rumbled with constant hunger. She began her own decay. Sometimes her mother fed her to make sure that she ate. She lay in bed for days, in looping spirals of woe. Sometimes she would read or watch her favorite movies and shows, but mostly she lay in her nothing. Haunted.

Once a week, she saw a therapist named Cathy. Cathy was a larger woman, jovial, her face always with the hint of a smile and a cup of tea in her hand. She sipped at it when they talked. Her clothes were ever a rainbow of color, with long flowing dresses that made Clarissa think she danced on air as she walked. Her mousy hair and hazel eyes added to the frame of her unusual beauty and her sense of calm. Always calm. Always slow words. Always kindness.

It was an hour-and-fifteen-minute drive to the north and west away from the city. It quickly became the only time she drew fresh breaths of the gathering winter air. In most of her sessions, Clarissa answered Cathy's questions with one-word answers, little cries of pain issued in singular syllables. Shouts in the dark. Nothing she said captured or caged her torment. Words were small things, an insignificant planet in the orbit of a black hole, fighting the inescapable gravity of mourning.

Yet she listened, and some of Cathy's words were stored for later use, seeds of transformation planted. Later, during Clarissa's final confrontation with the creature that tormented her, she told this to Demon. Told it that, "Sometimes you hear things you can't possibly understand yet. Then one day, you resurrect them, so that they stand before you with their wisdom and burn away your ignorance, a sun evaporating shadows."

The holidays came and went, and with it her tenth birthday. Her mother invited a few people she thought would celebrate. No one came, not even James or Margie, her only remaining friends. Both gave what sounded like valid excuses, but Clarissa was sure they were afraid of her, and they were right to be afraid.

Soon after Clarissa's birthday, Monica's parents left. There was no warning or explanation. One day their car was parked on the street, and then it wasn't. Shortly after, a moving company arrived and packed up their things. Clarissa never saw them again. Later in life she would wonder what happened to them, but not much. For in the days ahead, she would know so much more suffering and loss. Monica, the boy, and the detective were only a prelude to war. And she would go to war against Demon and his kind. Within her, a little fire was burning, growing, the sadness shrinking, a thing evaporating day by day from the heat of her rage.

She didn't go back to school until after the holidays. Her mother knew the town needed time to settle, time to spin out their gossip before she thrust Clarissa back into their world. And it was their world now. She was just an observer, a passing shadow that brought with it only coldness and fear. In a way, she became a cousin to the very monster that hunted her, the very monster who seemed to have vanished. Children in school avoided her, and most of the teachers wouldn't call on her. Mrs. Rollins was short and courteous but no longer her defender.

She found some solace in art. Where before she was unable to do more than just a simple scribble and stick figures, she found that she had a new ability to make lines and colors into recognizable forms. This puzzled her. Had something about what happened with Demon suddenly given her a new leap in ability? But her themes were dark, twisted, so said her teacher who had called home with concern one day. Shadows, blood, bones, the meadow, they all appeared at the center of her work. And why not? Hadn't her art teacher told her that art was an expression of your life and soul? Clarissa's life had only the shroud, the meadow, the monster.

A few nights after the phone call from the art teacher, Clarissa sat playing *The Secret of Mana* on her Super Nintendo. Ted had bought the console to help cheer her up. Although, Clarissa suspected his motivations were not entirely unselfish, as she routinely saw him on it at night when her mother was at work. She wished that she had magical powers for the umpteenth time. Sometimes she wished that she had the power of the One Ring to disappear (without all the dark lord side effects, of course), and she felt a kinship with Frodo now that she had finished *The Lord of the Rings*. Other times, she wished she had the power of the Wishsong, like Brin Ohmsford, able to reshape reality. Books and words were easier for her now. She understood almost every word she read, even in adult books. Little did Clarissa know there was a kind of magic in her and it was growing, despite its weighty cost.

The air outside was still in the grip of a winter's chill, spring still weeks away, and Clarissa could feel the air nipping at her, even indoors. The old baseboard heaters in the house, which Ted complained about frequently because of the high cost to run them, never did a good job of dampening the chill in the air.

Clarissa sat in the living room, with her back to the front window, her eyes fixated on her game. So far, she had gathered three of the Mana seeds to help save the Mana tree, and she was working on the fourth when she heard a car speeding by out front.

It wasn't the sound of the car screeching around the corner that drew her attention away from the screen. Clarissa didn't even notice it. Later she would remember hearing it, and the distant alarm bell ringing in her head. No, what caught her attention was the sudden tearing open of her world. In one instant, there was only the quiet of the game and then a loud crash as the window exploded. At the same time, Clarissa felt a terrible pain in the center of her back, a dull and thudding ache as if she had collided with something. All of her attention shifted to focus on the creeping, climbing, white-hot pain that now radiated not just from the center of her back, but through her entire body. Clarissa screamed, almost drowning out the sound of the tires screeching for a second time as the car carried away the ones responsible.

Trying to stand, to get away from whatever was happening, Clarissa cut open her hands as she thrust herself upward from the carpet. Then, taking a few steps the glass bit into her feet. She wobbled, feeling the pain spike and then collapsed into shards slicing other parts of her body.

She lay there, a small piece of glass digging into her cheek, unable to move because of the pain crippling her. She lay there as Ted or her mother, she would never remember which, scooped her up and moved her away from the window. She lay limp in their arms as she saw the reflection of Monica in every piece of glass across the floor. As she was carried away, she saw what had flown through the window, what thing had hit her in the back. It was a brick, and tied around the brick was a yellow note. The torn page was jagged at the edges as if pulled from a spiral notepad. But even in that single moment, Clarissa's eyes caught the gist of the note under the fraying twine that held it in place. In a red, angry scrawl with sharply-lettered writing it said,

"Devils Aren't Welcome...."

It was all she could see of the note, and she would never see the rest for her mother wouldn't allow it. But it was enough. She thought she knew who had written it and why. After all, had she not seen his daughter reflected in each of the glass shards on the ground?

After the ambulance came and the police arrived with their pads and questions, Clarissa lay again in a hospital bed. The doctor said she had two cracked ribs but should heal just fine. While there, Audrey Lamont, her mother, had announced in a voice trembling with fury, "I've had enough of this mother fucking town, and it's time we leave."

Ted didn't protest. Neither did Clarissa.

A few days later, as they began packing and searching for a new life, a reporter came by for a tabloid on the supernatural. He said that he wanted to interview Clarissa for a piece they were doing on the brick incident and the mysterious deaths. Ted slammed the door in his face. A picture of their house still ran on the front page of a tabloid a few days later, with the headline, "Man Claims Demon-Possessed Child Killed His Daughter!" and below that in smaller white print it said, "He tried to kill her with a drive-by brick."

Clarissa was no longer allowed to go to the skate park. Nor did she want to. Her mother and Ted took her out of school while they tried to find a path to a new life. There were many long, boring days sitting in her bedroom.

But now, she had something to occupy herself. For the brick incident had relit the fire under Clarissa to find a way to destroy Demon. One morning, Clarissa had asked if she could go to the library to check out some books. She checked out *The Scions of Shannara*, but when Ted was distracted she snuck into the folklore section and stuffed several of the books she and Monica had found useful into her backpack. Neither Ted, nor the Librarian noticed. She found that, like the other books she had read recently, she had far less difficulty understanding the meaning, though she always kept a dictionary close at hand.

2.   Six weeks after the brick incident, as Spring took hold, the house sold and moving day arrived. It was hard to say goodbye to the only place Clarissa had ever called home, but there was also a part of her that was eager to leave all of the bad memories behind. Besides, what was left for her but people who hated her?

Clarissa sat on the front step of the porch, watching as Ted loaded the last few things into the back of the truck. The for-sale sign on their front lawn swung back and forth in the gentle spring breeze, making a gentle clacking sound against the new 'sold' sign just below it. Clarissa could smell the first bloom of flowers in the air. Looking across the street she saw Mrs. Everson peering through her curtains. Clarissa didn't need to see her face to know what she was thinking. All of the neighbors seemed relieved that they were going.

James and Margie had shown up in the final days to say goodbye and helped Clarissa pack her things. James had helped Ted move some of the larger furniture that morning, while Margie had sat and talked to Clarissa about the things happening in her life. Clarissa just nodded and listened. But now, both were gone, and in a few minutes, she would be too.

Clarissa had seen them both several times after the brick incident; her mother would no longer let Clarissa turn them away. High school was a busy time for them both. Margie had a rock band, and her boyfriend and James had a job. They both promised to keep in touch, and Margie said that she would come to visit and skate with her once she got her driver's license in the fall.

Demon had made no further appearances, nor the strange white raven. A few days after the funeral, Ted discovered the salt circle. It led to a huge fight between her mother and Ted. It was Cathy, Clarissa's new therapist, who convinced Ted that he should let her do it. "It is important for Clarissa to feel safe," she said. Ted gave in, saying, "As long as you clean it up every morning and recycle the salt."

Out in front, Ted rolled down the rear door of the moving truck after he loaded the final box of knickknacks. Then he climbed into the truck and started the engine.

"Time to go." Her mother said, from just behind her.

Clarissa nodded, stood, grabbed her skateboard, and followed her mother to the car. As they pulled out of the driveway, Ted pulled forward. They followed.

Sitting in the front seat, her mother offered her M&Ms and Clairissa took them, munching silently and looking out the window as she watched her old stomping grounds pass out of her life. She couldn't help but wonder if she would ever come back here. Her reading had suggested she might need to return to the meadow someday, but she had a lot to learn first.

Her mother, following behind Ted as they drove toward the highway said, "Are you ready for your new life?"

Clarissa hugged her skateboard. "Do they have a skate park where we're going?"

Her mother smiled. "Yes. I made sure that we found a place that had a skate park nearby." Her mother grabbed her hand and squeezed it once before letting it go and putting her hand back on the steering wheel.

"Everything will get better now, Clarissa. Sometimes you need a fresh start."

Clarissa watched her mother's face as she drove. She did seem happier. Maybe a new start was what they needed. Maybe being further away from Demon would mean fewer encounters with it? Thinking of the meadow, she thought of something else.

Clarissa said, "Will I still need to go to Cathy?"

Her mother nodded, turning on her left blinker to enter the on-ramp of the highway, where Ted was already speeding up. "Yes, for now at least. Clarissa, you've been through things that most adults haven't gone through. Besides, she actually lives closer to our new home than she does here. It will only be a forty-five-minute drive south from our new home.

Clarissa nodded. She wanted to feel hopeful, truly she did. But it was hard. Because even though Demon hadn't visited since Monica's death, somehow she knew that one day it would return, and if she wasn't careful, if she didn't find a way to destroy it, it would all begin again. For now, at least, she had the salt circle. No matter what Ted said, she would keep using it.

She thought maybe Demon was sleeping. She read about several kinds of monsters that were said to take a handful of victims and then sleep for a long time. Clarissa would be ready when it woke up, she hoped. For all of her anger and determination there was still the shroud, still the fear and doubt. In those times that she felt hopeless, she remembered her success with the salt circle. Despite what it had cost her, at least she knew that there was magic in the world.

As they entered the highway that led to their new life, Clarissa made a vow to Monica. She would destroy Demon.

Interlude I
The Boon

Clarissa felt the cold of the meadow nip at her skin and she drew her coat toward herself. The telling was far from finished.

Demon, still in its humanoid form, said, "Monica was your third sacrifice and your first boon."

Clarissa felt the pressure of both anger and grief in her chest. She thought of how she had used the boon over the years, how Monica, the detective, and the other sacrifices had helped her get this far. So many had fallen to Demon, and with each death, Clarissa grew stronger.

"I didn't understand what that meant then. I didn't understand anything about you or what happened, or the contract."

Demon chuckled. "I suppose a nine-year-old would struggle to understand a sudden leap in art, reading, writing, and deductive reasoning."

Clarissa said, "I knew something was different, and that maybe it had to do with you, but I didn't know about Draygon of Antioch yet, or the contract you had made with him...or others."

Demon laughed. "Oh, Draygon. I have not thought of him in an age. My centuries with him were among my favorites."

"Are we only your playthings?" Clarissa tried to keep the rage out of her voice, she could not give into her anger, not if this was going to work. She had to stay focused.

"And what else would you have me do for all eternity?"

She could not hold down all of the anger; some of it seeped through the cracks of her control.

"Suffer. Suffer for all the terrible things you've done."

The words were out before she could even stop them. But then she took a breath and regained herself. Clarissa realized that Demon probably wanted her to lash out, to make a mistake. She didn't think it suspected what she had done just yet, but it was impossible to tell. She needed to keep going, to buy time.

"Perhaps we should conclude your tale then, and we can see who suffers." It showed its white teeth, though they were less visible as the snowflakes grew and the storm gathered itself for a mighty blow. Clarissa wondered if, by the time she finished her story and finished the ritual, the snow would be too deep to navigate back. But she couldn't worry about that; besides, there might not be anything to worry about anyway.

"No, Demon. I have a right to finish my story. You agreed, and we both know that you are bound by that agreement."

She tried to sound more confident than she felt. In truth, she was not sure how much longer she could continue. The weight and burden of what came next hung heavy on her heart. She had been so foolish, and she wished she had understood the terms of the contract. If she had, some of her friends would still be alive. So much had happened in those late teen years when she first came into her power, when she had created and anointed her blade, Makhaira.

It smiled. "Very well, Clarissa. You may continue. "

The cold pressed in on her and the wind slipped right through her layers, inviting her to lie down and rest, and never wake again. Was Demon controlling the wind and cold here, or did the blizzard stand alone in its power? Suddenly so tired, she knew that she had to keep going, keep telling, to buy time. If her plan to stop Demon failed this time, two lives would be forfeit, and hers...well, she tried not to think about it. It was her last stand, her last hope to stop Demon once and for all.

The pressure inside her to concede grew. Before realizing what she was doing, she sat in the snow, ready to give in. Demon's smile broadened.

"Are you ready to surrender to the inevitable?"

Clarissa almost said yes, almost laid down in the snow and let the cold and Demon take her. But as she sat there, she saw something out of the corner of her eye. A soft, brilliant glow. She shifted her gaze for just a moment, making sure that she did not take her eyes off of Demon. The light seemed to land on the branches behind it, a creature that illuminated the darkness of the meadow.

It made no noise. It only fluttered its wings. But around its gleam, the color of the meadow was normal, as if it transcended Demon's power over this place. But there was something else. A warmth spread inside of her, softening the cold that nipped at her exposed skin. The White Raven watched from behind Demon, and Demon didn't notice.

The bird shook her out of her stupor, and all at once, Clarissa shouted at the monster.

"You're cheating!"

"Cheating?" It feigned innocence.

"You're using your power to make me feel drowsy."

It said nothing.

"Admit it. You're cheating. You're breaking the contract."

The sleepiness faded away almost instantly, and Clarissa stood back up, her strength and will renewed.

"I don't know what you're talking about." It smiled broadly.

Clarissa scrunched her face in anger, almost spitting her words. "It's time to continue the tale, Demon, time for you to accept my last request."

"You were always a clever one, even without your boon. Very well, continue your story."

Clarissa glanced briefly back up at the branches where the white raven had sat, but it was gone. She was alone with Demon again. But she shook off the cold and said, "I was twelve when you returned...."

Acknowledgements

There are a lot of important people in my life that I need to recognize who helped me either directly or indirectly in the creation of this book. A lot of people tend to think of writers and readers as solitary creatures, but in reality, the writing or reading of a book is a deeply social act. It is the amalgamation of countless ideas, experiences, and relationships throughout the writer's life.

First, I'd like to thank my friend, Dr. Stephanie Harabaglia, who helped me with some of the medical questions in the story. It's always helpful to know a doctor with answers to those kinds of question, and her input on Clarissa's time in the hospital was important. Luckily, I don't think she's ever been punched by a patient waking up from a ventilator.

Fellow author Stant Litore was an invaluable resource for his discussions with me about ancient Greek words. This is less important in this first entry of the series, but he helped me to determine the name of the blade mentioned in the final pages of this text. There's going to be a lot more of that blade in the next book, *Through an Endless Darkness Gleaming*. I'm grateful to know such a talented and brilliant writer.

Of course, my beta readers need mentioning as well. Lietzal Kilman, Kelley Mitchell, and Linda Andrews all gave me some invaluable feedback on earlier versions of this volume that helped me reshape some of the key moments of this tale for the better.

My editor, Sharra L. Schwartz, helped me catch all those little errors, and helped me clarify some key passages in the texts. Editors are magical beings and Sharra is both a taskmaster when it comes to the process (which, frankly I need one of those since I can be quite stubborn), and also seems to really understand the core of what I'm trying to do with a scene.

I also have a wonderful and supportive family. My parents, siblings, and of course, my four children have put up with all of my eccentricities and given me the space I need to write. I'm also grateful to my partner, Linda Andrews, who is a constant source of support for my art and craft.

I need to also thank Louis Estre. He has been a huge supporter of mine for several years now and offers endless words of encouragement. He's a true fan.

This book also exists in part because of a number of individuals who contributed to a crowdfunding campaign, and anyone who made a contribution deserves to be recognized here. Thank you to Louis Estre, Adriana Carlson, Gavin Ross, Christina Sachi Nakata, Linda Andrews, Craig Wee, Laurel McHargue, Francis Kilman, Blakesley Burkhart, Michael Kilman (my father), Bonnie Kilman, and the good people over at LMS radio/Podbean.

There is one person whom I cannot fail to mention in the creation of this work. Joanna Perry, whom this book is dedicated to, is the chief inspiration for this volume. The real story behind this book begins with the writing of a eulogy for Joanna. She passed away in May of 2023, and it shook me to my core. I had lost touch with her for the better part of two years at that point. We always tried to connect, but we just kept missing each other with our weird schedules. In fact, we were supposed to get a drink for her birthday that same May, but she didn't quite make it to her birthday.

We had a lot of shared battle scars, Joanna and I. I met Joanna when I was 17. A friend in high school asked me one day if I'd like to learn to sword fight. Being the sci-fi, fantasy, horror nerd that I am, and particularly a lover of swords and armor, I said, hell yes.

The next thing I knew, I was meeting this husband and wife couple who had a pair of small children. The wife, who was 34 at the time, very quickly became one of my best friends. But our relationship was more than friends. In a lot of ways, she acted as a mentor. She guided me through some of the most difficult experiences of my life. She offered me advice, and her door was quite literally always unlocked and open. She believed in keeping the door open for others, a quality I always loved about her. If you were having a problem, no matter what it was, Joanna always welcomed you. You could either talk through it, or hack at each other with swords to blow off some steam.

Teen years are tough for everyone. Joanna helped me remember the depth of my curiosity, and return to my love of books after a brief teenage respite from them (I got really obsessed with the guitar for several years). It's fair to say that Joanna was someone who helped shape me into the man I am today.

So, a eulogy.... This book was born at the same time I was writing her eulogy. Anyone who knows me, knows I am not a person who lacks words. I talk and write...all the time. But for the life of me, I could not write her eulogy. It just kept eluding me. After all, how do you write words for one of the most profound friendships of your life?

The night before her memorial I decided to go for a run. It was a late summer afternoon, and as sometimes happens here in Colorado, storms blow in. I was about three miles from home when this one hit, and it was a big one. Thunder and lighting were crashing down all around me and it was pouring rain. I was soaked to the bone and took shelter for a few minutes under a pavilion. My adrenalin was pumping, and despite the storm, the cicadas were singing and I just felt overwhelmed by the whole experience and began to cry. With those tears, the words just fell out of me.

Right then and there I wrote her eulogy on my phone, and sat and reveled in the beauty of that moment. I sort of fell into a state of joy and gratitude at being alive. But also, missing my friend terribly. I kept wishing that her life would have a different ending. But wishing does not make a thing so. That's why we have stories, isn't it?

The storm died down and the thunder rolled away, and a beautiful rainbow came out. The brilliant colors in the sky were reflected in the lake that I was running around. At the same time, the sun was setting and the lights of downtown Denver were lighting up in twilight. Rarely in my life have I seen anything so beautiful. Despite the grief, it was a perfect moment. I felt almost as if Joanna was with me right then. I got up and started running again. I let my grief roll down off of me and enjoyed the light rain that was still spitting from the sky.

Then it hit me. Joanna loved my writing. She was often the very first person to purchase and read my books upon release. We had written together a number of times and critiqued each other's work when I was in my late teens and twenties, and we always used to sit around dreaming about what we would do if our only job in the world was to write books.

Joanna, like so many of us, had a whole host of demons she had to contend with. As I was thinking about this, a young woman was skateboarding next to me as I was running. She seemed so happy and free. So, an idea was born. I thought of two things, the darkness and pain that follows us through life, and a young girl with a skateboard fighting some kind of shadow monster. Her name, Clarissa, popped into my head and I went back and wrote the first draft of the first chapter of this volume. This book is a love letter to my incredible friend, it is a way of expressing my gratitude for how she shaped my life. It is my gift to her, one last story I'll tell her before our paths diverge in the woods. Of course, what was one last book has really turned into a four volume series...but like I said above, I don't normally lack for words.

Now Joanna goes to find the Yew, to stand watch and wait for her loved ones to come join her to the other worlds. We must all stand watch for someone. Remember who will stand watch for you. Keep them dear to you, because nothing lasts forever and we don't always get happy endings.

- Michael Kilman

August 6th 2023 – April 12th 2025

Don't miss out!

Visit the website below and you can sign up to receive emails whenever Michael Kilman publishes a new book. There's no charge and no obligation.

https://books2read.com/r/B-A-ZUBG-KHDAG

BOOKS 2 READ

Connecting independent readers to independent writers.

About the Author

Michael Kilman is an anthropologist who occasionally visits other worlds and reports back what he finds. When he isn't writing fiction he is lecturing at a few universities in the Denver metro area, or working on his YouTube series 'Anthropology in 10 or Less.' Michael can be found at his website, loridianslaboratory.com, and on Twitter at @LoridiansLab.

Read more at https://loridianslaboratory.com.

www.ingramcontent.com/pod-product-compliance
Lightning Source LLC
Chambersburg PA
CBHW031338020726
47499CB00005B/1317